DEEPEST ROOTS
OF THE HEART

DEEPEST ROOTS OF THE HEART

Chautona Havig

Waterfall
PRESS

Published by Waterfall Press, Grand Haven, MI.

www.brilliancepublishing.com

Amazon, the Amazon logo, and Waterfall Press are trademarks of Amazon.com, Inc. or its affiliates.

ISBN-13: 9781477826744
ISBN-10: 1477826742

Library of Congress Control Number: 2014943614

Printed in the United States of America.

Dreams are cultivated in the soil of home. The richness of family fertilizes and gives those dreams roots, while love waters them until they flourish and thrive, unless drowned in a torrent of misguided affection. And time—time determines the quality of the fruit produced in that soil.

—Avelino Carrillo, 1994

CHAPTER ONE

THE PURPLE VALLEY

September 1945

Many thousands of feet have stirred the dusty roads of Napa Valley over the centuries, but on a September morning, one pair of army-issued boots tramped over familiar hills, down rutted lanes, and toward el Valle de Morado and la Casa de los Sueños.

The man scanned the countryside, drinking in the familiar sight of a sea of vines stretching themselves over the hills as far as he could see. His strong, brown hand gripped the strap of a kit bag. His senses heightened with each step as his nostrils took in the subtle scents of his homeland. The grapes were nearly ripe—almost time for harvest.

Around a bend in the road, he just had a few hundred yards to go at most. There was the corner of the house. Had it been four years? Would it be neglected, or had Gregory Lyndon found someone to rent it? Had it been sold? Would the agreement Mr. Lyndon signed hold up in court if it had?

As his childhood home, the house of his ancestors, stretched into view, Avelino Carrillo's heart constricted. For almost four years he had dreamed of the house, the land, and the heritage he'd left behind. Four years of dreaming of la Casa de los Sueños. *How fitting*, he mused as he stood there. *How fitting that I should dream of a "house of dreams."*

It was clean, with windows shining and fresh curtains fluttering in the noon breeze. Someone lived there. *Is it a family? A man wealthy enough to employ a housekeeper? Will they feel threatened at the sight of me?*

A young woman rounded the corner of the casa, the very corner his great-great-grandmother rounded a century ago. Her hair, although tied up in a kerchief, looked red from his vantage point. *"El pelo como rosas,"* his grandfather always said. Hair like roses. He strode forward, trying to hide his eagerness to see his home—to be near his home again.

She stopped, dropped the handles of the wheelbarrow, and shaded her eyes with one hand. "Can I help you?" Her eyes searched his sleeve. "Corporal?"

"I . . ." He didn't know how to answer. What could he say that would not seem strange?

As he hesitated, she observed. He saw her eyes take in his uniform, the garrison cap, the khaki trousers and shirt, and again the corporal's stripes on his sleeve. She didn't flinch at the patch over his left eye. Her eyes didn't fill with pity; that was a relief.

Unable to explain himself, he did the only thing he could think of. "May I use your water spigot? I've been walking—"

"Sure, come in. I'll make lemonade." Her hands waved him up the little incline. As he neared, she added, "Have I met you? You seem familiar somehow."

Probably because my grandfather's portrait hangs—or did hang—in the hall of your house. "I don't think so. I've been gone a few years."

"Europe?"

Avelino shook his head. "Philippines."

"You got home quickly . . ."

"Got injured and arrived back in June. They wanted men who can see from both sides."

"Well, we thank you."

That was a first. Oh, there had been bands playing, people cheering and everything when the ship came in, then more again just four days earlier when Japan officially surrendered. People were polite—even eager to help a soldier. However, no one had thanked him. In fact, Avelino had not considered thanks as something owed to him, but it was nice. *But how to answer?*

"You're welcome." It seemed pompous, inadequate. It was an honor to serve his country. *But thanks require a response.*

She led him into the house. The familiar choked him even more intensely than the unfamiliar. She had moved things, changes that illogically he resented despite having wanted to do them himself for a lifetime. Other parts of the house she had kept just as they were the day he locked the door behind him.

"You can set your bag there by the door." The young woman, hardly more than a girl, blushed. "I wouldn't want it to swing and catch something. This house is full of beautiful things, and none of them are ours."

"Thank you."

He set it down without hesitation and followed her into the kitchen. Memories flooded Avelino's mind as the girl poured a glass of water and offered it to him. The gesture warmed his heart with recollections of stories he'd heard since birth. *"'Would you like a drink of water?'"* he remembered his *abuelo* saying. *"Her hands pointed to a pitcher on a little table. 'Sí. Agua, por favor.'"*

"Did you say something? I'll just get out the syrup. I made some the other day and it was perfect."

From the icebox, she pulled a mason jar of lemon syrup and reached for the ice pick.

"I'll get that for you. Just let me wash my hands."

"The water is tricky, but it will come eventually."

"You just have to turn it on and off a few times. That seems to prime it—like that."

Water splashed into the sink as he rolled up his sleeves. Automatically, his hand reached for the soap dish, but it wasn't there.

"Soap's on the right, and here's a towel—but how did you know about the water? I didn't know that."

He flashed a smile, trying to be as reassuring as possible. "It's always been that way—ever since I can remember. The soap, though, it was always on the windowsill, where *abuelita* liked it."

"You are Avelino Carrillo?"

How does she know my name? "Yes."

"I should get my grandfather. Please wait."

The kerchief fluttered as her head bounced in her haste to exit the house. Before her grandfather arrived and ordered him from the premises, Avelino drank in the sights of home. The table, chairs, even the dishes had been etched into his memory, and being back in the familiar home became a balm to his lonely spirit. *It's been a very long four years.*

A shadow fell in the doorway as a tall man entered—taller than any Carrillo as far as he knew.

"You are Mr. Carrillo?"

"Corporal, Granddad. See?"

"Corporal Carrillo?"

"Yes, sir. My name is Avelino. I'm no longer in the army . . ."

"My name is Kearns, Joe Kearns. You've met my granddaughter, Amelia."

"Well, I didn't introduce myself," the young woman admitted. "I was a bit stunned." She glanced at the empty water glass. "Oh, the lemonade."

While she mixed the drink, Mr. Kearns gestured for their guest to be seated. "Have you had lunch? Amelia already brought me a sandwich, but—"

"I ate on the road, but thank you."

The older man gazed at him through clear gray eyes. Deep wrinkles etched the man's face, but Joe Kearns was not as old as he'd first seemed. In Avelino's estimation, the man had lived a hard life—a very hard life.

"Have you seen Mr. Lyndon?"

"Not yet. I had to see home first—for a couple of reasons."

"If you left your agreement here, it's long gone. I know that Mr. Lyndon searched every inch of this property himself."

"I did leave it here, but I doubt he found it." He swallowed hard. "Will I offend you if I ask to retrieve it?" The last thing he wanted to do was sneak onto the property at midnight. *But I'll do it if necessary.*

"Not at all! I hope you do find it." Mr. Kearns's face was a hard study, but it seemed as though the man did not understand that the agreement would put him out of his home. *Or perhaps he doesn't care—hard as that is to imagine.*

"There isn't a person in this valley who wouldn't like to see Lyndon forced to keep that promise," Mr. Kearns said.

"It means that in seven years—"

"I'll be looking for a new home, yes. I know that. But I'll have the satisfaction of seeing a man reunited with his history. Who could resent that?"

He could not help but glance at the granddaughter, Amelia. She stood stirring the lemonade, lost in the conversation.

"Oh, the ice. I'm sorry. I promised."

Avelino hacked at the small block she handed him. Amelia scooped the ice chips into glasses, and Avelino drank in every movement. *So like* mamá. *Graceful, even in the little things.* That thought shook him. *Don't be so foolish. She's just a girl.* Amelia handed him a tinkling glass of lemonade, and Avelino swallowed hard before he could even take a sip. *Just drink and do what you came to do.* Though he expected it to be excessively sweet or much too sour, the lemonade proved perfect. "Delicious."

"No one can cook like Amelia."

"How long have you lived here?"

"Only a few months. The house was a mess—needed a lot of cleaning and a bit of upkeep. Amelia did most of it. I've been busy with the vines. Fool Lyndon left them untended until this year."

"He probably assumed that I wouldn't want the place if the vines were in bad shape. Bet he thought that if I hadn't come back by this year, I wasn't coming, so he might as well get the wine flowing again." Avelino sighed. "The man cannot understand *familia. Los raíces.*"

"*Los raíces?*"

Avelino smiled at the tentative attempt to copy his words—just like his *abuelo* had described. "Roots."

"I see. You're right. He doesn't understand. All he can see are dollars and cents and acres."

They talked until the lemonade was long gone and he'd forgotten what Joe had said about retrieving the agreement. Avelino stood, shuffled his feet, and said, "I feel strange asking, but I do want permission if I can get it. I'd like to retrieve that agreement."

"Certainly. We can stay inside if you'd prefer . . ."

Even as Mr. Kearns spoke, Amelia turned away, grabbed a broom, and left the room as if her grandfather's words were an order to scram.

Avelino spoke quickly. "That's not necessary. You're welcome to come."

The man glanced after his retreating granddaughter, a question in his eye. Avelino nodded, and Mr. Kearns called after her, "Amelia, why don't you come with us? This kind of thing is right up your alley." To Avelino he said, "My granddaughter loves any hint of a story or mystery."

As they neared the great *secoya*, he slowed, a childhood habit. "My great-great-great-grandfather is buried here."

"Oh, but there's a family cemetery over there . . ."

"Yes. They buried the rest of the family there, but the first woman of this house had to bury her father alone beneath this tree." He smiled at the faces that listened with such attention. "I was surprised to see a girl with red hair when I came today. My great-great-grandmother—about your age when she came here, I suspect—also had red hair; hair like roses, they said."

"Carrots is more like it."

"Well, they said roses. It's legendary in my family."

As he spoke, he worked the stone cross from the ground, gently prying the dirt away from it. A foot deeper and his hand found what it sought—a small sample bottle for wine.

"Is it there? Really?" Amelia's excitement, while strangely quiet, was palpable. "Granddad, look! He's really going to be able to do it."

"Take the sheriff with you, son. You don't want to risk an 'accident.'"

"Who is the sheriff now?"

"Callum. He's clean from what I hear—something that Lyndon is working to rectify."

A shout from one of the workers in the vines closest to the house turned all heads, and Mr. Kearns began jogging toward it. "Be careful. Let us know how it goes."

Avelino turned the bottle over in his hand as he considered the man's words. Amelia began dragging the cross back to its place in the ground, snapping his attention to the present. "Thank you. I can do it."

She hesitated, her hand still on the stone. "Do you mean that you *can* do it or that you prefer to do it yourself?"

"I meant that I can, but yes, I do care about showing respect for *abuelito* Tandy's grave myself."

"Tandy? That is a very un-Mexican-sounding name."

"He and his daughter were *gringos* from Texas. The stories say that she had a voice that you never tired of listening to."

The young woman pointed down the hill. "I don't want to be rude, but I really did want to get that front flower bed cleared today. If you don't need me, I'll get on with it."

"Not at all. I'll be going. It looks like I need to get down to the phone box and call Callum."

They walked back to the house together, Avelino pausing only long enough to wash the dirt from his hands and grab his pack. As he started down the drive, her voice called after him, "Do you have plans for supper?"

"No . . ."

"Come back. Granddad would love the company. We're having chicken."

"Are you sure? It's not necessary—"

"We eat at six o'clock. If you're not here, I'll put a plate in the oven for you. If it rots in there, I'll expect you to clean it out."

Avelino grinned. "I'll be here. Thanks."

He took another step before she called after him once more. "If you're coming back for supper, there's no reason to haul that bag around with you. You're welcome to leave it inside if you prefer."

CHAPTER TWO

THE CONTRACT

An eerie sense of déjà vu filled him as Avelino stepped into the same walnut-paneled office where he'd received the last hope for his family's legacy. The same man who had made it possible for Avelino's older brother to borrow heavily against la Casa de los Sueños and the vineyard sat behind the same massive desk that had engulfed him that awful December day. *The day after Pearl Harbor. I'll never forget the date—the day our country went to war, and I vowed to fight for it* and *for la Viña de los Sueños.*

"So it's true," said the man behind the desk.

"What is true, Mr. Lyndon?"

"You've returned alive." The deceptively warm eyes flicked to the sheriff behind Avelino. "And you've brought our fine sheriff with you. I'm wounded, Avelino. I have never threatened your safety, have I?"

"No. I bring him only as a witness."

"You wish me to honor our agreement." It was there—a sneer—but almost imperceptible.

"I do."

"Have you the paper I signed?"

"I do."

The surprise in Lyndon's face evidenced the man's confidence that he'd never be required to uphold his end of the bargain.

"Let me see it."

Avelino produced the paper that promised a chance to redeem the family land, but he did not relinquish it.

"I want to know if you will honor it. I won't waste our time if you will not."

"I heard you returned and had a legal contract drawn up, one that covers everything we discussed in detail. My lawyer, Mr. Baines, worked all night to have it ready for you. I will honor my word."

Avelino handed over the still-curled piece of paper. As Mr. Lyndon grabbed it, the younger man added, "And I have had a picture taken of it. The film is being protected, undeveloped, until needed or not."

"You don't trust me."

"I know things happen—often unexplained, whether or not deliberate—and I want to protect my interests."

The man read the paper. Resignation entered his tone as he stated, "This is the paper I signed." Lyndon started to slide it into a drawer. "My lawyer will take possession of it. You have the film."

He pushed a multipage contract across the desk.

Lyndon's eyes narrowed as Avelino shook his head. "No. I will take the original document. The contract is all you need for your records. You lose nothing without that paper. I stand to lose everything." Avelino hesitated before adding the request that could kill his chances. "I need a place to live—even if it's just a cot in the office. If I'm going to work for you to pay off our debt, I will need somewhere to sleep."

"Your house has been rented."

"I met the Kearnses. They seem like nice people. Miss Kearns is an industrious young lady."

Gregory Lyndon rolled a gold pen between his thumb and index finger, lost in thought. At last, he laid the pen down perfectly parallel to the desk pad and folded his hands. "I know just the place." When Avelino did not respond, he continued. "You don't ask where. Is that because you do not want to know, or because you do not want to give me the satisfaction of answering?"

"I won't sign a contract that does not include provision for a place to live."

"You can have the room over the garage."

"At la Casa de los Sueños?"

"Yes. That's my only offer. It keeps you close, so you don't need transportation. It'll save you money in the long run."

Lyndon sent the contract into another room, with instructions for an addendum regarding housing.

The walls closed in on him as Avelino waited for the contract that would set him on the path to reversing the losses his family had suffered in the past five years. His mind ordered his lungs to breathe even as he answered inane questions about his time in the South Pacific and the injury that had sent him home only days before he would have shipped out anyway, his commitment to the army satisfied. Relief washed over him as the secretary scuttled into the room with the updated contract. *Almost there.*

Lyndon read it, nodded, and signed before passing it to Avelino, along with the gold pen he'd toyed with as they talked.

Avelino shook his head. "I will take the contract with me to review with my lawyer."

"Your lawyer?" Suspicion entered Lyndon's eyes once more. "Who is your lawyer?"

"I've spoken with a man in Napa." Avelino flipped open a padded folder and slipped the contract inside. "I will bring it back tomorrow."

"I gave you a good offer—one that'll save you money, as I said."
Lyndon folded his hands in his lap. "Considering you'll still need to
find a way to earn your food, I don't see how you can refuse."

The man's words were true, but Avelino heard something
beneath them. Even as he strolled out into the lowering afternoon
sun, Avelino dug through the underlying meaning of what Lyndon
hadn't said. He pruned each unnecessary shoot from the problem
until the root was exposed. A grin split his face as he turned toward
the road that would lead him to la Casa de los Sueños. *He wants to
torture me by making me watch others live in my family's home. He will
be disappointed.*

* * *

An apron covered the skirt and short-sleeved sweater that replaced
Amelia's dungarees and blouse. She'd removed the kerchief, reveal-
ing two rolls of hair sweeping up the sides of her head and pinned
on top in what Avelino had overheard women call a Victory Roll
hairstyle. Her beauty struck him unexpectedly, and he didn't think
his lifelong preference for women with red hair biased his opinion
in her favor. *She would be beautiful with any color hair or eyes. I
wonder if she knows—*

"It's almost done. I'll just toss the salad. You're welcome to go sit
on the patio. We thought we'd eat out there. It's so nice."

"Is the garden . . . ?"

"It's growing well. I need to can the last of the tomatoes next
week, but there's still some lettuce and a few other things."

"May I—?"

"Oh, help yourself!"

Despite the nonchalant attitude and words, her curiosity
showed.

He strolled to the edge of the garden, his hands gripping the fence posts that kept it protected from animals who considered it their personal buffet. The tomatoes were overgrown—unmanaged—but plentiful. He grabbed four and searched for onions. At first, it seemed as though the cilantro had all gone to seed, but he found a small fresh patch growing at the edge. Happy with his take, Avelino strolled back through the yard to the house.

He worked with swift ease. Being the youngest child—the baby—had advantages and disadvantages. Being stuck in the kitchen with the women had never sat well with him as a child. However, now, after years of K rations and mess-hall meals that never quite satisfied, he ached for the flavors of home.

"You are comfortable in the kitchen."

"I spent hours cutting vegetables as a boy. My *mamá* had a hard time letting me grow up."

"What are you making?"

"*Ensalada fresca*—one of many that my *mamá* called *pico de gallo*."

"What does that mean?"

Avelino grinned. "Beak of the rooster."

"Beak of the rooster." She leaned closer, the clean scent of her soap swirling around her. "You are teasing me, right?"

"No. I'll show you. I just need salt and pepper . . . and is there a lime?"

She passed him a lemon. "Sorry, it's all I have."

Avelino took it, thanked her, and tossed the ingredients into a bowl. He washed his hands once more and reached to pinch a little of the salsa. "What does this look like?"

There it was—that smile. *She is truly beautiful—probably has men swarming the place. They won't like to find me here.* Another surreptitious glance her way prompted another thought. *Tough luck.*

"It does! It looks like the beak of a chicken!"

"Rooster. *Gallo*. And it has a 'peck' to it . . . like striking you."

"What is chicken in Spanish?"

"*Pollo*—but only if you eat her. Otherwise, it's *gallina*." His throat constricted as he spoke. *So familiar. How can something I've never experienced feel as if I've lived it all before?*

"Those green leaves. What are they? I thought they were weeds. I've been digging them out every time I find them."

"Cilantro. It makes everything taste like home to me." He sighed, contentment filling him as he added, "I didn't expect to find it. It goes to seed so quickly. I think it is called coriander *en inglés*."

They carried plates and bowls of food to the table on the patio, Amelia's eyes following him and a smile on her lips.

As they returned for the remaining dishes, Avelino could no longer contain his curiosity. "I amuse you."

"Oh, no—well, I suppose. I just noticed how you slipped from no accent at all into perfect Spanish and back again. It seemed almost effortless." Her eyes dipped to the platter in her hand and back up at him. "Do you speak fluent Spanish?"

"*Sí.*"

Mr. Kearns overheard them and asked, "What are we seeing?"

"No, Granddad, *sí*, like yes in Spanish. I asked if Mr. Carrillo was fluent."

"I would assume so. From what I hear, the Carrillos have been in this part of the world for over a hundred years."

"We have. We've been in this house for over a hundred years, and before that *la familia* lived in la Casa de Vida just over those hills. It's gone now."

"A hundred years of history in this house . . ." Amelia sounded lost in the past.

Memories overwhelmed Avelino as his mind traveled into his past and the stories his family had passed down through the years. He could hear the gravelly tones of his *abuelo*'s voice as he told Don

Edgar's story. When he was a little boy, it had been his favorite—full of exploits and excitement, battle and friendship. The romantic nonsense that permeated so many of the later tales was blissfully absent in favor of guns, swords, intrigue, travel—in a word, adventure.

"Tell us."

The words tickled his consciousness like a whisper in the ear. "I'm sorry, did you say something?"

"I asked you to tell us," Amelia repeated. "I see a story in your face; it's itching to escape. Who was the first man to live here?"

"Avelino Aguilar . . ." He took a bite of his meal, enjoying flavors that can't be produced in institutional cooking. Well-spiced, juicy chicken, creamy potatoes that didn't taste like papier-mâché, and roasted vegetables not cooked to utter tastelessness had become a luxury in recent years. "This is so delicious."

"Let him alone, 'Melia. He'll tell us when he's done eating. I'd lay money that he hasn't had a good meal in years."

Twilight paused, holding the world in that magical time before dusk rips it away and hands it over to darkness. Amelia cleared away the food, stacking dishes for later washing, and carried out fresh glasses of lemonade.

"I'm not letting you have dessert until you tell us more about your namesake."

"What is for dessert?"

"Lemon meringue pie . . ."

"I'll stay and tell. It never was a favorite of my aunts and cousins. They preferred to hear of Cherith Tandy . . ." He paused. Once he tempted her with the story of a woman, she would not care to know about poor Señor Avelino.

"Someday I want to hear it all, but tonight you promised to tell us about Señor Aguilar."

He took a long drink of his lemonade, allowing the refreshing citrus to trickle down his throat. *No rush—there's no rush. Relax.* If

15

he had learned anything from the storytellers in his family, it was that a tale must unfold slowly. *"Like a flower blossom,"* his *abuelo* had always said. *"Let the words open so that the fragrance of them is not swept away in the wind before it can be enjoyed."* *Abuelito* had been such a poet.

"It's a long story. Too long for one night."

"Then you'll have to come back. Won't he, Granddad?"

"You're welcome anytime, son."

It was the perfect time to tell them the bad news—that he would be closer than they might expect for the foreseeable future—but he didn't want to veer into any unpleasantness on so fine a night. The story held prisoner in his heart ached for a chance to break free and intrigue a new listener. He smiled. Mamá *always said that one day I would catch the Carrillo fever for telling a good story.* Avelino glanced heavenward. *You were right,* mamá.

He steeled himself for practicalities first. "That is something we should talk about."

Mr. Kearns leaned closer. "What is?"

"When I saw Mr. Lyndon today, I told him I needed him to add a provision for lodging to our contract. If I'm to work for debt alone, I need a place to sleep."

"Debt alone? How will you eat? Shouldn't you insist on a small wage for necessities too?" Amelia's outrage on his behalf only endeared her to him more.

"Miss Kearns, I—"

"Granddad, he can call me Amelia, can't he?"

"Certainly. You should call me Joe too."

Avelino shook his head. "I couldn't, sir. *Mi abuela* would rise up from her grave and thrash me. 'Do not fail to show honor and respect to those who are old enough to be your parents or grand-parents. It is the downfall of society when youth places itself on par with age.'"

"But surely she would not object to those of similar ages or younger . . ." Amelia pressed.

"If Mr. Kearns does not object, I don't. However, I do have awkward news, so perhaps he would care to hold his answer until I tell him what Mr. Lyndon decided."

"Oh." Her eyes roamed the patio and out into the yard. "We're being evicted, aren't we? I knew it would happen, of course," she hastened to add. "It is your home by right, but I hadn't expected us to leave so soon."

"No, he is not removing you. I wouldn't have agreed to that." With his eye on Mr. Kearns, Avelino explained the arrangements, finishing with, "If it is unacceptable, I can try to find something else. I won't pretend it wouldn't be wonderful to live at my old home. It is convenient distance-wise and I think separate enough from your house that it shouldn't feel too intrusive, but I will look elsewhere if you prefer."

Where the words developed, Avelino didn't know. He had not intended to make such an offer, but it was impossible not to once he began speaking. Perhaps it was the disappointment in Amelia's eyes or the wariness in Mr. Kearns's. Whatever the reason, once he'd spoken the words, he did not regret them.

"That isn't necessary, son. I didn't even know there was a room up there. I just thought it was storage. I haven't had much time to explore the outbuildings."

"Thank you, Mr. Kearns. I'm not blind to the trust you're giving me. I won't break it. Being home means more to me than I could ever explain."

As Amelia refilled their glasses, she said, "I'll help you get settled. It must be dusty after all this time. It'll need a good airing at the least, but," she added with exaggerated impatience, "right now we want to hear about the first Avelino."

Before they could make further misguided assumptions as to the storage area above the old garage, Avelino took another sip of his drink and leaned back against his chair. "Avelino Aguilar . . ."

CHAPTER THREE

SAN JACINTO

April 1836

Avelino Aguilar sat on horseback waiting for orders and the arrival of His Excellency General Santa Anna. The men around him prepared to march. A lane of trees hardly wide enough for two horses abreast was their path. As the detachment assembled, the way filled with soldiers moving forward from New Washington. After the recent victory at the Alamo, Santa Anna's army felt confident that they would drive out the Texians and quell the revolution at the next confrontation. The soldiers spoke arrogantly, assuming that the next battle would be swift and end the war once and for all. They were correct, but instead of a victory, Santa Anna's army waited in the lane to march to their doom at the Battle of San Jacinto.

Nerves attacked Avelino's mind, heart, and soul. After torrential rains and the burning of the warehouse and the houses in town, it seemed as if there was nothing left for them there. *Where is His Excellency?*

Cries and shouts reached him, but he could not understand. Horses stamped impatiently, fearfully. One animal screamed, and the men seemed to back away from the center of the lane. There he heard, "The enemy are coming! The enemy are coming!"

His heart raced, panic nearly overtaking him. All around, men's faces drained to a deathly pallor. *Houston.* The distressed men began frenzied attempts to flee. Having a horse was both an advantage and a disadvantage. *Through the lane. I must get through the lane.*

It took hours, seconds, days—Avelino didn't know how long. Fear drove him onward, while that same fear begged him to retreat. It became a double-edged sword—one that would get him killed. A horse threw one of the *capitanes*, and the frightened animal nearly stampeded over others in its desire to escape. Hating himself for it, Avelino dismounted and offered his superior his horse.

"*Gracias,*" the *capitán* said as he mounted the animal. "Keep going. We will meet them on the plain, and we will defeat the upstarts!"

The man's tone belied the confidence of his words. He was terrified—just as unnerved as any of the others were. "*Sí, mi capitán,*" Avelino answered.

How he reached the prairie, Avelino did not know. The chaos there was even worse than that which had ensued upon the *general's* announcement. Commanders issued conflicting orders, trying desperately to form a column of attack. He and the men around him followed instructions, sometimes several opposing ones in the space of minutes. With great trepidation, he followed *coronel* Delgado, searching with the others for the position of the enemy.

Flankers were sent into the woods. Not for the first time, Avelino thanked the saints and Jesucristo that he was not a scout. Then he heard a new order—one that filled him with dread. "Drop your *mochilas* where you stand." *My knapsack! How will I survive if I'm separated from the others and without my knapsack?*

Onward they marched, Avelino's muscles tired and aching. His beard was overgrown, his body underwashed, and he had not slept well in months. Long past noon, they saw the enemy's pickets at the edge of a large wood. Some began firing, but Houston's men returned fire instantly and then drew back into the wood.

General Santa Anna rode among the troops, preparing to call for attack, but he could not locate the enemy. Furious, he sent Avelino's comrades to set up the cannon and another detachment to skirmish among the trees. Avelino trembled as he helped move the great cannon in place and packed it.

"*Fuego!*"

The cannon fired; Avelino and the others covered their ears to protect against each deafening explosion. The enemy countered with a spray of grapeshot. Men and horses fell. Avelino watched in horror as *el capitán* Urrezza's horse screamed with unearthly terror and dropped dead. The *capitán* was severely wounded. Two men, risking their lives as grapeshot sprayed across the prairie, dragged the *capitán* over ground to safety.

Avelino tried to quell his increasing panic as they rammed another cannonball into place. Hands covered ears again, but this time there was more to block out than the explosion beside them. The screams of dying men and beasts wormed their way between the fingers of the artillerymen and lodged in the most fearful places of their hearts.

Someone ordered *coronel* Delgado to send the pack mules back to Barragan to retrieve the knapsacks, the first logical thing Avelino had heard all day. He tried to do his job but found himself distracted by all that occurred around him. It made him sloppy and earned him several sharp words from his comrades, but he didn't care.

At last, *general* Santa Anna chose to encamp along the San Jacinto Bay shore. An hour later, Avelino listened as another *coronel* ordered *coronel* Delgado to bring the cannon, the artillery, and the ordnance stores. His throat went dry as the next order came. The company of Toluca was to leave immediately. *No one would come to their aid? The* generales *are leaving us alone and unprotected with orders to drag the stores to camp without the pack mules?*

Delgado protested, but it did no good. The words of *coronel* Bringas seared their way into Avelino's heart: "His Excellency does not listen to the observations of mere *coroneles*. In his present state, I would not wish to speak to him about anything. The man is mad—raving."

In no time, Houston's army reaimed their gun and took out the caisson and limber. The Mexican ordnance boxes exploded, along with the mules, their flesh coating anything nearby. Avelino and the others worked swiftly to carry the ammunition down to the shore, but the constant attack from the enemy made the tedious work terrifying. Two hours passed before they finally managed to move everything.

Just as they entered the camp, Avelino's gut clenched again as *general* Santa Anna gave orders for *el capitán* Aguirre to send his company to fight back Houston's men. Terrified, Avelino drew his sword, prepared once more to die. The enemy fell back for a moment and then bore down upon the dragoons. One of Sam Houston's men advanced toward him, but Avelino dodged behind a comrade and worked his way across the lines, avoiding combat wherever possible. Avelino watched as blade met blade, but without much bloodshed. *How is it possible?*

He wanted nothing more than to rest. His muscles ached; his spirit felt shattered. They had no hope. He would not live. The others around him all held the same defeat in their weary eyes. Then, to everyone's astonishment, His Excellency went to bed, leaving the rest of the army to set up camp.

The *generales, coroneles,* and *capitanes* barked orders as the excitement of the skirmish died down. The Texians were less than a mile away yet invisible down at the bayou, hidden by trees. Avelino helped pile everything they could find to assemble breastworks. They piled crates on trunks and saddles above that. If only the soldiers weren't bone weary.

Grit seemed permanently lodged in his teeth, and his scalp crawled with lice. *If I live through this,* he thought to himself as he did nearly every day, *I will leave Mexico and go to California. I will build a casa and plant viñas—vineyards. I will marry a pretty señorita and have children—many, many children.*

To Avelino, the dream was almost unimaginable. Such a long journey. He felt as if he would not live through the war, despite Santa Anna's prior success, but if he did the trip would be arduous. He'd have to go by sea. The de Anza Trail was still closed and controlled by the Yuma Indians. *Intelligent people, those Indians. Let foreigners through and they'll take over every inch if given half a chance.*

"Avelino! Get moving. We must have this finished before morning!"

"Avelino," he echoed under his breath, "*rápidamente.* Work like a slave, sleep like a dog. Be the target for some Texian's practice."

It had seemed so glamorous; he would be a *caballero.* He would ride into battle and send those usurpers back into American territory. The filth, the work, the drudgery day after day had never occurred to him. Battle was sweat, grime, blood, and screams of pain from the men around him. He was a coward like most of his untrained comrades. *Pray God that my family never learns it,* he thought often to himself. In fact, his prayers each night included a petition to *la madre de Dios* for enough courage not to disgrace himself. Distinction he knew he did not deserve. Even for life, he had no hope. His family should only not hear that he failed his duty.

The supply wagon did not arrive; the Texians intercepted it. Furious, the *generales* drilled the men harder long into the night and then ordered them to sleep until dawn, when the bugles would blow again. Avelino prayed.

* * *

Their flags fluttered in the morning breeze. Reinforcements would arrive soon over Vince's Bridge. But smoke rose in the distance just as some of the reinforcements arrived. The Texians had burned the bridge. *His Excellency underestimated the Texians, or more likely overestimated his own skills*, Avelino thought as he loaded guns and waited for the order to attack. There was always an order.

It never came. The morning passed, and with the afternoon came their siesta. To Avelino's astonishment, the *generales, coroneles,* and *capitanes* retired to tents to rest. *I do not understand—why?* he mused as he lowered his hat over his eyes and allowed the warmth of the sun to lull him into a lazy half-conscious state. Though not a proper siesta, it would do.

A bugle sounded attack. Avelino's head jerked as he awakened.

Coronel Delgado climbed up on ammunition boxes and surveyed the situation. "There are a lot of them—one long line. There are cannons on each side and—"

Gunshots and cannon fire deafened him. After the first man went down, screams of pain piercing the air through the noise around him, Avelino retched and refused to shoot again. Until then he'd been able to avoid close combat, but no more. Avelino moved mechanically, lowering the gun, raising it again, and lowering it for the next few minutes. Anyone watching would think he was a wonder with his weapon, firing endlessly at the enemy. He never pulled the trigger.

"Aguilar, get some water and bring more back with you," one of the *capitanes* called. The tone of the man's voice was approving. His efforts, worthless as they were, had caught the attention of those in charge.

Do they not see that I produce no gun smoke? Or do the guns of my comrades cover for me there too? I should be ashamed.

A glance out at the battle told him they would lose. *It's only a matter of time—a very short matter of time in fact—before we are overrun or we flee.* Men ran helter-skelter, overpowered by fear and panic. The only thing that had kept him in place was the illusion of safety from his spot.

I will die then. Despair tried to strangle him, but a primal instinct, one he did not know he possessed, reached into his heart and whispered a plan—*I will escape while I can.* He ran, crouched lower than the breastworks in hope that they would catch any bullets that flew into the camp, to the water and filled his canteen. A fallen soldier nearby held one as if he'd taken a last sip before dying. Water trickled out as Avelino moved it from the still-warm hand.

He found a dozen other canteens nearby as well, but Avelino only allowed himself two more. The *coronel* would expect him to bring back a few canteens, but if they saw too many, it might give rise to questions—questions he could not afford to be asked. Men began fleeing toward the bayou. Even *coronel* Delgado, as the men scattered, gave up trying to encourage his soldiers to fight, and rode toward the awful marsh.

Dried beef. I need more than I've saved in past days. How can I get into the supplies without being noticed? A bugle blast told him it was too late. He had no time. If he stayed, he'd die. His only chance, a small one at best, was to run. In a desperate moment, he grabbed yet another abandoned canteen.

As he scrambled between men, dropping over the bodies of fallen comrades when necessary, Avelino learned something of himself that he'd never known. He had a talent for evasion. Each time he thought he'd be caught by a bullet or commander, he managed to slip past yet again.

The marsh would be the easiest place to hide. He'd start there, work his way around the camp, and head north toward enemy lines. The rest of Santa Anna's army was running south and then later, possibly west. He'd follow the river northeast and away from the army. *It is my only chance.*

The marsh grasses were different from the high grass of the prairie, where the battle still raged. Trees showed him the path of the river, but the wetlands of the marsh made it difficult to trudge through it. His boots squished in the muck, and the mud tried to rip them from his feet; mosquitos stung his face and neck mercilessly, but still Avelino continued, determined to get away, and quickly.

He listened from time to time, adjusting his direction to lead him closer to the enemy, something that terrified him. One wrong move and they'd kill him as a spy at best.

He was weary from little sleep, much work, and a long day of pretending to shoot; his muscles screamed for him to stop. However, from somewhere deep within, Avelino Aguilar found a reserve of endurance that carried him through the marsh and across the river. He hid in the grasses and anything else he could find until nightfall. He drank fresh water, washed his face with his kerchief, and allowed himself half an hour's rest.

Stars twinkled overhead when he woke with a start several hours later. Furious with himself for wasting precious night hours, he plunged onward. He had to make it to Arkansas and stay hidden for a couple of months. Once the furor died down, he would travel back down to the gulf and find a ship sailing for California.

His hand fingered the pouch inside his underclothes. His *tía* Maria had given him enough jewels and gold to set him up anywhere. "For bribes," she had said. "If you need to use it to save yourself, do it."

That day had arrived. If he survived, he would go to California, where land was plentiful and the Californios lived like kings, with natives doing the work while they partied, traveling from rancho to rancho. *Un día a la vez.* He must survive somehow, one day at a time.

* * *

". . . one day at a time."

Only the chirping of the crickets and the occasional squawking screech of a bat broke the silence as Avelino ended his story. Moths flitted around the light at the back door, sending strange shadows against the side of the house. He waited, his stomach twisting in nervous anticipation of their—*Okay, her reaction*, he amended to himself. *Will she understand, or will she see my namesake as a coward?*

"He makes it come alive, doesn't he, Granddad? I studied the Battle of San Jacinto. I only read about how Sam Houston stopped the Mexican army there—crushed them in retaliation for the Alamo. I never thought of it from the other side."

"It only lasted twenty minutes," Avelino murmured. "Twenty minutes that changed the course of my family's history."

"I want to hear the rest. I want to hear how Avelino escaped and made it to California. Was he a great-great-great—or more—grandfather?"

"No relation at all," Avelino assured her.

That worked. She sat up straighter.

"Really? Oh, you can't stop there," Amelia protested. "Tell him, Granddad. He has—"

"To get some rest, 'Melia. He's had a long day. He can tell us tomorrow or some other day." Joe pushed his chair back. "Sorry. She gets a bit . . . focused . . . when things interest her." The older man leaned forward and asked, "Do you have somewhere to stay for the night? That room can't be habitable yet."

"The veterans' home said I could stay there for a night or two until I get settled. They have a few spare beds."

Standing, Joe beckoned him to follow. "I'll drive you." To Amelia he added, "I'll be home in a bit. If you wash the dishes, I'll dry 'em when I get back."

CHAPTER FOUR

HOME AT HOME

September 1945

His heart clenched once more as he started up the drive. *Home.* How long would it be before he could arrive without the now-familiar pang that reminded him he truly was home? His eye sought the garage—that place that once had been the low stable for horses and the cow. Something was amiss, but what?

Faintly, he heard the cheerful tune of Glenn Miller's "Kalamazoo" from the upper windows. *That's it—curtains.* Snowy-white curtains fluttered in the upper windows of the room over the garage. The *clean* window of the room. *How?* Avelino shook his head. He knew how: Amelia. Were there not the same curtains dancing in the breezes that flitted through the house as well? *She must have been up at dawn to get the windows clean and the curtains hung.* Barrels of trash half blocked the stairs leading to his new home. *Yes. At dawn.*

They'd listened to that song in the South Pacific—his friends and he. He could almost feel the heat, the tension. As Avelino jogged up the steps, he wondered what happened to some of the men—James, Ted, Jerald, who wouldn't let anyone call him Jerry. Victor didn't make it back. He died in the same blast that took out Avelino's eye and Ted's arm.

Bile filled his throat at the memory, but he stuffed it down again. *I lived. That's more than I can say for so many of the others—like Victor.* The music swelled just as he stepped into the large storage room. He'd forgotten what it was like in there; the junk littered nearly every inch. Some things had probably been there since the first days of the Carrillos.

His senses went on high alert as the shadow of a gun barrel grew on the wall in his peripheral vision. His eyes darted around the room but saw nothing he could use as a weapon. Avelino reacted instinctively. That Jap wouldn't get him—not this time. He dove for the screen that blocked the gun and pinned the enemy to the wall. Something clattered to the ground as a scream pierced the air.

His body froze in place, and his mind struggled to identify the weapon—if it even was a weapon—on the ground. Something or someone rushed past him, but he didn't see who or what. His concentration remained firmly rooted on long poles that lay on the ground. *A trap? Bamboo hiding a hole filled with Japs?* His senses grew more alert with each passing second as he deliberated. Thunder like rapid fire from a distance descended upon him, but he had nowhere to hide. He dove for the poles. His hands shoved away slimy snakes that seemed riveted to one of them, and were scratched by thin, spindly, needlelike spikes.

He whirled to meet his foe, determined to knock a gun from the hands of that scrawny little—*recognition.* Avelino dropped the stick. "Wha—?"

"What do you think you're doing, attacking my granddaughter?"

"Attacking?" Avelino leaned forward as if to prove to himself that the visage was no mirage foisted on his confused mind. "Mr. Kearns?"

"Yeah! Amelia just ran out of here, terrified. Said something about you attacking her."

"I didn't . . ." Even as he denied it, his mind cleared a little, giving him a memory of something he didn't care to see. "Oh! I—what happened? Why?" He covered his face with his hands and sank to the floor. *"No comprendo. Ayúdeme, por favor."*

"Did you say help? Help the man . . ."

Avelino raised his head, meeting the fading, infuriated glare of the older man. That one action softened Mr. Kearns's face. "Oh, son. I know. I am so sorry."

"You know what? What do you know? I don't know. I don't understand. One minute I am listening to a favorite song, ready to clean my new flat, and the next you tell me I attacked Amelia. How could I do such a thing! *Mi abuelita estaría furiosa conmigo."*

"You lapse into Spanish when you are emotional," Mr. Kearns noted as he reached out to help Avelino to his feet. "It is a flashback. Amelia's cousin came back from the Great War with them. The strangest things would set him off—almost always from something he saw out of the corner of his eye."

"¡Sí! It was like that. I saw the shadow almost from behind." The trembling in his hands settled as the explanation seemed reasonable, but beads of perspiration still glistened on his forehead and upper lip. "I did not hurt her? She is good?"

"She's fine. Not a scratch on her, but you did shake her up a bit."

Avelino wanted to ask permission to find Amelia and apologize, but her grandfather had no reason to trust him. He could not do it. Then again, Mr. Kearns had been understanding—more understanding than Avelino felt toward himself at that moment.

"Would you explain? Tell her how sorry I am. I would do it myself, but I could not ask—"

"Go ahead. If I know my granddaughter, she's in the kitchen with her hands wrapped around a cup of coffee or scrubbing . . . something."

Avelino nodded his agreement and took steps toward the door before glancing back. "Are you sure?"

"I'll be close. I'm not going to risk her, even if I do think you are okay now. Go ahead."

Somehow he felt better knowing that someone would be watching him. The sensation of distrusting himself clenched his gut. Still, he walked slowly and resolutely toward the house. The kitchen door had been propped open. He stood in the doorway, waiting for her to notice, before finally speaking.

"Amelia?"

She jumped, and the cup she clutched in her hands slipped and crashed to the floor. "I don't think—"

"Your grandfather said I could come and apologize."

Doubt flashed in her eyes. "My granddad said—?"

"It's okay, 'Melia. He had a flashback like David used to have."

Compassion—how did she shift from fear, anger, and doubt to compassion with just a few words? He watched the emotions flicker across her face until at last she said, "You'd better come in then. Coffee?"

His hesitation—he hated it. One strange move had paralyzed him emotionally. He could see the scene, now that he'd had time to relive it. The shadow, the taste of fear on his tongue, the saliva building as he prepared to charge. Her scream.

"Thank you." What else could he say? His gaze drifted to the door, where Mr. Kearns watched as promised. "Won't you come in, sir? I think we'd both feel better."

"I'm okay now, Avelino. Really." Amelia waved her granddad into the house, though, as she reached for new cups. "Do you want some too?"

Mr. Kearns backed away, shaking his head. "I need to get down to the vines. We're testing sugar today."

"Already?" Avelino frowned. "Are they that close?"

"It's been a good year. I am just being cautious. The last thing I need is Mr. Lyndon blaming me for an inferior wine."

And that was how it would be for seven years—always looking over his shoulder to see if his creditor was satisfied. "You are wise. He'd replace you just to prove a point to others who have no authority."

Amelia's eyes grew wide as she listened, and then she whispered, "He'd accuse you of sabotaging him, wouldn't he?"

"He might," Avelino agreed, "but he'd be a fool to believe it. I will want a profitable vineyard and winery with a solid reputation when I pay it off. Running it into the ground to spite him only hurts me."

"Shall we get to work?" Amelia filled two cups with coffee and handed him one. "There's a lot to do in there. That garage is packed with stuff. I don't know where we'll put it all."

"I don't need the entire space. We can stack as much as possible against the back."

She smiled at him as she passed, rubbing her nose as if able to feel the dust assaulting her sinuses. "Let's go then."

"Thank you."

"What for?"

Avelino stared at his shoes, his thumbs hooked into his pants pockets. "For understanding—for forgiving. How I could—how I . . ." Again he sighed. "*Lo siento*, Amelia."

"Forget it. Truly. Now that I know, I might be able to help next time. I think I remember how Mom and Grandmom calmed Da . . . vid."

"Please don't. Please. Just get away until you know I'm 'back' if it ever happens again. I hope it will not, but . . ."

Avelino was not prepared for the resistance that built within him as he followed Amelia up to the room. Amelia skipped up the stairs as carefree as any girl on her way to a party, but he had to force each footstep. The emotions that roiled in his heart left him uncertain and confused. *Is it because I expect another lapse into temporary insanity?* That thought shook him once more. *Do I really dread the return of the memories? Surely, the past—my past—can't be the cause.* Avelino swallowed hard and steeled himself against memories that threatened to betray him.

Relief washed over him as he stepped in the room and saw nothing but dirty floors, walls, and jumbles of junk everywhere. "It's a mess."

"Well, thank you very much! I'll have you know I've cleared out several barrels of trash—you should go through it so Granddad can burn it later—and cleaned the windows."

"And curtains. Those weren't here before. I don't think those windows ever had curtains."

"I made spares for the kitchen and the side of the house that gets the most sun. I'll make more later. You have so many old sheets, and they make perfect curtains." She gestured toward a pile in one corner at the front of the room. "That was stuff I didn't know what you wanted me to do with. There's a lot of papers in there—things that look interesting, but I can't read most of it."

His fingers flipped through letters, documents, and the now-useless deed to la Casa de Vida and the first Carrillo rancho. He stacked the box aside and flipped through other things. There were clothes from decades ago—things that no one wore anymore but were beautiful and traditional. His children would like to see them someday.

"May I put these things in my old room of the house?"

"Sure. We'll do that when we're finished for the day. We have a lot to get done first."

With the mop that had felt like snakes to him, she scrubbed at the walls. He wondered why she didn't use a rag, but a closer inspection showed rough patches.

"Want me to do that?"

"No, thank you. I really need you to get through those piles so we can determine how much room you're really going to have. Put the stuff for the house in that corner, the stuff that stays against that wall"—she gestured to the one opposite the first corner—"and if you want to get rid of it, take it down."

News droned on the radio at times, but for the most part he enjoyed a recap of all the music he'd missed and never heard. As he worked and listened, Avelino couldn't help but watch Amelia occasionally. She danced with the mop, humming along with each song. It was catching, but so many of the songs he didn't know—just what he'd learned in the army.

After peeling back years of layers of junk, he found a trunk— one he recognized. *How did* abuelita's *trunk get so buried?* He raised the lid, and a hint of musty roses filled his nostrils. *It smells like her too.* He lifted piece after piece of fabric, linens, and a few blankets from it.

"What do you think about these?"

Amelia dropped her mop so quickly that he had no doubt she'd been watching him as well.

"Let's see . . ." Her hand stroked the heavily embroidered blanket—*colcha*, if he remembered correctly—folded it back to reveal another one even more beautiful than the last. "These are amazing. Did your grandmother or great-grandmother embroider?"

"*Sí.* Both. This they called *colcha.*"

"What does that mean?"

He grinned. "Bedcover or bedspread. But it is the embroidery, not the piece—not anymore."

"You must preserve these. I should take them inside, where they'll be more protected. They could have gotten ruined out here. What else is there?"

"Cloth—not a lot of it, and it's not that useful."

Even as he spoke, Amelia's hand spread over a green piece of fabric. "This is my favorite color. Isn't it beautiful? I wonder what it was for . . ."

He tried to remember but failed. He'd never seen the fabric. "I don't know. Maybe *mamá* bought it to make herself something and then never did."

"And green is still so hard to find. I think you might find a store that would buy it."

Now he recognized the tone. Longing. "No, you take it. Maybe you can have green curtains in your room."

"Green curtains? Are you kidding? This is rayon—lovely rayon. There must be four yards here—maybe five! You should take it down to Whitby's. I bet he would—"

"If you want it, take it. Otherwise, it can go in the burn pile."

Once he spoke, he knew he'd never do it. He felt like a liar, the words searing his throat. Avelino started to confess, but her smile silenced him.

"Thank you! I've wanted a new nice dress for ages, but you know how it is. No one can afford anything—well, we can better than a few years ago, but still . . ." She set the fabric on top of the pile she'd appropriated for the house. "I'll take it in when I bring these."

A chocolate velveteen piece appeared next. "Have any use for brown?"

"Are you serious?"

Taking that as a yes, Avelino dug through the trunk and piles until he had several pieces of cloth. "Here. Do whatever you want with them. I care about the *colcha*, the clothing, and some of the linens, but this can burn for all it interests me."

"Well, you take it inside then, where it's protected, while I finish the walls. You can fill that thing with other—stuff."

They made slow but steady progress, and as they worked Glenn Miller dueled with Bing Crosby and Judy Garland and "The Trolley Song."

"That's a fun one," Avelino remarked as he stacked unused saddles in the corner, unsure what to do with them.

"You know, I wouldn't have really understood it until I saw the cable cars in San Francisco when we came here. Granddad tried to get work in the shipyards first."

"And then found la Viña de los Sueños?"

"No . . . we went to Fresno next. Well, we went to Bakersfield first—all the folks from Oklahoma went there first. It was just too full. No work for an old man, so Granddad decided to try the shipyards. It was closer to Los Angeles, but he thought there might be more work the further north we went."

"And then you went to Fresno?"

She nodded as she dumped the bucket out the window and went to refill it again. "Yes. It was nice there. Granddad learned a lot about grapes from the owner. He liked Granddad. They were close in age, had similar family stories. Mr. Delaney taught Granddad all he knows about grapes."

"You were sorry to leave."

He couldn't see the nod this time, but he heard the agreement in her voice as she blasted water through protesting pipes into the bucket.

"Grandmom had just died. We had to leave her in a place where no one would visit the grave." A sniffle followed, nearly choking him with the raw emotion in it. "She's all alone there. We're all alone here. I just hope when Granddad can't work anymore we can go back there. Start over. Maybe by then I'll be able to support us."

The world had become an upside-down place when a girl—hardly more than eighteen if his guess was anywhere near close—expected to support herself and her grandfather alone and without a family to assist her.

"You wouldn't go back to Oklahoma? There is no family there?"

Before she could answer, the radio began playing a song, one he had loved as a child. Avelino didn't recognize the group, but the song . . . *I can still hear* abuelito *singing as he examined the grapes, searching for the white powdery dust that clings to the dark clusters to see if the yeast would be sufficient for a good wine.*

The rhythmic chink-chink of the mop back and forth in the corner of the room seemed to keep in time with the song. Unaware at first that he did, Avelino sang along with the refrain, allowing it to pull him into the past and wash him with soothing memories.

". . . *Cariño, mi querida, por favor, ven conmigo.*"

The next song cut off abruptly, making Avelino turn to see what had happened to the radio.

Amelia stood resting her chin on her hands atop the mop handle. "What does it mean?"

"What?"

"The song. It's one of my favorites. I've heard it in English—but Granddad says that the ones with the English words are different, changed."

"It's a love song—one about home and family, as well as his sweetheart. He wants her to come with him now and not wait for tomorrow, because tomorrow may bring sorrow with it." Avelino smiled and said, "It was my *mamá's* favorite song. She liked the sad ones. She insisted it made her feel better when she sang. She'd say, '*Music, Avelino—singing—it makes the heart glad.*'"

"It's true." She shrugged at the questioning glance he tossed her way. "It is. Whenever I was sad as a little girl, Mama or Grandmom would get me singing 'Bye, Bye, Blackbird' or 'Four Leaf Clover,' and it just didn't feel so important anymore that I didn't have a new dress or a fancy doll."

"Does it still help?" He couldn't imagine that it did.

"Some, yes. It gives you a chance to set your troubles down and rest awhile before you have to carry them again. That helps." She gave the mop a shove before she added, "It's prettier in Spanish. I think Spanish is such a lovely-sounding language. Not like English. We sound so clipped and flat in comparison."

"I won't argue that *español* is lovely, but English can sound different depending on who speaks it. A Californian sounds very different from someone from New York or Boston or Michigan." He grinned, remembering the stories of the Texians. "And in America's south, they sound even more different. I wonder if you sound like the Tandys that Avelino Aguilar left this house to."

"Texians then were probably from other states."

"Yes, they were originally from Virginia. The stories that my family tells of her voice—they loved to listen to it. Just as you say you like ours. I think people like what is different."

"Wait, Avelino met a Virginian while he was in Texas? He left this house to her? How is that possible?"

"Well—"

"You should be writing your stories down, you know. Your family will appreciate it someday."

Avelino gave a short shake of the head. "I have no skill with a pen. I can tell you the stories my father, grandfather, great-grandfather, and others have told for generations, but I was never able to put the ideas in my head on paper in a way that made sense. It frustrated my teachers, as you can imagine."

"This is what I get for being lazy about studying that shorthand book."

"Shorthand?"

"I thought I might get a better job with a better wage if I knew shorthand." She sighed. "Now I wish I learned it, so I could take down your stories for you."

With that, she shoved the mop in the bucket, wringing it out again, and went back to scrubbing the floor. To his surprise, he heard her mutter, "But I will learn it now. Yes, indeedy I will."

* * *

Mr. Kearns interrupted their work to ask about lunch, sending Amelia flying down the steps and into the house. The men glanced at each other, shrugged, and followed. They found her in the kitchen, slicing onions. Avelino watched, hands stuffed in his pockets, as Mr. Kearns pulled out a butter knife and began scraping a thin layer onto the bread.

"May I help?"

Amelia didn't hesitate. She pointed to a tomato on the windowsill, saying, "Sure. If you'd slice that, I'd appreciate it. Thanks."

He'd never had an onion-tomato sandwich on buttered bread. Even as he sliced, his taste buds screamed for a few peppers and some cilantro. *Would it offend her? Surely not.* He couldn't do it. *With all her help, to change her food—rude.*

"Avelino might like peppers on his. Didn't you say you found some?"

She nodded and gestured toward the door. "Go see. I'll fini— oh." The pile of sliced tomatoes stopped her. "You're fast."

Once more they ate on the patio, Mr. Kearns filling Avelino in on the condition of the grapes, the likely day they'd begin the harvest, and the excitement among the workers that morning as they discussed his return. Amelia ate in silence, but the moment Avelino swallowed his last bite and washed it down with water, she grabbed their plates and rushed inside, returning moments later with a small plate of cookies.

"Tell us more. There's a little time." Her eyes sought her grandfather's. "Right?" At Mr. Kearns's nod, she added, "Please?"

Avelino slid his thumb along the edge of a cookie. *How would* abuelito *tell it? Would he talk about running from snakes and the long, uncomfortable nights?* He glanced in Amelia's direction and saw her eager expression. *Don't show too much of his fear. She might not understand—not yet. But she wants the adventure,* another part of him argued. *Don't leave out the adventure.*

"April gave way to May, and with it, long, hot days and even longer nights as Avelino tramped across Texas . . ."

CHAPTER FIVE

LIFE AND LONGING

Texas, May 1836

Harsh, cruel, the Texas sun beat down on Avelino as he forced himself toward Arkansas. So many nights he'd walked in circles, unsure of where to go and how to reach his destination. *Since when does a soldier need a sense of direction?* he mused to himself as he tried to find shade again. *A soldier should only have to follow the lead of his* capitán.

He saw a settlement ahead—one he prayed was not Waterloo. If so, it meant that he had not come nearly as far as he'd hoped.

His boots had disintegrated into tatters, food gone. He'd managed to forage strange plants and had even managed to crush a snake, but raw snake flesh was a hard thing to choke down even when starving. Oh, he'd stolen an egg or two when he found shanties erected on the prairie. He'd even milked a cow once, but the animal's lowing had brought out a vicious-looking woman with a mustache he would have paid for as a boy.

The canteens were empty—again. *Why are they always empty?* The dried beef hadn't lasted two days. *I should have rationed them,* he chided himself, but his recrimination was short-lived. *How do I know how much to save and how much is necessary to be able to continue?*

With each step that drew him forward, Avelino began to realize that it was no settlement; it was the battlefield he'd left almost three weeks earlier. *How—how?* Inwardly he raged as his feet stumbled toward the rotting corpses. He retched and turned, desperate to get away again. He ran. *This cannot be happening! I will die out here, and for what?*

A sound sent a shot of panic into his heart. In terror, Avelino tripped through the marshes and hid. There it was again, that sound. A whistle. Someone nearby whistled an unfamiliar song. Avelino poked his head up and saw a man—much older than he—strolling along the river, carrying a rifle and a dead turkey. And still whistling. Always whistling.

Avelino crept through the grasses, hoping to make it to the river undetected. It felt safe going the opposite direction from the man, but his heart still panicked. A pool of water drew him to it. It couldn't be as fresh as the river, but his feet ached. *I'll cool them for a few minutes until the man is long out of earshot.*

No sooner had he eased his sore, blistered feet into the water than a horrible pain seized him. Attached to his foot was a snake—*mocasín*. His scream of pain echoed around him, mocking him in the late afternoon air. The hunter called out, asking *en inglés* if someone needed help. When Avelino didn't reply, the man tried again *en español*.

"*¿Dónde está usted? ¿Algo le duele?*"

The foot swelled quickly, and the pain grew excruciating. He had not the courage to kill himself, but perhaps the man, seeing a Mexican in a soldier's uniform, would shoot out of fear. *"Sí. Ayúdeme, por favor." Help me, please.*

To his astonishment, the man arrived empty-handed. He pulled Avelino from the water, reaching for a knife on his belt. Avelino watched in horror as the man went to slice his foot—cut it off, it seemed. Screams pierced his ears. *Where did they come from? Who . . . ?* Realization dawned as his dry throat choked and sputtered, refusing to cooperate any longer.

The pain—he had never felt anything so excruciating. The man tied his belt around Avelino's upper thigh, cinched it tightly, and then squeezed the foot until it felt like there should be no blood left. Relief came when the tourniquet was released. The pain remained—ever throbbing and increasing—but at the same time somehow lessened. *It makes no sense.*

"Gracias, señor," he gasped.

The taller man grabbed Avelino's arms and jerked them over his shoulders. Every few minutes, the hunter paused and lowered his burden to the ground. Crazed with pain, Avelino wondered, *How much farther will he haul me before he leaves me to die on the prairie?*

Not much farther. Was that what the man said? It sounded like it, but the buzzing in his brain and the burning in his foot made it impossible to be sure. He wanted to ask—the man obviously knew some *español*—but the words refused to form.

From somewhere inexplicable, a voice called out, "Papa!"

Why does someone call me papá? *I have no children. I chose excitement and glory in the army over family. Such a foolish decision. I will die here near the battlefield—not of wounds received in brave combat but from the bite of a viper.* As his father had repeatedly pounded into him as a child, Avelino Aguilar could do nothing right.

The man's voice answered the girl. *Ah, yes. He is the* papá. Though Avelino tried to raise his head to see the child, his vision seemed contorted by the poison. Fire consumed the girl's head as she raced back toward what must be a house. *How long before the hallucinations end and I die?*

Softness—comfort. Death would be soon. His cousin had died when he was a boy. The young man had cried in such pain for so long before the silence came, and then the surprising words *"Hay paz ahora."* It is peaceful now.

The fire began again, burning hotter, searing. His eyes resisted, but at last he opened them. The flames grew closer and closer.

"Here," they said. "I have water."

Avelino knew water. *Inglés* for *agua.* The flames touched his cheek as the cool liquid poured over his lips and trickled down his throat. Soft. The flames—so soft. *Will they scorch the flesh from my bones before I feel their heat? Why do I feel the burning in my foot when the flames are near my face?*

Another splash on his foot sent the agonizing pain shooting up his leg once more. He cried out, choking on the liquid that had been so refreshing.

"¡La madre de Dios, sálveme!"

*   *   *

Heaven was not what Avelino had envisioned. Rich cities full of jewels and gold and pretty señoritas and angels . . . It certainly wasn't this shabby place with little light and no beauty—no beauty aside from the jar of wildflowers on a barrel next to his bed.

Avelino jerked. Bed! *I am in a bed. It is the house of the man who helped me.* A shadow drifted toward him, but not until it stepped out of the shaft of light through the now-open door did he see what it was. A girl, small but older than he expected, leaned over him and spoke. He didn't understand anything but that same word. Water.

"Sí, por favor."

The fiery head—it was hers. Her hair no longer swirled around her head in a riot of waves that looked like flickering flames; it now hung in one long braid down her back, with a few tendrils at her temples. *It looks like the roses that* abuela *tended so faithfully at home.*

"*El pelo como rosas,*" he whispered.

"Most would say carrots," a voice from the doorway said.

His eyes traveled to the black silhouette of his rescuer in the doorway. "*No, rosas,*" Avelino insisted.

"She doesn't understand *español*, but if she did, she'd think you were crazed from the poison, the fever, and likely a little drunk from all the alcohol we've poured down you."

"How long? How long has it been?" He feared the answer, but from the dullness of the pain in his foot, Avelino knew it must be at least a day or two.

"Better part of a week. The poison did a number on you. I thought I was going to have to take off that foot, but it seems to be healing now. You're going to limp, though. I am sure I cut things that shouldn't get cut, trying to keep out the poison."

"*Gracias*, I thank you," Avelino assured the man. "I would have died. I wanted to die, but I was also afraid."

"You fought with Santa Anna's men?"

Terror gripped him once more as he contemplated being turned over to the Texian militia. "I think it is more truthful if I say that I was with Santa Anna's men. I was better at pretending to fight than truly fighting." He frowned. "I deserted."

"So did half the army, from what I could see. Your running probably saved your life, but I don't know how." The man waved his daughter away from the bed, sat on her stool, and offered him the water again. "Most of the men that fled were killed or captured."

"I went the other way. I knew where they'd run, so I tried going the other direction."

"Tactical man—smart. They should have had you planning strategy."

Avelino could not repress his curiosity any longer. "How do you speak *español* so well? I have never met a *gringo* who didn't flounder over every few words."

"Always had a head for languages. Learned a lot of French from a fellow I met after the Battle of New Orleans. He'd grown up down there, so the Frenchies taught him a lot."

Avelino pointed to the girl, who stirred something in a pot. "Your granddaughter—"

"Daughter."

"Daughter," he corrected, smiling at the older man. "Does she have your talent with languages?"

"I don't know. I haven't had time to teach her anything."

"She has a pleasing voice." Avelino flushed at the fierce look the man gave him. "I mean no offense. *Perdóneme.*"

The girl, confused, smiled and asked in English, "What is your name?"

Avelino looked to the man for translation. When the reply came—asking for his name—he grinned. "Avelino Aguilar. *¿Y usted?*"

"Edgar Tandy." He pointed to the girl, who seemed to be trying to imitate the words she'd heard. "This is my daughter, Cherith."

"Cheer-ith. Unusual name."

"It's a river in the Bible."

The men stared at one another until, weary and ready to fall asleep again, Avelino whispered, "What are you going to do with me?"

"Get you well and help get you home."

He choked down the water Cherith tried to give him and then rasped, "But I do not wish to go home."

"Where were you going?"

"California. I long for California."

*   *   *

Amelia sat entranced, hanging on every word, but a glance at Mr. Kearns told Avelino that he needed to stop there. "I could tell stories for hours, but I only have today to get settled, and I think Mr. Kearns is anxious to get back to the vines."

She started to protest—Avelino saw it in her eyes—but as she glanced over at her grandfather, she sighed and nodded. "I will look forward to the next one. Waiting'll be good for me." At Mr. Kearns's snicker, she protested, "It will!"

CHAPTER SIX

FIRST TENDRILS OF FRIENDSHIP

A green ribbon of fabric divided the floor. Avelino sat on the seat his *abuelo* built beneath the window that looked out over the front of the house and listened to the radio program with his hosts. Across the room in his *mamá's* favorite chair, Mr. Kearns sat shelling peanuts, while Amelia crawled around the floor, pinning pattern pieces to the cloth.

As the show ended, Mr. Kearns snapped off the set and closed his eyes, listening to the crickets outside.

Amelia sat cross-legged, arms akimbo, and stared at her project in disgust. "Is there any pop in the icebox, Granddad?"

"Not that I know of."

"Lemonade's gone too. Shoulda made sweet tea today."

The older man's eyes opened and rested on his granddaughter, his fondness for her shining in them. "Hankerin' for something cool?" He winked at Avelino.

"Yeah. Was hot up in that room—not sure how Avelino is going to stand it in summer."

"I won't be up there during much of the day anyway. I'll be working."

She shrugged. "That's true, but I'm not sure how that's any better. It's hot among the vines too."

"After the heat in the Philippines, I don't think I'll ever think of Napa as hot again," he murmured.

The Kearnses just nodded.

He could offer to walk down to the gas station. Hank Rhimes kept a cold soda machine just outside the door to his office. It wouldn't take that long to hoof it up there and back at a slow jog.

"I could run down to Hank's. What sounds good? Orange? Grape? Coke? Does he still have them all?"

"Oh, that sounds perfect!"

He stood, not even hesitating, and tucked his shirt back in as he stepped gingerly around her sea of fabric, pins, and paper. "What'll it be?"

Amelia hesitated, as if trying to decide, before she turned to her grandfather. "I could go with him—it'd be colder if I got it right away. Is that okay?"

"Sure, but—" Avelino broke in.

She whirled to face him. "Do you mind?"

"Not at all." As if compelled to attempt honesty, Avelino heard himself say, "I would have asked, but I thought you probably wanted to rest. You really put in a hard day's work today."

"Amelia doesn't know the meaning of the word 'rest.' I try to lead by example, but I'm afraid she caught her grandmom's industriousness." Mr. Kearns stood and stretched and grabbed the bowl of peanut shells from the end table beside him. "Meanwhile, I think I'll take a bath."

"Can we bring you something, sir?"

"I don't think so, but thanks." The man dug his fist in his pocket and pulled out a few nickels and a dime. "Here."

Before Amelia could take them, Avelino spoke up, moving toward the door. "That's not necessary. I've got it, but thanks."

It seemed impossible. Only a week ago he'd been trapped at the Presidio. First the islands with their recurring horrors, then the awful weeks with a thousand other men on the hospital ship. Since June he had been in and out of the hospital and temporary barracks, and now he walked along the road to Hank's with a girl—one who looked like every dream he'd ever had about the first mistress of la Casa de los Sueños. She was quiet, this girl with the hair like roses, and she loved the stories of his family.

"I hope you didn't feel obligated . . ."

He flushed, grateful for the darkness that hid his embarrassment. *How do I tell her that I would have asked last night if I had thought it proper? How do I make her understand without making her uncomfortable?* "Perhaps," he began, hesitating, "I should apologize for not inviting you in the first place."

"You're not obligated to bring me along just because we live on the same patch of land."

Her protest sounded almost comical.

"But my apology would be for being dishonest, not because of obligation."

"Dishonest?"

Avelino glanced at the girl beside him. It was much too early to know if he was truly interested. He had little enough knowledge of the girl's family. She might take offense, or her grandfather might. Some *gringos* considered themselves above a "dirty Mexican." Even as he thought it, Avelino knew that wasn't true of the Kearnses, but that didn't mean he was welcome to ask her out for a walk or a date.

"I implied that I only offered to be an errand boy," he said at last.

"I don't understand."

Of course she didn't. *How can she? I'm being deliberately evasive.* "I meant it when I said I wanted to ask. I just wasn't honest about why I didn't."

"You thought I was tired—no, you didn't think I was tired?" Her eyebrows drew together as she riddled his disjointed explanation. "I feel very foolish and obtuse. What did you say again?"

I dug the hole. I might as well jump in and let her bury me. Please God, don't let me make things awkward at the house, he pleaded silently before forcing himself to answer. "That is my fault. I will be blunt. I didn't ask, because I didn't want you to refuse. If I offered to go alone, you couldn't tell me you did not want to walk with me."

Though his words remained ambiguous, the relaxing of her shoulders told Avelino that she understood him.

"Well, that's a nice thing to hear—and a scary one."

"Scary?"

"What if I had wanted to go but really was too tired?" She sighed. "Or, you know, Granddad was right. I usually keep working on a project. Usually, I wouldn't leave that dress unfinished and on the floor. I could have said no for that, and then you wouldn't have asked again."

"And that is scary?"

The moon remained hidden, with not a thing lighting their way except for the flashlight she carried. He'd hoped for lovely moonlight, but at the sight of a dark sky Amelia had grabbed the flashlight from a toolbox in the bed of her grandfather's truck. Still, he tried to read her expression in the faint glow of light that showed her face. *Failure. I can't see a thing.*

At last she answered, her voice quieter than ever.

"You would have thought I said no because I didn't want to. I wouldn't have thought to say something like 'Maybe next time' so you would ask again."

"And you would have wanted me to ask again?"

A cold sweat came over him as he caught her nod in his peripheral vision. The instinct to dive for cover, dragging her down with him, almost overpowered him. He reached and then stepped aside.

Avelino paused in the middle of the road and leaned his hands on his knees, taking deep breaths to calm the rising panic.

"What is wrong? Oh!" She knelt to try to read his expression. "Are you okay? Is it another flashback?"

He swallowed hard. "Yes. I recognized the feeling this time. That's good, I think. It never had a chance to throw me into the past like it did yesterday morning."

"That is good. What caused it?"

"I saw you nod out of the corner of my eye. I don't know why that affects me so. Yesterday the movement combined with the shadow of the broom handle looking like a gun did it. Tonight . . ." He shrugged as he stood. "I feel so crazy—*loco*."

"I think you'd be crazy not to. You were in battle. The things your mind has to deal with are things I don't think we were created to handle. Of course, it means you will react sometimes."

"I think," he said at last as he forced himself to stand upright and continue to the station, "I think God watched out for me when He sent your granddad and you here. Not everyone would be as understanding."

"I hope that isn't true."

The softness of her voice hinted that she thought it false hope as well.

"That isn't the first time you've hinted that you like the idea of people being better than you truly think they are. It's a nice mixture of realism with hope."

Amelia didn't respond. In fact, they were nearly to Hank's before either of them said another word. At first it had been awkward, but as they walked any unease melted away into a comfortable stroll.

The single light over the door of the station prompted an incredibly astute observation from Avelino: "There's Hank's." *Idiot. You couldn't say anything more obvious.*

"I've lived here for months, and I don't think I've ever thought to walk down for a soda. I've ridden along with Granddad a time or two when he had to get gas or have Jim look at something on the truck. There were a few days when I was bored out of my mind. Why didn't I go down?"

"I'm having a hard time imagining you bored."

She shrugged. "The house was clean, supper half-ready, I'd read everything I could several times. I'm just not used to so much time on my hands—being done with school and all."

"See, you could have had that shorthand down by now," he teased.

"Ugh. Don't remind me. When I think of the days I've wasted . . ."

"Now you'll be busy with dressmaking." The little bounce in her step brought a smile to his lips. It had been a good decision to give her the cloth. "My *mamá* always loved to have a new dress. She'd wear it every day the first week and then only once a week or every two weeks until it was almost worn-out. Then she'd wear it every day she could until she could throw it in the ragbag with a clean conscience. She called it *un placer máximo*—maximum enjoyment."

"Well, I won't be wearing the green one every day! I'm just hoping to get it done in time for the dance."

"Dance?"

"There's a Victory Dance in Rutherford on the twenty-second. My friend Helen's birthday is that day, so she invited me to come with her and her boyfriend."

The soda machine hummed beneath the single lightbulb of the station. Avelino fished a few coins from his pocket. "I thought these would be a dime by now. With the cost of everything going up, I just assumed . . . These were a nickel when I left."

She accepted the bottle of orange soda and stared at it before shaking her head. "During the Depression, people just didn't have an extra dime, but they might be able to scrape up a nickel. I think they're just now starting to get around to luxuries like soda. It'll probably be a dime soon enough."

"My brother always managed to find a nickel anytime he wanted one. I think he kept this machine going by himself."

Amelia passed the bottle back to him. "Can you get the top off? I broke the last one I did."

"The top?"

She blushed, visible even in the strange light of Hank's single incandescent bulb.

As she accepted the bottle back from him, Amelia said, "Yes, the top of the bottle. I guess I didn't have it hooked onto the opener right or something. Granddad said I'd scare people if I went around breaking off bottle tops—says they make good weapons, though." Amelia enjoyed a long drink before she asked, "What did you mean about your brother keeping the machine going?"

"Paco remembered the good years and couldn't grasp that times had changed. He could never go without things that gave him pleasure, even when we didn't have the resources. When Prohibition was over, he got so excited that he extended us too far. In seven years we lost everything."

"Why? How?"

Their footsteps slowed even more as Avelino explained how his brother had expected higher orders with the prices they'd commanded before Prohibition. When it didn't happen, Francisco, affectionately called Paco by friends and family, thought he'd be able to expand the business, hire more people, and people would start buying more wine.

"But his employees didn't buy wine. They paid the rent, bought shoes, had rice *and* beans at dinner instead of just one or the other."

"You can't fault him for his motives," Amelia interjected.

55

"Paco lived beyond his means—for a good cause, sure. He wanted to keep the business flourishing for more than our private bank accounts. He didn't want to lay off workers when times were tough. We've always had migrant workers during harvest, but Paco caught the vision of helping people have steady income—his own vineyard version of the WPA."

"Noble dream, though. Isn't it?"

"If your business can support it, sure. He was in the wrong business for that. All he did was ensure that those migrant workers had to find other work the next few years while Lyndon let the vines run wild."

He felt her hand on his arm and tried to meet her gaze as she spoke, but she did not look at him.

"Is that why he killed himself?"

There it was. He'd wondered if the Kearnses had heard the rumors, but Avelino had hoped not. It would be better if they heard the truth from him first.

"It looked that way; I know it did, but Paco didn't commit suicide."

The loss of the pressure of her hand on his arm felt like a kick to the gut. *Why did she move it? Is it because she doesn't believe me?*

"May I ask how he died? Mr. Lyndon just said—"

"Lyndon says what he wants people to believe. Paco was a weak man. The pressure became too much, so he began drinking. It was legal to buy it then, you know." He sighed, remembering. "Once, when he was very drunk, he told me, 'I got the wrong name. I should have been Avelino. I should have been named after the coward who ran from battle.'"

"He thought Avelino Aguilar was a coward?"

Echoes of voices from raging debates at a dinner or party bombarded him as Avelino nodded with more emphasis than necessary.

"*Sí.* There was always debate in my family as to whether Avelino was a good man or a criminal—a deserter."

"Your parents obviously didn't think so!" A toss of her head sent one roll of her hair sagging. Amelia's fingers flew as she pulled pins from it and groused, "Oh, I knew I needed to take it down."

As tempted as Avelino was to look, to see the waves of hair that must be spilling over her shoulders already, he didn't allow himself the pleasure. *Daylight. It'll be most magnificent in daylight. I can be patient. I'll have to be.*

"No," he said finally. "They saw him for what he was: an undertrained soldier, like most of the others, who all ran just as he did. They just weren't as intelligent in where, and didn't have Aguilar's good fortune to meet Edgar Tandy."

"But your brother disagreed."

"When morose with liquor, yes. Not usually, though. Paco was weak, yes, but if *papá* had lived, he would have been an asset to the business. He was a genius with numbers. Those numbers were his downfall."

"But if he was so good with numbers, how did he not see that his ideas weren't realistic?" Amelia questioned.

"Because his dreams blinded him." Avelino struggled to explain. "Pride goes before a fall, Proverbs says. Paco's pride was definitely his downfall. He had *sueños grandiosos*—grandiose dreams. He thought because he could make them work on paper, people would just do what he projected they would." He strangled a sob and choked it back as he added, "When they didn't—"

"So he began drinking . . ."

She wanted to hear the end just as much as he wished to avoid it.

"It wasn't pleasant, Amelia. He drank too much. He got sick. Then he drowned. It was not suicide. In fact, the doctor I spoke to said it was his opinion that Paco was too drunk to have made the decision to end his own life."

The lights of la Casa de los Sueños beckoned them. Avelino stood in the drive, gazing out at the valley before them, unseeing. The hundreds of rows of vines stretched tendrils that had reached into the heart of those first Carrillos and held them fast to the earth.

"Thank you for walking with me."

Amelia handed him her bottle. "Thank you for the soda." She turned as if to leave and then hesitated. "Avelino?"

"*¿Sí?*"

"I hope next time you won't make me ask," she murmured so quietly that he almost didn't hear her.

She was halfway to the door before he called out to her. "I won't, Señorita Kearns."

CHAPTER SEVEN

DANCE AROUND THE TOPIC

Coward. What kind of man cannot bring himself to ask a simple question? Only one. A coward. Three days of inward turmoil; thirty-six hours of self-doubt and recrimination; dozens of failed attempts to reach a decision—they all preceded Avelino's eventual knock on the back door.

"Come in . . ."

Amelia sounded distracted. As he rounded the corner from the kitchen to the long dining table at the end of the great room, he smiled to himself. Shorthand. It wasn't the first time he'd seen her poring over the book, writing out sentence after sentence with painstaking precision. The squiggles looked like gibberish—interesting, but gibberish nonetheless.

"How is it coming?"

He heard rather than saw the smile that spread across her face. "I'm getting there. I'm slow, but I actually know most of the symbols now." After flicking her braid out of the way, she glanced over her shoulder. "Give me a sentence. Let's see if I can do it."

"May I take you to the dance next Saturday." Though it was a question, he worded it without the expected lilt at the end in order to make it sound like a statement.

So intent was Amelia on her task that she didn't grasp the meaning until she went through her symbol cards to make certain she'd done it correctly. "I—wait." This time she turned in her chair. "Was that a real question?"

"Yes."

Avelino saw the answer in her eyes before she nodded. "That would be wonderful! Thank you. Granddad will thank you too. He wasn't looking forward to sitting in the corner, waiting for me."

The way she could light up and show utter excitement while remaining the same quiet girl amazed him. His cousins would have squealed and chattered a mile a minute.

"Well, just tell me when we should be there." He stopped abruptly. "How is your dress coming?"

Without responding, she moved to her room and returned with a dress that looked like it'd be beautiful, assuming she ever finished it. "The skirt is just basted on, and the collar isn't on at all." She pulled her arms into the sleeves to show it off. "Your mamá had great taste in fabric."

"The color suits you."

"It's my best color. I've always looked best in that exact shade of green, but I haven't found it very often lately." Her fingers pinched the back together as she twirled a little. "Look at that skirt! I made it fuller than the pattern. I think skirts are going to get fuller now that the war is over. They've been so straight since the twenties."

"That is very wise," he agreed. "You will find a way to close the back, I hope. It might get a bit chilly—"

Avelino ducked as she whipped the dress off and tried to snap it at him like a dishtowel. Something in her expression made him laugh louder.

"Your granddad said the same thing, didn't he?"

"I think it might be a mistake having you two in close proximity." She folded the dress carefully and smoothed it one last time before she glanced at the clock and sat back down. "Can you give me another sentence?"

"What do I wear?"

"Your uniform. All the soldiers will be in uniform, I think." She held her pen poised, ready for the sentence, and then giggled. "That was the sentence, wasn't it?"

"Well . . ."

"Hey, weren't you supposed to start work today?"

"No, tomorrow. We signed the contract today. I just left the bank with my lawyer."

"Bank?"

"We put the contracts and all the proof in a safe deposit box."

An unexpected flash of anger in her eyes took him aback, but the calm, quiet fury in her words was even more astonishing.

"That man is like the Al Capone of Napa. He gets away with everything. No one should be forced to put a simple contract behind steel and locks and keys to protect it."

Before he could respond, she glanced at the clock again and stood.

"Bread is done. Hungry?"

"No, thank you. I have laundry to do."

"I could—"

"That's kind, but no. Your job isn't to do my laundry."

"Will you have supper with us?"

Avelino waited until he reached the back door to make up his mind. He needed to stop accepting invitations; it was wrong to take advantage of their hospitality, but each time they asked, he couldn't say no.

"If I can bring something."

"Yourself."

"And don't say yourself." He frowned. "Come on, what can I bring?"

She glanced through the cupboards and the icebox and finally at the fruit bowl. "Lemons. If I had more lemons, I could make more lemonade syrup."

"Lemons and sugar. Got it."

Before Amelia could argue, he stepped out the back door, berating himself inwardly for the cowardice of not refusing. *You must get a grip, Avelino Carrillo.*

* * *

Once more he sat in the same seat after a filling dinner, alternating his gaze between the front yard and Amelia working on her dress. Dinner had been good as usual. Simple but filling. Beans with ham hock, cornbread—Mr. Kearns ate his in a glass, covered in milk—and okra breaded in cornmeal and fried. He'd dumped the *ensalada fresca* on top of all of it as many men would use salt. He ate it with relish usually reserved for wealthy men and steak or hummingbird tongues.

Amelia had finished basting the collar. His *mamá* would be pleased. *"Your cousins, they are lazy. They try to pin and sew, but how can they know how it will look without a basting so it can hang properly? Marry a woman who takes the time to do her tasks correctly."*

He'd been seated in the very chair she now occupied, basting the cuffs onto a shirt sleeve, when his father came in and ordered him out to the vines. That had been the last time the men left him in the care of the women. He had just turned twelve. For years he had resented the wasted time learning domestic chores to help his *mamá* and *abuela*, but now they were good memories. *Strange how that happens*, he thought to himself.

"What do you think about the grapes, son?"

The question startled him from his reverie. "How do you mean?"

"You've had time to inspect them, haven't you? How is this year's crop?"

"Excellent."

"What'll you recommend regarding yeast?"

The question seemed odd. Anyone who knew anything about grapes at all could see that they wouldn't need to supplement the vats with any extra yeast.

"I would advise against it."

"And is that what you will tell Lyndon?"

Now the purpose of the questioning became clear. Mr. Kearns suspected, as Avelino himself did, that Gregory Lyndon planned to insist that they do the opposite of whatever Avelino recommended. Here was a good chance to test his idea of a solution before he had to implement it.

"I hadn't planned to tell him anything. My job is to get the harvest in, to keep the vines healthy, to make the wine, and to turn him a profit so that he more than makes up for the money he put into this place. If he wanted to be that involved in the business, I doubt he would have hired you."

Before Joe Kearns could comment on his opinion of Avelino's plan, Amelia's quiet voice interjected a surprising statement. "I think it would be wise to keep your plans to yourselves. If one or the other of you were a spy for Lyndon . . ."

"Amelia! Accusing our new friend—"

"I was not accusing him or you, Granddad, but since no one knows who is listening to what, I think it is a bad habit to get into. It's just something to consider."

The men exchanged amused but also impressed glances.

"I think I'll make popcorn. Either of you want any?" Mr. Kearns asked.

"I do." Amelia waited for their guest's nod and then added, "Avelino too."

The minute Mr. Kearns poured the kernels in the pan, Amelia shifted closer. "Granddad is too trusting, even though he thinks he's shrewd. Mr. Lyndon will pit each of you against the other without you realizing it. I've heard of people saying things they never intended to because he knew just enough information to put them too much at ease. He's sly."

"I don't think you give your granddad enough credit, but I'll be careful."

She tapped her stenographer's notebook with her pencil. "I don't suppose you feel like telling a story? The syrup might be set enough by now to make lemonade to keep you from getting parched . . ."

"You just want a chance to practice."

"That too . . ."

"Of course I will. The first Avelino needs to get out of Texas after all."

He started to rise to help her.

"Oh, I've got it." Amelia glanced over her shoulder to ensure her grandfather was still in the kitchen before moving closer to Avelino. "May I ask a question?"

"¡Sí, señorita! A la orden."

"What?"

The concentration she put into trying to learn the words shouldn't have surprised him. Repeating himself once more, he said, "*A la orden*—at your service."

"Oh." Again she glanced to be sure they were alone. "I was wondering . . ."

The hesitation seemed out of character. She was a quiet girl but not a timid or shy one. "Yes?"

"Why did you ask if I would go to the dance with you?"

There it was. *She wants to ensure I didn't make more of her acceptance than she'd meant to give. After all, her first thought had been for her grandfather.* This gave him the perfect opportunity to save face, and he knew it.

"I . . ." He what? *You're a fool, Avelino Carrillo. This isn't the first misunderstanding in your family. It won't be the last. Prove you're not the coward she probably thinks you are and be honest like a man.*

"It's just that I wanted to tell Granddad, and you know how he talks about everything. He'll want to know if you're just being polite or if it's a real date." She blushed. "He'll feel cheated if he doesn't know he has teasing rights."

That didn't sound like a kind way of saying she wasn't interested. Then again, sometimes girls managed to be even more encouraging when they tried to soften a blow. Her nervousness seemed to imply she did have true concerns.

"Would it be better if I asked him?"

"Oh! I hadn't thought—that is, I didn't mean—but he would like that. Grandfathers like to be kept in the know and all."

"I'll take care of it."

"Take care of what?" asked Mr. Kearns as he reentered the room bearing a buttery bowl of popcorn.

"Oh!" Amelia flushed a little deeper. "I'm going to make lemonade, and Avelino is going to tell us another story. Do you want some?"

"Sure."

Avelino waited for her to round the corner to the kitchen before he pulled a fluffy white kernel of corn from the bowl and stared at it. "Mr. Kearns?"

"Yes?" His hesitation must have sent a strange message, because the elder man added, "You don't have to tell another story if you don't want. Amelia is the most persistent little thing on the planet. She's so quiet that you almost don't notice at times, but she is."

"Oh, it's not that. I just . . ." He forced himself to meet Mr. Kearns's eyes. "This morning I asked her to the dance next weekend. Then I realized maybe I should have asked your permission first."

"The dance, huh. Hmm . . . Why?"

"Sir?"

"I asked why. Why did you invite her?"

"I don't think I understand." The moment the words crossed his lips, Avelino knew they were a lie. He started to retract them, but the other man had already begun a response.

"Are you being a considerate neighbor, or is there something more personal involved in this invitation?"

The distinctive clinking of metal on glass as Amelia stirred the lemonade ceased as Mr. Kearns asked the question. *So, she is listening. Great. Your* papá *would be disgusted with you, Avelino,* he admonished himself. *Be true to your heritage. Be a man—an honorable man.*

"I asked her because I like her and wanted the chance to get to know her better. I will understand if she chooses to tell me that she is only interested in being my friend. I hope for that at least."

It had never been easy to show interest in a girl. He remembered how difficult it had been to ask a girl to walk home with him from church or school—all the tittering *mamás* there crooning their delight at the blushing boy.

Mr. Kearns's voice interrupted difficult memories. "I am sorry, Mr. Kearns; I didn't hear you. What did you say?"

"I said," he added with a knowing twinkle in his eye, "let's see how she perceives it."

The moment Amelia returned with their glasses, Mr. Kearns pounced. "So, Avelino was just telling me about your date."

So that's how he'll do it. Avelino accepted the glass. *"Gracias."*

She hesitated before answering, *"De nada."*

"I've been speaking Spanish for years, and she never echoed me once. You show up, and in less than a week she tries it."

"Granddad!"

"And you ignored me."

"If you want me to tell you all about a date we haven't even had yet, I think your romantic little heart will just have to palpitate alone for a while longer. There's nothing to tell yet!"

With a handful of popcorn ready to fill his mouth, Mr. Kearns gave Avelino a pointed look. "Seems Amelia is looking forward to your date."

"As am I."

Amelia glanced at each man, confusion written on each line of her wrinkled brow, and picked up her notebook again. "Are we going to hear a story or what?"

"Where did I leave off last time?"

Her pen poised, she didn't even look up from her tablet. "Avelino said he didn't want to go home, that he wanted to go to California."

"Right. California."

CHAPTER EIGHT

TO CALIFORNIA

May 1836

The slow recovery surprised him. Edgar said often that he was too impatient, but Avelino could think only of getting as far away from Texas as he could. He'd be sorry to leave—now anyway—but he had to go.

Life in the Tandy home was very different from his life back in Mexico. They were poor, these *gringos* from Virginia. They worked hard every day just to exist. They had no natives for servants or old family money to keep things going. Avelino would sell a few jewels and sail to California. If he made it alive, he would buy land from Don Ruiz and have enough money to live on indefinitely. Edgar had said that he sold everything they owned just to get to Texas, where land was cheap and opportunity ripe. They now had nothing but that land. Well, Avelino suspected there was a little cash hidden somewhere, but as friendly as the two men had become, Edgar had no reason to share that kind of information with a relative stranger.

As he pondered these differences, a shadow filled the doorway. He knew the shadows now. This was the girl with the strange name—Cherith. She carried a basket indoors and began folding the sheets that had been on his bed that morning. *Where is Edgar?* He didn't allow her to stay behind when he had to go very far.

Crack! The distinct sound of ax meeting wood. *That's where he is.* Avelino pointed outside. *"¿Está su padre allí?"*

She laughed and threw up her hands as she always did. "I don't understand, but Papa is in the yard."

With a cane in each hand—both carved by Edgar in the evenings—Avelino shuffled out the door, blinded by the bright sunlight. "A warm day, Don Edgar!"

"Don now, is it? And look how well you are walking. Try using both canes in one hand or put one under your arm."

He felt like a child, hobbling about the yard with one cane and then two, displaying his newly acquired walking skills. He made it around the whole yard four times before he felt faint and accepted Edgar's help inside.

"A day's work. How pathetic."

"For a sick man, it is an excellent day's work." To Cherith, Edgar added in English, "He made it around a full four times."

"That is excellent! I made extra cornbread just for him. It'll be done soon."

As Edgar relayed her message, Avelino smiled at the girl. "It is too bad that you live here and not in California—and that your daughter isn't a few years older."

"Don't be ridiculous. She's a child."

"She is today, but in a few short years you will have your own battles right in your front yard. The *caballeros* will arrive in droves to fight for the chance at her heart."

To his surprise, Edgar laughed. He spoke a few words *en inglés* to his daughter, and Cherith too laughed, tugging her own hair with a look of disgust on her face.

"I am a father. I think my daughter is lovely, of course, but she is freckled and her hair—"

"Is her beauty," Avelino interjected. These strange *americanos* with their odd ideas about hair. *That red hair—like roses—you take for granted.*

"Some man will appreciate it, certainly, but not as you do."

"If she was a woman, I would try to convince her to run away with me when I left."

Edgar's eyes narrowed. Never had Avelino seen the man look so unfriendly.

"Then I am thankful that she is only a child. I would not wish to be concerned that a guest in my home might forget that."

"*No quiero ofenderle.* Truly, I would not wish to cause offense. I meant only to compliment my host on a charming daughter."

It took some time before the other man's face relaxed. "Don Avelino, I believe you didn't. I think I am not ready to accept that my little girl will ever be a woman."

Relief was so marked that he nearly wept. *Don Avelino.* It meant respect and friendship. He had first felt terror at being thrown out of the house before he was able to walk the distance to catch a ship; however, those cold eyes had created a fresh fear of losing his new friend.

"I must get well soon, though. I cannot intrude on your hospitality indefinitely. You will want your bed back!"

"It's a long way to California. What will you do when you get there? Why there?"

"When I was a boy not much older than Cherith, a man came to us." Avelino told of the terrible earthquake, the many people who were crushed in their homes, and the widows and orphans left behind. "Don Ruiz Carrillo came all the way from California to bring back some orphaned relatives to California, a girl and a boy—Miguel—who was always so quiet. Oh, to listen to Don Ruiz speak of his home—it must be paradise."

"He traveled from California to Guerrero to help orphans? He sounds like a good man."

"He is. My *madre* cried when the children left."

Edgar listened for some time, hearing all the stories of the wonderful place called California. "You've wanted to go ever since, haven't you?"

"*Sí*, but *mi madre* did not wish me to leave, and then when she died *mi tía* Maria gave me the money to go and be a soldier." He hung his head. "I suppose I seem ungrateful not to wish to return to such a good family."

"I think you've been given a blessing to go and make your own way in the world. It is understandable. But how will you get there? You can't go overland."

"No. I could go through Mexico and then up, but *bandidos* would find me, take my gold, and kill me."

Cherith arrived with bowls of beans and freshly buttered corn-bread on a napkin. Not until the meal was nearly finished did Edgar speak, but when he did, he offered a solid, wise plan. "You'll go to Virginia. I'll buy you a horse here, and you sell him when you get there. Mail the money back to me. I have family there who'll help you get the money you need for your jewels. They'll get you to a ship, and you'll sail around Cape Horn like everyone else. It's dangerous in its own way, but not nearly as bad as trying to make it overland."

"But you cannot—"

"I can do what I want to do. I can't tell you how freeing it is to follow a dream. I've always wanted to go out west. California sounds like heaven, but Texas is probably all I'll ever be able to afford. That's okay too. We'll have a good life here once we get established. I want *you* to have your dream."

"But a horse!"

"You'll never make it on foot, Avelino. We both know that I destroyed your foot when I cut it so badly."

"You saved my life," the younger man argued.

"Mebbe so, but I still did some serious damage. You'll be fine eventually, but not if you don't let it heal properly."

"How do we know you'll get that money back? What if it gets stolen? You can't afford to lose it."

"I'm willing to risk it. Now this is what I think we should do . . ."

Cherith sat with her elbows on the table and her chin resting in her hands and listened, starry-eyed, as the men talked late into the night. Occasionally, Edgar stroked her hair or winked and updated her on the plans they made—plans that included her riding out with her father in search of a horse the next day.

*   *   *

They were gone. It felt strange to be in the Tandy home alone for so long. Avelino walked around the room, taking in every bit. How could such a humble place feel so warm and welcoming? He'd be leaving soon, and now a part of him wanted to stay.

It is not possible. Every day that he remained tempted fate. His hand slid over the worn Bible. *Santa Biblia.* His family had never owned one. He opened the pages, his eyes trying to make out some of the words, but it was not in Latin—*en inglés.* He closed the cover with a snap, his hand trembling. *La lista de libros prohibidos*—the List of Prohibited Books. The Church forbade translations of the Bible into common languages. His *abuela* said it was for the priests to know the words of God and to share them as the Church decided best.

These people were bold to go against the Church. Some might say heretics, but Avelino could not agree. Had they not been like the Samaritan? He remembered that story—something the priest had told a few boys who had ignored an injured child. It was probably in that book somewhere. Avelino's eyes slid to the cover again. *I must not ask.*

These Tandys love their books. His eyes rose to the three books on the mantel. He could not read their titles. He could not read—not really. The little girl with the red braids could read. He would have to learn. In California he would find someone to teach him. As his eyes fell on the covered plate left for him, he reached for the chair and mentally added, *And write. I will learn to write.*

The sun had begun to set before Don Edgar and his daughter rode back into the yard, so Avelino could not see what the new horse looked like. His gut clenched at the idea of a weak animal who could not outrun a posse or wild animal, but twisted further at the thought of the expense of a good one.

The dilemma he'd faced all day now seemed ridiculous. He stepped behind the curtain and fumbled for his uniform. By the time the Tandys entered the house, they found him picking at a jewel-encrusted necklace with the tip of a knife.

"What are you doing?"

Without answering, he continued to pick until the tiny ruby fell onto the table. "There." The look on Edgar's face prompted him to take the jewel to the daughter. He set the tiny stone onto her palm and smiled at her confused expression. *"Tómela. Sálvela para su dote, pero permítame que haga esto para usted."*

The girl's beautiful eyes turned to her father for translation.

"He said to take it and save it for your dowry." To Avelino he said, "It isn't necessary. You shouldn't ruin your beautiful jewelry."

"Let me show my gratitude, Don Edgar. It is a small stone. It won't bring much, but I want to do something—show my appreciation."

"Well, thank you. We found a good animal, but you'll have to leave in the morning."

"So soon?"

"Everywhere I went, people wanted to know why I wanted another horse. Implying it was for Cherith to ride brought out all kinds of inferior animals."

"You lied?"

"Not exactly," he grinned. "I pointed to the one horse that we rode in on and said the animal shouldn't have to carry us both around the area and back home again. They could infer from that what they chose."

"You are a shrewd man, but I do not understand the need to leave."

"They're going to talk, and then they'll come around. I want you far from here so no one recognizes the animal. I had to turn down a good mare because she was too distinctive. Lovely roan with a white blaze and forelocks."

Edgar's sigh told Avelino that his friend loved good horseflesh. Eager to reassure him, the younger man protested. "We wouldn't want such a fine animal to leave the area, although I could have taken your horse, I guess."

"I thought of it, but I think people are more likely to notice me on a new horse than not. You must go. Once you are in Louisiana, I will feel more confident. Cherith will pack you food and water. This animal will make a good thirty miles a day. If the weather holds, you could be in Virginia inside two months."

"And I go to Richmond. I ask directions to the home of Sidney Tandy, and present to him the letter. I say *en inglés*, 'Señor

Edgar Tandy requests that Señor Sidney Tandy read this letter of *introducción.*'"

"Yes. Sid will take care of everything for you, but I have been thinking, and I don't think you will like what I think."

"What is it?"

"We should ask Sid to try to sell your jewels for you—alone. They might try to cheat a man who does not speak English. Sid might be able to get more money for them."

Not like—what an understatement! Don Edgar would not cheat him, but what of the others? *How can I trust these men—strangers—with my fortune?* It seemed foolish, but Edgar's statement was true. The jewelers would try to cheat him. *Who wouldn't? In the same situation, I would be tempted as well.*

"I don't know. It is wise, but . . ."

Without another word, Edgar pulled out another piece of paper and began writing. How swiftly the pen scrawled across the page, making the letters that would tell Señor Sidney Tandy this new plan! *But do I want this? Will I be forced to trust these strangers?* Weathered hands folded the paper just as they had the last one. Cherith passed him a candle, and all three of them watched as each drop piled on top of the others, sealing it. Below the seal, Edgar signed it again, but this time he added an extra flourish to the *y* in Tandy.

"This is an additional note. If after you meet Sidney you feel comfortable, give him this one as well."

"Thank you. You are kind to me. I show distrust, and you are not offended. You are a good friend."

Through the night, he wrestled against his own fears. Edgar had no reason to lie to him. After saving his life, what would the motive be? Night sounds drifted in through the window, but still he questioned and pondered. Tossing and turning, he tried to relax but failed.

At last he heard the man stirring on the floor. "Since you're not sleeping, let's get you on your way."

Avelino grinned at the words. *So true.* Had he slept at all? Cherith stirred, but Edgar told her to stay in bed.

"Good-bye, Mr. Aguilar. May God go with you."

Avelino listened as Edgar translated, tears springing to his eyes. "And you," he whispered. "Tell her that I will pray for both of you every day."

At the door he heard a sound and turned just in time to see the girl dash across the room and fling her arms around him.

"Be safe. Please be safe."

A lump welled in his throat as he nodded. He didn't understand the words, but he knew what she meant. She was sorry to see him go.

"*Gracias*, Cherith Tandy."

The men saddled the horse, another debt to the older man. He would have to find a way to help them—show his gratitude. They stood together, looking off into the distance.

"*Vaya con Dios*, Don Avelino."

"I will not forget you or your kindness to me. I promise you this. I will make this right."

The sun blasted over the horizon just as the little house was no longer visible when he turned the horse to take a last look back. A sense of loss washed over him when he strained but still saw nothing. Once facing east again, he took a deep breath, drank in the glorious sunrise, and rode toward it.

CHAPTER NINE

CONFESSIONS OF THE NIGHT

September 1945

Glenn Miller's "In the Mood" echoed into the evening air as Avelino hurried around the Kearnses' truck to open Amelia's door. Her hair, styled in that familiar Victory Roll, tempted him even more than usual, but he couldn't decide why. Her dress swished against his legs as she stepped down from the truck onto the gravel of the parking lot.

"What about your purse?"

"I put it in the glove box. I don't want to have to take care of it."

"My *mamá* would never leave without access to her favorite tube of lipstick," he teased.

Amelia slipped her hand into a side pocket and pulled out a golden metal tube. "I am prepared for urgent repair jobs. If my hair needs help, then I'll have to fetch the purse."

Never had he seen anyone so quietly excited. Amelia nearly burst with exuberance, but she said almost nothing. Her feet didn't hop, her hands didn't twitch, but her eyes sparkled with a joy that could only be called excitement.

"If someone gave you a gift—something you've wanted for ages—you wouldn't make a sound, would you?" he asked.

"Make a sound? How?"

"Squeal, scream, jump up and down . . ."

She shook her head. "No . . . I don't think so, why?"

"Just something I suspected about you."

The band switched to "Don't Sit Under the Apple Tree" just as they entered the door to the Grange Hall. Amelia clung to his sleeve as they threaded their way through the groups of people.

She pulled back against the wall and nodded to the dance floor. "There—in the red dress. That's Helen. She's seen us, so she'll come introduce herself when the dance is over."

A glance at Amelia's toes saw them tapping in time to the music, but the heels made him wonder how she'd be able to dance in them. "How do girls do it?"

"Do what?" Her eyes followed his to her feet. "Oh, dance in heels? It's not hard."

"Looks like torture."

Her face flushed, and he knew she'd just noticed that she now stood a solid inch taller than he.

"Oh, I didn't think. I could have worn—well, no, I couldn't. I don't have any nice shoes that aren't heels. When I grew out of the last ones, these were what we found."

"I don't mind." The doubt clouding her eyes made him smile. "Truly. I just can't imagine how you don't fear for your life walking on those things—they're like stilts!"

"They're reasonably low actually. Look around you."

As his eyes followed several feet dancing past them, Avelino had to concede. Most of the shoes were nearly an inch taller than hers. "I yield to your superior knowledge."

A man passed, glowering at Avelino. Amelia stepped closer and wrapped her hand around his arm almost possessively.

"Who was that?" he asked.

"That's Raymond Welton. Don't you know the Weltons? They're ever-present around here."

"That's little Ray Welton? He was just a freckled little pipsqueak whose voice hadn't changed the last time I saw him."

"Well, now he's all grown up in his own estimation and thinks he's the progeny of the gods."

The derision in her tone told him she could have come with Ray had she wanted to. "He didn't take no very well, I take it?"

Flushing again, Amelia shook her head. "Not too well. He'll be madder now that he sees me with someone else."

"Let's give him something to seethe over then. Next dance anyway. This should be nearly finished."

As she glanced up at him, smiling her agreement, the smile dissipated into a frown. "Your patch . . ." Her hands, so gentle that he held his breath for fear of missing the sensation of their touch, reached up and adjusted it slightly. "I think it might have slipped a little. That's better."

"Gracias."

"De nada."

Her wink nearly undid him, but he managed to contain his amusement until she added, "See, I can learn too. Granddad thinks he's the only linguist in the family."

A linguist after learning half-a-dozen words. *That'd make me a linguistic genius. First Spanish, then English, and a dozen or two words in Japanese!* "I think your friend is coming."

Helen was almost Amelia's antithesis. Tall, elegant, with dark—nearly black—hair, she embodied sophistication. In comparison, many girls would have felt like a bumpkin, but Amelia seemed oblivious.

Helen accepted the younger woman's hug and birthday wishes and then asked for an introduction. "Who have you brought for us tonight?"

"Helen, this is our friend Avelino Carrillo. His family owned the vineyard where Granddad works." She smiled at him. "Avelino, my friend, Helen Moreau."

"Owned?"

Had her voice not been the perfect model of courtesy and cordiality, he would have assumed venom lingering behind the word.

"The last years before the war were hard times. I am now working to regain it."

"That is wonderful. I wish you great success." She smiled back at Amelia, fawning over having another soldier to honor. "She is such a little patriot. I hope you have a good time. I'll steal her away now for a few minutes. I have a friend I want her to meet. He's been awaiting her arrival."

"Oh, Helen. I'm sorry, I can't. Avelino and I were going to dance after I introduced you."

As if on cue, the band began playing "I've Heard That Song Before."

"Oh, I love this one too. We can meet your friend later. I'm sure he'll understand."

Something in Helen's expression told Avelino that even if the "friend" did understand, she wasn't happy about it. However, Amelia and Avelino entered the dance floor a second later, and with the delight shining in Amelia's face, he chose to ignore the probable social awkwardness ahead. *I do not think your friend would care for you to spend too much time in my company, Amelia Kearns.*

"Everyone is still giddy. Look at them!"

Why should they not be giddy? Only three weeks had passed since Japan signed the Instrument of Surrender. *The war is over. Sons, husbands, brothers, and sweethearts will be home soon—not soon enough for most people, but soon.* "You should have seen the cheering at the Presidio. I think I saw legless men dancing."

"Oh, how beautifully tragic. You are a natural storyteller, aren't you? I thought you were just reciting what you'd heard, but I don't think you can help it."

"I suppose not."

Helen pounced upon them the moment the dance ended. "Oh, Amelia. How convenient. This is the friend I wanted you to meet. Amelia Kearns, this is Robert Flynn." She turned, flashing a smile at the man—a knowing smile that hinted at a matchmaking scheme. "Robert, this is my friend I was telling you about, Amelia. She brought a soldier with her too. I can't remember your name. Amarillo?"

He had no doubt that she remembered his name, but Avelino had no intention of playing the game. "You were close. Avelino Carrillo."

"Yes, Mr. Carrillo. Their family has been in the area for some years, I believe. But I think Avelino is the only one left."

How it happened, he didn't know, and by the look on Amelia's face as Mr. Flynn led her across the dance floor, she was equally confused, but he found himself alone. Amelia seemed to try to engage—to be pleasant—but from his vantage point, Avelino could see that she was none too pleased to be torn from him. *That's a nice thing to know*, he mused.

Helen danced past on the arms of the same man she'd been dancing with when they arrived. Her smile, genuine for the first time since their introduction, told him his suspicions had been correct. Either Helen Moreau did not like him, or she had other plans for Amelia, so he was just an unwelcome complication—or both.

A glance around him showed that women outnumbered men two or three to one. Courtesy demanded he ask someone to dance, but who? His teenage habit of choosing the shyest-looking girl would likely get him refused, but that wasn't fair to girls who might like to dance—even if with a one-eyed Mexican ex-soldier. A face, a familiar one, caught his attention from a chair near the corner. *Margretta Mendoza—or Sanchez now, I suppose.* Her eyes met his, and she offered a tentative smile. *Go say hello. She probably thinks you hate her.*

Avelino inched his way around the room and to the corner. The nervousness in her eyes buoyed his spirit.

"Margretta! It is good to see you."

"I thought it might be you. The mustache and the patch did make me wonder."

"A friend suggested the mustache as a way to draw attention from my eye." He swallowed hard and forced himself to ask, "Would you like to dance?"

They passed Amelia on the floor, and Margretta laughed when she saw his eyes follow the couple. "I saw you come in with her. She is pretty."

"One of the loveliest things about her is that she doesn't know it. She thinks she's ordinary."

"She has *el pelo como rosas.* You always did like the red hair. Pedro used to joke that you would make your wife dye her hair unless she came that way straight from God."

Rather, he used to joke that I would make you *dye* your *hair when we* were *married.* Eager to change the subject, Avelino asked the question he knew she expected. "Has there been word of Sal?"

She shook her head. "He's still listed as a POW. *Mamacita* Sanchez thinks we'll get more news now that the war is over."

"You must miss him. I will keep praying." Avelino ignored the echoes of family arguments in his past and added, "I'll light a candle at church."

"Thank you," she whispered.

Awkwardness grew between them, and Avelino couldn't help but notice the way Amelia's eyes followed them. "And how is the rest of your family?"

"The war helped." A poorly repressed sigh escaped. "It is strange to say that, but it's true. Diego went to San Francisco to work in the shipyards. He made good money even with his bad hearing."

"That's good to know. As soon as I can, I want to visit your parents."

"You just want some good food!"

He smiled. It was true that he missed some of the more traditional foods he'd grown up with, but no one could say the Kearnses didn't eat well. "I have good food, but your *mamá's albóndigas*—I have dreamed of it when eating MREs, until I wanted to throw them at the enemy as a weapon of torture."

"Just like all the boys. You can only think of food—and girls." She tapped her index finger on his shoulder. "See there. She watches you too."

It was true. Each time he allowed himself to follow Amelia's movements for a moment, her eyes caught his. She didn't speak to her partner, but she did seem to try to listen.

"She is probably concerned that I not be left out of the fun. I think she was under orders to bring all the lost and forlorn soldiers she could find."

"She is friends with Helen Moreau. That woman wanted to dredge up the veterans from the Great War and bring them along, but none of them wanted to come."

"Miss Moreau doesn't seem to like me much."

"It isn't you. Well, not you in particular. I think she's one of those people who forget that your family has owned a good portion of this valley for longer than her family has been out of France."

"I am Mexican in her mind."

"And if she is like Raymond and his gang of gargoyles, you are not just a Mexican. You're a 'dirty Mexican.'"

"I knew I forgot something before I came."

Margretta's head cocked in that same way it had when she was seven and couldn't understand how she'd been left out—again. "Forgot what?"

"To bathe."

* * *

It became comical. The more Helen tried to keep them apart, the more self-assertive Amelia became about refusing others' offers to dance. She was kind, often using the many girls waiting for partners as an excuse, but refusals came swifter with each attempt. On the times she did accept, he found that his chance of offending someone by asking them to be approximately one in five. Twenty percent seemed high, but as long as the majority didn't gasp and turn away, he couldn't complain. *Margretta has always been oversensitive. They may fear my patch more than my ancestry. Besides, Ray was never opposed to me before I left.*

The final notes of "Yes, Indeed!" played, and he escorted Mabel Dorling to the punch table before he found Amelia again. The delay had unexpected consequences. Minutes later, he spied Amelia by the door. Avelino wove through the crowd. A flash of red skirt told him she was with Helen—again. He wondered who was next on the string of potential *novios* that Helen seemed determined to parade before her.

Determined to save her the awkwardness, he hurried to reach her but pulled up short when he overheard Helen's hissed reprimand.

". . . will think you are . . ." She paused, apparently hunting for words that wouldn't raise Amelia's hackles. "Well, it's just that you wouldn't want to give him the wrong idea, and you wouldn't want to waste the opportunity to meet other eligible men."

His choked snicker sounded like a sneeze, prompting a woman passing to smile and say, "Bless you."

Amelia's dismissive response entertained him simply by how easily she showed utter disgust without raising her voice—at all.

"I don't care what other men think. I like him, and if he wants to dance with me I'll do it. From what I've seen, he's definitely the best man here."

"Oh, I don't doubt that he's a fine man, but Amelia, I mean that people—*he*—might misunderstand and think you are *romantically* interested in him." The stunned expression on Amelia's face seemed to soften Helen's voice. "See, I knew you'd understand my concern."

"Actually, I don't. If people think that, then they'd be right."

Nothing pleased Avelino more than stepping in just then and whisking her off to the dance floor. From that point on, Helen didn't bother to interrupt their dancing. They hardly spoke until the band played "Cariño Mio."

". . . *Cariño, mi querida, por favor, ven conmigo.*" As the song continued, Avelino sang softly, some words hardly more than a breath or a whisper. "*Tu madre mira de la ventana . . . Me da un abrazo . . .*"

Amelia's eyes watched his lips as he sang the words and widened as she heard him sing *abuelito* instead of *madre*.

"What does that verse say? You said something about a window, and when they said mother, you said grandfather. I caught that much."

As the singers sang, "*Cariño, mi querida*" again, Avelino leaned closer and murmured, "The man in the song says that my mother—or your grandfather, as I sang—waits at the window for—well, you."

His hesitation produced a skeptical expression. "Avelino, I think there were more changes than that."

"Well, the song says to give me a kiss before I go and one more when I leave you at your door. I changed it to hug." He laughed at her surprise. "I feared facing Mr. Kearns at the end of a shotgun barrel."

Her eyes twinkled. "Suggestions like that could be dangerous."

"Or delightful—depending, I suppose."

A scuffle near the door arrested the attention of the entire room. Raymond Welton, face contorted with anger, spewed verbal venom as two soldiers forcibly ejected him from the hall. Two friends, young men who had been boys when Avelino last saw them, slunk after him as he stumbled off into the darkness.

"I wonder what that is all about."

"Ray's always in trouble these days. Granddad thinks it's because he wanted to enlist and Mr. Welton wouldn't let him. Granddad says the military is usually the making of a spoiled boy like Ray."

"Well, it couldn't hurt. I'm just sorry to see him like that. He was always a smart kid." Avelino shrugged and turned, with the rest of the room, to applaud the band. "These guys are good."

"All 4-Fs. They couldn't join, so they formed the band and traveled all over Northern California on weekends, giving concerts in parks and halls. They donated the proceeds to the Red Cross and the USO. We were lucky to get them."

"As Time Goes By" signaled time to go. It was the fourth slower song in a row, usually an indicator that the evening was winding down.

Avelino's eyes slid toward the band and then over to the door. "Care to go after this one?"

"I was just going to suggest it. I'd say let's go now, but I do love this song."

It took a little strange maneuvering, but Avelino managed to have them near the door by the time the song ended.

"Do you want to say good-bye to Helen?"

She scanned the crowd, looking for her friend, and shook her head. "I don't think so."

The truth of what she didn't say was even more evident than what she did. Amelia's friend chose to overlook her while she stood with him. Avelino almost offered to walk away for a few moments, but the serene look in Amelia's expression as she stepped into the night with him stopped him. *Why ruin my date's happiness because her friend had other goals for the evening?*

The truck was pinned in by other vehicles. It took him several attempts to back out of the parking space, before he allowed the Kearnses' old pickup to chug along to the road. His arm hung straight out the window as he prepared to make a left turn, but he hesitated. Amelia glanced at him, questioning. Seconds ticked past as he debated within himself. It would be stating a lot, but would it be too much? Too soon?

His smile flashed as he made up his mind. He quit signaling his intended turn, gripped the steering wheel, and laid his other arm across the back of the seat, beckoning her to sit closer.

"Care to keep me company?"

Relief, joy—innumerable emotions spread from the fingertips that rested on her shoulder and coursed through him as she slid across that seat. Amelia tapped the steering wheel and said, "Are we going, or are we going to hold up the exodus out of here?"

Unlike the chatty ride there, the drive home was a peaceful ramble along the highway and then through the vineyards of Napa back to la Casa de los Sueños. Only the great harvest moon shining down on them and the hum and rattle of the truck broke the silence of the night. Avelino, still amazed to be seated next to a girl as near perfection as he'd ever imagined, drank in every moment as if to wash out all the unpleasantness of the past decade.

The truck rattled around the bend, up the hill to the house, and stopped with a jerk.

"Sorry. I think I was letting the truck take the reins a bit."

Her hands fidgeted, but she didn't move, and Avelino wasn't ready for the night to end either.

"May I ask a personal question?" she asked with some deliberation.

"Of course." He wanted to say anything but yes. Something about the way she hesitated made him nervous.

"Helen said something tonight, and then I overheard the pretty girl you danced with first talking and I wondered . . ."

So the gossip does bother her. It's best to learn it now before it becomes too difficult to walk away. "Talking about what?"

"The vineyards."

The slow exhale did little to calm his nerves. What could Margretta or Helen have said to make her ask about that? "What would you like to know?"

"Everything? Anything?" Something in him, an involuntary response perhaps, urged her to add, "I just know how important it is to you that you regain them, and I can understand that, but then I wonder, why?"

He stared out at the moon for several long seconds before he sighed, nodding. "Care to go for another soda? I'd talk better if I could walk."

Her agreement made him feel better, until he saw her shoes hit the ground. His pointed stare produced a giggle. "I'll go put on my oxfords. Be right back." Amelia took two steps, glanced at him, skipped back, and gave him a quick hug. "The song said to," she explained as she hurried away.

A sliver of a cloud, like a single wisp of cotton candy from a carnival, slid over the moon in what seemed an ineffectual attempt to darken the valley. It wouldn't darken his spirits. He hadn't had so much fun in years. He had invited her to the dance, had monopolized her as much as possible, and had ridden home with his arm almost around her. He behaved like a *novio*—a boyfriend.

If you are going to show interest like this, she has a right to know your plans and the motivation behind them. Papá *would tell you, "Avelino, do not show interest in a girl whom you would not or could not marry. It's foolish and cruel."* That thought sent his mind reeling with implication. A future, combined with plans for relationships—Amelia appeared midthought.

"Are you ready? Do you need a sweater?"

A shake of his head assured her that he would be fine. They walked several hundred yards before he swallowed hard and said, "So, *la Viña de los Sueños* . . ."

"If it's none of my business, I won't be offended."

"I think your friend and mine both know me, Margretta from—childhood—and Helen, I suppose, by reputation, and well enough to have an idea what it—the land, of course—means to a Carrillo."

"What I wondered was if the vineyards are what you know or what you love."

"I would say both." As casual as he sounded, even to himself, Avelino knew the answer would take deeper explanation.

"So you are not settling . . ." Exasperated, Amelia tried again. "That's not what I mean. You see, Helen suggested that you were trying to relive the past and only out of some kind of duty or obligation. She seemed to know something about your family and made it sound like you would work yourself to death for your family's honor and hate every minute of it." Her voice, even softer and gentler than usual, became almost a whisper when she added, "Helen thinks that kind of pressure would eventually be taken out on close friends and family."

His stomach filled with rocks, pushing bile into his throat. So this was it. How quickly and simply her friend had ripped the fledgling root of their relationship from the ground and exposed it to the elements. "And you believed that."

"Not any of it really, and certainly not the last part. I couldn't see you taking out frustrations on people you care about."

"Thank you. So what made you ask if you didn't believe her?"

"Something that girl, Margretta, said to someone when I passed by for punch. She mentioned your commitment to your family and the tradition of winemaking. It made me wonder if Helen hadn't taken something partially true and understandable and turned it into something ugly." As if compelled, Amelia added, "It wouldn't have been the first time tonight."

"Why would it matter? If duty and family honor were all I concerned myself with, would that be a bad thing?"

"Not if you chose them. I just wondered if you'd ever wanted to do anything else that you might enjoy more. I would hate to see you work for seven years to regain these vineyards, only to realize you hated the work."

How could he explain? What could he say that would make her understand the heritage he enjoyed?

"For a hundred years the Carrillos have lived in that house, worked the vineyards, made the wine. We survived all of the changes in California from the Gold Rush through the Great War, Prohibition, and the Depression. I know every story ever told about anyone in my family. Not all are pretty and honorable, but most . . ." Emotion choked him.

"Avelino, I do not question the honor of your family. You know that, don't you?"

"I hadn't considered it," he admitted. "I love my family. We Carrillos are a little fanatical about family. As *mi abuelo* said more times than I could ever count, '*La familia es el corazón de la vida*'— family is the heart of life."

"And for a Carrillo, the vines are the veins and arteries?"

"*¡Sí!* Yes. That is beautifully put."

"Has anyone in your family chosen something different?"

He laughed. "Of course. I have cousins, aunts, uncles. During Prohibition, most of the family abandoned the vines. Some moved to San Francisco or to Los Angeles. I have an uncle who grows oranges now. Carrillos from our branch of the family have become doctors, politicians, merchants; most did not stay with the vines."

"And when your brother lost the land, did you consider anything else?"

The light ahead told him that they were nearly there. He slowed, taking her hand as he did. "I want to tell you that I did. I can't help but think you would be comforted to know it. I can't. From the moment I realized we'd never dig ourselves out of that debt, I became consumed with finding a way to do it anyway. Mar—a friend's father—suggested that I work hard, save my money, and buy land in Sonoma or somewhere else. Get a fresh start. But I didn't want *a* vineyard. I wanted *ours*. Can you understand that?"

"I think so. I remember what it was like for Granddad to leave that little farm in Oklahoma, and there was no rich heritage like yours connected to it. I can only imagine . . ."

"I think when you hear more about how the vineyard grew and developed, when you learn to love the people who are at the roots of it all, then you will understand."

Silence settled around them as she stopped again and surveyed their surroundings. "I want to ask a question that really *is* none of my business."

"And what is that?"

She did not hesitate but asked in a near whisper, "Where is your sweetheart?"

A cold fear gripped his heart. *Who told her what? Why cannot the past stay the past?* "I don't have one—not anymore." Then, because he simply couldn't resist, he added, "Well, I could say not yet too."

"Was she not willing to wait, or was it not that serious?"

Amelia's face turned up to his, and the picture it made caught his breath and held it for a moment. She smiled and interrupted her own question. "'Not yet' is an even nicer thought than 'not anymore.'"

She's flirting—actually flirting with me. How did that happen? How did I come home with nothing and find everything I ever wanted? The moment that thought formed, Avelino shoved it aside. He resisted the temptation to touch her face, her hair. Instead, he nodded. "I want to say something clever or witty, but my thoughts are must."

"Do you mean mush?"

The desire to touch her grew almost impossible to resist, but Avelino shook his head. "I don't think your grandfather would approve of me getting 'mushy.' I meant must—the first pressing of grapes into new juice. It's just a mash of jumbled grape parts. That's how my mind feels—like it's all squished in odd ways."

Their laughter danced in the night air and in Avelino's mind, finally resting on the vines. *Next year's wine will be happy wine.*

Feeling foolish about his flight of fancy, he brought the conversation back to her question.

"I thought I was in love."

"You thought?"

"I am older now. I see things with different eyes. I had an understanding with a girl who grew up with me. We could have married and had a beautiful life. I know that one day, maybe early on or maybe not for ten or twenty years, I could have looked across the table and truly fallen in love with her, because a good marriage does that. I saw my parents fall in love with each other several times in my life—a new, deeper, richer love than they'd ever known."

"Avelino, that is beautiful."

"It is true. But my love for Margretta was immature, selfish." He winced inwardly at the shock on her face as she tied the name of the girl from the dance to the girl who had once held his affection. Avelino struggled to explain—to reassure her that Margretta hadn't even kept a small piece of his heart. "I loved her beauty, her admiration of me, and how much fun we had together. It was enough to start a life together perhaps, but not to sustain it without sincere commitment. I suspect her affection for me was similar. I was the boy who protected her from taunters, who told her she was pretty, and who promised to make her happy always. She believed me."

"And you would have tried to do that."

"Yes, but I would have failed. I don't know if she knew that, but I didn't—not then."

They continued walking again, drawing close enough to the soda machine to hear its humming lullaby in the evening air. He felt her eyes on him and wondered what she saw. Was he hopelessly ordinary, or did she find him handsome? Did the patch make him mysterious, or did it only hint at the repelling injury below? What would she do if he removed it?

Her next words offered the kind of healing balm his heart had needed for years.

"I feel a little sorry for her. She doesn't know what she missed."

CHAPTER TEN

TROUBLE

For much of his life, Avelino regretted one thing most about that evening. It wasn't the dances with the other girls and Margretta, sharing his stories with Amelia, or even the sleepless hours that came as he rehashed what could have been different until dawn broke over the eastern horizon. No, he regretted standing at the soda machine with the various insects buzzing around the glow of the lightbulb, talking. Why hadn't they left immediately as they'd done the last time?

"This is good. Exactly what I needed," Amelia whispered as she chugged the last few drops and set the bottle in the crate beside the machine.

"I'm almost tempted to buy a second one for the walk home."

"I've got lemonade at the house. We can work up a thirst walking home, and it'll be even more refreshing."

The few coins in his pocket agreed with her. Just as he set down the bottle, he heard something. "Did you hear—?"

Amelia's scream sent his blood pumping faster than he'd felt in months. He whirled to see one man holding her hands pinned behind her, while Raymond Welton and Dave Adams advanced on him, obviously prepared for a fight.

"What seems to be the trouble, boys?" The effort it took to keep his voice nonchalant nearly undid him, but he'd learned that aggressive tones with a hostage present meant danger to the hostage. The change in Ray's face showed he took it as an insult.

Ray charged like a schoolboy on the playground, fists flying and without purpose.

"I'll teach you to paw one of *our* women, you dirty Mexican."

As he stepped aside, Avelino's eye met Amelia's, and he shook his head at the protest he saw on her lips. Resignation followed, giving him confidence. She'd obey orders—be the distraction while he took on the offensive and completed the mission.

Ray crashed into the soda machine, while Avelino spun to locate the other boy. Working with one eye was awkward, and it crippled his instincts. The boy holding Amelia shouted for Dave to jump Avelino from behind. He whirled and rammed his head into Dave's stomach, knocking down the stunned boy.

Several times Dave and Ray charged, and, thanks to their "coach," Avelino had an idea of what the next moves would be, but Dave finally managed to land a hard slam to his jaw, splitting his lip. A scream pierced the air. He spun to see what they'd done to their hostage and in his peripheral vision caught Ray charging. He sidestepped that charge, but the result was disastrous. Ray crashed into the window, shattering it. Blood poured from glass cuts on his head.

"Ray!"

The boy holding Amelia tossed her aside and rushed to the aid of his friend. Dave managed to land a blow to Avelino's temple, and it felt like a land mine exploded in his eye. Blinded, he took another hit to the gut before he could get his arm beneath Dave's neck.

"Take your buddies and get out of here, do you understand me?"

"I'm going to kill you."

"No, you're going to kill your friend unless you get him to a doctor. Do you understand me?"

"Get. Off. Me."

"Not until I know you're going to get Ray help immediately."

Before Dave could respond, the other boy cried out, "We'll go. He's bleeding everywhere. Just let us go!"

With a shove to Dave's back, Avelino released him, prepared for a charge, but the boy ran. Ray groaned and screeched as his friends half dragged, half bullied him to a car behind the garage. Dust flew as they peeled out of the station and onto the road, but Avelino couldn't see a thing.

"Are you okay?"

Gentle fingers wiped blood from his lip.

"Don't . . ." He reached for his handkerchief and passed it to her. "You'll ruin your dress."

"Who cares about a stupid dress! Are you okay?"

"I'm fine. Really," he added as he sensed her disbelief. "I might need help getting home, though. I'm not going to be able to see out of this eye for a while."

"Let's go."

"No. I've got to call Hank first. He needs to board this up tonight."

"Like you can see a phone. Got another nickel?"

Avelino fished change from his pocket and offered his open hand to her, not bothering to try to differentiate between nickels or pennies. She plucked a coin from it and closed his hand back over the change. "Be right back."

"Not like I could go anywhere without killing myself," he muttered.

As he waited, he relived the fight. In a strange way it seemed almost like one of his flashbacks, but he knew it wasn't. He'd been aware of his surroundings, but his training had kicked in as if he were once again fighting for his life. *Will I always see things through the lens of my war experiences, or are they just still too fresh?*

Footsteps crunched across the gravel, and he felt her near before she spoke.

"Hank is on the way. He said we could go, but I think we should wait. The place is all open and exposed."

"Yeah. I'd rather not leave it like this. How bad is it?"

An instant feeling of loss tingled his senses as she moved to examine the door more closely.

"It's pretty bad. There's only one good-sized piece of glass left. I could reach in and open it without hurting myself."

"Don't risk it."

"No, really. There is just nothing on that side at all. Look!"

He heard the door swing open. "Are you nuts?"

"That last piece of glass is going to fall. I'm going to see if I can find a rag and take it out."

"Amelia . . ."

"It'll be nicer for Hank if he doesn't have all of this to clean up. Maybe I can find a broom too."

Only once in his life had he felt more helpless—the morning he'd left la Casa de los Sueños in the hands of its new owner. *At least I could see then—see all that I'd lost.* The tinkling of glass sounded deceptively delightful—almost like wind chimes—as Amelia swept up the mess, depositing it in what sounded like a pasteboard box. It was thoughtful and, if he was willing to admit it to himself, exactly the kind of thing he would have wished someone to do for him, but Avelino hated the abandoned feeling he had standing against the soda machine, the rumble of the motor serving as backup to the music of her sweeping.

"I've gone crazy."

"Why do you say that?"

"All night I keep thinking of the oddest things. I thought about happy wine as we laughed on our way here, and just now I thought about how the glass and your sweeping and the machine behind me all sounded like parts of a band. It's weird. There were a couple of other things too. Maybe I wasn't ready to leave the hospital after all."

Her laughter sounded farther away than he expected.

From inside the building, she called out to him as she put back the broom and dustpan. "I think it's just your tendency to add the little details that make a story come alive. I can't wait to write those down."

A cool cloth covered his forehead, dabbing gently at his eye, and then swiped across his cheek.

"Dave really got you good. Ray isn't going to like that."

Her words made no sense to him. "Why not?"

"Because he wanted to do it. He failed where Dave didn't. That's gotta hurt his pride."

"I suppose—ouch!"

Her giggle made him want to tickle her. It's what his father would have done to his mother, and he'd almost reacted instinctively. *How quickly my mind seems ready to think of her in more personal terms.* "I think I should be glad you don't have iodine or something."

"It needs it."

He gave his head a slight shake. "I'll survive."

"I think I hear Hank's truck." She stepped away from him, apparently watching for Hank's headlights to come up over the rise. "Yep. I think that's him. Either that or Ray got some fast stitches."

"Do you think he needed them?"

"Hard to tell. Most of the blood was on his head. You know how head wounds are. His arm looked pretty bad, but I don't think it'd *have* to have 'em. Nice, sure, but he'd be okay with a good bandage."

"Hank'll offer to drive us home. Back me up when I say 'No, thanks,' will you?"

"It'd be easier—"

"Ever ride with Hank?"

She hesitated before answering. "No . . ."

"Trust me."

The lights of the truck must have blinded her. He felt her turn toward him, shielding her eyes with his shoulder.

"Hey, you look pretty bad, 'Lino. Tell me the other guy looked worse," Hank called out as he slammed his truck door.

"He did." Amelia spoke with unmistakable pride. "Went to get stitches. I don't think Dave would have landed a single punch if Avelino had both eyes. He was amazing!"

"Well, I'm just glad you're okay." Crickets chirped in the night air, but Hank's shoes crunching on the gravel weren't much of an accompaniment. "You cleaned it up?"

"The glass is in a box in the garage. I didn't know what to cover it with. Sorry."

"Thank you, 'Melia. I can work with sharp metal all day and not get a single cut, but if there's a piece of broken glass within a mile of me, I'll slice something."

"Then you better let someone else throw that box away," Avelino teased. Before Hank could keep them talking, he added, "I can't help much, but I can hold a board while you screw it in."

"Nah, I'll be good. Why don't you just go sit in the truck, and I'll take you home after I get this covered?"

"I think we'd rather walk, but thanks."

"That's crazy! You can't see a thing with that eye and the other one covered and all. Just hang on a minute and—"

"Mr. Rhimes, that's so nice of you, but walking home gives us a little more time." What he wouldn't have given to see Amelia's face when she added, "I'm sure you understand how it is . . ."

"Oh, sure. Sure. You take yourselves off home. I've got this."

They hadn't gone three steps before Hank called after him, "Heard someone say you were lookin' for work of a Saturday. That true?"

Avelino turned and tried to face the general direction of Hank's voice. Amelia adjusted him slightly with a giggle that again tempted him to tickle her.

"That's right. I have to feed myself somehow."

"I could still use help on Saturdays. You man the station, and I'll fix the cars or go fishin' if there ain't any." Hank misread his hesitation and added, "Can pay you more now. How 'bout seven fifty a day?"

Avelino wanted to protest—to say that their prior five-dollar arrangement was all the job was worth—but practicality won out over pride. "If you think it's worth it, I'll be here on Saturday."

"Good. It's more'n worth it. Gives me time with my grandson. Only time that boy opens up to me is if we's fishin'."

Avelino waved, grumbling under his breath about feeling like a charity basket, but Amelia put a stop to it.

"Your pride is making you foolish. Hank isn't going to take food out of his family's mouths so that he can pay you what you don't think you're worth. Wages have gone up during the war. You've been away. Accept it."

"Yes'm."

She nudged his arm and muttered, "That's better."

Disappointment hit him before they reached the road. First, she'd held his hand and led him a little like a child, but he'd still stumbled several times, and it made him overly cautious. The idea of falling was mortifying, but taking her down with him was simply unacceptable. She tried taking his arm as if he were an elderly gentleman, but it felt awkward.

"Just give us to the bend up there, and we'll work something out," she murmured. "We don't want Hank to decide to push it if he thinks we look like we need the help."

The way she insisted on saying "we" when the problem was clearly his charmed him. "I'm sorry. Maybe it would be safer in his truck."

"Maybe, but it won't be as nice as walking along at a snail's pace on a beautiful fall evening. Come on, where's your spirit of adventure?"

"Teetering on my throbbing lip?"

Her snicker was exactly what he needed to hear. *She isn't taking the awkwardness seriously, so why should I?* Several steps down the road, he slipped his arm around her waist and instantly felt more stable. "Do you mind?"

"Not at all, but I wish it wasn't necessary."

Once more disappointment doused him with reality. *This must be so awkward for her.* "I could put my hands in my pockets maybe. You could steer my elbow."

"I like this just fine, but like I said, it'd be nice if it was just because we were walking along, not because you have to. Does your head hurt?"

She hadn't said that clearly at all the first time, but now her words drove out his doubts. "My head's going to hurt for sure, but not quite yet. I think adrenaline is keeping me going for now." Several steps later, he added, "Thank you, by the way."

"For what?"

"For letting me take care of it."

"I could have gotten away. I think I would have done it too if I didn't think it would distract you. Peter assumed that because he caught me, I couldn't get away."

"Wait, Pete Silverman? I thought he looked familiar. He wasn't at the dance, though."

"No, but Jimmy Randall was. His dad has been a stickler for being home before midnight—cuts off allowance if he doesn't make curfew—so I doubt Jimmy'd risk it. I bet they went to get Peter after they were ejected."

"Do you think they followed us?" He couldn't imagine how they wouldn't have noticed, but no one knew they'd go to the station.

"I don't think so. I think they went, got a soda, started to get back in the car, and heard us coming. We stood out there for a bit; remember? Laughing. I bet they just pushed the car around the corner and planned it on the spot."

It made sense, but it still bothered him. Amelia could have been hurt. Just as he started to say something, she leaned her head against his shoulder and sighed. "It sure is beautiful out here. It's driving me crazy that you can't see it. Is the eye swollen shut?"

"Completely."

"I should have bought another soda. We could have put it on there to reduce the swelling."

"At home is good enough."

"I'm glad you don't have to work tomorrow."

"I'll never make it to church like this. Father Ortiz will not be pleased after I promised to be there."

It felt just for the briefest moment as if she stiffened, but he attributed it to hearing a sound or seeing something in the road. Whatever it was had been so brief he couldn't be sure it happened.

At last she said, "I hadn't thought about your church. You're Catholic, of course."

The way she spoke meant only one thing. She wasn't. Avelino believed that those who tried to say that history did not repeat itself were fools. This time, however, the similarities in the past and present did not comfort him. It had worked a hundred years ago when the only church around was Catholic, but now? Would a Protestant even consider him? It wasn't likely, and being Catholic was more than a faith—one that his family did not wholly subscribe to; it was part of their culture. It was part of their history.

"And you are not."

"I am not. Our family has been Baptist since—since I don't know when, but we are."

The priest would not bless marriage to a Protestant. It didn't matter much to him, but should it? He'd have to think about that. Read the Bible. Pray. His family had always been in trouble with the priests, but he hated to disappoint men he respected so highly.

"You go to that little white church near the school?"

"Yes."

"They won't think much of you going around with a Catholic."

Now her arm slid around his waist. They walked together without a single stumble for a quarter mile before she answered him. "No. Pastor Fletcher won't like it."

"How many Mexicans are in your church?"

She shook her head. "None. We have a few Negroes—a lovely widow with four of the cutest children, an older man who can sing like you've never heard anyone sing, and a nice couple from Alabama. Sometimes the migrant Chinese come."

"But no Mexicans."

"No." He felt her head rise as she looked at him. "Why?"

"Do you know why?"

"I thought it was because the Catholic Church is very good at instilling loyalty and fe— . . . things like that into their people."

"Fear." He voiced the word she'd started to speak. "Is that what you were going to say?"

"Yes."

"There is some truth to that, but it's not the kind of fear that you might think. It's more respect—like for authority." He sighed. "There are no Mexicans in your church because to be Mexican *is* to be Catholic. It is a part of our culture—of who we are as people.

Maybe someday that won't be true anymore. I don't know. I think it would be sad, but some things would be easier then, I guess."

"Easier?"

"Carrillos are not very good Catholics, Amelia. We show respect for the Church. We attend Mass. Some of us attend confession; others do not. We read our Bibles and we pray, but—"

"Why don't some of you attend confession? I thought that was an integral part of Catholicism."

"My father attended confession. He believed it was something we could do with a clear conscience. He didn't think it was commanded—not the way it is done—but he really tried to yield on anything he could. My uncle disagreed."

"I've never heard of a Catholic who did not go to confession."

"*Tío* Raul said that it interfered with confession to other Christians. He thought it was too easy to confess to one man, say a prayer for forgiveness, and be done with it. *Papá* disagreed."

"And you?"

"I think they are both right. I will go to confession out of respect for the priest and tradition. I think it serves me well to consider my sins and confess them. I, like my father, do not speak the traditional Act of Contrition. Ours is a little different, but no priest has ever condemned it."

"But what about forgiveness? Doesn't the priest forgive you?"

There was the slightest trace of horror in her voice and, surprisingly, he found it charming rather than insulting.

"He does. I, as many in my family do, consider it him reminding me that God forgives my sins."

"Are there many Catholics like this?"

"I don't know. I know that we are different enough that many mothers would never permit their daughters to marry us, but even more don't care. We go to the right church, we observe the right holidays, we show respect, and that is what matters."

"And I go to a church where the pastor semiregularly condemns the Catholic Church from the pulpit."

He heard more in her words than Avelino thought she intended. The Catholic Church wasn't an option for her. Not being a part of the culture, despite the many aspects of the faith that he rejected, was not an option for him.

"You would want your children to be Protestants."

"Just as you would want yours to be Catholic."

The catch in her throat as she choked out the word "Catholic" nearly undid him.

"Amelia?"

"Hmm?"

"Can we talk about faith sometime—not about churches or traditions, but about what we believe in regards to our faith?"

"Do you think it'll do any good?"

"We've had a Presbyterian, an Episcopalian, a Methodist, and a Baptist all marry into the family without compromising their faith. I think it might do some good. You will see."

A stiffness that he hadn't noticed forming disappeared as she relaxed. "We'll talk then."

* * *

It galled him when she had to see him to his own door. She helped him inside, found his pajamas for him, and hurried down to get him an ice bag. She turned down the covers, brought him a drink, and muttered something under her breath about the lack of room left by the pile of junk in the corner.

"We really do need to find a way to put that downstairs somewhere so you can bring in a nice couch and a radio maybe. You liked listening to mine while we worked."

"Trying to get rid of me of an evening, eh?"

"Scratch the radio, but surely a couch would be nice—or a chair?"

Avelino tried to pull off his tie with one hand but couldn't. He started to set down the ice bag, but Amelia stopped him.

"Here, I'll get that." As she tugged on the knot, she asked, "Can you get your shoes or—?"

"I'm good. Thanks."

Awkwardness hung between them, until he felt the faintest touch of her lips on his split one.

"Good night, Avelino. Thank you for taking me. I'm so sorry you got hurt."

Without a word she fled the room, her shoes making the now-familiar rat-a-tat-tat on the stairs as she hurried to the ground. From the sound of it, she ran. Pajamas forgotten, Avelino lay on his bed, ice bag resting over his eye, and relived the night in his memory.

CHAPTER ELEVEN

AN ISSUE OF FAITH

Gunfire, short bursts of it, woke him from the precious little sleep he'd managed all night. He jerked upright in bed and realized someone was knocking. "Coming."

Amelia, looking much too perky for his comfort, smiled at him. "We're . . ." Her expression changed to horrified. "You look terrible. That eye! Can you see?"

"Well enough not to break my neck."

A finger touched his swollen, cracked lip.

"Still hurt?"

His flinch answered for him. "A little." He stepped aside for her. "Do you need something? Want to come in?"

"No, we're leaving for church in half an hour. Granddad says we can drop you off on our way if you wanted to go to Mass."

How he managed not to say "No, thanks" and close the door for another few hours' sleep, Avelino didn't know. Instead, he nodded and promised to be ready. "Thank you."

"You didn't get much sleep, did you? Do you need some aspirin or something?"

"That'd be nice."

"We have some scrambled eggs left. Want me to put them between some bread with a tomato or something? You could eat on the way . . ."

"I'll be ready for them in a few minutes. I've just got to go down and wash up in the garage."

"That's not necessary, you know. We have—"

It was already an "old" argument between them, but Avelino refused to use the house as if it were still his home. "It's fine. I'll be there soon."

Avelino allowed himself the pleasure of watching her skip down the steps and wave at him before she returned to the house. She did it every time. The way her blue dress swished around her knees and her hair bounced against her shoulders—the guys in his platoon had talked about such things. They'd said they were fighting for the little things like that as well as the freedom to work where they wanted, go to school if they wanted, and go to any church—or none at all—if they wanted. They were fighting for the big ideals and the little pleasures of life too. Now he understood.

Avelino snatched up his clothes and hurried down to the sink in the garage. It was just a laundry tub—not very pretty but it worked. He filled the bottom with water and scrubbed one foot and leg at a time. He drained the water and refilled it, working on his chest and arms. Finally, as fresh water rinsed out the dirty, he scrubbed his hair, toweled himself dry, and pulled on clean clothes as quickly as possible. *I'll freeze come winter*, he mused.

He'd hung a mirror over the sink—a small little thing that was meant for use on a vanity, but it worked. Slowly, he shaved the dark shadow from his jaw, careful not to catch his mustache or jar his lip. The reflection before him always discouraged him, but today's looked particularly gruesome. Half of him appeared perfectly normal, but angry red scars crisscrossed over where his left eye should be. Someday they'd be pale, but now they were a constant reminder of ugly days.

The patch slid easily over his eye. He hated it. Every time he put it on, it felt like he had something sinister to hide. *Instead, it's just revolting—I'm revolting.* With a still-puffy black eye and a split lip, he looked like he'd just crawled out of battle. *I guess I have.* The thought did little to comfort him as he hurried toward the house.

The back door stood open, so Avelino knocked on the screen before entering. "Morning."

"Oh, Amelia said it was bad, but . . ."

"I'm fine. I've been hurt worse just goofing around with my brother."

Amelia breezed into the room and stopped short. "You really should have iodine on that lip."

"Not if I plan to eat. It'll be hard enough to do that without causing more pain first."

A sandwich on the table with a glass of milk beside it beckoned. As much as he dreaded opening his mouth wide enough to take a bite, Avelino was hungry.

Mr. Kearns started to leave the room, muttering something about looking for his Bible, when he stopped short. "We'll be leaving in five minutes. That doesn't give you much time. Sorry."

"I appreciate you thinking of me. Father Ortiz would be disappointed in me for breaking a promise, but I would have slept through."

A look passed between Mr. Kearns and his granddaughter. Amelia nodded and went in search of the missing Bible while Joe sat down.

"Son, you didn't sleep well, did you?"

"No."

"Care to talk about it?"

He gestured to his sandwich before taking a bite. Once he swallowed, Avelino realized he couldn't ignore it indefinitely. "Not really. There are a few things I need to work out in my own mind first."

"She likes you."

The words were a kick to the gut. "I know. I like her too, but—"

"But you are Catholic."

"It's not just that. Really. I think if we talk, you will understand that. I don't think you'll have a problem with it. There's more than that."

"Such as . . ."

He stared at the sandwich, suddenly not very hungry. A napkin in a basket caught his attention, and he covered his plate before getting up and putting it in the icebox. "Sir, in the eyes of some, I am a dirty Mexican." He pointed to his eye and his lip. "Last night she could have been hurt by those fools."

"Most people don't think like that, Avelino."

"No, maybe not, but even some of *my* old friends might object to me dating a *gringo*—maybe. A hundred years ago it wasn't an issue. For some reason it seems to be one now."

Amelia's voice at the front door called for them: "Granddad, Avelino, we're going to be late."

*   *   *

The familiar holds people in tender arms, cradling them with comfort that the new can never achieve. Carved woodwork, flickering candles, and the distinct scent of incense tantalized Avelino's senses, making him feel like a boy again. How many times had he walked through that same narthex, hand in his mother's, and slid into their usual pew in the nave? The Stations of the Cross that had fascinated him as a small child now intrigued him on an intellectual level.

The beauty of that familiarity struck him deep in his heart. Avelino's still-swollen eye welled with tears as he listened to the singing of the psalm, and the truth of the priest's words at the blessing, "Blessed be God: Father, Son, and Holy Spirit," filled his heart. All around him people sang, *"Glory be to God on high . . ."*

He could not take communion. As the others went forward, Avelino knelt and prayed for those receiving it. *I knew I should have gone to confession yesterday. I was too focused on myself. Forgive me, Jesus.*

The solemn reverence of Mass in the church his family had worshipped in for almost half a century lingered with him as he stepped into the sunlight again. The two blocks to the Baptist church seemed longer somehow, his mind still swirling with recent events. Music, a wheezy organ accompanying a rousing congregation, filled the air as he neared the little white church.

". . . the Lord be with you and keep you . . ."

He sat in the truck, waiting through what sounded like a prayer. *How different is church in this pretty white building with the tall spire and the many large windows?* He knew there were differences—big ones in fact. From the stories handed down through the years, it seemed that in Texas they'd all met in a barn somewhere until the community had raised enough money to build a little combination schoolhouse/church. People sat in desks on Sundays, and the preacher spoke from the teacher's desk.

Would it be wrong to go and see—learn the difference? Father Ortiz would say it was. But then there were the words from the Bible—"where two or three gather in My name . . ." To miss Mass seemed unthinkable, but perhaps once. It might prove his commitment to truth, assuming that this church also had such a commitment.

The doors opened, and people spilled out, laughing and talking. The preacher, Pastor Fletcher, shook hands with all while his wife hugged the ladies or admired their dresses. The atmosphere was very different here. The quiet devotion of those in his parish was almost antithetical of what he saw here. He wanted to dislike it—find it offensive—but he couldn't.

A few people saw him in the truck and frowned. Was it his eye? Did the big black bruise imply that he had been in trouble? Was it that he had obviously not gone to church there that morning? The cold eyes of Mr. Welton showed disapproval of him, and Avelino had no doubt of its cause.

Amelia saw him first and hurried from a group of chattering girls to greet him. "Come meet my friends."

"I—"

"Please, Avelino. I would like you to meet them and Pastor Fletcher."

If she can be so open about her interest, I can as well. Despite his resolve, Avelino's heart was heavy as he climbed from the truck and followed her to where her friends whispered behind their clutches. Amelia, on the other hand, seemed oblivious.

"Girls, I'm sure some of you know Avelino Carrillo."

He recognized two of the girls, but one was new to him. "I'm sorry, I don't know you," he said to the stranger, "but it is nice to see you again, Rosemary and Caroline."

"Barbara, this is Avelino Carrillo. His family owned the vineyards where Granddad works. He's just home from the Pacific."

A genuine smile on Barbara's face told him that at least one of the girls did not find his intrusion distasteful.

"It's nice to meet you. I think I saw you at the dance last night."

"Yes," Rosemary agreed. "I thought that was you. How did you like our Victory Dance?"

"I appreciated the efforts everyone made to ensure the soldiers had a good time."

Amelia's face fell when Caroline murmured to Barbara, "He must not have met Helen." A few titters erupted, until the girls saw her expression. "I'm sorry, Amelia, but you have to admit that she can be uppity."

"She was kind to me when I first arrived—"

"And won't be if you don't follow her around like a lost puppy."

He wanted to protest—to protect her from the pain of Rosemary's words—but he couldn't. Instinctively, he knew they were true. Something his aunt had said often echoed in his memory until he gathered the courage to share it. "'A person's flaw does not negate a virtue any more than a virtue negates a flaw.'"

Rosemary's forehead wrinkled. "What does that mean?"

A smile formed before he could prevent it, making him wince as his lip tried to reopen. Rosemary never had been exceptionally bright. "Just that we don't have to overlook Helen's kindness to Amelia. What she did was a good thing, and I am glad to know that someone welcomed Amelia and helped her get to know people."

"I wouldn't know any of you if it wasn't for Helen," Amelia agreed.

"That's not true. We would have met you eventually. Everything is just so busy in spring around here . . ." Even as she spoke, the expression on Barbara's face showed she knew the excuse was weak.

"How is your brother, Caroline? Wasn't he commissioned?"

The conversation easily diverted to the war and those they knew in it. The crowd of worshippers slowly evaporated until even Rosemary had to leave.

Amelia pulled Avelino toward the church door. "Let me introduce you to Pastor and Mrs. Fletcher."

Despite awkward introductions, the middle-aged man and his wife seemed genuinely interested in him, his family, and his connection with the Kearnses. The brief conversation ended with an invitation to the evening service. Avelino started to refuse, but the hope in Amelia's eyes made it impossible. "I would like that, I think. Is a Catholic welcome?"

"Always."

"Then I will come. Thank you."

As they bade the couple good-bye and climbed into the truck, a mantle of disappointment settled over him. It made no sense. Amelia was happy; he was happy to please her and to learn what the differences between the churches and what they believed were. So why was he so disheartened? As they passed his church, Father Ortiz's robe flapping as he rounded a corner, Avelino realized the source of his dejection.

He could go. He could sit and listen to the pastor of this church teach. He could sing their songs and enjoy the service with Amelia by his side, but she would never be able to do that with him. Sunday Mass took place simultaneously with her Sunday morning worship.

CHAPTER TWELVE

THE CRUSH

The crush erupted in full force. All the modern machinery that Paco had leveraged to purchase did the crew no good without the skills to use it properly. Avelino considered it a risk to try it and an even bigger risk to assume that Mr. Lyndon would not complain about the archaic methods he would have to employ. *Lyndon will complain no matter what I choose. Even if it's a success, he'll have expected a bigger one or something.*

Grapes poured into the wine house, ready to be stomped. But would he do it?

"Still haven't decided?"

Mr. Kearns's question cut to the heart of the issue.

"Actually, I have. I just keep trying to convince myself that there is a choice that is both safe and effective."

"I'll have them call in crushers."

How the man knew what he wanted, Avelino could only guess, but he did. *I know traditional winemaking. I've never used any of that modern equipment that Paco insisted would make us wealthy beyond our wildest dreams.* He knew vats, crushers, and premium wine in small batches. They had a reputation for making some of the finest wine in the world—even if much of that world would not yet admit it. *We've won awards. Our process is flawless. Why risk it?*

By the time Mr. Kearns returned, Avelino felt more confident, but it didn't last.

"Amelia has been missing your company of an evening."

"I get home late—too late to visit. It's our busiest time."

"Yes, but you avoid her when she's outside."

That truth he couldn't deny. After days of wrestling with his conscience, Avelino had come to a decision. Their relationship would not work. He couldn't risk Amelia getting hurt because of fools like Welton.

"I am sorry."

"Don't tell me; tell her." Mr. Kearns laughed. "Well, not quite. You tell her you're sorry. You tell me why."

Avelino pointed to the sickly olive green around his eye and the ugly scab on his lip. "This is why. What use is it to ignore the inevitable? Even if she is never physically hurt when some fool decides I've overstepped my place, her heart will be hurt."

"How so?"

"She'll hurt to see people reject me. She'll hurt when people reject her because of me. If we married, what about our children? Would she be able to stand by and watch them scorned by the children who should be playmates because some of their father's ancestors came from a different part of Europe than is currently acceptable?"

"That's not fair, Avelino. Most people don't think like that."

"And yet enough do that they held her and made her watch as they tried to attack me." He swallowed hard. "I endured enough of that kind of prejudice in the army—men like my sergeant ranting about the worthless Mexicans who didn't belong with the pretty white men."

"That kind of ignorance—"

"Exists. I didn't know it before I left here, but I do now." He gripped the side of a vat as workers poured grapes into it. "It isn't right. We are too different. I am a Catholic whose family has been in trouble with the priests for a hundred years. She is a Baptist who can't understand why I stay where they sometimes teach what I do not believe."

"I don't understand that either, son."

A lifetime of explanations, careful teaching, and impassioned encouragement welled up in him. "Have you never heard anything taught by one of your pastors that you disagreed with?"

"Well, of course! For one thing, I work at a vineyard where they make wine. Baptists are temperance people, you know."

"And yet you keep going. Why? Why not find a church where everything they teach is exactly what you believe?"

"That church doesn't exist, and if it did it'd be a church of one. Me."

"That is why I remain a Catholic. For a hundred years, Carrillos have broken rules and rejected some of the tenets of our general faith. We have done it out of love for family, culture, and tradition. You do the same thing in your church for your family, your culture, your tradition. Do you see?"

"Did you tell Amelia that?"

That was the important question, and one he hadn't intended to consider. *Why discuss what won't change the impossible to the possible? Why cause that kind of pain to her or to me?* It seemed cruel to suggest it, but the kind of silence he had brought between them hadn't been pain-free either.

"I'll talk to her."

"Go. She's probably doing laundry about now. I'll make sure things go well here."

"Lyndon—"

"I'll tell him you'll be along to see him if he shows up. I doubt it. He'll wait until nothing can be salvaged and then he'll come in, complaining."

He hadn't taken two steps before Mr. Kearns spoke again. "I'm sorry about this, Avelino. I like you. I had hoped . . ."

"Me too, sir. Me too."

"Call me Joe. It'll take some of the sting out of it all."

"Yessir—Joe."

*   *   *

A familiar snap greeted him as he climbed the drive to the house. She really was doing laundry. How many times in his youth had he chased between the sheets, looking for bandits to drive away from the castle he pretended to defend? Even now he recognized the distinctive snap of a pillowcase versus a shirt or pair of pants.

Her head turned at the sound of his feet on the gravel. A lump filled in his throat when a smile lit her face.

"What are you doing . . . ?" The smile faded. "Granddad—?"

"He's fine. He's overseeing the crush." To his disgust, he found he couldn't meet her eyes. "I wondered if we could talk."

"I'm almost done, but the sheet will sour if I don't get it up first."

Without a word, he pulled the sheet from the basket, offering one end to her, and pinned it to the last line. His mother had hung sheets back there too—privacy for the rest of their clothes and undergarments. Thankfully, there were no undergarments on the line to embarrass either of them.

"Are you thirsty?"

"No, I'm fine. Thank you."

She'd picked up the basket, but something made her drop it. "What's wrong? You've avoided me since Sunday night, and now I can hear it in your voice. What did I do or say that offended you?"

"Nothing."

"I don't believe it."

Unsure what else to do, he led her to the steps to his "apartment" and sat beside her. "It's true, Amelia. You did not offend me, and yes," he added reluctantly, "I am avoiding you."

"Why?"

The whispered question hung between them. Answering it meant no turning back. He wouldn't spin her on an emotional yo-yo. "I think you know why."

"You didn't like my church."

"It was different, but I didn't have a problem with it."

Seconds passed—minutes. How could he explain without hurting her? That was the real problem. Amelia would be hurt no matter what he did or didn't say.

Determined to put the awkward task behind him, Avelino began talking. He explained his misgivings, the pain he wanted to save her, the wisdom in recognizing the problem now. When she didn't respond, he started in on his regrets, the hopes he'd allowed himself to entertain. When she still kept silent despite the obvious disappointment and hurt in her expression, he added the one thing he thought would harden her to him.

"I've always dreamed of a wife with hair and eyes like yours. After the stories my family has recounted every week of every month of my life, how could I not? Add to it your personality, and how could I ask for anything else?"

"How indeed."

There. That was something. Maybe now she'd react in some way. "You love my family's stories." He ducked his head. "It seems like you enjoy my company . . ."

"I do."

"Can you see why this is so hard for me?"

"Yes."

His mother would have yelled, argued, wept, beat his chest, and then demanded that they work it out. His grandmother would have done all that and brought every other woman of the family in to back her up. The utter silence and apparent acceptance, while a relief on one level, seemed unnatural. Then again, his *tía* Elena was one of those quiet types—just like Amelia. She would seem quiet and accepting while seething with white-hot anger.

"I guess that's it then," he said, standing. "I'll keep to myself. I don't want things to be awkward."

"It's too late for that."

"I'm glad you are taking it well . . ." The moment the words were out of his mouth, Avelino knew he'd said the wrong thing.

"That's a lie." Amelia stood and concentrated her gaze on Avelino's one eye. "I am not taking this well. When you asked me to go with you to the dance, I had hopes that you might like me. At the dance and afterward, you said . . ." A tear splashed on her cheek as Amelia choked back the emotions that threatened to overwhelm her. "It doesn't matter what you said, I guess."

He hadn't expected to feel loss. Not so soon. This was why he'd decided to cut it off now—before either of them got hurt.

"Amelia . . ."

"You should know," she continued as she brushed past him, more tears flowing, "I'm not giving up. I am here, and I am praying every day that you see that we are above this. Not everyone is like Ray. Most people aren't. But even if every single person in this valley . . ." She stopped abruptly, thinking. "You know what? Even if every person in this country was against it, I wouldn't care. It sounds silly and dramatic—something a schoolgirl would say—but it's true. I don't care. I care if I find something out about you that won't work. Maybe you are a drunk and I don't know it yet. That would make me say, 'Forget it.' If you have a temper that you can't control and I haven't seen it yet, then yes. That's not going to work. If your faith rests in icons, prayers to saints, and Mary instead of in the work of Jesus on the cross, then we are incompatible. However, if the only problem between us—don't interrupt me," she added with just a hint of impatience, "is that your ancestors came from Spain and mine came from a thousand miles north of there, then I will keep praying, keep fighting to be your friend, and I will not give up."

He stood on the bottom step, staring after her. Convincing himself that his heart was the only one that would be affected had been easier than watching the realization of just how wrong he was. Maybe Lyndon would have the last laugh after all. It might well become torture to see her daily and know he had to keep his distance. *It would be worse not to see her daily*, he mused to himself as he turned back to the road. *At least she's where I can keep an eye on her—make sure no one hurts her.*

* * *

Avelino's lungs filled with the perfumed air of crushed grapes as he stepped into the winery. The free-run juice already flowed into tanks as women and children stomped the grapes in vats. Old men, too old to help with the harvest, could still earn a day's wage in the vats, and seeing so many men washing their feet in preparation to take their turn swelled his heart. *Traditional is better. It helps an elderly man feel needed and useful and produces superior wine.*

"You have a good operation here." Joe Kearns leaned over the railing, where Avelino watched the workers with an experienced eye.

"I think so. Is something wrong?"

"We found about fifty vines infected with bunch rot."

"Rip them out and burn them—twenty feet beyond the last one in all directions."

"Are you sure? That seems aggressive."

"They've been left unattended too long. We'll have more next year. This might give us a jump start on it."

A man behind Joe nodded and went to give the orders, but Joe stayed. "Did you find Amelia?"

"Yes."

"Want to talk about it?"

"Not particularly, but I will tell you that she is upset and that she says she's not giving up."

"And she won't. I told you, there isn't a more persistent girl on the planet."

The men stared down at the tons of grapes pouring into the wine house, each lost in his own thoughts.

At last Joe nudged Avelino's elbow and said, "So, did the first Avelino ever make it to Virginia?"

How could he not, Avelino protested to himself. *He—oh. He wants the story. Brave man to risk Amelia's silent fury when she learns he got the story from me.* Realization crept over him slowly. *He'll go back and tell her. He just wants her to still get her stories. He's a good* abuelo. Abuelito *would approve.*

"He did. After a long trip to Virginia, he found himself on a ship bound for Yerba Buena—becalmed."

CHAPTER THIRTEEN

LIFE BY THE HORN

August 1836

Becalmed. It was a stranger feeling than dancing over the water at the speed of a racing horse. The gentle rocking of the ship on the waves was deceptively restful and a great relief after several days heaving up whatever he managed to get down at a meal. In stark contrast, the sailors raced around the deck, doing odd chores that made no sense to him.

For the first time in three weeks, Avelino did not regret that he climbed aboard the *Milton*. Señor Sidney Tandy had teased him about wishing to return to Texas, but he had denied it. It was a lie. From the moment he rode out of sight of the little homestead by the river, doubts plagued him. People were unexpectedly friendly along the route through Louisiana, across the tip of Mississippi, into Tennessee, up through North Carolina, and finally into Virginia to Norfolk.

It had taken him four days to recover from the journey. He'd arrived weak and emaciated, but Sidney Tandy had been eager to learn of his cousin's success in Texas. They'd found an interpreter, a young man from Florida who had foolishly come searching for his sweetheart despite the fact that she had obviously not come to Virginia.

He got me a good price, Avelino reflected as he gazed out over the water. *I have plenty of money and still a few jewels for later.* Of course, once there were the funds, the real questions had to be considered. They'd debated the price differences between a clipper ship and a frigate. The *John Henry* had a fare half the price of the *Milton*, but choosing between around a hundred days of sailing and two hundred fifty, he had considered it a bargain. With the roughness of the seas and his apparent inability to stomach it, Avelino now thanked El Señor that he'd cut travel time nearly by a third.

They would reach California by November. Don Carrillo would find him a good place to grow the grapes that had always tempted him. Good wine was part of his tradition—and hard to find—and the climate there in California sounded perfect for them. Little frost, temperate weather, plenty of rain but not too much . . . *It will be a good life. A very good life.*

*   *   *

The worst of the journey was over after the storms that raged around Cape Horn. How many times did the *capitán* tell him this? The sailors all smiled as if they had arrived already, but they still had seven thousand miles to travel. Much could go wrong in those miles. It galled him to realize that he would sail past the place where he'd begun. Had he not been a coward, he could have traveled down to Veracruz, crossed Mexico, and boarded a ship from there, saving thousands of miles of journey by sea.

That thought amused him as well. As a coward he avoided land and confrontation with anyone who might accuse him of being a deserter. No, he preferred to climb aboard the wretched deathtrap-like coffin they called a ship and risk drowning instead—*Because I am a coward. I am a fool.*

Accustomed to a life of ease and leisure, Avelino bemoaned the past two wasted years of his life. His grand plan for adventure in the army had failed him. There was no great honor and glory in the slaughter of men. *Perhaps for the* generales, *but not for me. My childhood dreams failed me, but I will be content as long as my new dreams are not quite as disappointing.*

However, I will have to work in this new place. I will have to oversee the natives who build me a house and plant my vines. I will have to travel to find vines for cuttings. Riding was painful now—not as painful as walking—but still painful. *But if I plan to have a leisurely life in California with my own delicious wines at my table, I will have to walk my vines and care for them.*

A priest too. I must find an educated man or a priest to teach me to read and write. I must learn. I will write to Don Edgar and tell of my new home. This will please him.

Memories of the man who saved his life filled him, and not for the first time regret followed. *Why did I not beg him to pack up their things and go with me? I could have built a home for them too. Edgar was older but strong. He could have supervised the land and the workers while I found a wife and began my family. The señorita could have made friends with Don Ruiz's family. They would have enjoyed a much finer life than their impoverished Texian one.* That thought filled him with remorse.

Once the land was his—once he had a rancho or portion of a rancho of his own—he would make a will. The land would belong to Señor Edgar Tandy and his daughter Cherith, should he die. *Yes, the house, vines, jewels, and all my money.* The longer he thought, the more confident he became. Ruiz or one of his sons could hire someone to take the news to Don Edgar, along with enough money to get them to California. Maybe by then the overland route would be open and they could avoid the long journey by sea.

For weeks Avelino planned his new life, not truly believing that it would ever come to pass. Each rough day, calm night, or strange wind that seemed to blow them off course and never did sent a new fear and renewed determination through him. He knew what he wanted his house to look like, how he would plant his vines, and the things he wanted to learn first.

He could have been educated. Some in his family were; the opportunity was always there. However, he had ignored it, played ignorant and unteachable until those trying to teach had given up. It hadn't taken long. In his former lazy life, he'd had little need for reading or writing. They need only count their money, know the worth of things, and know how to choose servants wisely. *I know my name, recognize that; it is a start.*

The sight of land—of California—brought renewed hope. Sailing grew harder there, but the long trek up the coast only took two days before the ship arrived. It was November 4, 1836, 116 days after they left the port at Norfolk. *A new life—home.*

CHAPTER FOURTEEN

RUMORS AND REJECTION

October 1945

"Independence is an expensive luxury for all. Men die for it, while others sell themselves into slavery, mistaking it for the independence they seek."

He'd heard the words all his life—wise words spoken often by his *abuelo*, his *mamá*, and his *papá*. The Carrillo family valued independence. *If only Paco had understood the importance of financial independence as well as personal independence.*

Wash the beans. Soak the beans. Drain the beans. Cook the beans on a hot plate, stirring often. The work it took to make a simple meal—one to last him the week—astounded him. It would take all afternoon and evening just to have food ready for the week.

A knock on his door surprised him. How had he not heard someone climb the stairs? Expecting Amelia to stand there waiting for him, he opened it slowly.

"Oh, come in, Joe."

"I was just going to see what you're doing for supper, but I smell it."

"I have it taken care of, but thanks."

"Amelia is spending the night with Rosemary, so I thought maybe you'd like to listen to the radio with me—maybe tell me more of that ancestor of yours while the house is quiet."

While the house is quiet. *While Amelia is gone is more like it.* "That'd be nice. I'll be along after I eat."

Joe pointed to the ice chest in the corner. "Just so you know, Amelia will have ice for you in the house every few days. Don't fight it. Just get it. She'll buy it whether or not you take it, so don't be stubborn about it."

"It's not necessary—"

"Maybe not, but she's going to get ours anyway, so don't be difficult."

Without another word, Joe turned and hurried downstairs, his feet as light as a cat's. Not ten minutes later, Avelino heard more steps on the stairs, footfalls like drumrolls, which were followed by a sharp knock and shout of "Avelino! Come quick."

Frustrated, he snapped off the hot plate and dashed to the door, grabbing his shoes on the way. "What?"

"Señor Lopez fell in the vats. He refuses to get out—says he'll be sent to the corner with the old women at home."

Avelino followed Pedro to the wine house, listening to the story and trying desperately to invent a solution that protected both the winery and Señor Lopez's dignity.

"Is he hurt?"

"No, I don't think so. His pride is, and he can't continue. He's just too feeble to do all that stomping."

Several solutions presented themselves, but none would be fiscally responsible. However, the other employees watched to see what he would do. How he handled the situation would either garner loyalty and respect or further disdain for the injury his family had caused so many. He could not afford not to take that into consideration.

"Bring him up to the walk. I want to see how he handles it."

It was a risky move; some might consider him cruel to expect an old man who fell in the vats to make it across the floor and up a flight of stairs. However, he had to judge the man's strength for himself.

Hector Lopez had no trouble making it across the wine house floor. The stairs took more effort, and the man seemed quite unsteady a couple of times, but once on the walk, he ambled to Avelino's side without trouble.

"You asked to see me, señor?"

"I can't keep you in the vats, Señor Lopez. You know that."

"Don't send me home—*por favor*," Hector hissed. "You know what it means to a man my age."

Avelino pointed to the stairs. "I won't send you home if you can walk and climb those stairs. You had trouble just now."

Pedro interrupted before Señor Lopez could protest. "He has been working for several hours. His legs are probably tired. Treading grapes is much harder work than walking and climbing stairs now and then."

So, Pedro anticipates my plan—seems to approve of it. Abuelita *would call it a sign and get a scolding from* abuelito. "Good. Then we'll give you a trial on Monday. You'll run errands. It doesn't pay as well as treading—a boy's job really. But I'd rather keep a boy in school and give the job to a man I respect."

"*Sí.* I can do that, señor! Thank you!"

Avelino smiled at the pride in the man's voice. "Okay then. Monday. Right now you go home and rest those legs. I need them in the best shape possible. You're going to be a busy man."

The hour away from home to tend to his staff meant that his beans cooked slower. There was no time to make rice and tortillas.

He'd do that tomorrow. A new thought occurred to him as he ate the bowl of beans without benefit of his favorite salsa. He would ask Señora Mendoza if she would sell him tortillas. That would save much time. Perhaps the next week he could make tamales. That would be a wonderful breakfast in the mornings. *Huevos y tamales*—if he could buy eggs too. Or, again, Señora Mendoza might be willing to sell him some. He would ask after church. *Buying, if I can afford it, would save a day of hard work. Making tamales is so time consuming*, he reminded himself.

*   *   *

They hadn't spoken when Avelino arrived at the house. A plate, covered with a plaid napkin, sat on the table waiting for him. Joe simply picked it up and thrust it in his hands before turning on the radio. Now, with the rhubarb pie devoured, Avelino sat awkwardly, listening to the program.

He hadn't meant for things to be this way. His eyes slid across the floor, across that same swath of rug that had once held a ribbon of green cloth. He could hear the rustle of the paper as she adjusted it and pinned it. The gentle whoosh-whoosh of the scissors as they sliced through the fabric—gone.

The dress—beautiful on her. He could still see the skirt—so much fuller than the other girls' skirts—and watch it spin as she danced. From the compliments she received, Avelino had no doubt that she'd been correct regarding changing dress styles. *Will the brown be as perfectly suited?*

Program ended, Joe snapped off the set and crossed his arms, grinning. "Heard what happened with Hector. How do you think that'll go over with Lyndon?"

"Our agreement states that I will do whatever I can to restore our family's success with this business. This is what my father and my grandfather would have done."

"I think," Joe mused after a minute of reflection, "you have hit upon the real success of the Carrillos."

"What is that?"

"Integrity and true Christian charity," Joe said. "God has blessed it."

"And when we got greedy, God withheld His blessing. How could He not?"

"God's mercies rain upon the just and the unjust, Avelino."

Almost before Joe finished speaking, Avelino's head shook. "But those who know what is right have a responsibility to do it. It isn't just a matter of just and unjust; it is a matter of the just behaving like the unjust. We did that."

"If I didn't know any better, I'd say you sounded an awful lot like a Baptist."

"If I didn't know any better," Avelino countered, "I'd say you sounded an awful lot like a Carrillo—and we are Catholic."

"You hinted to Amelia that your beliefs were not so very different from ours. You reminded me that I don't believe everything my pastor teaches. Are they really not so very different from ours?"

"They are not."

Joe waited for several long seconds before asking him to explain. "I'd be curious to know if we have misunderstood the beliefs of Catholics all these years."

"I don't think you have. Name something that you know you disagree with."

"The Marian doctrines. Who was Mary?"

"The woman chosen to be the mother of Jesus."

"Not *madre de Dios?*"

"Yes . . . in a sense. Jesus is God, so she is the mother of God in that sense."

As Joe contemplated his deliberate ambiguity, Avelino watched. It seemed as if the older man expected a trick of words. "The ever virgin . . ."

"I do not believe that, nor has most of my family for almost a hundred years."

"Isn't that a serious part of your church's doctrine?"

"Yes."

"The pope."

"The head of the Catholic Church."

"Sinless?"

If Avelino wasn't mistaken, Joe had barely suppressed a smirk as he asked. *This was where he expects to trip me up; it won't work.* "No."

Eyes widened. "That surprises me, obviously."

"I expected it would."

Again Joe tossed out another question. "Priest gets authority to forgive sins direct from God?"

"Do you believe in the priesthood of believers, Joe?"

"Yes."

"Then that is my answer. Yes."

It took Joe a long pause to grapple with what Avelino meant. "If I had said no . . ."

"I would have said yes and clarified that I included myself. Then I would have asked to show you a Bible."

"But I thought the Bible in common languages was on the *Index of Prohibited Books* or something like that."

Avelino hated this. He always felt like a traitor to his church, but how much worse to be a traitor to the Gospel? "It is."

"But you read it."

"I do." He sighed. "You want to ask why I remain faithful to a church that I don't agree with."

"Well . . ."

"Mr. Kearns, you know why. Why are you?"

"But these are big points of doctrine. It isn't comparable to attending a church where they preach against my livelihood. I make wine that I don't drink, because it feeds my family."

"So that is your only disagreement with your church? Whether or not it is a sin to make wine?"

"Well, no . . ."

"What other things?" Avelino hated that he would likely put his friend on the defensive, but it seemed necessary.

"I don't believe that Christians under the new covenant are required to tithe. My church does."

"Anything else?"

Joe thought. "I guess I see your point. When I start thinking of it, I can find quite a few things. Even Amelia disagrees with me on a couple."

Lights swept across the front window, and the familiar rumble of the Kearnses' truck hummed outside before the engine died.

Avelino stood, ready to leave, but Joe waved him back down. "Don't make things more awkward, son."

Amelia appeared out of seemingly thin air. He didn't hear the truck door slam shut, the back door open, or any footfalls. One second they heard the truck turn off, and just a few more later she stood in the doorway, the anger on her face louder than any sound she could have made. One look at Avelino seemed to send her over the edge.

"I hope you are satisfied," she said in little more than a whisper.

"Wha—?"

"'Melia, you know we can't possibly know what you're talking about."

"Rosemary and Caroline were asking about you." A strangled attempt to control her emotions only made them worse. "They wanted to know if you'd be coming to church again, what we did for fun, my favorite things about you . . ." She sank into the chair, her feet tucked beneath her. "It was mortifying."

"Mort—?"

"Well, what did you think would happen? People saw us at the dance. We were quite exclusive whenever possible, if you remember. People heard about Ray and his stupidity. They're all on our side for what little good that does us, by the way. So they know we walked a mile home together, in the dark—"

"But—" The third time did not charm her at all.

"No 'buts,' Avelino." Now she really did whisper. "I had to admit that you weren't coming back, that we weren't going on any more dates, and do you know what they said?"

"No . . ."

"They let me have it. They said I've been spending too much time with Helen and her narrow-minded friends. That I don't know a good man when I see one. Any one of them would be proud to go out with one of *the* Carrillos of Napa County."

Tears spilled onto her cheeks before she could cover them. "I couldn't even defend myself."

"Why not? It wasn't your decision. Why didn't you tell them that I—?"

"She wouldn't do that." Joe stood, moved to her side, and wrapped an arm around her shoulder. "It might make you look bad. She'd never risk damaging your reputation—especially now."

"But—"

Joe sagged. "You'd better go."

"No." Amelia's head snapped up. "I just endured the dressing down of my life. Now I want something in return."

Avelino's throat went dry. She wouldn't make him refuse—she wouldn't! "What?"

"I want you to finish whatever story you were telling about the first Avelino. I want to hear every word. I want to try to take it down. I want to take my mind off this, and you owe me that much."

"But—"

"I'll get you some water, son. Looks like you've got a story to tell."

Hands gripping the arms of his chair, Avelino prayed for wisdom. "I am sorry, Amelia."

"Did you hear what happened? Did you really?"

"Yes. They thought you rejected me and were upset by that. I don't understand."

Her eyes closed. "You thought you were being a gentleman, I suppose. Let people think I didn't want you. Well, that's what they assumed all right."

"I hadn't planned to tell anyone anything. I was leaving that for you."

"Don't you see, Avelino? You said it would be too hard—that people would object to it. Well, they object to me 'rejecting you.' They object to your objections. Think about that."

With those words, she stood and left the room.

Joe brought the water, but when Avelino began to tell about the arrival in California, the older man held up his hand. "She'll be back. You don't want her to miss anything. We'll never hear the end of it, and she'd never have to say a word."

It was true. Amelia could say more without a word than most females could while flapping their tongues nonstop.

Once settled in her chair again, Amelia nodded and said, "This better be good."

CHAPTER FIFTEEN

CALIFORNIA

November 1836

The bay at Yerba Buena teemed with excitement as the sailors of the *Milton* rowed Avelino to shore. Within minutes of landing, Avelino had heard the news of an uprising against Governor Gutiérrez.

"Two hundred men—"

"No, it was three hundred with the *americanos!*"

"I heard almost five hundred by the time they reached . . ."

Rumors spread like wildfire, and Avelino's stomach churned at every one of them. He'd escaped war, fighting, and for what? He had come here to live a life of quiet ease and richness. He did not want political battles and squabbles to interfere with it.

"I need to find someone who can help me find a friend."

The sailor stared at him before turning away to stroll into Yerba Buena. Unsure what else to do, Avelino followed, watching everything around him with an excited but suspicious eye. One great source of comfort was understanding what those around him said.

Yes, some spoke the *inglés*, but most conversation was in his native tongue.

After a minute or two of internal deliberation, Avelino decided to start by inquiring where he could purchase a horse and find somewhere to sleep. He needed a guide too.

Negotiations were difficult. Avelino did not have the skills to barter effectively, but a new sense of panic settled in as he realized his gold wouldn't last forever. Thankfully, the name of Ruiz Carrillo seemed to garner some respect among a few of the locals. Everything he needed could be found in Sonoma, they said.

By the next morning he felt more confident. Several men offered to take him, but Avelino hesitated. What if they waited until they were out in the country somewhere and killed him? He would have to carry his pistol—loaded. Once more Avelino thanked Don Edgar in his heart for wisdom. He would never have thought to purchase a weapon before embarking on that ship.

After three days of searching around Yerba Buena, he decided to visit Mission Delores. Perhaps the priests or friars could help him find an honest guide to take him to Señor Carrillo. It wasn't a long walk, and it was definitely a pleasant one despite his still-stiff gait. After so much time at sea, he remained a little unsteady on his legs.

Alas, the mission was closed. No natives worked the land, and no priests waited to hear his confession or give him advice. Disheartened, Avelino turned back to Yerba Buena. Someone there must be trustworthy—but who?

He heard one name repeated in every corner of the tiny place—Juana Briones. Known for her kindness to sailors and her service to anyone in need, she seemed the perfect choice, and Avelino was growing desperate. Not knowing what else to do, he set off for the house of the señora.

It was a small farm combined with a cattle operation. Avelino didn't know how successful it could be, but the woman managed somehow to provide for herself and what seemed to be a dozen children. She served him a drink, offered him a meal, and listened as he told his story.

"I know Ruiz Carrillo. He is a good man. He will help you."

"But how do I find him? I don't know this place, and I don't trust strangers who are eager to help me."

"I know someone—Marco. He sometimes acts as a guide for me when I need to know where to go," the woman insisted. "I'd take you myself, but I am needed here to help with illness." She sighed, looking weary for the first time since he stepped onto her property. "Every day someone comes. They say, '*Viruela*, Señora Briones! What will I do?' but so far it is only *sarampión*—measles or a rash."

"Is the smallpox really here?"

"Two years ago, there was some just north of here. It was a hard time."

She offered to allow him to stay and sent a native to bring his things from the ship. Not having to row back out every night would be a blessing by itself. It seemed, if the woman's words could be believed, that his dream was soon to be a reality.

*   *   *

"Dreams are tied up in this place, aren't they?" Amelia murmured as she rose, holding her hand up. "I'll be right back."

Most dreams have come true here, Avelino agreed as he considered her words. *This new dream of mine died before it had a chance to form a strong root. Just like Avelino.*

"Be gentle with her," Joe warned, misreading the pained expression on his face for frustration.

"I wouldn't hurt her—not if I could avoid it. I do not want this, Joe. But regardless, I must do what is right."

Amelia's voice startled him as she entered the room again. "That's my only consolation. I know you'll always do what is right."

"Amelia . . ."

"Tell me about Marco and Avelino and the first Carrillos." She picked up her pen. "What was the name of the rancho again? Casa de Vida—is that *v-i-d-a*?"

"*Sí.*"

* * *

The rancho at la Casa de Vida had been built on a gentle hill—more beautiful than anything Avelino could have imagined. *I will build my house on a little hill. There are many hills here. It will be good for rain too—no water in the bedrooms.*

As his guide led him along the road to the lovely hacienda, he grew nervous, his stomach twisting into knots. *What kind of crazy plan is this? I was a small boy when Don Ruiz came to Guerrero. He probably won't remember me.*

"There it is. I have heard good things about your friend."

"He was kind to children from my home in Mexico—brought them here after their parents died."

"This is a large rancho. Look at the buildings and the vineyards and the fields. He is a wealthy man. I have heard that he owns the property for many miles around—given to him by Diego de Borica!"

Though the information was helpful, Avelino was more interested in the awe and fascination in Marco's tone. This man, Carrillo, seemed a more important person than he had supposed. As a boy, he had seemed kind, down to earth, but the stories he told . . . Now, as Avelino took in everything before him, he grew overawed.

A man rode out to meet them, smiling and waving a welcome. *This is good, is it not?* "That can't be Señor Carrillo. He is too young."

"That will be one of his sons. I don't know their names, but I know he has three still living. Who lives here and who has moved to expand their holdings, I don't know."

"*¡Bienvenidos!* Welcome."

"I am Avelino Aguilar. I met Señor Carrillo in Guerrero many years ago and have come to visit him." He nodded at his companion and added. "This is Marco. Juana Briones sent him to guide me."

"My father will be pleased to meet you again," the man assured them. "I am Nicolás."

The usual questions of time at sea, weather, the journey overland— they all wearied him—but Avelino tried to be patient. It seemed that the closer he came to realizing his dream, the more desperate he became for it to happen.

Marco took the horses to the stables while Nicolás led him to a covered patio in a garden. Emotion choked him. It was the first time since he'd left Guerrero that anything seemed familiar and comfortable. The fountain, the roses, the . . . air. The air itself seemed scented with genteel ease. *There is no sweeter perfume.*

"*Papá*, an old friend—Avelino Aguilar from Guerrero."

"Little Avelino? The boy who listened spellbound as I told of California and the trip to Mexico?"

"You remember me!"

"How could I forget such an eager listener? I almost asked to bring you home with me, but your *madre* was ill—"

"I did not know."

"Few did, but my own mother died in much the same way. I recognized the symptoms. Your *madre* knew, but she did not want anyone else to."

"*Gracias.*" The emotion that choked him upon his arrival now overflowed. "I would not have liked to leave and miss that last year with her."

"And now you are here." Ruiz accepted a drink from a servant, smiling his appreciation to the older woman before continuing. "What do you hope for, my young friend? How did you come to be here?"

Nervous, Avelino began to tell his tale—how he left Mexico with Santa Anna's army, fought against the Texians at the Alamo, and then ran just in time to save himself at the Battle of San Jacinto. He told of his friend Edgar Tandy, how the man saved his life and helped him get to Virginia, the voyage to California, and finally the short journey from Yerba Buena.

"And what do you hope for now that you are here? You must have some kind of plan. Will you stay here, or do you expect to return to Mexico?"

Somehow he sensed that Don Ruiz knew he had no desire to return home, but this only made it more difficult. He thought of all that Edgar and Cherith had done for him. The money spent on the horse, the hours spent nursing him, and the longing as they spoke of going as far west as California.

"I have had a dream—almost since you came to us fifteen years ago." *How do I explain?* He sat in the shade of a well-manicured manzanita tree, trying to find the words.

"And what is your dre—?"

A young girl flew across the stones, interrupting Don Ruiz before he could continue.

"*Tío* Ruiz! Miguel says I have the nose of an *asno*! Why does he hate me so?"

"Boys his age do not know how to say, 'Sarita, you are *una chica bonita*.' Instead, they pretend they do not think you are pretty; they tell you that you are homely to hide their admiration."

The girl turned laughing dark eyes to Avelino. "Is this true, señor? What do you think?"

"I think your uncle speaks truth."

Happily, the girl kissed Don Ruiz, waved, and skipped across the stones, all troubles fallen from her shoulders. The older man shook his head. "If all of life's cares could be resolved so easily."

"A touch of *amor* in the air?"

"Perhaps—most likely Miguel simply wants to warn off the boys by making her seem undesirable. He's a protective one." Don Ruiz reached for an orange in the basket beside him. "Would you like one?"

"No, thank you."

"Then tell me about your dream."

"When the gunfire exploded around me that last day in battle, all I could think of was coming to California, buying a piece of land, and planting vineyards. I want a home, a family, children around my feet. I remember when there were vineyards at home, before disease killed them. That always interested me."

"You could raise cattle too—as a source of income. There is always a market for cattle . . ."

Avelino did not speak. It seemed as if Don Ruiz did not understand. The disappointment nearly crushed him. After a minute or two—it seemed like much longer—the older man nodded. Leaning forward, he clasped his hands together eagerly.

"Yes. I will speak to my friends. They will help us get you a nice rancho nearby. I know exactly where I want it. Perfect soil for your grapes, and plenty of grazing for the cattle. I expect that you will need servants. We'll see what we can do about finding you a few natives too. Come." He stood and beckoned Avelino to follow. "Let's go write those letters."

*   *   *

Avelino's story ended abruptly as he remembered the many arguments over whether Ruiz Carrillo had steered the first Avelino in the direction of a commercial enterprise.

Amelia's voice broke through his reverie. "Did he keep talking about cattle when Avelino so wanted to plant a vineyard? It's a little frightening to think of what might have happened if Avelino hadn't had a vision for a winery."

"He didn't," Avelino countered. "He just wanted to have a vineyard. He was like the farmers of England—the wealthy country gentlemen who had others doing their work for them. He wanted a hobby, a family, and a place for all of it to exist."

"Then why—?"

"Give the man a chance to explain, 'Melia. He's still wearing his storyteller's cap. Let it unfold," Joe interjected.

"Sorry."

"There is no need to apologize. I am glad you see it. Ranchos were required to have so much cattle or cultivated land. Cattle meant money. Vines meant roots and home. Avelino Aguilar needed both." Avelino waited for her nod of understanding and watched her scribble a few symbols on the paper before he rose. "I need to go. Thank you for dinner, Joe."

Without a tear or even a catch in her voice, Avelino heard the cry of Amelia's heart as she whispered, "Good night, Avelino," and hated himself for it.

CHAPTER SIXTEEN

FROM ALL SIDES

November 1945

Once again the solemnity of his worship wrapped Avelino in comforting arms and shielded him from the coldness of his life. He was early for Mass, but he didn't mind. The quiet nave gave him a chance for sanctuary from the outside world.

Not for the first time, his eyes darted around the church, trying to see it with a fresh perspective. Hers, of course. Would she be offended by Mary in the alcove? The candles? Would she like the Stations of the Cross as the visual reminders he thought them, or would they seem heretical to her? What about the crucifix? No, Baptists had crosses. There was one in the church that night that he went.

He had wanted to go to church with her again, but each time they climbed into the truck, he couldn't bring himself to ask. The informality of the service appealed to him. Did he prefer it? *Not at all, but it was nice as an addition.*

Shoes clicked across the narthex and entered the nave—women's shoes. They stopped so soon that the woman must have chosen the very last pew. Strange. He hadn't seen people sit there unless the building was full. *"Don't turn around. That's rude. Show respect."* His mother's words chided his temptations just as they'd chided him as a boy.

The Mendozas arrived—Margretta with them—and he stood to allow them into their usual place in the pew. Things had changed in the years he was away. They had once sat one row ahead of the Carrillos, but now another family—one with many more children—filled it. As Señora Mendoza inched her way to her spot in the pew, Avelino glanced at the back of the building, still curious about the person in the last row.

Amelia. He sat, stunned, and wrestled within himself. Why was she there? There was no reason for her to come.

She didn't know he had seen her. In that last pew, all alone she sat, head bowed, her silly little hat atop her distinctive red hair. *Is she praying?*

"I see your young lady has finally learned to appreciate you."

His eyes widened as he glanced at Señora Mendoza. "Oh, no. I—"

"Margretta says you want me to make more *tortillas y tamales,*" she whispered as a few more people filed in around them.

"If you would."

"I will. I will bring them and a pot of *albóndigas* . . ." She reached for one of the little boys—the name escaped him—and pinched the child's arm, a silent command to behave, before adding, "Tuesday."

There was no more time for chatter—even whispered. Mass began. How he wanted to watch Amelia. *Perhaps I should have gone to sit with her, but if I did, would she not see it as me weakening? Would others not perceive . . . something?* He could not do it.

The distraction of her presence made worship a jumbled, disjointed affair. Señora Mendoza poked him twice when he missed a response or forgot to kneel. *If it will be like this, I hope she stays at her own church.* That thought germinated, and new ones sprouted. *Was she this unsettled when I went to her church? Did I make her uncomfortable?* It hadn't seemed like it. He wanted to ask, but of course he could not.

The pew sat empty when he left the building. In fact, there seemed no sight of her at all. Outside, a few boys snickered as they listened to another boy tell a funny story.

Father Ortiz stepped close, listened, and then laughed as he came to greet Avelino. "It seems our Baptist friends had an unwelcome guest today. A skunk thought it needed a little religion in its life."

"That's why she came," he murmured before he could catch himself.

"The girl in the back? Is that Miss Kearns?"

"Yes."

"She is lovely."

He agreed but added, "And she is a Baptist."

"I do not know why that should matter. It has never stopped your family before." The priest clapped a hand on Avelino's shoulder. "There is so much talk—speculation about why she will not date you."

"It's not true. She will."

"Anyone can see that you care for her. Why not . . . ?"

His eyes refused to leave the ground. "You saw what they did to me for daring to take her to that dance. She had to watch that." Avelino choked before he continued. "They held her—"

"Fools like Welton are few and far between." Father Ortiz turned to greet another parishioner but added under his breath, "And will you really let them win?"

All of the yielding and softening that began as the priest spoke froze solid again with those last words. Amelia was not a contest.

She would not be caught in the crossfire of a silly battle between *gringos* and Mexicans—not if he could help it.

The walk home was more pleasant than the last few Sundays—primarily because Avelino enjoyed the memory of Amelia's head bowed, that hat with its little bit of netting covering her forehead, and the glorious shine of her hair peeking out from behind it. *What would she look like in prayer with a traditional mantilla over her head?* He swallowed hard, trying to put the thought out of his head, when he heard a sound ahead of him.

Avelino followed it around the bend and saw Amelia examining her arm as she walked. To his astonishment, she seemed to bite it. "Amelia?"

She turned, her mouth still attached to her arm. "Hmm?"

Avelino jogged to her side. "Are you okay?"

"Fine," she mumbled, examining her arm again. "Crazy bee stung me absolutely unprovoked. I don't know what his problem was."

"Her."

"Hmm?" She flicked her finger over the red circle on her arm.

"The female stings. Males can't."

"Could have fooled me."

She spoke the words so quietly that he almost didn't believe he'd heard them. He chose to ignore it and bent to examine her arm. "Did you get out the stinger?"

"Well, I don't think so, but I don't see it either. I keep trying to suck it out, but I can't find it."

"Are you sure it stung—well, I guess with that mark it had to have."

They were another half mile down the road before either of them spoke again. "You were at Mass this morning."

Amelia nodded. "There was a skunk at my church. We couldn't have sat there if we'd tried. Pastor Fletcher got a good spray too, so we all went home."

"Except for you."

"Granddad offered to go with me, but I knew he didn't really want to."

A dozen yards passed before he brought himself to ask another question. "Why did you?"

"You came to my church. Why wouldn't I come to yours?"

"You don't agree with it."

"That doesn't seem to stop you," she snapped. Immediately, she apologized. "Oh, Avelino. I'm sorry."

He felt terrible, seeing the tears she fought ineffectively. "I think I deserved that. I just meant that you had no reason—"

"You think I have no reason, but that is because you choose to believe that, not because it is true."

A car rumbled past them, and two eyes bored into his from the back window. Ray Welton. This would just be fuel for the fire of hatred in the Weltons' hearts.

"See that?"

She nodded. "Yes, but—"

"You do have a reason to stay away. You just refuse to acknowledge it."

"And you use it as an excuse."

They did not speak again until they reached the drive at la Casa de los Sueños.

She turned to him before following it to the front door. "I have one question for you, Avelino. I would appreciate an honest answer, even if you think it doesn't matter—that it is foolish."

"Okay."

"If my last name was Ortiz or Lopez, or if yours was Jones or O'Malley, would you have held my hand on the way home today?"

"I—"

"Just yes or no, please."

Against every instinct within him, he finally answered honestly. "Yes."

"Thank you. I feel like less of a fool anyway." Her finger touched the corner of his eye. "The bruising is all gone." As she turned, Amelia murmured, "I only wish hearts healed as quickly."

He stood there, watching until she disappeared behind the front door. "So do I, *querida*," he whispered. "So do I."

*   *   *

A sink of sudsy water, bar of laundry soap, a washboard, and a pile of dirty clothes. Avelino pulled a sock from the pile, picked up the bar, and scrubbed. Sock after sock, shirt after shirt, each piece of filthy clothing went through the same motions. Soak, soap, scrub, and rinse. He repeated each step as automatically as he had in the Pacific.

As a young man, he thought he understood—held more respect for—the work that went into running a household. Things like laundry appearing in drawers was something Paco and *papá* took for granted, but not he. Avelino had spent too many years as his *mamá's* right-hand boy not to know that it was hard work. Doing it all alone, however, without the aid of his mother's trusty Thor wringer washer was harder work, but scrubbing out his skivvies in his helmet in the Pacific might have been a little worse.

A shot rang out, and Avelino ducked, glancing around him for something to use as a weapon. His eye fell on his shovel, and he grabbed it. The building was full of places to hide—it must be a storage building. He ducked behind an old upturned bathtub and waited, furious that his gun was back at camp. *I know better.*

The enemy advanced without hesitation—*Bold, arrogant fools.* They never tried to hide their movements, always pressing onward and forward. This one would never march another step.

"Take the left," he hissed to Jerald.

"What?"

Movement at his right sent him charging, yelling as he drove the end of the spade into the neck—glass shattered.

Avelino stared at the fragments of the mirror and then at the shovel in his hand. His breath came in ragged gasps as he tried to comprehend what had happened.

"Avelino. Over here. Look at me."

That voice. He knew it. Safety. *The voice is safe.* "Amelia?"

"Put down the shovel, please. I need to know you know I'm here."

He stared at the handle and dropped it as if it burned. "I . . ." Avelino sank to the floor.

"May I come over there?"

The realization of what was happening, the memory of what had happened, all assaulted him, fracturing his confidence. A toe kicked a shard of mirror that glinted in the afternoon sunlight. The creak—it returned. His head whipped toward the sound, panic filling him once more. That safe voice spoke again, telling someone to wait outside.

"Amelia?"

"I'm coming over. See my shoes?" Every move she made she chronicled as if for the minutes of some meeting. "It's just me. Amelia. Look up at me."

His eyes rose, relief washing over him to see her. "You're okay."

"Of course, I'm okay."

"I thought maybe I—"

Amelia lowered herself next to him. "You didn't hurt anyone. The mirror isn't going to survive surgery," she teased, "but everyone else is just fine."

He couldn't help but smile. "I don't understand. One minute I was scrubbing clothes and the next I heard gunfire. Was there a coyote out there or something?"

Confusion was etched in her eyes as she examined his hands, face, and arms, looking for cuts or scratches from flying glass. "There was no shot, Avelino."

"I heard a shot—then a creak. I saw the light shift; that must have been you opening the door."

"You told me to take the left."

Avelino shook his head. "No, I told Jerald to take the left. I was going to take you out—thought you were a Jap."

"What happened then?"

Her hand brushed a sliver of glass from his hair. He caught it in his and held it for support. Unfazed, she used her other hand to brush something from his shoulder—probably that sliver.

"Movement to my right. I turned, saw something, and charged."

"I don't know if you saw yourself or me in that mirror, but . . ." Amelia watched him closely as she asked, "Are you really okay?"

"I'm fine. I just wish I knew what triggered this one. We've always known before."

She frowned. "I think I should be a little insulted that I'm always the trigger."

"Not always," Avelino admitted. "I nearly took out Pedro in the wine house the other day."

"Did he understand?"

How he dreaded to answer that one. "He didn't know," Avelino whispered.

"Oh, I'm so sorry. Still, do you know what caused that one?"

"He dropped a metal box. Sounded like an explosion. I just dropped and reacted."

"And today you heard a shot?" Her eyebrows drew together as she considered what could have sounded like a gun. "Margretta's door! When she slammed the car door shut. That probably sounded like a gun from in here."

"Margretta?"

"She's out there with a box of some really great-smelling stuff."

With his mind clearer, he noticed something in her voice that he couldn't have just minutes earlier. Irritation. *She is jealous.* Had he not decided that there was no hope for them, he would have found it charming. *This just hurts.*

"Oh, I should go pay her."

He stood and offered Amelia his hand.

As she pulled herself up, Amelia asked again, "Are you sure you're okay?"

He nodded. "Thank you." Her smile made him realize he hadn't let go of her hand. As cruel as it seemed, Avelino decided to push the point just a little further. "I think we've just discovered another reason for you to stay away from me. I'm a danger to you until these things stop."

Amelia didn't respond. She walked to the door, opened it, and stepped outside, smiling at Margretta. "Here he is. Make him carry that up there, though." To Avelino she said without turning to meet his eye, "You're wrong."

Margretta stared after her and turned to him. "What was that all about?"

"It's hard to explain," he began, taking the box from her. "Come upstairs. My wallet is up there."

As they stepped into his unorthodox apartment, Margretta's eyes wandered the room. "It looks better than I remember. It used to be a great place to hide."

"You know we didn't look, right?"

The girl rolled her eyes. "You did too."

"No, really. We just played outside, calling for you now and then to keep you hiding—well, until the time you passed out from the heat and your *mamá* gave us a thrashing."

The memory seemed to flicker in her eyes until it burned brightly. "Oh, I do remember that. I felt sick for days."

"So did my backside."

"Still, it's nice up here," she conceded. "Well, nicer than it was."

"It works."

"What were you doing in the garage?"

The vision of shattered glass and the frustration with repeated flashbacks almost tempted him to say, "Fighting the enemy," but instead he told the less interesting truth. "Washing my clothes."

Margretta watched him pile the food in his ancient icebox. "I heard something break."

"Mirror over the sink. I'll have glass in my laundry now. Great."

"She was worried about you."

He had no doubt as to who "she" was. "Amelia still thinks we could work."

"And yet everyone I know thinks that she won't look at you. I feel sorry for her."

Avelino grabbed his wallet from the makeshift end table and pulled out the money. "Why?"

"People are going to start treating her badly. They're all disgusted with her."

"They shouldn't be. I decided not to pursue a relationship, not her."

"No one believes that. Everyone thinks that she considers herself too good for you—like she's one of the Weltons or something."

Avelino followed her to his door. He stood at the top of the stairs and waved until Margretta began backing down the driveway.

153

He'd hoped to protect Amelia from the *gringos'* disapproval, but he hadn't counted on reverse indignation from his Mexican friends. Amelia stood on the patio gazing back at him, until an alarm buzzed in the kitchen. His *mamá's* windup alarm clock still got plenty of use as a cake timer.

CHAPTER SEVENTEEN

BOYS 'N' BUCKSHOT

The next evening Avelino dragged himself up the stairs, each step more difficult than the last to his sore, aching body. *I can't even rest*, he grumbled to himself. A long day of sulking over the injustice of life had soured his attitude—much as his clothes, still in the sink with shards of glass covering them, had probably soured. *I work hard all day and come home to more work—the domestic work* papá *insisted I didn't need to do anymore.* Shame filled him. *"You are not too proud to do honest work, Avelino."* How many times had his mamá said that? *She would protest your attitude too. Like Ecclesiastes says, "There is nothing better for a man than that he should eat and drink, and that he should make his soul enjoy good in his labor."*

A change in his room alerted him, but he couldn't determine what—not at first. His eye scanned the windows, the bed, and stopped. He hadn't made that bed. After oversleeping, he'd tossed on his clothes, tied his shoes, and rushed down to the wine house, ignoring the mess. The sergeant would have chewed him out for it. That thought made him smile.

Something else was off about the bed. Clothes at the foot. He frowned. Avelino's hand smoothed the pressed shirts and pants that lay folded in neat piles. Socks, pajamas, undershirts, underwear—she'd washed his underwear? Another pile of clean, folded sheets told him why she'd made the bed. *Fresh sheets too. It's too much.*

A mason jar on his nightstand held chrysanthemums. Avelino stared at the russet petals, wondering how something so small could make such a difference, and then hating himself for liking them. *They're flowers, you dolt,* he chided himself. *What kind of man are you?*

However, even after all he'd seen, Avelino wasn't prepared for a covered plate and a glass of ice water—the ice nearly melted—waiting for him at his little table. His first inclination was to storm down the stairs and tell her she had no business messing around in his apartment like that. The very thought produced a wry smile at himself. *Sure, Avelino. Go tell her that she is out of line for doing exactly what you'd want your mother, sister, or*—he choked at the next word—*wife to do. Hypocrite.*

A sound outside, this time easily recognizable as a car door, pulled him from his internal self-flagellation. As he stepped from his door onto the landing, Avelino's heart sank. Ray and his buddies were back. A quick glance at the house showed no movement from the Kearnses, giving him some measure of relief.

"What do you want, boys?" The moment he spoke, Avelino regretted his choice of words. It'd just antagonize them.

"We have a score to settle with you."

Without Amelia to worry about, Avelino didn't dread a fight in the same way as he had the first time. However, he did feel like a fool. *I should have expected this.* "This isn't necessary."

"You brought one of our girls to a dance. You walked with her at midnight. Then, after we taught you a lesson, you still kept seeing her."

Taught him a lesson? The urge to laugh nearly choked him, but Avelino managed not to succumb. His eye scanned the trio, trying to anticipate the first move.

"It's hard not to see someone who lives next door, but if you mean dating, we're not."

"So," Ray jeered with his friends, "you're not just a *dirty* Mexican, you're a dirty, *lying* Mexican."

"And you're trespassing." The unmistakable sound of a shotgun being pumped to load accompanied Amelia's announcement. "Get off this land."

"Don't you threaten me, you little—"

"Watch your language, Welton. I'll let her handle you unless you sully us with more than your presence. You heard the lady. Get out."

It galled him to say it. He felt like a weakling hiding behind a girl's skirts, but the only thing worse would be to leave her unsupported. From the look on her face, Amelia was furious at Ray.

"Since you think so little of me anyway, I can't imagine what my preference for a man like Avelino would matter to you."

"I invited you to that dance, and you said you couldn't go."

"No, I said I didn't want to go with you; granted, I tried to be polite. I think my actual words were something like, 'Thanks for the invitation, but I'd rather not.' That doesn't sound like I was saying I wasn't going at all." She pulled the gun into her shoulder as comfortably as if she did it every day. "Are you leaving?"

"He needs a girl to fight for him. Coward."

A spray of buckshot scattered pebbles and dirt at their feet. "He doesn't need anything. I'm just sick of him having all the fun. I take it you're going," she added as the boys backed up the driveway a bit.

"You deserve each other."

"Thank you." Her smile almost made Avelino snicker again. The trio looked stunned. "Now, if you would be so kind as to convince *him* of that, we'd all be happy."

Avelino covered his mouth with his hand. "You heard her. Time to go."

He didn't move until they backed out of the driveway and roared down the road toward Hank's. Hands in his pockets, Avelino turned to where Amelia stared after the car. "Nice show."

"Morons, the lot of them." She unloaded the shotgun, visibly unwilling to leave. "Um, Granddad has been telling me your stories."

What could he say? "Has he?"

"Yes. He's not a good storyteller like you, but I'm getting them down. I've even got some of them typed up."

"I don't see how you have time." He took a deep breath. "I had a nice surprise in my room today." When she didn't respond, he stepped closer. "I really appreciate it. Of all the days, today I needed not to have those sour, glass-sprinkled clothes waiting for me when I got home. Thank you."

"It was a bribe."

The second he heard her, Avelino knew it wasn't completely true. "What kind of bribe?"

"Eat supper with us? Tell us how Avelino ended up here and what parts of this house are original and what have been added?"

His hesitation must have lasted too long, because she sighed and turned as if it was a no. "There's enough supper for you. I'll bring it up after a while."

"I'll come." He couldn't help but smile as she turned, obviously not quite believing him.

"Really?"

"*Lo siento*, Amelia. I didn't mean to be ungracious."

"You don't have to be sorry. You have no obligation. We want you, of course," she added. "But it's just—well, thanks. We'll eat at six."

"May I help?" Avelino kicked himself for asking. There was no reason to put them together any more than necessary.

"If you wanted to make more of your salsa . . ."

"Do you have any tomatoes left?"

"I might have a few left on the vine. I canned most, but we haven't had a hard frost . . ."

He nodded and turned to go back upstairs. "I'll be down in a bit to see what we can find. We can always use canned if we have to."

Just as he stepped into his room, he glanced back down and saw her staring out at the road, a look of contempt on her face. She was still seething that Ray and his sidekicks dared to show up at all. *You should have said no to the invitation. She'll take it as you softening, Avelino Carrillo.*

Self-doubts and recrimination seemed to paralyze him for a moment, and then he moved into action. Clothes he placed in his trunk; the covered plate—with a sandwich inside—into the icebox. He'd eat it for lunch tomorrow. Suddenly thirsty, he downed the water and reached for clean clothes. He could at least arrive clean.

The glass was gone, and a new mirror hung where the old one should have been had he not lost his mind for a moment—again. The nightmares had grown worse too—strange things where his friends' mouths all assured him of their admiration and appreciation while Sergeant Miller's voice erupted, screaming insults about him and his heritage.

Avelino stared at his reflection in the mirror as he scrubbed his arms. *Let the flashbacks go to your dreams. If they stay there, you can control your response. No more attacking mirrors and losing yourself in a battle that we already won.*

The ingredients for salsa waited for him on the cutting board by the sink. A hot frying pan sizzled with a little oil, but Amelia seemed to be waiting for it to be just a little hotter.

"What goes in the pan?" he asked.

Amelia lifted a cloth-covered plate from the counter and pulled the towel from it. "Fish. I don't want it to stick . . ."

He chopped the onion in half and cut a slice from it. After dipping it into the pan, he nodded. "It's good. Do you want a few onions for the pan?"

"It won't overpower the flavor of the fish?"

"I didn't think of that. I'm used to adding onion to everything."

She hesitated and then nodded. "Yes. I'll take a couple. Thanks."

He watched as she let the onion sizzle for a minute and then he began chopping. There wasn't much—only three tomatoes, and they were a little mushy—but it worked. He allowed the juice to drain between his fingers into the sink before he added them to the bowl, fully aware that she watched him. *How long will it take her to ask—?*

"Why are you doing that?"

"It keeps the salsa from soaking the food. It'll work. You'll see."

Joe burst through the door before she could respond. "Are you all right?"

"Of course! Why?"

"I was getting gas at Hank's. He said that Ray and his shadows showed up, whining about getting shot at here. They're headed to Callum's to press charges."

Amelia snickered, which caused Avelino to lose what hope he had for a straight face. "Well, I hope he does. I'd love to see the sheriff's face when he hears what Ray has been up to." Her eyes twinkled as she looked back at Avelino before turning over the fish. "Supper's almost done."

The men exchanged amused glances, and Joe sighed. "I can't wait to hear this one."

"She was quite impressive . . ."

"Morons."

Joe didn't even attempt to hide his amusement, but he did make a token attempt at a rebuke. "Amelia . . ."

"Sometimes the truth isn't flattering." She waved the spatula in his direction. "Oh, and you might thank Avelino. He didn't let that oaf call me a nasty name."

"Thank you."

"I might thank her for saving me another black eye, split lip, or both."

"But I stole the satisfaction of you running them off by yourself. I think we're even."

Once again, the men laughed, shaking their heads.

"Amelia," Joe said as he went to wash his hands, "you make people underestimate you, and it is a scary thing sometimes."

No one said another word until after Joe finished saying grace. Then Avelino chuckled. "You should have heard that shotgun pump and the buckshot spray dirt on their shoes—looked like something out of a Wild West show . . ."

Before Joe could ask another question, Amelia passed Avelino the salsa and laughed. "I can't believe I listened to you about the onions. Look at that. There's no way you can taste the fish with all that on it."

"But the fish tastes great." Joe took another bite. "Just a hint of onion . . . delicious."

"She doesn't trust me."

"She's a woman. She'll only trust you on her terms."

Amelia ignored their teasing, eating her meal in silence. However, when she went to clear their places, she paused by Avelino's seat and whispered, "It's good to have you there again."

"Dinner was delicious. I haven't had a good fish in years."

She paused, staring at him. "Not even in the Pacific? That seems strange."

"Just because it's abundant doesn't mean we had the means or the skills to cook it properly."

"Avelino, will you help her with the dishes?" Joe interjected. "I'd like to take a quick bath before *Inner Sanctum* comes on."

Their previous banter and ease as they worked disappeared, and if Amelia's face was any indication, she felt it as keenly as he did. This was his fault. She wouldn't be uncomfortable and hurt had he not been so premature. *This is what you get for letting your heart lead when it should follow. You've hurt more than yourself.* Abuelito *would be ashamed of you.*

"Did you say something?"

"Did I—what?"

"You looked like you said something, but I couldn't hear."

Relief poured down his spine, nearly making him shiver. "I must have been thinking."

"Trying to find a legitimate excuse to leave?" She sprinkled cleanser over the sink and began scrubbing.

"No."

"Good."

"I should have given our circumstances more thought before I . . ." Before he what? Enjoyed the company of a girl? What kind of comment was that? "Anyway, I didn't think, and now I made things awkward between us. I'm sorry."

"I'm not."

He almost didn't hear her. "You're not sorry?"

"Nope. Not at all." Before she continued, Amelia rinsed the sink, rinsed her hands, and dried them on a towel. She turned to him and waited until he met her gaze before she spoke. "I would have admired you whether you showed any interest in me at all or not. Because you did, and because I know your only objection can't hold water forever, I don't have to pretend that I don't like you. We both know that would be a lie."

"Amelia—"

"Oh, no. You brought this up. I met a wonderful man. I liked him. He showed interest in me. We had fun together. A fool acted like the fool he is, and my wonderful guy tried to do the right thing. He's wrong. But he tried." She leaned forward and smiled. "Someday he'll see that. Until then I'll just get to fall in love with him from a distance. That's probably good for my impatience problem."

Without waiting for a response, she pulled a pie plate from the top of the icebox, cut slices, and carried them into the living room without a glance back at him. Avelino dried the last of the dishes, his thoughts bouncing between her words and the promise of what looked like a pumpkin pie. Somehow that combination seemed a little out of balance.

Ay, yi, yi . . .

* * *

The snap of the radio knob at the end of *Inner Sanctum* prompted Amelia to pick up her notebook and pen. Avelino stood, collected their empty plates, and carried them to the kitchen. Low murmurs in the living room told him to hurry before Amelia misunderstood him. *You will not hurt her again—not tonight. She was happy. Go tell her of Avelino and the mamás who tried to snare him as a husband for their daughters. She'll like the romance of the story.*

He hurried back to the living room and took his usual place near the window. "Let's see . . . where was I?"

"Don Ruiz was going to write letters to get Avelino a rancho," Amelia offered. Her eyes slid around the room and out the window. "That means this—the house and the vines. It's amazing to realize that they spoke of here—of this place."

"Yes. The letters. It took a long time then—to write a letter, post it, and wait for a reply. Even with it going only as far as the capital in Monterey, it could be a month or more before they heard anything back. In the meantime, Avelino settled into life at la Casa de Vida . . ."

CHAPTER EIGHTEEN

NEW BEGINNINGS

December 1836 to December 1837

Don Ruiz's home was a paradise. A large party of guests welcomed Avelino without hesitation; one man even knew an uncle of his. Señoritas, lovely as anything a man could hope to meet, danced with him at *bailes*, never complaining about his awkward limp. It seemed as though the family at la Casa de Vida enjoyed one fiesta after another, and though he enjoyed himself, Avelino began to worry that his hopes for his own little hacienda were fading from Don Ruiz's mind.

The señoras all teased him into eating more, drinking more, and enjoying the parade of daughters that they each hoped would catch his eye. Avelino, on the other hand, refused to be lured into matrimony prematurely. Yes, he desired a wife and family, but first he must have land, build a house, plant his vines. *Then I can relax and enjoy life with a pretty* esposa *of my own.*

Christmas neared. The young people were all abuzz with plans for *las pastorelas*—the journey of the shepherds to the star of

Bethlehem. The hombres built elaborate sets, while the señoritas painted them and sewed costumes. The *madres* worked with the children to decorate the enormous seven-coned piñata, all in great anticipation of the festive season.

Inez, a small servant girl, appeared at his shoulder one afternoon while the house was enjoying the afternoon quiet. "Señor Carrillo wishes to speak to you in his rooms."

The door was partially open, but Don Ruiz asked Inez to close it as she turned to leave. "I have received news—good news."

"Have you?"

"My friend, Vallejo has offered you a rancho. It will border mine, and on the short side, so only a few miles away from here. Will that suit you?"

Knuckles white from gripping the chair, Avelino nodded. "I am most grateful. When can we begin to build a house?"

"He is already eager to leave us," Don Ruiz said to a statue of Mary in an alcove on the wall.

"I am eager to begin my new life, yes—never eager to leave your gracious hospitality."

"And will you want a wife in this new life of yours?"

The air in the room changed. Avelino swallowed a dry choke and tried to think of the least offensive way to postpone matrimonial plans without seeming to reject the daughters of fine families. "As I told you, I wanted to come to California, build a home, plant my vines, and raise a family. Not nine months ago I was half-dead on the Texas prairie. I still limp terribly, and I have no home to offer."

"So your answer is no."

"My answer is not yet. In a year or at worst two, when I have a house and have recovered from the toll these past months have taken on me, I will eagerly seek out your advice as to how to choose a bride."

"Well then," Don Ruiz said, pushing a piece of paper to the middle of the table that separated them. "Let's plan a proper house so that we can begin to make some of these dreams come true."

"Do you think that we could also find someone to teach me to read and write? I think it would be beneficial."

"How did you manage to avoid it? I know your *mamá* wanted it for you."

"It wasn't necessary," Avelino explained. "I played stupid, and the priest left me alone."

"That wasn't playing, my friend. That really was *estúpido*."

* * *

Construction of his adobe home did not begin until March. Before that, Avelino rode to his property nearly every day and walked the perimeter, planning the best places for his vineyards and drawing diagrams in a large empty book one of the servants had made for him. In the evenings he sat with anyone who would help him and wrote each word of his notes into the book.

Before walls were constructed, Avelino and four helpers had built the first trellises for the grapes. Before the workers covered the roof, he'd ridden to the mission San Francisco Solano several times and carried back hundreds of cuttings. By the time he had windows and doors, most of the green shoots thrived.

He worked tirelessly on his journal, his reading, his writing, and his vines. In good weather, Avelino traveled to any vineyard he could reach, asking questions of the vintners, and putting their helpful hints and lessons in his notes. In one of those travels, he met Ana Maria.

At Christmas, 1837, he spent the holidays at Rancho El Molino—the home of Ana Maria. Several days before the holiday, Avelino stepped outside to take a walk among the vines, planning to sketch how they should look in winter, and stepped back in the shadows as Ana spoke to someone.

". . . cannot be too choosy. He is a good man and a handsome one. He seems to have money, and, thanks to Vallejo, the governor did give him a small rancho."

"But his limp—and he is so uneducated," the other woman said.

"*Mamá*! I am almost thirty. No man has shown interest in me, aside from one or two looking to raise themselves in the world. He is learning to educate himself. What more can I ask for?"

Consuela de Garza, Señorita Ana's mother, pleaded with her daughter. "But how can you love—?"

"How can I not? He is a good man who admires me; not my money—me. That means something."

"And how do you know it is not your money?"

The silence that hung in the air was filled with Avelino's inward answer before Señorita Ana answered, "Because I did not tell him, nor did *papá*."

Avelino reached for the door, opened it, and closed it a little louder than necessary. "Shh! You'll wake up the house. *Puerta estúpida*—stupid door." He stepped onto the veranda and stopped. "Oh, pardon me. I did not mean to interrupt."

"That is fine, Don Avelino. My daughter and I were planning the day's work."

"Then I suppose I should not ask for you to walk with me to the vines."

"Always with your vines, Don Avelino. One would think there was nothing more interesting to admire here." For a mother who seemed disinclined to recommend him to her daughter, Señora de Garza did not veil her hints very well.

"A man has to have some excuse . . ."

"Go along with you, but take Ramona, of course."

The chaperone would be easy enough to bribe. His Ana—he really could call her that now, it seemed—would see to that. She had managed it in previous outings. However, it was imperative that he keep his behavior honorable. He would not risk an outraged father sending her to Mexico to get her away from an undesirable man—himself.

"*Lo siento*, Don Avelino. *Mamá* . . ."

". . . is a good mother. She protects her daughter. No one can fault that."

"Did you enjoy our conversation? Were you surprised to learn that I have money in my own right?" Ana asked.

Heat flamed up his neck and into his face. He had not intended to listen but could not honestly say that he had not chosen to continue to do so. "It would not matter to me."

"I did not think it would."

"I should not have stayed quiet. One never knows how to react in such situations."

"If I had not wished you to hear what I had to say, I would not have said it."

They walked, Ramona far ahead of them and ignoring their slow steps. At the vines Avelino sketched while he struggled for the courage to compliment Señorita Ana, who simply watched.

"Why does the heart strangle the voice?"

His words had their desired effect. Ana's beautiful laugh filled the foggy air, muffling it just a little. "And what would your voice say if I removed the stranglehold of the heart's hands?"

"So many things." Avelino paused, his pencil lying flat on the page, forgotten. "I think it would admire your beauty, your kindness, and it might marvel that you do not share your mother's opinion of my limping leg and modest purse."

"I suspect your purse is not as modest as you imply, or my father would not be as eager to combine it with mine."

"It is nothing to yours, my Ana. I have sufficient to live on for my lifetime, but not for a lavish existence. I certainly will not leave grand fortunes to my granddaughters for their dowries."

"You knew of the money then," she added with a sigh.

"I did. Don Ruiz told me. I still insisted that he not invite you to la Casa de Vida on my account. I was not interested then."

"And now?"

"And now I hope that you will come to the grand *baile* in February. I would like to dance with you at the home of my friend before I leave for my own house."

"And will you invite our family to your house as well?"

"I hope that your father will come and inspect my vines and that Ramona might be persuaded to chaperone you as I show you my plans for expansion. It is small for now—only a dozen rooms— and they are building a barn soon. But as the family I long for grows . . ."

"Ramona would delight to visit, especially since I think she has hopes for your Diego."

"They are twenty years our seniors. Why play these games at their ages?" To Avelino, waiting now was silliness, but at fifty and older—*loco*!

They stood staring across the long rows of vines. Avelino reached for her hand and squeezed it gently. "In the army, all I could think of was the day I would have my own vines in California. I dreamed of a wife and many children."

"It is a good dream."

"I did not expect to have it come true so quickly. I have only been in California for a year, and already I have a rancho, a house that is almost ready to move into, and vines."

"Why are the vines so important to you?"

This was something he could not easily explain. "I think because for me they represent life—family. The way the tendrils wrap themselves around each other to support one another. I like how they hold to the trellis; it is almost like a cross." Now he was growing fanciful. "Even as a boy I was very good at making things grow. After my failure as a soldier, I want to feel the satisfaction of success."

"You were not a failure."

He hadn't told her of the cowardly way he'd run, hiding from both the Mexican army and the Texians. "I'm afraid I was. Shortly after the battle, I fled—deserted."

"But you said the battle didn't even last half an hour. Didn't the others run too?"

"Yes, but . . ."

The dark fringe of her lashes seemed to tickle his heart as she swept her eyes across her father's vineyard. "I had never thought of these as anything but a foolish hobby—an excuse to go off by himself when *mamá* pesters so." Eyes back on him, she smiled, that lovely curve of her mouth seeming to mock him without trying. "You wish to see yourself as a coward, but I think it is because you feel guilt."

"Guilt?"

"You survived where so many others didn't. You choose to see your actions as uniquely wrong. I don't know battle and armies and things. It sounds to me like everyone, including your leaders, ran for their lives."

"Yes."

"Then you are only guilty of being cunning enough not to get killed. You don't know who ran first; it doesn't matter. You kept yourself alive. There is no glory in dying so that your comrades do not die without you."

Her words, as simple as they were, soothed his wounded pride in a way that his own attempts had failed to do.

"Ana Maria, *tú sanas mi corazón*—heal my heart."

* * *

As he ended the story, a slow smile tugged at the corners of Amelia's lips. She stood and without a word crept from the room, hugging her notebook to her chest.

Avelino's eyebrows rose in question, but Joe didn't answer. Still curious, he said, "I missed something."

Joe leaned back, hands behind his head, and nodded. "Yes you did, but she didn't. Good night, son."

CHAPTER NINETEEN

NEW YEAR'S DECISIONS

January 1946

"The pruning comes at the New Year as a reminder to cut away the dead and useless from our life in order that we can grow and flourish as we were intended." How many times had his father or grandfather said those words as they walked the vines on New Year's Day? Resolutions were not about what new things would become a part of their lives in the coming months but about what old things were no longer profitable for their physical, spiritual, intellectual, or emotional health.

As Avelino inspected each vine, a handful cultivated from the original ones planted by the first Avelino a century earlier, his mind wandered to what things he could cut away from his life. Bitterness—it should go. He'd allowed too much of it to take root in his heart. His brother's mistakes, the occasional digs by self-important soldiers in his platoon—there were so many things. Bitterness must go.

He examined a row, comparing it carefully with another one, and marked it with a red flag. It needed to be treated. Row after row, vine after vine, trellis after trellis, Avelino walked, and as he did he skipped over the truth he refused to acknowledge. *I must prune her from my heart this year.* Frustration grew within him, making him kick a rock, which only made his toe smart through his worn shoe. *I don't want to cut her out of my heart, Lord,* he prayed. *I know I should. It is only right. But if I do, another dream dies. Has not la Casa de los Sueños suffered enough attacks on the foundation of our dreams?* He gripped one of the trellises with hands that seemed immune to the splinters that pierced his skin, leaning against it as if to push it over. *How can I do it? How? Mi Dios, mata el corazón.*

Kill his heart—would it really? Margretta hadn't. She didn't have the lovely red hair and green eyes he'd always admired. She didn't have the quiet resolve that fought for him when he'd given up. He once thought he loved her; could he not love someone else as well? He didn't know. It wasn't about his history anymore—not with Amelia.

Amelia was beautiful—not like a pinup girl, no, but *bonita* definitely. She loved his family despite having met only him, and that appealed to him in a way he could never hope to explain. Her interest wasn't in their standing in the community or in the honor of his notice. She loved the history, the stories, the people. She talked about Ana Maria as if she could visit and hear the other side of Avelino's story.

His arms shook as his muscles protested against the strain on them. As he'd told of the house, what each room looked like in the original, Amelia had wandered around the room, trying to see it with Don Avelino's eyes. He'd caught her running her finger along the doorjamb after he'd told her where Don Ruiz had scratched his hand before the wood had been sanded to a smooth finish.

How could he lose someone like that—someone who valued the things most important to him? She hadn't given up on him yet, despite his continual refusal to engage in more than pleasantly civil conversation and interaction. Each time he accepted an invitation to dinner, he told more of his family, and Amelia would take down the stories in her little stenographer's notebook. She'd filled several and then spent hours typing them up. Often he returned home to find a sandwich and a few sheets of paper on his desk, waiting for corrections, changes in wording—anything he'd give her. She even asked him to retell a few of the stories in order to capture more of his style of telling the tale.

She seems so unhappy when she thinks no one can see her. What else can I do, though? She doesn't know what it is like to be rejected for your ancestry—regardless of the prior nobility of that ancestry. His questions seemed to have only one answer. Keep working. In a little over six and a half years, he'd be able to hire Joe as general manager. By then she'd have gotten over her attachment to him, and perhaps by then someone who could offer her an easier life would notice her.

The idea galled him. Avelino wanted to rail against the injustice of it all. He was an honest man, hardworking, and from a good family. There should be no objection, but the Ray Weltons and Sergeant Millers of the world knew how to create prejudice in the kindest of people. It would kill him to see her suffer for his selfishness.

Startled, Avelino jumped as Joe broke into his thoughts.

"I said, 'Are you trying to break that trellis, or is it merely an innocent bystander?'"

He stepped back, staring at his hands as if unable to account for the half-dozen splinters in each one. "I didn't hear you coming."

"Well, that's obvious. You think they're ready to prune?"

"Yes. Do we have enough experienced workers?" At least Joe hadn't asked him what was bothering him.

"Probably not. We'll be working sunup till sundown."

"I'll go visit my aunts—see if they can come for a few days."

He tied another strip of cloth to the place where he'd left off and turned to leave.

"I think you should know something, son. After any danger of frost is past, I'll be giving my notice."

Avelino's mouth went dry, and his heart squeezed until he felt choked. "Is something wrong?"

"My granddaughter. I cannot stand to see her hurting. She'll get over it sooner if we just go."

What could he say? It pained him to imagine not seeing her hanging clothes on the line or hear her singing as she did her work. "If it would help, I could move. I think the Mendozas would find a place for me or—"

"You'd be too close. We'll leave California, I think. Probably go home to Oklahoma—family there will help us."

In Oklahoma he'd never see her again. "I'd hate to lose you. Maybe—"

"It's no use, Avelino. I understand your concern. I do. Amelia is young and idealistic. She is also stubborn and determined."

He felt mollified in knowing that at least Joe saw the problem, but before he could respond the older man added, "I also think you're wrong. You refuse to see the whole picture."

"Joe—"

"No. For Amelia's sake, I'm going to say what has needed to be said for a long time now. Nearly every person in this valley has asked Amelia why she rejected the chance with a man like Avelino Carrillo. She didn't tell a single one that you rejected her. She could have, but instead she lets people think that she has the same prejudiced ideals that Ray and his cronies do. She does it for you."

"I think you must not have spoken to enough people."

"No. You go ask anyone in this area. Anyone. Ask how they would feel if you took her to a dance or a movie. Ask them."

He wanted to protest—to point out that his granddaughter had been forced to witness an attack and then protect him already—but Joe spoke again first.

"I want you to promise me something, son."

"What?"

"You'll ask. I want you to promise me that you'll ask every man and woman you can think of what they'd say to you dating Amelia—Mexican or not."

"I—"

Joe pulled off his hat and resettled it on his head as he interrupted Avelino. "I want that promise."

"I can't give you that promise, but I can promise—"

When Joe began to protest, Avelino rushed onward. "But I *can* promise to try to ask people I respect and those I think would object. I'll try."

*   *   *

No one answered the door when Avelino knocked the next afternoon. He stepped into the kitchen, calling for Joe or Amelia.

"Be right there . . ."

From the kitchen window, he watched the laundry flutter in the afternoon breeze until he realized that the sheets at the back were his. Guilt sent tendrils from his conscience to his heart and squeezed it until it ached. How had he let this continue? His claims of keeping a distance were mere words—lies meant to blind himself from the ugly truth. *I'm using her.*

"Sorry. I was . . . busy."

As his eye met hers, her busyness was apparent. She'd been crying. Joe must have told her his decision first.

"I—"

"Did you see Granddad?"

"Yes."

"He told you then." Amelia's fingers played with the corner of the tablecloth, and she seemed unable to tear herself away from the sight.

"Yes."

"I'm going to miss him."

"What?"

Her eyes rose to meet his. "I've decided that I'm not going. I can do decent shorthand now. I'm going to get a job and stay."

"You can't—"

"And you can't stop me. So what did you need?"

"We need more pruners. I thought I would see if my aunts could come for a few days."

"Okay . . . ooh! They'll need a place to stay. Of course. What rooms should I clean and air for them?"

It sickened him that he had to ask, but he continued. "Whichever you want to is fine, but . . ."

"What is it?"

Using her again—would it ever end? "It's just that they might have to bring grandchildren. I know *tía* Lucia watches Theresa's children while she works. If they have to bring the children . . ." He jammed his hands in his pockets in frustration. "It seems so wrong, but we need the helpers."

Her hand on his arm, the softness of her voice, the assurance that she'd be pleased to help—they all felt like burning shrapnel in his soul. "Avelino, I can't prune grapevines, or I would be out there with the rest. I can, however, play with babies and make small children laugh. I can do that."

"You shouldn't have to."

"Nonsense."

"I should probably go. I have to . . ." He frowned. "You can't stay, Amelia. If for no other reason than Lyndon. He won't let you stay in this house."

"Then I'll rent a room from someone."

It was a dumb question, but Avelino asked before he could stop himself: "Why?"

"You know why." She picked at the cloth again before adding, "Don't make me humiliate myself any more than I already am."

"Humiliate?"

"If you had not said more than once that you didn't like things 'having' to be this way, I couldn't bring myself to do it. If I had even a sliver of doubt that you weren't honest about that, I'd be packing already."

"Your grandfather isn't going to leave without you."

"Probably not," she agreed, "but I'm going to hurt him by defying him like this."

"Then don't do it. Get in that truck and ride back to Oklahoma, where some lucky man can love you without worrying about you."

She reached under the sink for a bucket and scrub brush. "Which rooms do you think they'd like best again?"

Frustrated, Avelino turned on his heel and strode to the door. "Whatever you like. I've never met a more stubborn woman."

"And considering you are equally stubborn and how well respected you are, I'll take that as a compliment," Amelia called after him.

At the top of his stairs, a new thought sliced through his mind, ripping open memories he hadn't anticipated. Seconds later he burst into the house, calling her name. He found her opening the door to his room—the one he'd shared with Paco until he'd outgrown his childish fear of the dark. *Strange. How did I not notice that I never changed it after Paco moved out?* "Amelia, I—"

"This was your room, wasn't it?"

"*Sí.*" He hated how emotions had the ability to jerk him from one language into another without warning. It made him feel weak, vulnerable.

A red Cardinals pennant still hung over Paco's bed. *I should have put that away.* The chest of drawers seemed to have an inch of dust on it. Paco's clothes would still be in there. How he'd fought *tía* Jacinta to leave those clothes where they were.

"Are you okay? You should have these things in your other room for now, don't you think?"

Raw emotion made his voice ragged as he shrugged. "Perhaps."

She surveyed the room for another minute before stepping a little closer to him and whispering, "Did you share a room with—?"

Avelino forced himself to say "Yes" instead of *sí*. "That was Paco's bed."

"Shall I lock this for now?"

He shook his head. Swallowing down the rising panic that appeared for no obvious reason, Avelino took a deep breath before answering. "If you would put the clothes on the left side of the closet and in that dresser in a box for me, I'd appreciate it."

"Of course. What about the things on top, or—?"

"If it looks personal, I'd appreciate it boxed. I'm sorry, but I've got to go to work."

She dropped the bucket and wrapped her arms around him. "It'll be okay, Avelino. I'm so sorry."

He stood rigid, unwilling to allow himself the comfort she offered. The loss of that comfort hit him much harder than he could have anticipated. As she stepped back, embarrassed by his cold refusal to accept her hug, Avelino pulled her back and squeezed her with a fierceness he seemed unable to control.

"*Gracias*, Amelia," he choked as he willed himself to let go. He failed. Seconds ticked into minutes as he clung to her for the support he desperately needed and knew he had no right to take.

CHAPTER TWENTY

AMELITA

Squeals of children greeted the Carrillos as they trudged back from the vineyards, spent after a hard day's work. *Tías* Lucia and Jacinta smiled, the weariness of the day seeming to melt from their faces at the sound of happy *niños* playing with Amelia. Avelino started for his stairs, but young Michael dashed around the others and raced up to him.

"Amelita says you are coming for supper and will tell us some of *abuelito*'s stories!"

Amelita. Already the children had given her a pet name. His aunts smiled at him with that knowing look that women have when they catch the scent of a heartsick man. "I am. First, I have to change. I am filthy."

"I like dirt. It grows fine grapes—Amelita said so!"

"Did you watch her scrub the floor or wipe the table today?"

"Yes. I helped," Michael added proudly. "Amelita said I did a very good job."

"Did that not remove dirt from the room? Dirt is good for outdoors, not for the dinner table."

"And she made it pretty with the red flower from the window."

The amaryllis from Christmas. All attempts to ignore her now failed. Avelino's eye followed a flash of red as Amelia chased a toddler between the sheets and towels on the line. When she emerged, the chubby boy in her arms giggling at her tickles, his heart seemed to thunder up the stairs to hide in his room without him.

"Avelino?"

"What?"

"I said, isn't Amelita beautiful? Just like Cherith Tandy, no?"

"Yes. She is certainly beautiful." He hunkered down on his heels, forcing himself to ignore the scene he wanted most to watch. "Do you know what makes her more beautiful than anything else?"

"She is kind. That is what I think—that and her *pelo de rosas*, like Cherith's."

He had created another boy obsessed with the history of the Carrillos and their lovely ancestress. A glance at his aunt told him that the boy probably had been helped a little by her stories as well.

"I'll be down in a minute. Why don't you go ask Amelia what you can do to help get ready for supper? Perhaps she'll let you set the table."

"That's for girls!"

"I must have been a girl for most of my childhood then. Perhaps I should ask Amelia if I can borrow one of her dresses."

Michael concentrated both of his eyes on Avelino's single chocolate-colored one and tried to find some kind of teasing in it. "Did you really set the table when you were a little boy?"

"Most of my life, yes. I have to set my own table up there each night that I eat alone."

"Yes, but that's because you don't have a woman to do it. It's okay then."

"So a man is not too proud to work in the dirt to buy the plate, but he cannot reach for it and set it on a table? Is that it?" Avelino smiled. "Never become too proud—too macho—that you cannot help a lady."

His little cousin seemed to study him before dashing off, calling to Amelita for permission to help set the table. To the boy's great delight, his aunt and grandmother beamed and lavished praise on him for being so helpful. Left alone at last, Avelino climbed the stairs to retrieve his clothes to change for supper.

As he so often did, he stood shirtless before his little mirror, scrubbing the grime from his arms and chest using the laundry sink as a basin. The door opened with that now-familiar creak that had sounded so much like the hatch cover on a tank months earlier.

Instinctively, Avelino reached for his towel. "Amelia?"

"No, silly boy, she is in the kitchen."

"*Tía* Jacinta." He tried not to let himself sound as deflated as he felt.

"Would you like me to get my sister? I think Lucia would not be as gentle with you as I will be, but perhaps that is what you need."

"Gentle—you?"

"Compared to what Lucia is thinking, my words will be a caress." His aunt stepped closer, her thumb tracing where his eyebrow should have been. "I am so glad your *mamá* is not here to see this. You were such a pet of hers—all those babies . . ."

"I lived—others didn't. I didn't lose an arm or my legs like some men did. Just an eye. I consider myself blessed." He went back to scrubbing, washing his hair and waiting for her to say what she'd come to say. "Did you need something?"

"I want to tell you something."

He knew what that something was. "Yes?"

"You are a fool, my Avelino."

"I suppose I am. What evidence do you offer this time?"

Jacinta grabbed his towel and roughly dried his hair as she began her loving tirade. "Are you doing penance for living when others didn't? Are you like Avelino Aguilar—too guilt-ridden to allow himself a bit of happiness? You lived because El Señor del cielo wanted you here. He knew our family needed someone to continue this rich heritage we have. He knew you were the right one for the job—the blessing of being Señor Carrillo of el Valle de Morado."

"The God of heaven willed that I should live so that our little family could continue—with Amelia Kearns as the new Cherith, I suppose."

"I don't care that she has the red hair. I don't care about much of that silly stuff. I do care, however, that you love her. I do care that you will break your heart and hers over this foolishness of yours. She is a very special girl. Don't let her go."

Avelino took the towel from her and draped it over the nail he'd pounded into the wall by the sink. A clean undershirt followed by a fresh shirt came next. As he dressed, his jaw worked to keep his emotions in check. It failed.

"You were not here, *tía* Jacinta. You did not have to watch as a man restrained her so his friends could attack me. You did not have to see the hurt she endured watching them try to beat me. You were not there to feel the pain she tried to hide as she cleaned my lip and iced my eye."

"We are talking of Raymond Welton. The Weltons have always considered themselves above our notice—well, ever since I told Ed Welton to go home, grow up, and learn how to keep his hands to himself."

A lot of things made sense as he listened to her talk. The problem was first that he was a Carrillo—that Carrillos were once Californios was secondary.

"If he was the only one, I wouldn't care. He isn't."

"He's the only one around here that I can find out about. I have asked every worker, and they have asked every person they can think of. I spoke to Margretta's mother. She says that every person she knows of—white, brown, pink, or blue, and a few green with envy—blames Amelita for refusing you."

"Well, they shouldn't," he growled. "I made the decision. I didn't tell anyone—didn't want her to seem rejected. It was the honorable thing to do." Even as he spoke, Avelino's heart chastised him. *You did not keep your promise to try—not yet. But your aunt comes to work, and in the precious few moments she has to herself she finds the time to poll the citizens of Napa about your relationship with Amelia.*

Jacinta pulled him into her arms, just as his *abuela* would have, and murmured every comforting word he could have hoped to hear. In familiar, affectionate Spanish, Jacinta assured him of her love, her understanding, and her complete support. Avelino's mustache twitched with repressed amusement as her voice then changed to the familiar scolding tones of the Carrillo women.

"But, despite my love for you, I will not allow you to disgrace our family. Your ideas of honor are wrong. The honorable thing to do is to accept with thanksgiving the gift of a wonderful girl. The Lord provided someone to love you and care for you and walk through all of life's blessings and trials with you, and you toss her aside while claiming honor. This is not honor, Avelino. This is cowardice. This is laziness. This is cruelty." Her hands cupped his face, fingers tracing familiar lines that must have reminded her of someone in the family. "My wonderful boy, you will not hurt her anymore. When we leave, you will pray about this. You will search that Biblia that you know so well, and you will see that I am right."

"What if I don't?" The words spilled from him before he could stop them.

"Then I will send Lucia." Her hands dropped, and she stepped back from him, her eyes searching for something she didn't seem to find. "And you do not want me to send Lucia. You remember what happened when you lied about the chickens at her house . . ."

The door shut with a soft whap, and he stood alone again before his mirror. *Are you a coward?* His reflection nodded. *Did tía Jacinta speak truth? Should I reconsider, or should I ask tía Lucia to give me my fifty lashings with her tongue before she leaves?*

Neither answer satisfied.

* * *

The great table in the dining room overflowed with people. Every chair in the house crowded up to it, children sitting on their grandmother's laps and in little seats beside them on stacks of books. Familiarity lived as a bittersweet guest in his heart.

The table was laden with delicious food—all a testament to Amelia's hard work. How had she managed to accomplish so much with all the children underfoot? Before he could ask, Amelia answered. "Mrs. Ramirez—"

"You are a dear friend, Amelia. You may call me Jacinta. And," his aunt added, "everything is delicious."

Amelia flushed, her eyes skittering between Avelino, her grandfather, and Jacinta. A smile grew from the corners of her lips and she nodded. "Doña Jacinta, I just wanted to thank you for your help in planning out the meals. I don't think we'd have anything worth eating if you hadn't told me what to cook before bed, how to juggle the choices so things didn't need the same stove and oven space—everything."

The eyes of his aunts bored into Avelino's forehead as he bent to take a bite. He heard their unspoken rebukes and admonitions distinctly. *She is a treasure. She wasn't afraid to ask for help, and she succeeded. The children love her. Don't let her get away.*

"Avelino?" Michael's wide eyes were deceptively innocent.

He took another bite of salsa-topped frijoles. "Hmm?"

"When are you going to marry Amelita?"

He choked on his beans, his eyes watering. "What?" The second the word escaped his lips and hung in the air, he regretted it.

"I said—"

"I think that's a question for Avelino and Amelia to discuss away from the table, Michael," the boy's grandmother interjected. "The family waits for good news without bothering them."

"Could have fooled me," Avelino muttered under his breath. To Michael, he said, "I promise that I will tell you right away if I ever get married."

"Did you get a lot done on the vines today?" Amelia sounded strained.

"We got the north quadrant almost done. Lucia says she saw a few rows that needed a bit more aggressive pruning, but it was a good week's work." Avelino smiled his gratitude to his aunts. "You are the difference. We wouldn't be half-done with that north section without you."

"It is what *la familia* does; we stick together and help one another through hard times. Without those harder times, we would grow lazy in our appreciation for one another."

It was another dig—another reminder of his foolishness in their eyes.

By the time he cleared his plate, he just wanted to go to bed, but his aunts bustled the children into the bathroom to give them quick baths so they could fall asleep to the gentle cadence of his voice as he told the next tale.

His eye rested on Amelia before he began. She held his little cousin Luis in her arms, the child sucking on his thumb. It didn't seem as if Luis even noticed his mother wasn't there whenever Amelia was present. He whimpered when *tía* Jacinta moved him, but Amelia just kissed his cheek and shushed him. "Tomorrow, little man. I'll hold you tomorrow."

Those words, that little kiss—it nearly killed him. Avelino raised his head, feeling *tía* Lucia's gaze on him. She smiled, knowing exactly what pricked his memory. How many times had his mother comforted him with those very words when he didn't want to go to bed at some family gathering?

"Well, the grand *baile*," he began when everyone was settled, "was upon them . . ."

CHAPTER TWENTY-ONE

ANA

February 1838

The gaiety of the dancers, the joyfulness of the music, and the beauty of the ladies as they tittered behind fans when they weren't dancing seemed a fitting celebration for the first milestone in the pursuit of his dreams.

Yes, his vines were already growing, the first dormant season upon them. Señor Avila had advised as to which shoots to save and which to prune, and the vintner from Rancho El Molino had been an invaluable help. Indeed, after perusing Avelino's extensive notes and sketches in his journal, Señor Avila had predicted a very successful enterprise, joking that someday they might plant more and more acres and expand into a commercial winery.

Ana Maria returned on her mother's arm, listening intently to something. She laughed, shaking her head at whatever nonsense Señora de Garza suggested. Surprise tickled his heart as he realized that Ana would come to him and tell him all her mother had said. Such a comfortable situation. Don Ruiz had suggested that he might prefer a younger bride, but there were advantages to a woman who had been overlooked thus far.

As she wove her way past the spectators, her eyes locked on his, and he allowed himself a moment of open admiration. "You will not guess what *mamá* has said now."

"I saw that she amused you . . ."

"It seems that I am doing an insufficient amount of flirting with you. How was I to know that you would never throw your heart at my feet if I did not flutter my eyelashes over the top of my fan?"

The exaggerated movements of her eyelids slowed into a definite provocative movement.

He smiled, enjoying the banter that he always found so delightful. Yes, a young and beautiful debutante was a great feather in a man's cap, but the sort of shy, simpering looks he'd received from that direction assured him that his heart had not failed in its choice. "I would not hesitate to throw my heart at your feet if you so desired it, *mi amor*, but such a short-lived romance would seem unsatisfactory, would it not?"

"Short-lived?"

"Would I not die without my heart beating in its proper place?" He leaned a little closer and murmured, "However, I can confess that it does not always beat properly when you are near. Perhaps it would work better under your care."

"Are you going to ask me to dance, Don Avelino? I do believe my mother's heart is going to explode with her temper if you do not."

"I will when you promise to allow me to give you a tour of my house and vineyards tomorrow."

"I will have to bring Ramona—and possibly one of the señoras."

"We'll hope that your *madre* will be content with just Ramona." Once more, he leaned close and whispered, "Perhaps if you were to intimate that you thought me a little shy in regards to issues of the heart? If I had a little time without as many eager eyes, I might work up the nerve to see if you would be receptive to whatever the *portador* might bring . . ."

"I think that can be arranged—particularly if I suggested that maybe she give Ramona a hint about not hovering quite so near all the time."

"Yes. Chaperones should be neither seen nor heard, I should think." He winked.

"My father will expect the *portador* to be a priest . . ."

"A woman of your beauty and grace deserves no less."

They joined the next dance, clapping and twirling. Though he limped at odd moments, Ana did not seem to notice. If she did, he knew she didn't care. As they were called to supper, he offered his arm, and as they followed their hosts to the great tables, he asked her for one favor. "And while you are there, would you help me choose a name for my house?"

Ana Maria nodded. "I think I already know what I will suggest."

* * *

A wide room opened from a small entryway into Avelino's house; in this room, he planned to put a padded bench, a few chairs, and a writing desk. It would be a fine place to sit of an evening and play with children, teach them to read, and talk with his wife—with Ana. It seemed as if every one of his dreams had, or would soon, become true.

Ana listened as he described the planned furniture—the things that were being made and those he had yet to commission. She made suggestions regarding color of rugs, and Avelino took careful notes, grateful once more for the lessons in writing. He was not a well-educated man, but he might be someday. He would never stop learning. *Never.*

The kitchen still amazed him. Don Ruiz had suggested the stove, the pitcher pump that brought water in from a cistern, and the long waist-high table that ran along the wall opposite the window. For baking, he'd said. A large cupboard with shelves from floor to ceiling stood at one end of the room, and a small table would one day sit at the other.

"What is out here?"

"We'll have a patio, partially covered, and then a nice fountain there in the middle someday."

It was the first time he'd allowed himself to include her in his future in conversation with her.

"I like that. So where is the vineyard from here?"

Avelino pointed out the kitchen garden area he'd planned, a pile of rocks meant to be the boundaries for it. "I'm hoping it'll keep out rabbits if I build it high enough." He pointed to where the foundation of a barn stood, and shared his plans for that. "Then, beyond those trees and along that little hill, I've planted the vines. Your father said there would be best so that frost would be less likely to kill the tender buds in spring."

He pointed at a flash of blue as Ramona disappeared around the back of a great *secoya* several hundred yards away from the house. "I think she has spied Diego in the vines."

"Then you must show me the rest of the house while we have a little time to ourselves."

He gave the little outhouse behind the coming barn an honorable mention before he turned back to the kitchen. "I've planned it so that we can build on each side as the years pass and we need more space. On that side, there are two rooms. One will be for storage—food and wine, once we start making it—and the other will be a quiet place for me to study."

"*Papá* says he has never seen a man so determined to learn all that he can. He is very impressed with you."

"I squandered my opportunities as a boy. I won't do that again."

"Why did you?" Ana asked as she allowed her fingers to trail along the walls.

"You will laugh at me." Avelino flushed with embarrassment before he confessed his childish motives. "The priest was brought in to teach me. I thought if I learned, I would have to be a priest too. I didn't want to live in the church and have no children or a pretty wife, so whenever they brought someone new to teach me, I played stupid. It worked."

Ana's eyes glowed with that expression he'd come to recognize as her peculiar form of flirting. "So what is on the other side of the house?"

They stepped through the dining room and into a small hallway that led to two bedrooms. "This will be my room, of course—being larger—and that is for the first children. We will add more rooms as needed, of course."

"Well, if that is for the children," Ana teased, "and that one is for you, and I am a part of this 'we' of which you speak, then pray tell me where I will sleep."

His whisper brought the deep throaty laughter that always sent his blood racing through his veins. It was time. He needed to be bold and yet tender. The speeches he'd planned all failed him.

Hesitation gripped him for several seconds before he asked, "May I send the *portador* today?"

It wasn't much of a proposal, but it was a courtesy to her while still holding to their traditions.

"I would like that . . ." Eyelashes swept rosy cheeks before she whispered, "I would like that very much, Don Avelino."

It was bold—inappropriately so—but Avelino chose the relative privacy of his new home to give his future bride her first kiss. Or so he hoped.

* * *

Celebration of their engagement was the most elaborate event Avelino had ever experienced. A week of feasting, partying, dancing, all combined with the rodeo that came with the spring cattle roundup. They held bullfights, contests, and other events designed to showcase the skills of the *vaqueros*.

The festivities seemed to wear down Ana Maria, and though she didn't complain, Avelino grew concerned at the fatigue in her eyes and the flushed cheeks that seemed to indicate impending illness. Despite his pleading for her to rest, Ana insisted on attending the grand *baile* held in their honor. People teased her about being lovesick, but she took it in stride, hardly blushing unless he mistook her delicate modesty for fevered cheeks.

He waited until their special dance was called before dancing with his soon-to-be bride, citing his semi-lame leg as an excuse. Her droopy eyes told him he'd postponed too long; she wouldn't last through the course of the dance. Indeed, he barely caught her as she collapsed. Men around them offered to carry her to her room, but Avelino refused their help. The struggle to stagger through the house was only slightly less difficult than to let her go too soon. However, the moment he laid her on her bed, the women bustled him out of the room, clucking their tongues at the impropriety of his presence now.

The news arrived at his home a week later. *Viruela*—smallpox. Fear of a kind he had never before imagined possible struck his heart. *There is nothing worse than smallpox*, he wailed to himself. Desperate to get help, he sent Diego to Yerba Buena with a note for Juana Briones, begging her to come to Napa and nurse his *novia*.

Each day the news came, and each day's news was more discouraging than the last. Avelino prayed, wept, and prayed some more. Hope seemed lost, but he refused to believe it.

The whispers enraged him. Scars—people said—scars would disfigure her. The once-beautiful Ana Maria would be covered in hideous scars. Diego's jaw was sore for days after daring to hint that she would lose her loveliness to the disease. His Ana Maria had a *corazón de oro*, a lovely heart that would outshine any pockmarks that might be left.

He would not lose hope. He would not lose faith.

* * *

Horse hooves pounded the fog-blanketed road between the house of Don Avila and la Casa de los Sueños, and a rider flung himself from the animal's back.

"¡Ana Maria está mejorando!" She is getting better. She will live.

He pounded at the door, but no one answered. Undaunted, he dashed around the corner of the house and rushed for the grapes, calling out to Señor Aguilar, but only silence answered him.

The barn was empty and the gardens were bare—not even the fledgling little shoots of coming growth tickled the surface. Halfway to the first row of vines, he met Diego with the good news. "Señora Briones says that Ana Maria is out of danger. I came to tell Señor Aguilar, but I cannot find him."

"He has paced the vines, praying and worrying for over a week. I will probably find him there. Thank you." Diego hesitated and then whispered, "Ramona . . . ?"

"Did not contract the disease. She is fine."

A grin split the man's face as he turned to find his employer. Somewhere in the small maze of vines, he was sure to find Don Avelino. The fog was thicker in the vineyard than at the house, and it was difficult to see more than a few feet in front of him. "Don Avelino! There is news. Ana Maria is getting better," he called.

There was no answer.

He stumbled, tripping over something he'd missed in the fog. "Don Avelino! *¿Está bien usted?* What happened?"

A groan that sounded a little like "Help me" was his only answer. With much difficulty, Diego managed to grab his employer's arms and hoist the man over his back, much as Edgar Tandy had in Texas. Step by step, he struggled to carry Avelino back to the house. They stopped several times, him resting, Avelino groaning and whimpering. The heat of the man's body felt almost scalding on Diego's back, but still he trudged onward, until at last he dropped Avelino onto the bed.

Throughout the night, Diego mopped Avelino's brow, trying to cool the raging fever. He offered water, but to little avail. By morning Diego was exhausted and frustrated. He didn't know what to do to help. His own fear at contracting the disease gripped his gut and twisted it into knots.

The housekeeper, Flora, took over long enough for him to ride to la Casa de Vida and beg for help. There were few enough servants at Don Avelino's home, none of whom seemed to know what to do with the sick man.

Don Carrillo promised to send help and to say prayers. "Be encouraged, Diego. Avelino is young. Look how much recovered Ana Maria Avila is! I was told she was sitting up in bed today."

"So many die . . ."

"Yes, but Ana lived, and many years ago I too lived through it. More live than die, my friend."

*   *   *

In the wee hours of the morning, long before light could be hoped for, Diego pounded once more on the doors at la Casa de Vida. It took several long minutes for Señor Carrillo to appear as requested, and even longer to find themselves riding over the familiar road to the sickroom at la Casa de los Sueños.

Ruiz Carrillo grew concerned as he listened to Diego's tale.

"He asked for me himself?" he said.

"*Sí*. He has been in and out of delirium all day, but the last time he was lucid, he insisted that I bring you immediately," Diego answered as he urged his horse forward. "I do not know when he'll be able to talk coherently again, though."

"What does Señora Briones say?"

Diego's answer came in a whisper: "She does not think he'll survive another night."

"I am very sorry, Diego."

To their surprise, Avelino was quite clear minded as he fought the desire to sleep. He gasped each word as an effort as he welcomed his visitor.

"Don Ruiz. *Gracias*."

"Of course I have come. I could do no less for a dear friend of mine."

"I must leave *instrucciones*—a will."

"I see. You wish to bequeath your rancho to Ana Maria perhaps?"

"No, señor. It must go to Edgar Tandy and his daughter, Cherith. They saved my life. Without them, I would not have come here and begun such a good life with you. You must arrange it for me. I beg you." A crazed panic filled Avelino's eyes. "*Le mendigo*—I beg you," he repeated.

It seemed that Avelino had planned his will for some time. It was simple yet thorough. Everything he owned, from the smallest vine, to the land, to the house, and each and every head of cattle, went to the Texian and his daughter.

Then came the startling revelation.

"There is a bag of jewels—take them home and save them for the Tandys, *por favor*. I want to be sure they are safe." After a moment's pause, he added, "The ruby brooch—the one with diamonds—give to Ana Maria, with her father's permission."

Ruiz watched as Juana worked hard to cool and soothe the miserable Avelino. Even to his inexperienced eyes, the efforts were futile; nothing seemed to settle the man. At last he whispered, "I will do it."

"There's a chain," Avelino rasped between struggling breaths, "to the cistern. They're at the bottom of it. Thank you, my friend." Tears filled his eyes, irritating them. "Tell Ana I love her and to be happy."

Five minutes later, Avelino spoke his last words before the priest stepped into the room. "Thank you for all you have done. You have been a very good friend to me. *Vaya con Dios*, my friend."

CHAPTER TWENTY-TWO

SAVE THE VINES

Early April 1946

His nose twitched in the cool air. One gloved hand held a flashlight as Avelino tramped through the vines, checking the outdoor thermometers nailed to the ends of the trellises every few rows. It hovered at the edge of the safe zone. Herein lay the dilemma before him. If he sounded the alarm and began the battle against frost damage even ten minutes too late, it could be financially devastating. If, however, he jumped the gun and began it unnecessarily, their profits would be seriously affected as well. Labor and the electricity to power the great fans didn't come cheap.

His watch said three thirty. Just another hour or two before they were likely in the clear. Avelino inspected vine after vine, bud after bud, and still remained uncertain. Fifteen minutes. He'd converge with the east quadrant at approximately a quarter to four. Maybe Pedro had ideas. *Lord, please let Pedro have ideas.*

* * *

A shuffle followed by a click and an exclamation jerked Avelino out of a sound sleep. He sat up in bed, glancing around for the source of the noise, but saw nothing, until the room exploded in light as Amelia jerked the blanket he'd put over the windows from the rods.

"Wha—oh, I'm sorry! I didn't know you were in here. I couldn't see . . ." Her hands fumbled with the blanket, trying to replace it.

His panic receded as he forced himself to take a few gulps of air. "It's fine. I should be up already, I'm sure."

"No, no. I forgot you were up last night—the frost threat."

Avelino swung his legs over the bed and yawned as he stretched. "It was a long one, but no frost. That's always good news."

"You hungry?" The eagerness in her voice twisted his gut. "I'll go get you some stew. I made some yesterday."

"That would be nice. Thank you."

She paused by the door, her hand lingering on the doorknob. "Avelino?"

"Yeah?"

Red tendrils swayed as she shook her head. "I'm sorry. Never mind."

Before he could encourage her to open up to him, the door closed behind her. Then again, he didn't have that right—to expect her to confide in him when he consistently closed himself off from her. Asking was wrong, but oh, how he wanted to go down there and . . . Avelino shook his head. He was ridiculous. She probably wanted to ask if he'd make it to confession or if his aunts were still going to the Spanish Baptist church in Oakland.

That had been a surprise. When she'd told him, he hadn't believed it, but it was true. There was actually a church—a Spanish church—that wasn't Catholic. *Tía* Jacinta said it was good—using the Bible alone to teach and exhort. Their culture wasn't lost, but the parts that conflicted—those were set aside. He wanted to go, but that wasn't likely to happen for years.

Stew waited, steaming in a bowl, as he stepped into the kitchen. In the dining room stood an ironing board, iron, and stack of clothes with a shirt that looked suspiciously like his on the top of the pile. Instinct told him that had been the unasked question. She'd decided not to ask if she could iron for him so he wouldn't say no. It gave him fascinating insight into who she was and how she handled things. His *mamá* would be proud of her. She would say, "Amelita, you know how to manage your man. *Tu eres inteligente—* you are smart."

"Your man." That's what mamá *would call me. Your man.* He could do it. He could be her man. It would only take a word, a touch. She would understand why he resisted—why he didn't think it was wise. She'd forgive the rejection. All he had to do was tell her he loved her. *Te quiero. Mucho.* He sighed. *Te amo.*

How much he wanted her to know he wanted her, but he couldn't. It would be wrong. *I must not be weak. I must not be selfish.* His family had already done so much damage to so many people in the past decade. He could not be responsible for hurting more. *I will not.*

"So, are you going to eat that, or do you like your stew cold?"

"I am sorry. How ungrateful."

Joe burst in the room. "Franco missed a section in the south quadrant. There is ten percent damage at least. I need you there— now." He glanced at the bowl. "Eat first. You'll be up all night. I guarantee it."

Without a word, Joe dashed out the back door with much more speed and agility than expected in a man of his age. The full import of Joe's words hit him hard. Loss. Already. He should have walked more—faster. Checked the rest of the area. *Loss. I can't afford more loss.*

"Avelino?"

With a mouth full of stew, he barely managed a generic, "Hmm?"

"It's not your fault. I bet you've had bud loss every year since the first."

"Not every year, but most." He tried to explain: "I just can't afford a single bunch lost. Not for the next few years."

She set two cookies beside his plate. After waiting for him to look up at her, she added, "You don't have to make up for anyone's failures but your own. You couldn't even if you tried. You can only do what you do best, to the best of your ability, and that's all. Extra is just that—extra."

"Wise twice in one morning. You're killing me."

"What?"

He stood and grabbed the cookies and downed the milk before him. "You're a smart girl, Amelia. I want to agree with you, but I can't. I know you're right, but I can't give in to it. I must succeed. Can you understand that?"

A short little jerk of a nod was his only answer—until he opened the door. Then, somehow traveling over the rustle of the wind through chimes on the patio, a whisper reached him.

"Your pride blinds you. Please try to forgive yourself when you trip."

* * *

He felt it long before the thermometer warned him. The bite of the air on a cold, clear morning—his most and least favorite weather in the world. The equivalent of whiskey to a drunk on the wagon. Avelino sprinted for the closest bell and jerked it repeatedly. The echo of several others followed. Though he couldn't see it, he knew the lights blared in the wine house as Pedro began making the calls.

The first smudge pot flickered and flared in the darkness. Again and again, row after row, he lit the pots. All around him gold flickered in evenly spaced rows. Heat reached desperate fingers to the sky, fighting back the brisk air that threatened the health and safety of his grapes.

Eventually, helpers spilled into the vineyards, lighting each pot, desperate to save the grapes. Something in the air felt different; Avelino didn't like it. He remembered the cold nights as a boy. The workers had sung, laughed, teased—almost made a party of fighting nature. The difference startled and unsettled him. Now everyone worked with calm, silent deliberation.

Joe passed him as if on a mission, hardly acknowledging him. More pots lit, and still he stood there at the corner of his quadrant, unhappy and thinking. A voice at his elbow nearly made him jump from his skin.

"What's wrong? Is it too late?"

"Amelia? Why are you here?"

"I wanted to help." She looked close at him again. "What's wrong? I know something is bothering you."

He scanned the groups again, listening and watching for the laughter. "We used to work together with joy. We had smiles on our lips while we fought the cold that tried to destroy our income. This"—Avelino swept his arm across the vines—"they look like it's . . ."

"Work?" She smiled at the sheepish look on his face. "If you want them to look less driven and more joyous, try being that yourself. They're taking their cues from you. How does that song go again?"

"What song?"

Amelia hummed a bar. "The one about the hug—or kiss, if you're feeling bold—before you leave me at the door."

Without another word, she gave him a quick squeeze and went to work in the west quadrant.

It took several more minutes before her meaning managed to burst through the cloud of confusion in his mind. *She is right.* The others mirrored his own drive and determination, and only he could make that change.

"Ahora puedo ver en tus ojos que aceptas el amor que espero traerle, a casa a mi mamá . . ."

The fields around him swelled with the refrain, as the workers pleaded with the girl of the song not to make her love wait for tomorrow. *"Cariño, mi querida, por favor, ven conmigo. No esperas mañana porque el mañana vendrá y traerá tristeza, yo sé que tú eres mía."*

It didn't take long. A few improvised verses, even more joyful choruses filled with parodies and exaggerated pathos, and the fields filled with music and laughter—just as they once had. The pots glowed with fire one after another, and those with thermometers worked harder than ever to stay one step ahead of the icy tentacles that tried so desperately to squeeze the life out of the vines.

Once more the south quadrant was threatened with the worst of it. Trucks arrived with generators and fans and blew the hot air back down on the vines. It felt good. His life was the life he'd always known, the life he'd dreamed of. He had it back. Even though it wasn't his—not on paper—his life had returned.

The eastern sky began to glow with that first light of morning. The workers, one by one, put out the smudge pots as the small white streak of light grew golden and pink as the sun crept up over the horizon. Soon the roar of the generators ceased, and the fans slowed and came to a complete stop. One more day, one more battle fought and won.

Joe found him leaning over the trellises as he watched the sun spread its warming rays over the leaves and buds that survived the night once more.

"Come on, son. It's time to go home. Amelia's making buck-wheat hotcakes."

"I didn't jump the gun, did I?"

"Temp got down to twenty-four. You did good." Joe took a couple of steps. "Come on. She makes the best hotcakes in the world."

They tramped past the rows of vines, around the wine house, and up the hill to the house. His body screamed for a bed and a few hours of sleep, but Joe was right. He needed food first.

"How can she do this? How can she work so hard all day, stay up all night with us, and still have energy to make breakfast?"

"It's just Amelia. I don't know anyone who works harder than she does."

The sizzle of pancakes on the griddle hit them as they entered the kitchen. Without turning from her work, Amelia said, "Wash up. The first ones will be ready in a minute."

Joe went for the kitchen sink, leaving Avelino to head for the bathroom. He stood gripping the white porcelain and staring at his reflection, pain etched on his face. *So like* mamá. *"Clean your hands, Avelino. Wash for supper. Don't tramp mud on my clean floor, Avelino. Supper is almost finished. Hurry and wash."*

Amelia's voice called from the kitchen, as if she did it every day. "Avelino, hurry up. They're getting cold!"

He stood in the doorway and watched her slide another hotcake onto the plate. *You should tell about Marco's journey*, his conscience prodded. *Stories at breakfast—too much like the old days—but how can I not?*

Avelino stuffed down the thought and seated himself at her insistence. But when Amelia sat down without a plate, explaining that she'd eaten as she worked, he relented.

"Acapulco Bay . . ." Avelino paused. "Well, Acapulco isn't that important. Marco just felt tempted to stay—twice: while there, and after enduring the storms around Cape Horn. Let's just say that despite much temptation, Marco did the right thing and made it to Virginia."

"But how did Marco know to go? Did Ruiz Carrillo send him? I want to hear more about Cherith, of course, but Don Carrillo just lost his friend. It must have been hard to send someone to tell Edgar Tandy that the man he'd saved died," Amelia protested.

Avelino and Joe exchanged amused smiles, and Avelino started again. "Ruiz Carrillo . . ."

CHAPTER TWENTY-THREE

BEARER OF GOOD NEWS

May 1838

Ruiz Carrillo stared at the will he had penned just six weeks earlier. Letters had to be sent—both to Avelino's family in Guerrero, and to this man, Edgar Tandy, in Texas. The question was the best way to do it. Should he send a messenger with it? *I must. I just don't want to ask it of anyone. But Señor Tandy should know of his inheritance.*

Marco sat across from him as he wrote with lazy swirls and slopes, forming each word with thought, care, and precision. After Ruiz finished the first, sealed it, and began the second, Marco began asking questions.

"I take the letter to the Aguilar family in Guerrero first?"

"Sí."

"Then I go across Mexico into Texas, and up the San Jacinto River to find Señor Edgar Tandy and give him the second letter and the money."

"Yes."

Ruiz did not wish to borrow trouble, but the recurring conflict between Mexico and Texas couldn't be ignored. "Ask the family in Guerrero. Do not go up to Texas that way unless they say it is safe. I will send enough to take a ship if that is best."

With letters in hand, Marco boarded the *Alexandra* for Acapulco Bay. From there he'd travel to Señor Aguilar's home. He'd heard the complaints about a long, hard trip down the coast, but he found it swift, beautiful. The days dawned bright and sunny; no storms troubled them as they sliced through the water at speeds he'd never felt in his life. His family had come overland back when he was a baby, trying to find a new life in a place where people without connections and wealth could have a new start.

It wasn't the wealth-filled paradise they'd hoped for, but it was a good life. His parents had a small house, a garden, chickens. They danced at fiestas and rested with a clear conscience during each day's siesta. They were not servants without property or the hope of it. His life was as good as could be expected.

These Tandys will have a good life—far better than Señor Carrillo seems to think they have now. Avelino Aguilar was a good man. He should have lived—should have married Ana Maria and had children. I do not understand El Señor's ways.

* * *

"Things are the same no matter where or who we are, aren't they?" Amelia mused as she jumped up to make a new stack of hotcakes when Joe stared at the empty plate in obvious dismay. "We don't understand why God does what He does. We think we know best, but if Avelino had lived, you wouldn't be here. This place might not be here—well, I suppose it would."

"Actually, you're probably right." Avelino sopped the last cold triangle of hotcake in the pool of syrup on one side of his plate and popped it in his mouth. "If not for Cherith Tandy, the Carrillos would have lost this property as they did la Casa de Vida, but that is a story for another day."

"And now I'm becoming interested in Marco's fate, so let's move this along. We have work this morning." Joe jumped up and poured himself a fresh cup of coffee. "More, Avelino?"

"*Sí.*"

Amelia whirled in place to stare at him. "Are you okay?"

Confusion furrowed his brow. "Why do you ask? I'm fine."

"You answered in Spanish. You usually only do that if you're upset."

Joe set a cup of steaming coffee in front of Avelino as he said, "And when he's emotional. We care about the stories that mean so much to him. Of course, it affects him."

She watched his reaction, nodded and carried more hotcakes over to the table. As she passed his chair, Amelia squeezed his shoulder. "Get Marco to Virginia, and save the rest for later. You're tired, and Granddad wants to go stare at the grapes. I think he thinks it makes them cooperate or something."

Joe stifled a snicker and shrugged. "Worked with you when you were little—very little. Doesn't work anymore, but grapes aren't as stubborn as you."

But Amelia ignored him, training her eyes on Avelino. "So in Richmond . . ."

She wants me to skip a lot. Aaah . . . she expects me to tell her details later when Joe's not in a hurry. I can do that. He winked at her and nodded. "Yes, in Richmond . . ."

*   *   *

In Richmond, Marco searched for the home of Señor Sidney Tandy. Finding someone who understood him wasn't easy, but at last he knocked on the door of the great house of the man who was supposed to help him. A servant answered, scolding him for something, but a young lady in voluminous skirts passed and smiled, saying, "Are you a friend of Mr. Avelino?"

Avelino's name brightened his eyes. He wasn't sure what the woman said, but "friend"—wasn't that the word for *amigo*?

"¡Sí! Estoy aquí a favor de Avelino Aguilar."

"He's not here. He left over two years ago."

These words were utterly useless to him.

"No comprendo, señorita."

She called a man, a man he learned to be Señor Sidney Tandy himself. They fed him, gave him a nice room, and pored over the letter, trying to make out the blurred, soggy missive in a foreign language. At last he was called to Señor Tandy's study and introduced to José Santiago.

Despite Marco's eagerness to continue on his journey, Señor Tandy insisted he wait for March . . .

* * *

The crunch of feet on the gravel interrupted Avelino's story again.

Pedro knocked. "Is Avelin . . . ? There you are. They found frost damage on the north side."

Dread sent trembles through Avelino's heart as Pedro nodded at Joe.

"They want you too—to see how bad it is."

Joe jumped from his chair and grabbed his jacket from the back. "First impression?"

"I think they're overreacting. It's just a row—two, tops—where the pots don't help as well. Happens every year."

The trembles subsided into a steady pounding—one he'd recently come to associate with Amelia's presence rather than loss of buds. *He is right. We always lose a few up there on the worst of frost nights.* Papá *thought it worth the risk of loss to save manpower. Don't overreact.*

His pep talk did him little good, but the confident smile and reassurance in Amelia's eyes followed him across the vineyards and up to the northernmost vines. *Take note: Pedro has good instincts. This is bad, but it's no worse than in* papá's *time. This is just the way of life on the vineyard.*

CHAPTER TWENTY-FOUR

TURNING POINT

May 1946

Shots rang out in the night, waking Avelino from the first good sleep he'd enjoyed in weeks. Bleary-eyed, he rolled to the ground, pulling on his boots automatically. The sounds came from down the hill, so he grabbed his weapon and crept down, taking cover at every new sound.

Silence. Not a single footfall or crack of a twig underfoot alerted him to the position of the enemy. Ted was out there—somewhere. It was his turn for watch duty. If those Japs got past the American lines, Ted and eventually every other soldier would be in danger.

"Ted," he hissed into the night air, dodging the leafy overgrowth of the jungle. "Where are you?"

Once more only the whispers of air rustling the leaves and the occasional cricket answered him. Still, without anything more than the occasional light of a partially cloud-covered moon, he stumbled along the line, listening, watching, praying.

"Ted!"

From behind he heard the scramble of feet and a cry—not Ted. Weapon drawn, he prepared to spray the advancing enemy with bullets, but his gun jammed. He reached for a grenade, but his belt was gone. *Where's my belt?*

Panic set in as beads of perspiration formed. *I have to hide, but how? Where?* The crunch of feet nearby sent him ducking behind the protection of the leaves, but they stopped too close. They'd hear him breathing in the night air. *Where are the cries of night birds and turkeys or the incessant chatter of monkeys to help hide me? Fear—it silences the wildlife every time.*

The feet moved again, and Avelino made his move. The moment the feet passed him, he dove, tackling the Jap from behind. The man cried out, calling to his comrades. Avelino straddled the man's legs as he shimmied up the Jap's back and hooked his arm under the enemy's neck.

The man fought, screaming with little effect, as Avelino's death grip crushed his esophagus. Hands grabbed him from behind and ripped him from his prey. Furious, he kicked, praying for a solid landing. At the sound of opera in the jungles of the Philippines, Avelino grinned. Success. A kick to his gut sent the air whooshing from his lungs, and a slam to the temple caused a familiar explosion behind his eyes. These were big men. Bigger than any of the Japs he'd encountered yet.

Training kicked in once more. He rolled toward the assailant, surprising the man. The satisfying thud and groan of body meeting earth told him his trick had worked—well. Swiftly, he flipped the man over and rammed his forearm down on the windpipe. The man glared up at him with bulging eyes as strange fingers fumbled for his . . . Avelino turned his head as the hand gouged at his eye. It fumbled again, fighting to tear out the other one, but he felt nothing. The Jap screamed in terror and jerked back his hand.

Through a rapidly swelling eye, he saw the face beneath him—Ray Welton. *What is little Ray Welton doing fighting for the Japs?* A voice screamed at him to stop, but still Avelino stared at the boy and his bulging eyes. What—?

". . . off him, man! You're killing him! We'll go!"

At that point he realized the source of the screams and the attempts to drag him from his victim: someone was trying to pull him off the Jap—off Ray. Ray. He heard screams for help, but Ray still struggled. Between the fight below him and the men trying to pull him from his prey, the boy seemed to get enough air.

Avelino jammed his elbow in the pants of the man on his left. Another tenor screeched in his ear. Strange for opera to erupt again in the jungles of—Napa. Napa. Grapes. The giant fronds weren't from ferns but grapes. *What—?*

He felt himself flung from Ray and into the trellises. A kick—pain. *I didn't know I could sing so high!* Another kick landed, this time to his chest, his back, his head. He scrambled toward it, trying to fool the attacker again but failed. This kick got him at least one loose tooth—probably a broken one as well. *Amelia won't think me handsome anymore.*

As if that thought conjured her from the night air, he heard her scream. So close. His mind and heart demanded that she return to the house—to safety—but he couldn't speak. Gasping for air required more work than he could stomach. Blackness felt like a comforting blanket as it swelled closer and closer.

Just as it dropped, Avelino heard the distinct cock of a shotgun and Joe's voice say, "Back off, fellas, and sit down. 'Melia, call Callum. This looks like a job for the sheriff."

* * *

With knees drawn to a wrapped and aching chest, Avelino held a cold compress to his swollen eye and tried not to shake. Each twitch of his body was agony, but the tortured memories twisted his gut further into knots. They were gone now—all of them. Callum hauled off the three young men, insisting Avelino go in and make a statement in the morning. Doc Metcalfe wrapped his ribs and agreed that they were either cracked or broken. His teeth supposedly would survive. All but the cracked one on the side of his mouth. How he'd pay for a dental bill, he couldn't fathom. Joe and Amelia finally left when Doc Metcalfe suggested he needed quiet.

Alone, his mind reviewing the night's drama, Avelino slowly grew terrified. *I could have killed him—Ray. I could have killed the kid. This has to stop. Oh God, please make it stop.*

Tía Jacinta's words regarding Ed Welton returned to him, mocking and yet teasing. Something about them whispered to his spirit and reminded of—what? Ed had felt rejected by a Carrillo. He probably, deliberately or not, instilled that hatred into his son. Then again Ray had always been friendly enough before Avelino left for boot camp.

Boot camp. Could it be that simple? Jealousy combined with his father's wounded pride and bigotry—a new thought slammed into his head, making the ache stronger than ever. She rejected him. Ray invited Amelia, and she rejected him—just like with *tía* Jacinta. Rejection by a girl who then clearly preferred him, his service in the army—it was immature but understandable. Ray wasn't much more than a boy yet.

What do I do? If I press charges, it'll follow him all his life. If I don't, he'll think his father's money can save him from anything. He won't quit until he's won. That's even worse. Amelia . . .

Amelia. She's endured enough. Thus far, the boys had blamed him for everything, but she would continue to fight for him—to defend him. *Fight for me. She loves me.* That thought overwhelmed him.

Eight months he'd known her. For most of those months—seven at least—he'd resisted it. *I love her too. To what purpose, though? A life of this kind of treatment?*

"Better to be rejected by a fool than by those you love." Where the thought came from, he couldn't tell. It didn't seem familiar. Avelino smiled to himself as he realized the thought was his. *Is it true? It sounds true, but is it really? It sounds like something* papá *or* abuelito *would say—*abuelito *has said similar things. I will someday be like him. I will say things that sound wise; but will they be?*

But her friends . . . He sighed. They thought she rejected him. They blamed her—all but Helen, he supposed. Helen Moreau was likely thrilled. Strange that he had not seen her visit. Very strange. Then again Amelia had not cared to say good-bye. Had she chosen him over her friend?

Tía Lucia had written just days ago with stern words for him. *Amelita is a good girl. She will be a wonderful wife and mother. Do not hurt her with your silly ideas. Do not let your pride drive her away.*

Amelita. His family loved her. *Why should they not?* Amelita. The endearment should have been his—would have been his. *I love her. I should have been first to call her that. Amelita.*

As he shifted, stabbing pain caused him to wince. Instinctively, he sucked in air, only to moan again as his lungs and ribs protested. The ribs would make sleep impossible. Once more he shook, the trembling waves creating a cycle of pain and misery that he couldn't control.

Somehow the pounding in his head, the twitching of his arms, and the confusion of his thoughts deafened him to her approach. He saw her feet first, a breath before he heard her whisper, "Avelino?"

"*¿Qué?*"

"You're okay?" She knelt before his bed, her eyes searching for his. "I was worried . . ."

"I am cold, but . . ."

She pulled the bedspread from the foot of his bed, tucking it around him. "Does that hurt? I'm sorry."

"No, Amelita. It is fine. *Gracias.*"

She knelt once more, examining his face with her eyes, before sitting back on her heels, apparently satisfied. "You will go in tomorrow, won't you? You will press charges this time?"

"I think I must. This cannot happen again. They're going to hurt you someday. I couldn't bear . . ." He stopped himself short. Saying such things would only hurt her more—would only strengthen her resolve to stay close until he relented.

"I know." Her hand brushed his cheek with the touch of a feather. "Does the tooth still hurt?"

"*Sí.* It hurts. They will have to fix it—or pull it."

"Granddad says that Mr. Welton will have to pay for it. Sheriff Callum will insist in hopes that you won't have to take him to court for it."

"His son is an adult. He doesn't have to do anything."

"But coming from the sheriff, there's a chance Mr. Welton won't argue." She smiled and traced his jaw with her finger, sending new shivers down his spine. "The swelling is going down a little. Do you need more ice?"

"No, thank you. I just need to try to sleep, but every time I try to lie down . . ."

To his astonishment, she turned and left without a word. He'd hoped she'd stay, talk to him. Make him sleepy enough to help him rest, but no. She just left. *Serves me right. I can't tell her that we have no future and then expect her to treat me as if we do.*

Just minutes later the soft rat-a-tat-tat of her feet up the stairs irrationally soothed his heart. She stared at him for several seconds, her eyes scanning the room and returning once more.

"You need to get up. I can't push that with you on it."

"I—"

Amelia didn't wait for his response. She eased his arm around her shoulder and slowly stood, pulling him up with her. His groans brought a new flood of apologies. "I'm so sorry . . . *Lo siento.*"

"You are picking up my bad habits, *querida.*"

"*Querida?*" she gasped as she tried to pull him to the windowsill and lean him against it. "What is that?"

Where did she hear that? Did I . . . ? He tried to clear his mind. *But I couldn't have.* "Depends on context, I suppose. Where are you going to move the bed?"

Her expression showed that she knew he changed the subject, but she let him do it.

"I'm putting it along that wall. Just—hold—on." Amelia grunted as she pushed the heavy frame across the floor. "I think I wish we hadn't found this. The cot would be so much easier."

He couldn't help. Walking would hurt. Pushing, lifting, moving—not possible.

"Sorry."

"I'm teasing, Avelino. You should have a comfortable bed. You work hard."

Avelino didn't respond. Instead, he watched as she fluffed pillows, her robe flapping around her ankles. She layered pillows and his winter blankets until the corner was well padded at an incline.

"Come on, let's get you comfortable." She sat with him, using herself almost like a crane to cushion his drop. Despite her efforts, he moaned, catching his breath with the pain.

They sat, his arm around her shoulder, while he tried to catch his breath. "*Lo siento . . .*"

"Shh. You're fine. Take it slow. Don't try to talk."

His eyes closed, and he tried to rest. The breeze ruffled the curtains near his head, but he could no longer feel it wash over him. As he rested, he listened to the song of crickets, a dog somewhere, and the slow, steady rhythm of her breathing. The delicate scent of her somehow permeated his defenses and wrapped fine tendrils around his heart.

A rooster crowed. Sunlight streamed in through the windows, and he turned to glance at the girl beside him, but she was gone. He closed his eyes, aching for the dream to return. It had been so real . . .

He bolted upright, almost screaming from the pain, but he smiled instead. His bed wasn't in its usual place. Half-a-dozen pillows supported him from behind. *It wasn't a dream.*

CHAPTER TWENTY-FIVE

NOT AS THEY SEEM

Dave, Ray, and Peter stood before the sheriff's desk, heads bowed and apparently obsessed with their own hands. Ed Welton and Terry Silverman stood to one side, their arms crossed, clearly displeased. Avelino gave his statement with as little embellishment as possible.

Sheriff Callum filled out his report, ordering the young men to keep quiet as he did. "You can tell your story to the judge. He's got witnesses."

"But—"

"Be quiet, Ray."

Ed Welton seemed more than a little put out, but Avelino didn't know with whom.

Once finished, Callum asked Avelino to step outside. "I need to talk to you once they're gone."

Amelia climbed from the truck minutes later and hurried to the door. He tried to stop her, but she shook her head. "I want to press charges too. They held me; they threatened me on my property. I'm done with this." Her calm, quiet demeanor belied the silent fury in her eyes.

He caught her hand and pulled her close, whispering in her ear, "Will you please go home and forget it? Will you do that for me? I'll explain later."

"I—"

"Please, Amelia. I'm not going to let this go with them, but Ed Welton isn't a pleasant man. You rejected his son . . . for the nephew of a woman who rejected him."

"Wha—?"

"It's salting a wound." Avelino squeezed her hand. "I'll explain later. Just go home before they see you. Please."

Her eyes flitted to Joe's in the truck. Something there must have encouraged her to trust him. "Okay, but I want to hear that story—and you have to tell me what *querida* is. I asked Granddad, and he just got a goofy grin on his face."

Another car pulled in just as the truck rumbled down the road. He saw the truck slow, but it kept going. Avelino couldn't help but admire the DeSoto convertible. The woman behind the wheel wore a scarf and sunglasses, but when the scarf came off, he recognized her. Helen Moreau.

She stepped from the car, smiling, and removed her glasses. "Did I get here in time?" She gestured with her glasses to the disappearing truck. "Where did Amelia go? What was she doing here?"

"I convinced her to go home."

"Why?" Helen stepped closer, examining his face. "Your mouth hurts. You're talking strangely." She looked closer and turned his head gently. "That eye looks bad too."

"Because she doesn't need to make enemies."

"That was generous of you after she rejected you."

"Can I help you, Helen?"

"No, I'm just here to tell Sheriff Callum what I overheard. I'm too late, it seems, but I'll tell him anyway."

Avelino's mouth went dry. "And what was that?"

"I overheard Ray and Dave talking at a party last night. They must have come straight for you if you're here this early. I'm sorry."

"No matter. We've evidence enough. Don't make enemies."

Helen seemed to consider his words before offering her hand. "I'm very sorry that Amelia chose not to pursue a relationship with you after all. You seem like a very good man." The woman turned to leave before adding as an aside, "I never would have imagined that she'd be one of 'those people.'"

"What people?" The moment he spoke, he hated himself for asking.

"Those who assume that some people are beneath them."

He watched as she put the car in reverse and pulled onto the road, following the direction Amelia had taken. What could that mean? Helen had been opposed to her having any relationship with him. He'd heard her objections himself. Why did she seem so very different now?

The door opened, and Ed Welton pushed his son out the door and onto the porch of the ancient sheriff's station. He nudged Ray, and the young man mumbled, "Sorry. I won't be bothering you anymore."

"Thank you."

"Avelino, if you could come in here, please . . ."

He navigated around the three young men and their parental escorts and entered the office, closing the door behind him. "So what now?"

"They'll be called before the court. They'll plead guilty, but you should go anyway." Callum passed him an envelope. "Give that to the dentist. Welton says he'll cover all expenses to repair your tooth. I didn't even have to insist."

"Thanks."

He turned to leave, but the sheriff pointed to a chair. "Let's talk."

"About . . . ?" Hesitant, Avelino sat.

"Amelia."

"Isn't that out of your purview?"

Bob Callum crossed his arms. "Perhaps, but she's a friend of my wife, Carol. Carol would talk to her if you think it'd help. Everyone is rooting for you. This just seems so out of character."

"I know you mean well, Bob, but I don't think that would be a good idea. I like to keep my personal life—well, private."

*   *   *

After Mass, the other parishioners flooded Avelino with support. The name of Welton engendered little charity, but he was appalled at how many people blamed Amelia for his beating. No matter what he said, people patted his arm sympathetically and told him what a good man he was to speak so well of such an unworthy girl.

He had never imagined opening himself up in such a public manner, but the situation had exhausted his patience.

"Can I make an announcement?" Avelino spun slowly until everyone in hearing distance glanced his way. "I would appreciate it if the rumors regarding Miss Kearns ceased. She has not rejected me in any way. There is no reason to feel sorry for me or antagonistic toward her, and I would also appreciate if my friends would correct such erroneous statements anytime you hear them. Thank you."

Before anyone could respond, he strode away from the church, trying desperately to hide the desire to double over from the pain. Walking home would kill him.

Five minutes later the Kearnses' truck pulled up beside him, and Amelia stepped out.

"Come on. You shouldn't be walking." He opened his mouth to resist, but she nudged him gently toward the cab. "There . . ." she whispered. "Just be careful."

Amelia pushed the door shut and climbed up on the running board before swinging into the bed with more agility than he would have imagined in a straight skirt and heels. Her hand pounded the top of the cab before she settled herself on the side. "Ready, Granddad."

Joe took curves slowly and avoided potholes and ruts in the road as he drove toward home.

"You should know we heard about your announcement. It's all over town."

"I'd forgotten how quickly news travels."

"Something must have happened to set you off."

"People were blaming her—her!" The accusations still pricked him. "And then Miss Moreau . . ."

"Helen? What does Helen have to do with it?"

"The other day at the station—she acted like she . . ." Should he even say anything? Then again, hadn't his actions caused enough trouble for Amelia? "She just seemed to think Amelia was wrong to reject me too."

"I thought Amelia said she seemed opposed to the idea at that dance."

"That's what I heard her say."

"Sounds like you've won everyone over but the Weltons."

"It's all so strange."

They rode home, each seemingly lost in his own thoughts until Joe pulled into the drive.

"I want you to think about something, son."

"What's that?"

"What is your true objection to Amelia?"

"Nothing!" he protested. "I only—"

"Then," Joe continued as if he hadn't been interrupted, "what are you really afraid of, Avelino?" He put the car in gear and hung his hands over the wheel for a second. "That was a rhetorical question, by the way."

Avelino's door opened before he could process the words. Amelia offered her arm, trying to help him from the truck. "We've got a roast for supper. The tomatoes have just been planted, so there won't be any for salsa . . ."

"In case you didn't understand," Joe interjected, "that's an invitation to supper and probably a bribe for a story."

"I was going to make a chocolate cake too . . ."

"I'll come." He couldn't have refused if he wanted to. The pain had kept him from cooking. It'd be a lean week.

The steps nearly killed him. His room felt awkward still with his bed in the corner, but the pile of pillows did make sleep easier. He tossed his jacket aside, removed his tie, and unbuttoned his top two buttons. His sleeves rolled easily, but the sharp crease in them brought a frown to his face. *She irons them still.*

Gingerly, he lowered himself onto the bed, shifting to get comfortable, and closed his eyes. Relief. The next five or six weeks would be torture. Lying on the bed, he forced himself to breathe as deeply as he could manage—in. Out. In. *What are you really afraid of, Avelino?* The words slammed back into his consciousness. What could Joe mean?

Others objected—or so it seemed. Though he tried to wrestle his thoughts into some semblance of order, he failed. Exhaustion borne from poor sleep, pain, the long trek to church, and the emotional distress of the day overtook him before he could answer the question that reverberated in his mind and heart. *"What are you really afraid of, Avelino?"*

*   *   *

"*La, la, la, la . . . Cariño . . . something . . . por favor . . . la, la, la, la, mañana . . . something, something . . . tristeza.*"

It is fitting, his heart scolded him, *that she would remember the words for "dear one" and "tomorrow"—well, and "sorrow." Do you hear her cheerfulness? She sings the song that you love—because of you. She sings because you are coming. You should be ashamed, Avelino.*

Somewhere between his first thoughts and his last, he could hear his *madre* take over, chastising him for his cruelty. *It seemed right,* mamá.

Joe stepped up behind him and pulled open the door. "You're allowed to go in, son."

"Avelino!"

There it was, that quiet cheerfulness. It spoke to him like nothing he'd ever experienced. There was such peace in her. "Can I help?"

"You can sit and heal. That will do more to help than anything else."

Joe nodded his approval as he washed his hands in the sink. "I'm going to go lie down for a few minutes. Call me when it's time to eat."

She kissed Joe's cheek, and the simple gesture nearly killed him. *That could be me. She could be so affectionate and attentive to me. The right words would do it.*

Amelia watched as Joe left and then shook her head. "I worry about him sometimes. I think he should not work so hard."

Unsure how to respond to something he couldn't help, Avelino pointed to the cake. "It looks beautiful."

"Thank you. Do you like chocolate?"

"Of course." The question of Helen burned in his heart, until he couldn't hold it back any longer. "When was the last time you spoke to Helen Moreau?"

Her head snapped up and her eyes bored into his. "Why would you ask that?"

"Just something she said."

"When did you see her?"

Against his better judgment, he answered. "Friday just after you left the sheriff's office."

"What—?"

"She'd heard about it, Amelia—before it happened. She heard the boys talking at a party and was coming to tell Bob."

Amelia gripped the sink as if to steady herself. "There's that anyway."

"That what?"

"I saw her Friday too. She came here and talked to me for a while."

"Will you tell me what she wanted?" Asking was cruel. Considering he was certain he knew what Helen had to say, it was also unnecessary. Still, he wanted—no, needed—to know.

"She suggested that I reconsider you as a—"

"That's what she told me."

"That you should reconsider me?"

He lowered himself into a chair and fought for a good breath of air. "That she thought you were wrong to reject me."

As she dried her hands, Amelia stared out the kitchen window. "I misunderstood her that night. I thought—she sounded like she didn't want me to *have* a relationship with you. But . . ." Her eyes sought his. "Avelino, she moves in circles that are—biased—against people whose skin isn't as pale as theirs. I took her comments in that light. I misunderstood her. She just thought I was being polite to the man who lives close to me. She didn't want me to lead you on."

He shook his head as she spoke. "But I heard her. She said something about not giving eligible men the wrong idea about you and me."

Here, she smiled and stepped close, her hand reaching to touch his face before she snatched it back again. "She's a matchmaker. I knew that. She likes to introduce people—set up blind dates."

Could Helen simply have wanted Amelia to take advantage of being in a group where she could meet someone? "So she just wanted you to mingle."

Amelia's shoulders sagged a little. "I said something to her a couple of days before the dance. I don't know what it was—Helen can't remember—but I guess somehow she inferred that I wasn't interested in you. She thought I *knew* I wasn't interested and assumed—well, that I thought you beneath me. That's why she was so disapproving that night. She said, 'Amelia, I was so disappointed in you for being so narrow-minded. I just wanted to keep you away from him before you hurt him. I could see how much he liked you.'"

Avelino swallowed the rising lump in his throat, tried to speak, and failed.

She took pity and changed the subject. "You said you'd tell me about Doña Jacinta and Mr. Welton."

The abrupt change, while welcome, sent his muddled brain spinning before he could control it. "It happened a long time ago. Apparently, Mr. Welton and she were dating, and he got a little too friendly. She dumped him, rather harshly, I guess. She thought that might be why Ray hates me—that his father turned his wounded pride against our entire family."

"And do you think so?"

"No." Even as he said it, Avelino knew he was right. This wasn't about something that had happened thirty years earlier. "I think, though, it helped fuel something. Ray was always pleasant before I left. He had friends who were Mexican. This came later. I think maybe he's jealous of me. I went to war when he couldn't, or something stupid like that. I took you to the dance and you rejected him. If you combine it all . . . maybe."

"It still seems excessive."

"Yes. That's what doesn't make sense."

She wiped her hands on her apron and turned to him. She pulled a chair forward to face him and sat in it, her eyes never leaving his. "He is the only one objecting to us, Avelino. You need to remember that. I'm not going to humiliate myself every few days, but when something big like this happens, I have to say something. Even Helen is behind us. There isn't a single person in this valley—with the possible exception of Ray and his two buddies—who objects."

"It would seem that you are right."

He wanted to say something more to encourage her—anything—but he couldn't. Not yet. He had to think it through. He had to know why he still resisted and overcome that first.

"You also promised to tell me what *que—quer* . . . great. Now I can't remember it, but you promised to tell me what it is."

"*Querida.*"

She repeated it several times, working hard to get the proper inflection. "It's a pretty word—*querida.*"

"*Sí,*" he answered with a smile on his lips.

"You can tease me, but I will not give up. You promised to tell me."

"The translation is simple. Dear, darling, beloved, sweetheart . . ."

"Oh . . ." The happy expression that began to form faded as a new thought occurred to her.

"What is it?"

"I just realized that people say things when they are in pain or semiconscious that they don't mean."

"Yes." The right words refused to come. Avelino fumbled, fighting to say something to make her understand without sparking too much hope. He still didn't know what to do. "And sometimes," he added at last, "in our weakest moments we find the strength to say what we can't at other times."

* * *

"He's tired," Joe protested as Amelia reached for her notebook. "Give the poor fellow a night off. He probably didn't sleep very well."

Though her face fell, Amelia nodded and pulled back her hand.

Avelino couldn't stand to see her disappointment. "Maybe a short one. Let's go back a bit and get Marco to the Tandys' home in Texas. Then you'll have something to look forward to."

CHAPTER TWENTY-SIX

AMERICA

May 1839

America—a fascinating place. The people were all so different. Some lived with great wealth in large houses with many servants or slaves. Others lived in tiny shacks that even the lowest native on a rancho would not use for the animals. Most were friendly, even to the man who could not understand what they said.

Señor Tandy had taught him several English phrases. He practiced them over hills, through valleys, while shivering beside a campfire on a cold night. *Cannot speak English. Going to Texas with news. How do I get to Texas?*

The Carolinas gave way to Georgia and Mississippi. The farther south he traveled, the warmer it grew. He made it to Louisiana before his horse became lame. Finding someone to buy the animal—for next to nothing—and sell him a good one proved difficult. *"Necesito un caballo fuerte,"* he insisted, but the men didn't understand his need for a strong horse.

He continued on foot, hoping to find someone who would not cheat him. He traveled slow—the trip long and arduous. The bugs—mosquitos—drove him nearly crazy at times. But at last he reached New Orleans, and there he found men who spoke *español*.

Strange how many languages they speak here. Even el inglés *is so different here from the Tandys'* inglés *in Richmond.* Some people spoke in voices that dripped like honey, soft and soothing. Sometimes he understood them simply because they didn't rush to speak. Others sounded harsh, like an out-of-tune instrument, and spoke so rapidly he couldn't hope to follow.

But on the other side of New Orleans, he found a breeder, José Gálvez, who gave him food, water, and of course a horse—for an exorbitant price. Marco protested, argued, threatened to leave without purchasing anything. Señor Gálvez just laughed at him and suggested a cobbler in New Orleans. "You'll need it if you intend to walk that far."

He deliberated—haggled—for almost a week. Mornings he rode over the countryside, trying to find the best animal for the price he knew he'd be forced to pay eventually. Afternoons he rested on the veranda and flirted with the owner's truculent daughter. Once more he was tempted to stay and forget the rest of his errand, and by the time he left he'd learned to love more than the respite from the journey.

His very expensive horse proved a blessing and a curse. Marco found it difficult to ride the animal as hard or as long as he might have had he not paid what seemed to be a criminal price for something that roamed freely at home. The horse, on the other hand, seemed eager to push forward, almost as if as anxious to arrive as he.

He didn't arrive at the Buffalo Bayou until June. Farm after farm, ranch after ranch—each one seeming shabbier than the last. At last he found someone who knew the Tandys. In halting *español*, a young man offered to show him. *Ocho millas*—eight miles and his job would be done. Sure, he would stay and help them pack their things, sell their things, whatever necessary to help them leave for California. However, the weight of responsibility would lift the moment he could put that letter in Señor Tandy's hand. *Sí, sí.*

They rode across the prairie, off the narrow trails that served as roads. Cattle roamed free with little supervision at all. The *vaqueros* at home kept a closer eye on their animals. Then again, even in California each rancho operated differently

"There. That house there. Um—casa. *La casa . . .* um *. . . es Edgar Tandy.*"

It was small but clean. A woman—she turned. No, it was a girl, maybe fifteen. His eyes slid sideways, watching his companion, but the young man seemed uninterested. "That's Cherith. She's Mr. Tandy's daughter." To the girl, he waved. "Hey, Cherith. You've got a visitor from California!"

The girl dropped the bucket she carried and flew across the space, eager to welcome him, but stopped short a few yards away. "Oh! You are not Mr. Aguilar. I thought—"

"Can you tell her my name is Marco and I have news from Avelino Aguilar?"

What the boy said, he couldn't tell. The señorita seemed cautious, almost suspicious of him. He did understand her words though. *Papá.* She would get her *papá.*

Marco thanked his escort, pulling a coin from his pocket. It wasn't much. Señor Tandy had called it a dime. *Diez centavos*—ten cents.

Edgar Tandy was a tall man—very tall. Older than Marco expected too. As the man read his letter, the muscle in his jaw twitched. It seemed he had cared about his friend Avelino Aguilar. That spoke well of the Texian.

"Señor Aguilar insisted that you have everything. He wanted you to come to California and live the dream he would not survive to enjoy." The words, provided by Señor Carrillo and rehearsed all the way there, seemed almost cruel in the wake of the news.

"He was a good man, Don Avelino. I cannot believe he left me his property and his money. I saw those jewels. It is a great fortune to a man like me!"

Edgar Tandy led Marco into the little house and introduced him to the pretty red-haired girl. "Avelino told me of her; he loved her hair."

"He called it 'hair like roses' when he was here."

"*¡Sí!* Such lovely hair. I had an aunt from Seville with hair just like it. The beauty of the family."

The girl blushed as her father translated for her. "My daughter is not accustomed to people thinking her hair attractive. Around here people don't admire it."

The gringos *are strange people; I have always thought so. There is no sense in their thoughts. She is beautiful, this girl with the* pelo como rosas. *Even* con pecas—*with freckles—she has such lovely eyes and clear skin.* Hermosa—*beautiful.*

* * *

Amelia stared at him, agape. "That was cruel." She leaned forward. "What was Marco's last name?"

He shook his head. "That is part of a story for another day."

"But he left his heart in New Orleans!" Amelia sent a mock glare in her grandfather's direction. "I blame you for this. I'm going to go nuts waiting."

Avelino didn't even try to hide his smirk as he stood. "Only Amelia can protest with utter indignation—and without raising her voice. Who else exclaims in a perfectly normal conversational tone?"

"You know one thing, son."

He waited for Joe to continue, but the man just gazed pointedly at him. Understanding dawned. "She'll be ready for another one soon."

CHAPTER TWENTY-SEVEN

BAD TO WORSE

Long hours of fitful sleep left much time for Avelino to ponder his situation. He had no answer. Walking the rows gave him more time to think and examine his aching heart. Answers still eluded him.

He saw her working in her garden, tending the flower beds, painting the trim around the windows. Laundry flapped in the breeze, and tantalizing scents greeted him and Joe each evening. Yes, his evenings became less about cooking and loneliness and more about stories, card games, and radio programs.

Each time he saw her, he wanted to talk to her. But what could he tell her? Though he had managed to acknowledge to himself at least that his prior objections were not valid, something—some ugly thing deep down inside him—warned him against yielding. He just didn't know what or why.

What could I say anyway? We're not in high school. I cannot ask her to "go steady."

"Avelino?"

He turned and stared at the man in the doorway. "Oh, Pedro."

"There's a problem with a few of the barrels. You should come."

"What kind of problem?"

"You should come."

Those words struck fear in him. It had to be bad. He'd been so careful—inspected every barrel of wine as it was sealed. A few barrels had failed—there were always a few—but nearly every barrel had been properly sealed and stored in temperature-controlled rooms. They shouldn't have to touch those rooms for two and a half years.

Lyndon wanted to bottle this year, of course. The man had no patience for fine wine, but the contract gave Avelino the power of decision. This would infuriate Gregory Lyndon and appease his pride at the same time.

Pedro led him to the storehouses and flipped on a flashlight. "Over here . . ."

Row upon row of crates passed, but Avelino did not need Pedro's help to find the problem. He could smell it. "How many?"

"An entire row—twenty barrels."

"Every barrel?" That seemed unlikely. In fact, it was almost impossible.

"Every barrel."

They dripped slowly, the spread of the wasted wine, now spoiled, creeping across the floor. "Get someone in here. I want one of those barrels outside for inspection."

Two men brought in the cart and loaded it with a barrel. Outside, Avelino found the source of the leak and examined it closely. "Dump it."

The men stared at him, dumbfounded. Frustrated, Avelino stormed inside and retrieved a brace. He drilled out the bung, his chest screaming for him to stop as knives of pain stabbed him with every movement, and poured the turned wine onto the ground. The men tried to help, but he ordered them to step back. Once empty, the barrel became easier to examine.

"This is fresh damage. Look. It's been scraped—probably an awl. Are the sheds locked?"

"Always."

"I want a guard on them," he gasped as a fresh wave of pain washed over him. "At all times we have a guard. I want a list of men who can do it within the hour."

"Avelino—"

"Just do it, Pedro. I've got to talk to Lyndon."

"He's not going to like this."

Avelino turned slowly. "He? *He* isn't going to like this? I do not like this! This is my livelihood on the line! This is my family's name and reputation, our home! I want the man or men who did this, and I want to ensure it never happens again. Do. You. Understand. Me?"

"Yessir."

As he walked toward town—toward Lyndon's office—Avelino tried to think. His chest begged for relief, and the coughing. Oh, the coughing nearly killed him. *Doing that yourself was stupid. You don't have to prove anything to anyone.* But still he thought, and the conclusions he reached unsettled him further.

Lyndon looked pleased at the yellowish green around his eye and the way he clutched his chest by the time he arrived. "I heard you got jumped, but that looks worse than I imagined."

"I just pushed myself a little too far. I've got bad news."

"What's that? If you tell me there's more bunch rot . . ."

"No. The vines are surprisingly healthy for four years of neglect."

"I see." Lyndon rested his head in one hand, his arm propped against the arm of his chair. He looked utterly relaxed, but Avelino was not fooled. Such a studied air of nonchalance was too deliberate for relaxation. The man pointed to him impatiently. "Go on. You said you have news."

"Someone broke into the storeroom and damaged an entire row of barrels."

"Someone damaged? How is that possible—and why?"

Avelino forced himself to remain as matter-of-fact as possible. "Sabotage is obvious. They used an awl of some kind to create a crack at a seam."

Incredulity—Lyndon didn't believe him. "That's not likely. Looks like you got a bad batch of barrels to me. Or . . ." He leaned closer. "Perhaps you did it yourself."

"I am the one who stands to lose the most by this. I'm the least likely suspect, and you know it."

"I suppose that's true, but it's my money on the line."

"Twenty barrels—"

"Twenty?" Lyndon sat up, leaning forward. "I thought you said one row. I thought there were ten barrels per row."

"We double-stack them. There's twenty."

Lyndon looked ill. "And how many bottles per barrel again?"

"Three hundred."

"Six thousand wasted bottles. That's—"

"A lot of money. That wine should have been perfect. There's no excuse for this."

"Thousands of dollars—gone." The man's forehead wrinkled as he realized where Avelino would take the conversation. "You have suspicions."

"I do."

Lyndon waited for several seconds before adding, "Do you care to elaborate . . . ?"

"I checked the sheds on Wednesday. The barrels were all fine."

"Why check the sheds at all?"

"Temperature, Mr. Lyndon. The weather is much warmer. We have to be sure the temperature stays as constant as possible."

"Aaah . . . so Wednesday there was no flood of wine all over my floors?"

It was an intentional dig, but Avelino refused to allow it to rattle him. *Your floors are almost one year closer to being mine again.* "Correct. On Thursday night Ray and his buddies attacked me in the vineyards."

"From how I heard it, you attacked them."

How—or rather why—could he have heard anything? That was strange. "They were in the vineyards, sir. You're missing the point. They were in the vineyards. The vineyards lead to . . ."

"Oh, I see. The evidence is circumstantial, but it is an interesting theory."

"I'll be talking to Callum about it." He started to share his other idea, and stopped. Something wasn't right.

"Without proof—"

"It has to be reported. Vandalism. It's important that whoever did this knows we won't take it lying down." He hesitated and then turned to leave. "I just wanted you to know what was happening."

* * *

"I think that's what they were doing there. They came, walked through the vineyards so no one would see their car by the storehouses, broke in, damaged the barrels, and came back through the grapes. I'm not even sure they planned to attack me that night. I was just there, and they took the opportunity." Avelino frowned. "Or, if Lyndon is right, I attacked them first."

"Lyndon. How would he know anything?"

"I don't know, but that's 'what he heard.'"

Sheriff Callum fiddled with his pen, occasionally doodling on the paper covering his desk pad. "Would Lyndon benefit in any way if the winery failed? What does your contract state?"

"Contract says I work for him for seven years, unpaid except for the garage room, and he keeps all profits during those seven years. As long as I work for all seven years, ownership reverts back to me at the end of that time as repayment for our debt."

"He's just giving it back. That seems unusually generous."

"He's making an enormous profit. We were in debt to him specifically. If we didn't pay by the date Paco agreed to, we lost it all. I didn't know the terms until it was too late. I couldn't raise the money."

Callum frowned. "I don't see the profit. The fields sat untouched for three years. People helped themselves to the grapes when they saw he wasn't harvesting."

"The profit wasn't there. I think he assumed that I'd come home to neglected vines and give up. When I didn't come home when he expected, I think he assumed I was dead, so he invested in the winery again. Now, the rent from our house, the wine—even low yield and inferior quality—will give him a large income if I keep costs down for him, and I'm trying."

"I suppose he sold a lot of that equipment your brother bought."

Avelino flushed. "I didn't even look to see. I don't think all of it, because Joe mentioned some. I bet he sold some, though—or could."

"So if the winery failed, he is the only one to lose." Callum sighed and leaned back, crossing his ankle over his knee. "Well, there goes the idea he's trying to sabotage it himself. Lyndon wouldn't risk money loss. That man's god is the almighty dollar."

"The only way he benefits from any loss is if it drives me away. He keeps it all then."

The men stared at one another. Slowly, Callum shook his head. "If he had plans to sell the place and you returned . . ."

Avelino stood and strolled to the door. "I'm going to talk to Mr. Welton. If anyone can get Ray to say if he was put up to it, his father can."

Bob Callum stood and gestured toward the door. "I'll drop you off. Perhaps the sight of my car will loosen the boy's lips as well. If nothing else, it'll save those ribs another trek across the valley."

*   *   *

The Welton home was even grander than Avelino remembered. Neoclassical architecture was flanked on all sides by perfectly manicured lawns. Callum waited until the housekeeper admitted Avelino before driving away slowly. It felt like a scene from a motion picture. All they needed now was a couple of bodyguards to step out and usher him into a dark-paneled study where—*Get a grip, Avelino*, he growled inwardly.

"I'd like to speak to Mr. Welton if I may."

"He's at home. I'll see . . ."

The housekeeper—skin darker than anyone else's he'd ever seen; he'd forgotten how dark—stopped short as Mr. Welton stepped into the foyer. "I'll see him in my study, Ruby Mae. Thank you."

Before Mr. Welton shut the door behind them, he asked, "What has Ray done now?"

"I hope nothing, but I do have to ask."

The study was dark paneled—exactly as his overly active imagination had pictured it—but no bodyguards waited to escort him from the property. Ed Welton gestured for him to sit, and instead of moving behind the desk, he took a chair opposite Avelino.

"What do you have to ask?"

"I need to know if Ray only came to la Viña de los Sueños to attack me again or if there was another reason."

"You have reason to think there was?"

The defeat in Mr. Welton's eyes surprised him, but Avelino answered honestly. "I do."

"Before I call him down, I want to know what you suspect. I don't know what's gotten into that boy."

"Someone, between Wednesday afternoon and this morning, broke into the storehouse and destroyed twenty barrels of wine. It was without question a deliberate act of vandalism."

Ed Welton stood to go, but Avelino asked another question, surprising himself. "Sir, do you have a personal objection to me or my family? Is that why Ray has taken such a dislike to me? If we have offended—or if this is about *tía* Jacinta . . ."

The man's laughter echoed through the room. "Jacinta. You think this is about her? That was thirty years ago, Avelino! I respect her for what she did. She made a better man of me by being the honorable girl she was."

"So you haven't held some kind of grudge or—"

"Jacinta said that, didn't she? She's a fine woman—was a great girl—but she has always had just a little too much of the Carrillo pride. I've spoken well of your family all of Ray's life. He idolized you as a boy—wanted to join the army to be like you. I said no, of course. He was too young. Not in age . . . maturity."

Embarrassed, Avelino nodded, his eyes on his shoes. "I see. I apologize. I meant no disrespect. I just can't understand why he took such a dislike to me."

"I can't tell you that. He didn't learn it from his mother or from me, that's for sure. He respected you before you left."

"And by the time I returned, I was just a 'dirty Mexican.'"

The man jerked his hand back from the doorknob. "He said that? I'll kill him! Your father was the noblest—your grandfather was . . ." He took a deep breath and opened the door. "I'll be right back."

Left alone in the room, Welton's words seemed to bounce off the walls, converging with other memories in an explosion of confusion in his mind. *Your father was the noblest—dirty Mexican— you're all lazy, worthless trash. Idolized you. Leave it for the Mexican; they make good janitors. Your grandfather was—*

By the time Mr. Welton returned, a surly-looking Ray in his wake, Avelino sat confused, panicked, and ready to leave. The sneer he expected on Ray's face when the young man saw the green around his eye didn't appear.

"Ray, Avelino has some questions for you. It goes without question that you should answer honestly."

"Without question," Ray echoed derisively.

"Someone broke into the storehouses between Wednesday afternoon and this morning. Do you know who is involved?"

"Why can't it be one of your people? Who says you didn't—?"

"Ray!"

"It's okay, Mr. Welton. I'll answer the question." Turning to Ray, Avelino explained. "If we make no money or if we lose money, it ruins the reputation of the winery. I have a little more than six years before it is mine again. I want it prosperous by then. To do that, I cannot lose thousands of dollars on a whim. Why would I sabotage my future?"

"Ray, answer the question. Do you know who did this?"

"What if I do?"

Before Mr. Welton could interrupt, Avelino asked the question he dreaded most. "Did someone pay you to do this? Did someone pay you to attack me and vandalize the barrels?"

They didn't need Ray to speak. The answer showed clearly in the boy's surprise.

Mr. Welton nearly exploded with rage. "What were you thinking? Who paid you? What did they pay you? You're going to work this off—every dime. You will be Avelino's personal slave until you pay back every penny."

"That isn't . . ." Avelino began.

"It is. He needs to learn that actions have consequences."

"I'm sure you will understand when I say I cannot risk my vines and my wine. He can work off his debt to Mr. Lyndon—his money is lost, not mine—however Mr. Lyndon sees fit, but not on Carrillo land."

A sickening pit lodged in his stomach as the boy's face changed. "That'll be better than working for a dirty—"

"That's enough, Ray."

CHAPTER TWENTY-EIGHT

TE AMO

Ruby Mae drove him home at Ed Welton's insistence. The woman chattered all the way there about everything from the price of eggs to how "her boy" seemed to have lost his way in the past few years. Avelino hardly listened. His mind still swirled with ideas that made no sense and yet had to be true. Lyndon paid Ray and his friends to attack him and destroy the wine. *That's why he was surprised it was twenty barrels. He'd already counted the cost.*

". . . let him join."

"Ray? He's not mature enough to handle it."

"My daddy said war made men out of boys. That boy has been coddled by his mama for far too long. Mmm hmm. He needs a good dose of put-in-his-place by a drill sergeant."

Drill sergeants can beat the fool out of a soldier or beat the life out of him. "I suppose."

"You look like you're healin'. You put some Vicks on that at night so's you can breathe good."

Welton didn't have a grudge against their family. That made more sense than the idea that he did, but it left things unresolved.

Why had Ray, who supposedly looked up to him, gotten involved in something so ridiculous?

Welton, Helen, the people in town—no one but possibly Ray and his buddies had ever objected. He'd hurt Amelia for nothing, and yet . . . Something Ruby Mae said grabbed his attention. "What was that?"

"I heard about your 'nouncement at your church. You're a good boy, Avelino. Your mama raised you right. That girl ain't worth the trouble if she can't see what a fine man you are."

"Ruby Mae, Miss Kearns would go out on a date with me tomorrow if I asked her. I told people that on Sunday. She hasn't rejected me."

The woman pulled up to the house and stared at him. "Then you'd better not let her go."

He stared at Ruby Mae. "I don't understand."

"That girl has been taking criticism and rebuke without complaint for months. If she did that without lettin' on that you're—"

"Thank you, Ruby Mae." He eased himself gingerly from the car and waved. "I appreciate you taking me home."

"Mmm hmm. You're a fool, Avelino. A good man, but a fool."

He saw Amelia hanging clothes as he started up the stairs. Her wave, natural and carefree, choked him. Without a word, he nodded and continued upstairs, seeking out the comfort of his bed. Eyes closed, he revisited every thought, every word, everything he'd ever heard about him, his family, his culture. It all poured into him, the ugliness rising to the top like pomace in the must at the winery. He could push it down, stirring it into his heart, and somehow hope that it would make him a richer man for understanding it. Or he could skim it off—less ugliness but also less depth of character.

Sergeant Miller—the man still held too much control over his mental state. He couldn't continue to allow bigots from his past make his life miserable. It was ridiculous. Shoving himself off the bed and fighting the desire to scream with the renewed pain, Avelino took a moment to regain his composure and then retraced his steps. *I must talk to Amelia.*

She stood at the clothesline, folding the last of the laundry, when he made it to the bottom of the stairs. By the time he crossed the yard, Avelino couldn't do it. She'd despise him—not that he would blame her. He offered to help carry in the basket, earning him a rebuke for not taking care of himself, and strolled past the yard and up to the old *secoya*. She followed him there a few minutes later.

"Avelino? Is it bad? Granddad said there was some trouble in the storehouse."

"It's bad but not devastating."

She stepped closer, peering into his face. "Your eye looks better. In the shade I can hardly see the bruising."

"That is the advantage of brown skin—it hides things."

They stood staring out over the rows and rows of vines—thousands of them. Amelia spoke first. "It's so beautiful. I know that up close everything is loveliest when the grapes are about to be harvested, but I love this time best. The leaves are so green, and the rows look like life itself."

The words choked him. They were so like things his *mamá* often said. Avelino glanced at her, knowing his troubled thoughts would show in his eye, and tried to say something. He couldn't.

"Avelino, what is it? Surely—"

"I can't do it anymore."

There it was in her eyes—fear—or was it anger? She asked the obvious question. "Do what? What can't you do?"

"Fight—fight what I feel." His head lowered; he stared at his shoes, defeated.

"Feel about what?"

She knew what he meant, but he didn't blame her for asking. *You are a coward, Avelino Carrillo. Tell her. She will feel used—tossed aside when it is inconvenient and then . . . Let her make that decision. It is hers to make, but you owe her the truth.* His mind softened its tirade against him. *She will understand, Avelino. She loves you. For some inexplicable and* loco *reason, Amelia loves you.*

"Avelino?"

"*Te amo*—I love you."

She smiled. "I know."

"I didn't mean to hurt you. I didn't want to."

"I know that too." Tears filled Amelia's eyes. "I knew why you did it. I understood." She tried to smile. "You were wrong, but I understood."

"Why did you—why . . . ?" He couldn't ask. He wanted to, but he couldn't.

"I love you. What else would I do?"

"You didn't then. You couldn't have," he protested.

"Perhaps I didn't, but I knew I would." Her tears splashed onto her cheeks, but Amelia brushed them away impatiently. "It was only a matter of time before you realized how few people are really so narrow-minded."

"I've begun to realize that my sergeant had a lot to do with it. He really hated us."

"Who?"

"The 'dirty Mexicans' who got lumped in with the nice 'white' folks. He wanted us segregated, like the Negroes."

"Ridiculous—on both fronts. When a man puts his life on the line for his country, no one has any right to say he is beneath any of the other men risking their lives."

"Thank you."

"*De nada.*"

They stood beneath the giant tree, the branches far above their heads, and stared out over the vines once more. His hand, tentative yet sure, reached for hers and held it close as he reveled in the realization of a lifetime of dreams come true. "I feel guilty," he whispered.

"Why?"

Why had he spoken? She might be hurt or insulted or, worse, she might think he wasn't sincere. "It's hard to explain."

"Well, you feel guilty if you must. I intend to enjoy my happiness. I thought it would take years. I thought you would find another girl—one like Margretta—and I would have to watch you with her until you accepted what I saw in you."

"And what did you see?"

Those eyes, beautiful green eyes, stared at him with such faith. *Faith in God or in me?* he wondered. *Likely both.* "That you loved *me.*"

He started to protest but realized she was right. As long as he loved her, he wouldn't have married anyone else. Some men could, but a Carrillo could not.

"Another story to add to the family collection—the story of foolish Avelino who almost lost the beautiful señorita with hair like roses."

"Carrots."

* * *

Joe knocked and opened the door as he entered. "Avelino? Are you . . . ? There you are. How're the ribs?"

"Sore but better. I can sit without wanting to scream now . . . just a groan. Standing, not so much."

"Amelia is singing again."

His mustache twitched as he tried to hide the smile he knew he couldn't. "Is she?"

"Want to tell me about it?"

"I thought she would want to—"

"I did too," Joe interjected, "but she says for me to talk to you about it."

"I—we . . ." he floundered, unsure what to say. What had they agreed to? What had happened? "I don't know what to say." He swallowed hard. "I love her."

"I know."

"That's what she said."

Joe frowned. "What?"

"When I told her. I said, '*Te amo*,' and she said, 'I know' just like you did."

"We both thought it would take much longer."

"The objections I saw—they were real. Well, they were real to me. I didn't want her unhappy for life. Better hurt now than every day forever."

He expected Joe to blast him for his foolishness, but the older man just nodded. "I respected you for it. I didn't agree, but I respected you for it."

This time he laughed, wincing at the pain such an instinctive thing caused. "That's almost what she said."

"What made you change your mind?"

"I realized I was wrong. I was seeing innocent—or mostly so—actions through the eyes of a man whose opinion I could never respect."

"Ed Welton is—"

"Not that man. He's a good man, Joe. He isn't behind this garbage. I think I know who is, though."

"We'll talk about that later. I want to know what this means."

"What what means?"

"You tell me." Joe pulled up Avelino's chair, turned it around, and sat on it backwards, his arms resting on the back. "You told her you love her, but what does that mean?"

He hadn't allowed himself to think that far. There was still the issue of his situation, the trouble brewing, and his secret. He could start there. "Before I can even think about that—about a future—I have something to tell her that could ruin it all."

"You want to run that by me, don't you?"

"Yes, sir."

Joe watched him for the better part of a minute—almost examining him. "Will you take off that patch, son?"

The idea galled him, but not as much as the reaction he expected. He pulled it up over his head and held it in his lap, never taking his eye off Joe's face. The older man didn't flinch. "It isn't as bad as I expected. In time . . ."

"It'll only be gruesome instead of grotesque?"

A pause; how long it lasted Avelino didn't know. Both men burst out laughing again, this time with groans of pain between guffaws.

"It's not that bad. It's not good. I'm sorry that it happened, but you're alive, your mind is all there, and your body is mostly whole. Not all men can say that."

"That's true. Not sure about my mind sometimes, though. The flashbacks seem to get more intense the further apart they are. I'd rather have them daily if it meant I could control them as easily as I did after that first one."

"I know what it looks like—that mental damage that comes from battle. I'm so glad yours is manageable." Joe rubbed his nose as if to signal the coming change. "Now that thing that's troubling you. Care to share it?"

"She's going to hate me. She won't trust me, and who can blame her?"

Joe inched the chair forward a little. "Why won't she? What is it?"

"You've heard of Cherith Tandy . . ."

"El pelo como rosas?"

"Green eyes, red hair," Avelino sighed. "Yes, like roses. I was an impressionable child. I heard the stories and grew enamored with the idea of it all. I wanted my own wife with red hair who tried to learn *español*, just as Cherith did a hundred years ago."

"And along comes Amelia as if ordered from the Sears and Roebuck, eh?"

"Yeah."

"Wasn't there a girl once before—Margaret?"

"Margretta, yes."

"But you say it with inflection. I take it she was Mexican?"

"Yes."

Joe continued, a smile on his face. "With red hair and green eyes?"

"No."

"Then if you could think yourself in love with a girl who didn't have everything you'd ever dreamed of, why should Amelia be offended that God saw fit to give her the things you did?"

"That seems too simple." He knew he sounded petty and ridiculous, but Avelino couldn't help feeling as if he were headed for disaster.

"Then tell her, and see what happens."

"Just as she's happy again."

"I think you'll find that being your dream girl is not something most young ladies resent."

"You really think she'll understand?"

Joe's eyes crinkled with his grin. "Certain of it."

"Now if we can solve the little matter of Lyndon being behind the attacks on me and the winery and the issue of church, all obstacles might be gone. Thankfully, we've got six years to do it."

"Lyndon? You're kidd—actually, that makes sense." Joe seemed lost in thought for a moment but jerked back as he asked, "Did you say six years?"

"Well, a little more, but yeah."

"You want to marry her."

"Of course."

As if determined to understand the incomprehensible, Joe added once more, "In six years."

"Right."

To Avelino's surprise, Joe stood and replaced the chair. "Come on down for supper. She'll probably have some kind of incredible dessert. We've got to celebrate."

As Joe opened the door to leave, Avelino could have sworn he heard the man say, "And she thought getting him to come around was the hard part. Poor girl."

* * *

His throat thickened with emotion as Amelia settled next to him in the window seat and made herself comfortable for another night's tale. The chicken scratches in her notebook did little to distract him, though he tried to focus on them instead of the nearness of her. He stole a glance at Joe and stifled a groan. *He's actually enjoying this.*

Her eyes met his as he gazed down at her again. "What are you waiting for?"

"I . . . I have to think of where to start." It was true—a partial truth, but truth nonetheless.

"Marco just arrived. He flirted in Louisiana, left part of his heart there, and is now admiring Cherith. I am beginning to think he's a bit doll dizzy."

Avelino's lips twisted, amused at the idea of a girl-crazy Marco. "I don't think Cherith Tandy would have recognized 'her' Marco in that description." *There. That'll send you after a nice little red herring.*

"Oh! He *was* a Carrillo. I hope Cherith didn't marry a man who just wanted her for her money."

"'Melia?"

She didn't even raise her head from her notebook as she sighed and said, "I'll shut my trap now."

"Thank you."

Laughing, Avelino began his tale. "Of course, they couldn't just leave the next day. They had to pack, to sell their property and any possessions they couldn't take with them, and as they worked to do that, Marco forged a friendship with the older man . . ."

CHAPTER TWENTY-NINE

RETURN TO LEAVE

July 1839

The property had been sold, many of the animals as well, and most of the household goods were gone. Only a wagon, two horses, and what they could fit in four trunks remained. Cherith packed and unpacked each one half-a-dozen times in order to fit in as much as possible. The rest they would leave behind.

As he and Edgar led Daisy the cow to its new home, the older man asked about his journey to Texas. "How was the trip—the boat? I'm not looking forward to that."

"It was good most of the time. I liked the feeling of the wind in my face, but Cape Horn. *¡Increíble!* I have never been so terrified in my life. The waves . . . I do not know how we survived. They say it is worse coming back."

The man seemed to age just listening. "You'll have to tell me if that's true once we get past."

Marco kept quiet. He did not wish to go back. He thought only of New Orleans and of Isobel, Señor Gálvez's daughter.

"Yes."

"What is it, son? You seem quiet all of a sudden." Then, as if prescient, Edgar laughed. "Ah, who is she? Where did you meet her?"

"Well—"

"Oh, I know! It's the one in New Orleans—the feisty daughter."

"How did you guess?"

"A man," Edgar said, amused, "does not become indignant when people ignore a nasty-tempered woman unless he is interested."

Marco began to regret telling stories of his journey and the señorita near New Orleans who had intrigued him.

"She is the daughter of a wealthy man. I have little—only what Señor Carrillo paid me to come. Everything else I have I left at home."

They arrived at Daisy's new home and made a swift transaction. On their return, Edgar asked a few questions and then offered a solution.

"You could sell me your things—give me a letter of ownership. I could pick them up when I hit Yerba Buena."

"What I own isn't worth much, but I will think about it."

During the rest of their walk back to the Tandy place, the men heard only the chattering of birds, the rustling of grasses, and the crunch of their boots as they made their way back to the yard.

Cherith waved cheerfully from her place in the wagon. "I did it! I got everything we need in the trunks!"

Edgar beamed at his daughter, praising her for whatever those words meant, and turned to Marco. "We'll be sorry not to have you with us. I'm sure you'll be very happy."

* * *

Her pen paused as she waited for him to continue, but Avelino took a sip of his water and nudged her knee with his. "Now what do you think of Marco being a Carrillo?"

"She said no, didn't she?" Amelia's eager eyes searched his face for confirmation. When she didn't find it, she frowned. "Well, just go on then. You obviously like to torment me."

"I thought I'd stop there. From here on out, my family has told the stories from Cherith's perspective. It seemed a good break."

"You wouldn't—you would! Granddad, tell him he can't do that!" she insisted. This time, her voice did rise—if just a little. Before Joe could respond, she sighed. "I was going to make a lemon cake tomorrow. I don't think I will now."

Avelino ignored her and appealed to Joe. "What do you think? Isn't this a good place to stop?"

"It would be—if I didn't want a piece of that cake," the older man hinted.

Amelia crossed her arms and glared at her grandfather.

"Okay, and because I'd like to know what Cherith thought of it all."

With an exaggerated sigh, Avelino stretched and began again. "Of course, they left their home in Texas to return to Virginia—a place they also once called home . . ."

*   *   *

The trip home—could she call it home if she would just leave again?—felt achingly familiar to a girl who had left it all behind at such a young age. Five years they'd been gone. Five years without her mother, her family, or her friends. Her excitement was tempered only by the understanding that it was temporary. They would stay only long enough to book passage on a ship. This time she realized that it would be unlikely that they would see any of them soon—if ever.

Papa would stay for a while—if I asked him. He would understand. That thought carried her out of Texas, through Louisiana, where they left Marco at a ranch west of the city, and into Mississippi.

The heat beat down on them. The jostling of the wagon bounced her so badly that most days she walked as much as she could—just as she had on the way there. This time, however, her boots gave out. It took a week to get new ones made, and then another of riding most of the day to break them in.

"Papa?"

Edgar glanced down beside the wagon as they climbed a hill in North Carolina. "Hmm?"

"Will we understand anyone in California? Don't they all speak Spanish?" She flushed. "Well, you will, but will I?"

"I think there are probably enough *americanos* there to give you someone to talk to."

"But shouldn't I learn?"

Her father shook his head slowly. "I don't think so—not yet. If you can't speak, you can't be insulted; you can't be pushed into a conversation that is unwise. Until I see what life is like there, I think it's better if you just stick with English. We'll have lessons as soon as I see what kind of place it is. For all I know, we might turn right around and come home."

"But Papa! Mr. Avelino! He was such a kind man. And Marco! Sweet Marco and his temperamental señorita! How can you say that about him? He is from California."

"They have all seemed like good men—honorable—but what do we really know of any of them? Avelino, yes. He was a gentleman. Marco seems to be, but how little time we had to see if his goodness went to the core or if it covered rottenness."

"Now you are getting philosophical! I'll learn in California. It'll give me something to do there."

"Grapes. We'll have grapes to do. Lots of grapes. That'll give you much to do."

"How many grapes do you think there are?" The idea of grapes in long rows like fields sounded strange and almost mysterious to her. Grapes were delicious—at least the wild ones that she'd eaten back home had been wonderful.

"I don't know. There's a lot of land, though. We can expand. According to the letter Marco brought, there's enough money to live on if we're frugal. So we can afford to put any money we make back into the vines. In ten or twenty years, we could have a full commercial enterprise. We'll have to learn to make wine, but . . ."

She laughed as they crested the hill. "Let me in. I'm not running down that hill. Not in this heat." Once on the wagon seat, Cherith added, "We're going to grow a lot of grapes, crush a lot of grapes, pour it all into bottles or jugs, and then pour it out on the ground when it's nasty, aren't we?"

"Probably—for a few years anyway. Maybe the wine will make good fertilizer." Her father sighed. "It's good that there are cattle there. At least I know cattle. If the grapes fail, we can fall back on beef. Beef will always be a good business."

"Maybe, Papa, but you have to admit grapes do sound more romantic somehow."

The road wound around a hill and out of North Carolina into Virginia. They were almost home.

Cherith was snatched from her reverie when her father said, "The romance of California . . . it'll be your romance too, I suppose."

"My romance?" As a girl of sixteen, the idea excited yet terrified her. "And who will I meet in this exotic place? A young cowboy who doesn't speak a word of English? Will I accept his proposal without knowing it? How silly."

Despite her flippant words, a small smile tickled the corners of her lips. There was something irrationally exciting in the idea of marriage to a dashing Californio with dark eyes, murmuring his love amid the rows of grapes, perhaps serenading her in the moonlight.

She shrugged off such nonsensical thoughts. "Honestly, Papa. The things you say."

CHAPTER THIRTY

FAMILY SECRETS

June 1946

It was the strangest argument in the history of arguments as far as Avelino was concerned. She stood before him, eyes flashing just as his *mamá's* would have, but without a word. And in the exact way she'd listened to his explanations without the emotional outburst he'd expected, she now argued with him on the one thing he couldn't change. Marriage. *Why did I mention it at all?*

"Come on, Amelia. You know this isn't what I want, but I have no money—none to support a wife with anyway. I get paid one day per week. Seven fifty a week—and only if I can work that day. It's not enough for two people to eat on, and where would we live? Do you really think I'd make my wife live in that grungy room above the garage—use an outhouse?"

"Because Granddad would object to us sleeping in the house, of course."

Had he not seen the sarcasm in the twist of her lips and the frustration in her eyes, he would have thought she didn't care. He'd have to pay close attention to her to know how she truly felt about things. He'd have to listen to her words rather than her tone, watch her face. What would have annoyed him as a boy now intrigued him. Life with her would never be dull, but in a way he'd never imagined.

"I should be taking care of Joe, not the other way around."

"So I'll get a job. I'll work to pay the rent and the food. Granddad can save his money. We'll make it work."

"You know why I can't do that. I know you know."

Yes, she knew, but even as he spoke, he realized that she disagreed. Amelia stood, arms crossed over her chest, and never wavered. In his mind the discussion was settled; in hers it wasn't.

We must look like stone statues, petrified in some calamity. I'm hurting her again. "May I hold you?"

She stepped into his arms without hesitation. "You know, if you hadn't told me that you've always dreamed of a wife with red hair and green eyes, I'd swear you were trying to get rid of me again."

"I told you what?" *When did I tell her?*

"The last time you told me you were distancing from us, you said you'd always dreamed of a wife with hair and eyes like mine. I assumed you meant like Cherith's."

"And that didn't annoy you?"

"Was it supposed to?" She smiled. "Because if it was, you failed."

He pressed his cheek against her hair, preparing himself for the idea of six very long years. "What kind of man would I be if I married a woman with no way to feed her?"

That he'd spoken aloud became evident when she answered a question he'd meant only for himself. "The kind of man who trusts that God will take care of that."

"I didn't mean to—"

"I know, but I answered anyway. It's true."

Joe stepped in the door. "Now that's a sight a granddad likes to see. When's the weddin'?"

"Six years, three months, and twenty-three and a half days if he gets his way." Amelia snuggled closer at his chuckle.

"Not that she's counting or anything."

He held her close, pleading with Joe for support. It didn't come.

"I give it two months—tops."

"Joe!"

She slipped from his arms and snuggled her grandfather. "Isn't he the best granddad ever?"

"Let's eat." Joe nudged Avelino toward the table. "A man is more tractable when his belly is full."

"I'm not changing my mind."

The Kearnses laughed.

"He is so innocent," Amelia snickered as she carried a platter of meatloaf and roasted vegetables and set it before the men. She eyed the table for several seconds and turned. "Forgot the gravy."

"She forgot the gravy." Joe reached for the platter. "The world comes to an end without gravy."

Amelia nudged his head as she passed. "I could let this end up in your lap." To Avelino, she remarked, "I'd certainly hear it if I didn't make gravy."

He couldn't respond. His throat swelled with emotion as he watched them banter. Instead, he took a bite, the flavor of the food overshadowed by something in the room—in his heart. *Amor*. Love filled his family's home again.

He raised his glass of sweet tea, smiling at the difference between his family's customary wine with dinner and the Kearnses' tea, and said *"¡Salud!"*

Joe winked at his daughter as he raised his glass as well. Amelia raised hers hesitantly and asked, "What does *salud* mean, Granddad?"

"I think tonight it means 'name the date.'"

* * *

Joe rose from his chair and bade them good night almost as soon as they finished up the supper dishes. "It was a long day, my back aches, so I'm going to go to bed early, I think." He paused at Amelia's crestfallen expression and added, "But you go ahead and tell her the next part of your story. I'll get her to tell me in the morning."

Avelino saw it—eagerness—but Amelia sighed and shook her head. "You should hear it from him. He tells it better than I do. I can wait."

Joe's lips twisted in a repressed smile. "Okay then. I'll see you in the morning." A moment later he heard him add, "Half an hour, 'Melia. He needs to go upstairs in half an hour."

They grinned at one another from across the room until she jumped up. "Let's walk."

"We can't make it to Hank's and back in half an hour."

"We can stroll through the vines. It's beautiful out there."

She grabbed a sweater from the back of her chair, threw it over her shoulders, and looped the sleeves in front, before tugging at his hand until he followed.

Hand in hand they strolled down the hill and over to the vines. He wanted to discuss how they could possibly marry sooner, but the magic of vineyards in the moonlight, combined with the wonder of having every dream of his heart surrounding him, silenced all thought, all words.

"Do you think Cherith Tandy wanted to come to California? Do you think she was happy to get on that ship, or was she terrified?"

"That is a story for tomorrow."

"But they were in Virginia for so long. She got to see friends, spend more time with family—and with money that she probably had never had before. I can't imagine how terrifying it would be to climb up onto that gangplank and wave good-bye to life as you knew it."

"Is that how it was?" He squeezed her hand. "Was there a boy with broad shoulders and a laugh that melted your heart?"

"Not until you came."

He pulled her close and kissed her temple. "Right answer. But truthfully, it had to be hard to leave."

"It was. Mama died; Daddy got worse until Granddad said we had to go."

"Daddy? Why did I think both your parents had passed?"

Amelia leaned her head against his shoulder as they paused at the end of a row. "Daddy fought in the Great War. Came back all wrong in the head. They told Mama he wouldn't recognize her, but he did—only her."

"Not you?" Avelino shook his head. "I guess you wouldn't have been born yet."

She leaned against his chest, staring out over the acres of vines. "At first Mama was sick—the influenza was so bad that year. They wouldn't let him see her, not that he asked. Grandmom said he used to sit in the chair, staring out at nothing. People walked right in front of him and he didn't even blink. Sat that way for weeks, except for when he caught something in the corner of his eye. Then he'd jump from the chair, dive across the room, tackle whoever was closest, and either smother them trying to protect them, or start whaling on 'em."

"Joe told me about him, but . . ." He stopped short.

"Granddad called him my cousin? He was, in a way. Mama's third cousin by marriage, or something like that. It's easier to talk about a cousin back home than explain why you left your granddaughter's father there."

Avelino wrapped his arms around her waist, leaned his chin on her head, and asked, "Why did you leave him? How can he live alone?"

"He's not alone. Aunt Ella has him now."

"Wait, but your name—it's Kearns, but your mother—"

"I've gone by Kearns most of my life. The Colberts didn't care much for us. We were beneath their notice. They didn't care enough to take care of Daddy, until it got to where he couldn't live with us anymore."

"Why not?"

An owl hooted nearby, changing the tone of the night symphony. "I said Daddy only recognized Mama . . . and it's true, but it was more than that. He didn't seem to realize anyone else was around. If she needed to go somewhere or get something done, we all had to help her get past without him seeing her or he'd want . . ." She sighed. "Well, he'd—"

"I think I understand."

"Whew."

"I just don't understand why that meant you had to leave."

Her head buried itself into his chest a little deeper—how, he didn't know.

"But I was getting older, and I look just like Mama did. I've heard all my life how I'm just the spit and image of her."

"A revolting comparison that I have never understood." His heart grew sick at what he knew she would say.

"You can imagine what happened. I walked by one day, he thought I was Mama, and it took Grandmom and Granddad both to hold him back so I could get out of the house. We couldn't let him see me anymore. He thought I was Mama." She sighed. "We had to leave."

"That poor man."

He felt his shirt grow damp as they stood—much longer than Joe had allowed. He didn't care.

Amelia stuffed her hand in her pocket and pulled out a handkerchief. "I miss him. He wasn't a bad daddy. Not really. He would hold me when I was a baby if they put me in his arms. He didn't talk to me or even look at me usually, but he held me close, and they said it was the only way I'd stop wailing sometimes."

"I was about to say that it might have been better if God had taken him, but maybe not."

"When I was little, if I got a scrape or a bruise, or if some girl teased me about my awful hair—"

"Hey . . ."

"That's how it was. I could go to Daddy, crawl up in his lap, and he'd hold me until I felt better. No one could hold you and make you feel wonderful again like him." Her head rose and she gazed up at him. "But I think you're going to change all that."

"I hope so." He swallowed hard. "But maybe not. Maybe I'll be different enough that it's not comparable."

"Probably."

"I'm so sorry that you had to leave him."

"Someday, Avelino. Someday I'll be older than Mama was—different. Maybe I'll get chubby after babies, or I'll go gray early. Then maybe I can send for him, and we can take care of him."

"I would like that." He pulled away and took her hand. "We've stayed out over double what your granddad said we could."

"He'll understand. He just said that to make you want to take over the job of telling me what to do."

"Is it a job?"

Her laughter filled the air around them. "How successful have you been?"

"Good point."

The final steps to the house, past the *secoya*, and up to the patio grew slower with each second that passed. Her hand reached for the doorknob, but he stopped her.

"Amelita . . ."

The regrets that had bombarded his heart as he rode transport ships to and from the Philippines now amused him. All those wasted self-recriminations. He had been sure that someday he would find another girl—one who loved him regardless of his wealth or lack of it—and the memory of a few stolen kisses from Margretta would burn his heart and heap guilt on him. Instead, he marveled at the gift of God in a perfect choice for him.

"I love you."

She smiled, and even with the cover overhead, he saw the love in her eyes as she kissed his cheek, murmuring, "I know. Good night, Avelino."

CHAPTER THIRTY-ONE

YES

As the sun rose, Avelino sat at his table-turned-desk and recounted his money. *No matter how many times you count it, it'll still be eighteen dollars and sixty-five cents.* Eight months. Over two hundred forty dollars. Only eighteen sixty-five to show for it. *Living is expensive, even without a lot of actual expenses.*

No amount of stating the obvious would change the fact that he had to spend almost every dime he made on food or sometimes clothing.

Row upon row of expenditures stared back at him. With the exception of a dozen nickels for sodas, every penny he'd spent had been a necessity. *You could have made your own tamales—your own soup.*

Sunlight filled the room, prompting Avelino to reach over and snap off the lamp. *Should be giving Joe something to help with the light bill too.*

Avelino sat there, working the numbers in a dozen different ways, hoping to find something that would give him the opportunity to save more of his weekly earnings. *We could get married earlier if I knew how to live on less. Or, if I saved even a bit more, I might be able to buy her an electric icebox. It could be a wedding present.* That thought brought a hint of excitement. *If I managed to save enough for a new icebox, then we'd have enough to get married.* That excitement fizzled as he realized how long it would take him to save up that much at his current rate.

He turned the page, staring at the numbers that represented four years of military service—four years of separation from the life he loved. *It's enough—more than enough. I could just use only what I absolutely had to and replace it all when we get the vines back. Maybe I could get a night job too.* His father's words slammed into his heart at that thought. *"Never let yourself trade truly important things for money. Learn to live without it before you do that."*

Discouraged, Avelino folded up his hand-drawn ledger and carried it to his drawer. He slid it under his undershirts and grabbed a fresh pair of socks—socks his Amelia had washed, hung, and folded for him when she had no real expectation of much more than a begrudging "thanks" for her efforts. *You were rude to her. You should apologize.* Mamá *would be so ashamed.*

He tried to dress quickly, but his ribs ached—screamed really— begging him to go back to bed and rest. *Hank would understand.* A glance at his drawer across the room changed the direction of his thoughts. *Hank might, but Amelia is counting on you to do everything you can to shorten the wait. This isn't how you do that.*

With that thought, he forced himself to crack a couple of eggs into the little skillet on the hot plate and poured himself a glass of milk.

Amelia knocked just as he sat down to eat. "I thought—oh. I'm too late."

"For?"

"I thought you might want to eat with us. I made biscuits and gravy—been saving some pork grease for 'em."

He meant to resist, opened his mouth to decline, but the eagerness in her eyes stopped him. "I could probably relieve you of a couple biscuits if you think you have any to spare." At her smile he added, "Thanks for including me."

In the doorway she hesitated, opened her mouth as if to speak, and closed it again. "See you downstairs."

The rat-a-tat-tat of her feet on the stairs sent his heart racing. Avelino braced himself, fighting back the expected disorientation and waves of panic that he knew had accompanied that sound several times. It didn't come—none of it came. As he carried his dishes down to the laundry sink in the garage, questions bombarded him. *Is it because I expected it? I was alert and not caught unaware? Or are they getting better? Or I'm getting better at controlling them?*

* * *

The roar of an engine drowned out Frank Sinatra on the radio, but the crooner's plea of "five minutes more" had already driven Avelino to the brink of frustration. *Rub it in, Frankie. Just rub it in. How about five years more? Plus one!*

A Lincoln Continental convertible pulled up to the pump. Two giggling girls and a pair of fellows with them laughed and joked as Avelino began to "Fill 'er up!" He washed the windshield, but before he could finish, the man behind the wheel pointed to the right front tire. "We went through mud on that side. Are the whitewalls clean?"

Even before he looked, Avelino pulled out the hose and turned it on, kinking the end to keep it from splattering all over the ground. The words hit him just as he went to spray the walls of the tires. "My, his face could use a good wash too—filthy."

Jaw clenched to keep his words in check, Avelino sprayed the tires. His hands shook with repressed anger. His teeth ground together, and the laughing giggles of one of the girls pointing at him welled up resolve in his heart—*Don't let them see you react. They win if they get to you. Don't let—*

". . . that happen?"

Avelino stood, ready to take their money and send them back to wherever they'd come from—Stanford probably. The young man's eyes didn't leave his face.

"*Lo siento*, but I didn't hear the question."

"How did that happen—your eye?" The fellow flushed and began apologizing. "Sorry. Rude question. Just thought you might've been over there."

Before he could answer, the redhead—*She'd have to have the red hair*, he mused—passed him her handkerchief. "Would you mind getting that wet for me? Like I said, my face is filthy—could use a good wash, don't you think?"

Overt flirtation coupled with a decidedly dusty nose left little doubt of his mistake. *You're looking for an excuse to prove that the Sergeant Millers of this world get to decide what your life is like. Get over it.*

"Gigi, stop flirting. You're embarrassing him." The man in the backseat nudged Gigi and turned back to Avelino. "Ignore my sister. She's a nice girl, but . . ."

"He's got a doll of his own," the other fellow insisted. "He hasn't given either of the girls a second glance."

It took a moment for him to relax and accept their good-natured teasing. As he jerked the hose around the front of the car, Avelino tried to relax the muscles in his face and shoulders. "I do have a girl-friend—fiancée actually." He smiled to himself as he added, "I've never said that yet."

"Having second thoughts?" the driver asked with an exaggerated wink at the girl next to him.

"John's such a fathead." The girl tossed her hair over her shoulder and waited until Avelino stood before she added, "Don't let him get under your skin. He's a nice guy and all that, but he's got a kooky sense of humor."

The redhead—*Her name's Gigi*, he reminded himself—touched his arm as he passed. "When'd you ask her—your girl? When'd you propose?"

Avelino started to say, "Couple nights ago," but the words came out garbled.

The occupants of the vehicle spoke in near-perfect unison. "What?"

Avelino sprayed, not even trying to make himself understood. "I—well, I didn't exactly ask, I guess. We just talked about it as—"

The girls protested, and even the guys shook their heads.

John waited until Avelino hung up the hose and removed the pump nozzle from the gas tank before he pulled out his billfold and offered Avelino a few bills. "No dice! You can't do it. The rest of us fellows'll have to bite the bullet and ask."

As the car drove down the road, leaving a dust cloud in its wake, Avelino shook his head and went to fetch the broom to sweep the entrance to the little building. "Why wouldn't I *want* to ask her? What's so hard about that?"

* * *

As he helped her hang a large blanket on the line, his arrogant question mocked him. *This is what's so hard! I have every reason to know her answer, and there's still that hesitation—that question of "What if she says no?"*

"I can tell something's wrong. I'm not waiting ten years, Avelino. You should know that right now. We'll go for a license tomorrow, and you can get over your pride first. This is getting crazy."

"I wasn't trying to postpone anything," he protested. "I was trying to—well." His throat swelled, his heart raced, and twice in the space of seconds Avelino caught himself gasping for air. "I realized today that . . ." *Don't say that! It'll sound like you feel obligated to ask instead of wanting to. Remember how you* wanted *to back when you were so sure it would be easy? Do it!*

She shoved a clothespin onto the blanket, pinning it to the line, and crossed her arms over her chest. "What'd I do?"

"Besides agree to marry a guy who didn't bother to ask, nothing."

Amelia's nose wrinkled, producing an adorable picture he hadn't yet seen. "What?"

"We talked about marriage—discussed how, when, and when again. I never bothered to ask you." He dropped his head and shoved his hands in his pockets. "*Lo siento*, Amelita. So very presumptuous of me. So very arrogant of me."

The music of twilight crept through the vines and settled around them. Avelino swallowed twice, three times. He waited. Amelia didn't respond at all. He chanced a glance her way and found her smiling.

"What is it?"

"There's one way to fix that, Avelino."

Befuddled by the affection in her eyes, the warmth of her voice, and the nebulous idea that something incomprehensible had begun, Avelino asked the only reasonable question to present itself. "Fix what?"

She shook her head, waiting.

"Oh." Once more the emotions of his heart filled his throat, choking him. As he tried to find the words that he knew could never be adequate, Avelino reached for her hand and tugged her close. His arms wrapped around her, and he buried his head in her hair. "I'm sure you know how many days—probably how many hours too—until we can marry. When we can, will you?"

Of all the replies she could have given, of all that he might have predicted, her simple "Yes" spoke most eloquently.

How long they stood there, the blankets she'd fought to wash all day blocking them from view, he didn't know, but Joe's voice calling out for a pan of popcorn and a story broke the magic of the moment.

He stepped back, took her hand, and led her toward the house. "You get your book. I'll make the popcorn. Then I'll tell you about the trip around Cape Horn and how Cherith and Edgar tied themselves to the beams belowdecks to keep from being slammed against the walls of the ship."

"Shh! Don't tell me until I have my pen," she protested with a playful shove. "I want to hear about their arrival in California!"

"Well, they stopped in Acapulco first . . ."

CHAPTER THIRTY-TWO

AN UNFORGETTABLE JOURNEY

November 1840

With the terrifying trip around the Cape still fresh in their memories, Acapulco Bay seemed even more of a tropical paradise to the Tandys. Warm, lush—Cherith had never seen anything like it. Unlike during the stops at the ports along the eastern seaboard of South America, now her father led her from the ship with the rest of the crew and passengers, determined to enjoy a few days on dry land. They giggled as they struggled to walk without stumbling.

"Works both ways—getting used to the motion of the boat and then getting used to the stillness of land. My cousin calls it dock rock." Sammy, a young, freckled seaman, beamed as he shared his information.

"I'd heard of sea legs, of course," Edgar said, smiling at his daughter's chagrin, "but until now . . ." He stumbled and nearly fell over. "Until now I couldn't really grasp the idea."

Sammy winked at Cherith and said, "You'll get over it just in time to board the ship again."

Her mouth went dry, and her cheeks pinked. Cherith glanced at her father, silently begging for help, but he stared up at a seagull soaring overhead. After several stammered starts, she murmured, "I'll remember that."

Looping her arm in her father's, Cherith turned toward the inn. "I'm hungry, Papa. What do you say to finding some more of that delicious—what was it called? You know, the meatball soup." Over her shoulder, she added to Sammy, "Thank you. We'll see you on the boat, if not before."

She walked away, chattering about the soup and trying to imitate Edgar's pronunciation—*albóndigas*. "That is such an interesting name—*albóndigas*. What does it mean?"

"Meatball—so original." Edgar nudged her. "You handled that very well, my dear."

"Did I? I felt terribly rude."

"Sometimes," her father said in that special tone that meant he was about to impart some little tidbit of wisdom, "young women must learn how to dispense a little kind rudeness."

"Isn't that a bit of an oxymoron, Papa? A kind rudeness?"

"It is kind," Edgar explained, "in how you deliver it. Just a bit of cold dismissal, tempered with a smidgen of cordiality, tells a man that you are a lady, but an uninterested one." He covered Cherith's hand with his own as he added, "And you thought I was crazy when I expected you to find your romantic prospects a little greater on this side of the continent."

"I'm afraid I don't think much of romance if it comes in such an awkward way and from someone so . . ." She blushed. "Uncouth. He winked at me! I never gave him any encouragement, and he winked at me!"

"It was meant as a compliment. It's not a sin to try to show camaraderie."

Her head snapped up, and she met his gaze frankly. "But I do believe Solomon was correct in Proverbs when he wrote, 'He that winketh the eye causes sorrow.'"

"I believe you were in church the Sunday that Brother Farnsworth taught the meaning behind that wink—'deceitful or malicious,' I believe he said."

Cherith nodded. "I do not doubt it. I simply agree with the words 'causes sorrow.' They did. Now things will be awkward and awful until we reach San Francisco."

"I think I can take care of that for you."

They didn't board that week—or even that month. Repairs to the ship meant long, tedious work as the carpenters found more and more damage from the battering trip around the Horn. Still, Cherith and Edgar found their stay in the quiet fishing village pleasant. The locals treated them well, and the beaches were warm and beautiful—even in late November.

"Papa, why do you not teach me Spanish while we are marooned here on this beach?"

"I don't like to think of what you might hear. Your uncle Sid agreed that it makes sense to wait until we reach the security of our new home."

"Why? Do you hear things that are so very unsettling?"

"We anticipated rough speech aboard the ship—"

"A ship where nearly everyone speaks English," she rejoined.

"Or once we reach Yerba Buena."

"Oh . . ." She resumed her brushing as he described all he'd learned of the town. "I think it sounds exciting! I would like to know what people think of newcomers."

"You might not. We'll be foreigners there, sweetheart—even more than we were in Texas. After Houston defeated Santa Anna, we might find that we're not very welcome to assume ownership of Mexican land."

"They won't fight it, will they? We spent so much to get here."

Edgar beckoned to her. "Come here." Once she'd crawled up on her father's lap, he added, "Marco says Don Carrillo will take care of us. He witnessed the will."

She dropped her head to his shoulder. "We're really going to own vines—beautiful rows of grapes with huge leaves and purple clusters . . . And cattle," she added as an afterthought.

"This time of year, it's more like skeletons on trellises with no green at all." Edgar chuckled at her snort of disgust and added, "And we own them now. We just haven't taken possession of them yet."

Minutes later she stood at the window of the little house Edgar had rented and gazed out over the sunset. "The sky, Papa, the ocean. It looks so different from Virginia. Do you think California will be like this?"

Edgar sat in his chair, unmoving. "Will you be sorry to leave here?"

"I might. The pretty little girls with their big brown eyes, the young fishermen with their laughter and their songs, the beaches and the relaxed life—it's charming. I love it." She held out her hand. "But *our* new life will have just as many beautiful things. There will probably be pretty little brown-eyed girls, young cowboys who sing while they work—"

"*Vaqueros.*"

"*Va*-what?"

Edgar smiled. "Your first—well, second—Spanish word. *Vaquero*. Cowboy." He added a wink as he said, "Perhaps one will come to carry you away from me."

"I doubt it. With the pretty girls around, who would look at a 'redheaded chit' like me?"

"Oh, Cherith. That's ridiculous."

But Cherith protested. "Mrs. Pollard said—"

"Mrs. Pollard may have said something so ridiculous, but do you remember what Avelino Aguilar said? He called you the girl with 'hair like roses.' That's how they will see you in this place. Some Spaniards have red hair, you know. They have light skin and eyes too. That's probably why Avelino and Marco appreciated your beauty. Less common in Mexico perhaps, but still in their realm of experience."

"Hair like roses . . ." Cherith sighed. "I cannot imagine anyone saying anything so beautiful about me."

*   *   *

He heard the sigh Amelia didn't know she'd breathed as he finished his story, but before Avelino could remind her of how much he loved her hair, Amelia began pulling pins from it until it fell where she could hold out the ends and look at it.

"Why has red hair always been such a curse to women?"

"Who says it has? It hasn't been in my family."

"Well, it has been for a hundred years for a lot of American redheads." Amelia's nose wrinkled. "I often wonder if I hate it because I'm like everyone else, or if it's because everyone has made me hate it with their comments."

Joe stood, bade them good night, and left the room.

Avelino waited until he heard the door close before he pulled her close and murmured, "Couldn't you learn to like it for my sake? Maybe if people with *pelo como rosas* embraced their hair color, others wouldn't tease them about it."

"So saying I like the hair that everyone thinks is ugly is the way to make people stop disliking it?"

"No . . ." he conceded. "I just think that maybe I'm not the only one who likes it. I wonder if the children who tease about it do so because they secretly envy a color that isn't as common as their boring browns and dirty blonds."

"I feel like Cherith speaking to her papa, but honestly, Avelino. The things that you say."

CHAPTER THIRTY-THREE

SPECULATION

July 1946

Amelia tapped his shoulder. "Señor Lopez is here."

The words repeated themselves in his mind, but consciousness refused to make sense of them. A hand shook him, his head wobbling painfully. "Owww . . ."

"C'mon, Avelino." Her voice tugged him into semiconsciousness. "Wake up. It's important."

His eyes flew open. She stood close, bending over him as if in a dream. "Wha—?"

"I said, Señor Lopez is here. He needs you."

Only after several seconds did the words enter the proper section of his brain and trigger comprehension. "Lopez?" Avelino sat upright and blinked. "Oh, that is not good." The befuddled expression on Amelia's face told him he'd spoken in Spanish. "I'd translate," he muttered as he crawled from between his sheets, "but I don't even know what I said."

"I heard *bueno*. The rest sounded like gibberish." She turned as she spoke. "Señor Lopez says to hurry. He has news. I'll go turn your eggs into a sandwich so you can eat on the way to whatever new calamity he has to show you." Amelia took several steps before backtracking and kissing his cheek. "Good morning, Avelino."

Pain urged him to dress slowly, providing him with plenty of time to enter the realm of the conscious and coherent. It forced him to take it easy as he descended the steps, and it provided an unwelcome excuse not to hug his fiancée as she handed him his makeshift breakfast—or rather for her not to hug *him*. Within minutes of waking, Avelino set off for the Lyndon home, Señor Lopez's message filling his heart with dread.

"He said you must come—quickly. You must speak to him first thing this morning. When you weren't there early, he sent someone to see why. He wants to talk to you. You must go."

Talking to himself as he wandered down the dusty shoulder of the road kept him from losing focus. "I need to find out why he made me that offer. At the time I was so panicked and grateful that I didn't think about anything but hiding the agreement so he couldn't destroy it while I was gone." His voice sounded strange, unnatural in the fading morning fog. Unease filled him, but Avelino forced himself onward, forced himself to ignore the pain that still made physical exertion miserable. "And I need to know when this rib will stop hurting."

Lyndon's housekeeper answered the door with a nervousness he'd never seen in the woman.

"*Buenos días*, Consuela. Is Mr. Lyndon at home?"

The woman refused to look at him as she opened the door wider to allow him to enter. "You know where the office is," she murmured with a thicker accent than he remembered.

"Consuela? Are you—?"

Lyndon's voice called out from another room. "Was that the door, Consuela? Is Carrillo here yet?"

"He is in there. Go." She scurried away, only to return and whisper, "See Señor Welton tonight."

What does she mean by that? Why should . . . ?

He wiped his feet once more on the inside mat before crossing the foyer. The door to Lyndon's office stood open, his secretary was gone, and Gerald Baines sat in a chair to one side of the desk. The little man with his sniveling answers and whipped-puppy expression nearly shook with repressed emotion—what kind of emotions, Avelino couldn't imagine.

"Taking an early-morning siesta, Avelino? I expected you over an hour ago." Lyndon turned to Baines and shook his head. "And I thought our idea was such a good one. Now I wonder if I should reconsider."

Avelino watched the lawyer, feeling very much like he'd seen the little man rub his hands together with what appeared to be fiendish delight, but Baines only nodded.

"Perhaps."

"Mr. Lyndon, I have a job to do. I was up late last night, checking the vines for further vandalism, so of course I slept a little later today, but I don't consider nine o'clock to be proof of indolence." *And where did that eloquence come from? Indolence? You can't even define that!* Avelino chided himself as he stood before the two men.

"With your experience in the industry, shouldn't you be doing something other than playing security guard? That's not a job for a Carrillo!"

Taken aback, Avelino riveted his gaze on Lyndon, waiting for elaboration. None came.

"Sir?"

"You've spent too much time taking orders. The military isn't for men like you. You were meant to lead, not follow."

You've been treating me as if I were meant to be food for worms. Why the change? "A man who cannot follow another cannot possibly be trusted to lead."

"Aah . . . more of that Carrillo wisdom. See, Baines," the man said, "I told you that these Carrillos were intelligent people."

"I never doubted you."

"What is this all about? If you don't have something you need from me, I should be overseeing the vines."

"Take a seat, Avelino. We want to talk to you."

With more inner strength than he knew he possessed, Avelino seated himself without showing the fear those words dredged up in his heart. *They are going to contest the contract—some foolish violation I do not remember. Where will I get the money for the lawyer?* Aloud he simply asked, "Regarding?"

"Your future." Lyndon leaned close and folded his hands on his desk. What he'd surely meant to be a comforting gesture made Avelino even more nervous as the man continued. "We're concerned for you."

"Why? I mean," Avelino clarified, "why the concern for me or my future?"

"You're a young man—a good one. Unlike your foolish brother—"

"I do not care to hear your opinion of my brother."

He rose to leave, but Lyndon's next words stopped him.

"The Napa wine industry is all but dead. You went to Rutherford. How many vines were plowed under and replaced by plums, pears, and walnuts?"

And there we see your true motive. Avelino allowed himself to smirk openly. "Like the saplings you ordered last week?"

"Why—what would . . . ?" Lyndon glared at his attorney as if Baines were personally responsible for Avelino knowing about them. "I don't see how that has anything to do with you."

"But it has to do with the vines. I took it as a clerical error and canceled the order."

"What? You had no right—"

This time, Avelino stood and leaned against the desk, his face even with Lyndon's. "I have *every* right. My contract says that I have to show every effort to produce the most income I can from these vineyards. I cannot do that if you plow under my vines and plant trees. This is la Viña de los Sueños. We grow grapes and make wine. I will be successful at what I know no matter how hard you try to thwart me."

As he stepped through the door, Lyndon called out again. "Avelino, we are not trying to sabotage your efforts. Quite the contrary." He stood and led Avelino back from the doorway to the chair. "Sit down. I think we misunderstood each other."

Once more Avelino found himself sitting in the chair opposite Lyndon, his eyes flitting back and forth between the men before him. "What have I misunderstood?"

"Those saplings shouldn't have been charged to the vineyards. I suppose the bookkeeper just assumed that nursery products belonged to the land and did it that way. I'll be sure to have him correct that. But that's beside the point."

"And what is the point then? You're taking a very circuitous route to get there."

Baines smiled and lifted his pen. "May I?"

"Certainly. Perhaps Avelino won't be as predisposed to assume the worst of you."

Don't count on it. Avelino forced himself to smile. "I'm predisposed only to ideas that are best for the vineyards."

"Such a one-track mind. I had heard that you'd developed more mature interests as of late."

So help me, Lord; I'll slug him if he brings Amelia into this.

"Mr. Lyndon, I think he'd rather know why we have brought him here. Mr. Carrillo strikes me as a young man who prefers to keep his private life private."

Avelino nodded his agreement while his mind struggled to think of the word he wanted. He could hear Miss Forsythe speaking it, defining it, using it in a sentence. He knew what it was, but it remained elusive.

Baines droned on about providing for a future in a secure position. As a *war hero* he had earned the respect of men who were too young to serve in the Great War and too old to serve in the Second World War. *Men like you two, I suppose. An arrogant man who fancies himself a bit of a mafioso and his obsequious—that's the word!—obsequious sidekick.*

". . . think the position would be perfect for you. It's a fresh start in a new place with a good job. The salary is excellent, and there is a fine community. Kearns knows the area and the man you'd be working for."

"Wha—wait. You want me to abandon my contract to take a job at another vineyard. Where?"

"As I said," Baines began with more than a little huffiness, "the vineyards are Greigson's in Fresno. They are well respected, and the owner is looking for someone to groom to take over the business. We can't guarantee that you'll be that someone, but I think we all know you're an excellent candidate."

"Fresno." Avelino stood to leave once more. "You really do think I'm stupid. That I'll leave the land my family has owned for over a hundred years to chase after some dream I don't even understand. What do they do there? Raisins?" Silence answered him in the affirmative. "I don't know raisins. I don't know Fresno. I know wine and Napa. I know this little town. I'll make the vines successful again. We'll recover. And we'll do it because I refuse to give up, so you can do whatever it is you are so anxious to do."

At the door, he threw one more line over his shoulder. "You'll have to kill me if you want to stop me from earning back my heritage."

*   *   *

"You shouldn't have said that." Joe inspected the underside of the leaves on a nearby vine before standing and kneading his back. "You know he was behind the beatings—"

"Assume," Avelino corrected. "I just . . ." At Joe's incredulous look, he tried again. "I just know that legally speaking, we know nothing. We can only assume. I know what I think. Even Welton seems—"

"What is it?"

"Consuela. She acted strange when I was there, and her accent—heavier than I'm used to. She always had just a slight one leftover from childhood, but today . . ."

"You have an accent when you're emotional. Maybe she was upset about something—a child or parent is ill."

"I have an accent when I'm emotional because that is when I speak Spanish. We've all done that—even Cherith Tandy learned to do that."

Joe inched his way down the row, inspecting leaves, clusters, and vines. "You'll have to tell us about that."

"It'll be a while. At this point in her story, she still only knows two words *en español* . . ."

When Avelino didn't speak for several long seconds, Joe nudged him and muttered, "What is it?"

"I forgot. Consuela said to go to speak to Mr. Welton. That's how I thought of her now. Anyway, I don't see how I can. It'll take me forever to get over there once I'm done for the day."

"You'll take the truck. Take Amelia. Go get an ice-cream soda somewhere." He winked as he stretched again. "You need to celebrate that engagement before she drags you off to the preacher."

"We've got years to celebrate, but I'll take you up on that."

"She won't let you make her wait that long. She's quiet, but she is tenacious in a way that you cannot imagine."

All afternoon Avelino mulled the possibilities through his mind. *If Lyndon is behind the stuff with Ray and the vineyards—and he has to be—then why is he being nice about trying to get me this job? And why is he trying to sabotage things? The casks made no sense. Thousands of dollars wasted. Then again, he did neglect the vines while I was gone. He must be planning something else—probably fruit orchards. He could have sold the equipment, though. On the other hand, who would buy it?*

"You're daydreaming again." Amelia stood beside him in the south quadrant. When she'd arrived, he couldn't have guessed. "You need to be more careful. I could have been Ray."

"There is something wrong," Avelino murmured as he slipped his hand into hers, "when a boy's name can strike fear into a man's heart."

She watched him, her eyes never leaving his face, until she nodded. "But you're afraid for the vines and the wine, not yourself."

Avelino pointed to where there had been nasty bruises on his face. "I'll heal, but you can't get back spoiled wine. You can't replant vines in time for this year's harvest. I will heal," he repeated. "The vineyard can't."

She tugged at him. "C'mon. Granddad gave me money for supper. He says you're taking me out for burgers and ice-cream sodas."

"Oh, I am?" Avelino allowed himself to be led away from the vines and back toward the house. "Do I get to decide if I want to go?"

"You want to, even if you won't admit it. I'm going to change— you should too; that shirt is filthy—and then wait on the porch like a *real* date." Amelia leaned close and whispered, "I should warn you. If you honk Granddad's horn, I *won't* come running. I was taught better than that."

"And I was taught better as well." A sigh escaped before he could prevent it.

"What is it? We don't *have* to go."

"It's not that," Avelino assured her. "Of course, I want to go. It's just . . ." He swallowed the lump of pride that welled up in his throat and tried again. "I'd like not to be so poor that I can't even do something so simple. I can't buy you a present. I can't buy you a meal—can barely afford a bottle of soda once in a while—"

"But you gave me the only thing I wanted. That's more than most people get in a lifetime."

The words—so quiet and simple—said much more. In them he heard her love for him, for his home, for his family. He heard her happiness and her excitement. "And I got the girl of my silly child-hood dreams. How could a man want more than that?" He nudged her and laughed at the bemused expression on her face. "What?"

"So does that mean I'm your *señorita de la sueños*?"

Suppressing his laughter hurt—much more than he'd expected. Laughter felt only slightly worse. "Not quite. The words would be *chica* or *moza de tus sueños*."

"So, what you are telling me, Señor Carrillo, is that we can thank Spanish-speaking peoples for the deplorable American habit of calling females 'chicks'?"

Joe Kearns stepped from behind a tree, startling both of them.

"Sorry, 'Melia. You can thank Sinclair Lewis for that. He used it in *Elmer Gantry* to refer to a 'brainless little fluffy chick.' Avelino's ancestors are free of guilt."

"And from all of this I have learned never to call my Amelita a 'chick.' Thank you." He dropped her hand and inched his way to the stairs to his room over the garage. "I'll be down in a minute—gotta wash up."

* * *

They sat on opposite ends of a couch in the Weltons' spacious living room. Dorothy Welton nervously puffed on a cigarette, offering one to Amelia and Avelino at random moments.

"Would you like—no, you said no, didn't you? Perhaps a drink." She frowned. "No, you're a Baptist, aren't you, Amelia? I didn't mean to offend."

"I'm not offended, Mrs. Welton. My grandfather does work for a winery." Amelia shifted as the former awkwardness settled back over the room. "Did you take a vacation this summer? I heard you usually do."

"We did, yes. We—yes." Mrs. Welton puffed several times and stared at the door as if willing her husband to appear.

Amelia glanced at him, imploring him to do something.

"Mrs. Welton, this is a very beautiful room. My *mamá* would have loved the upholstery on this couch. She always wanted to re-cover ours in this very blue. She used to say that you had the best taste in all of Napa Valley," Avelino offered.

"My car broke down by your house once, and your mother took me in while I waited for Hank Rhimes to come fix it. She gave me coffee with chocolate and cinnamon in it and the most delicious bread. I've remembered that bread all these years. I tried to get her to make extra on baking days, but she said it had to be eaten hot."

As Mrs. Welton spoke, Avelino nodded. "*Sí*—*sopaipillas. Mamá* made the best." He tried to choke back the rise of emotion that swelled his throat and gripped his heart. "We had a neighbor from New Mexico who taught her, but *mamá's* were better—lighter." His words sounded strangled even to his ears.

Silence hung over them once more as Avelino struggled to regain self-control, Mrs. Welton fumbled for a way to kill the awkwardness, and Amelia sat miserable, unable to fix the strained air in the room.

Mrs. Welton spoke first. "She was kind to me."

"*Mamá was* kind."

Amelia sat up straighter, a small smile forming. "I have heard that Avelino takes after his mother, but I always think he looks like his grandfather. Now I know what they mean. He is like her in personality, in character."

The door swung open as Ray burst into the room. "Mother—oh."

"Raymond, Avelino Carrillo is here with Amelia Kearns. Wouldn't you like to come—?"

"No."

The door slammed shut behind him.

"I'm sorry . . ." Mrs. Welton lit a new cigarette. "He's not himself these days. I keep telling Ed that we need to take him away for a while. His friends are such bad influences. I'm sure that in good company he'd come around again."

The door opened again, and somewhere else in the house one slammed.

Ed Welton walked in looking exasperated and as if he'd aged. "Sorry for the delay. Ruby Mae hadn't had a chance to talk to me and then Ray . . ." His eyes slid toward the door. "Dorothy, would you mind excusing us for a bit."

Mrs. Welton stood, her eyes darting from person to person before she bade them good night and scuttled from the room, teetering on spiked high heels as she went. "Good night," she called before the door shut behind her.

"You didn't have to ask her to go." Avelino leaned forward, clasping his hands together and resting his forearms on his knees. "It's her home too."

"But this is private information—information I don't know what to do with—so I want to keep it quiet." When Avelino didn't respond, Mr. Welton moved his chair closer. "Consuela, Lyndon's housekeeper—do you know her?"

"Yes. I saw her today. She seemed a bit out of sorts."

"She should be. What she told Ruby Mae disturbs me. It's actually good news for you—I think."

Avelino inched forward and sat on the edge of his seat. "Good news?"

"Well, I wondered if you would mind if Ruby Mae told the story. Consuela was too afraid to stay."

Amelia kept quiet, but he felt her stiffen and saw her hands fold with deliberate precision.

"Why was she afraid?" he asked with the hope that he'd anticipated her question as well as his.

"She works for Lyndon, and you can ask that question."

"Well, if Ruby Mae is willing to talk to us, I'd like to hear what she has to say if you think it has anything to do with me."

"It does. Just a moment." Ed jumped up and strode to the door. He called out. Ruby Mae appeared within seconds.

Avelino noticed something different about the woman, but not until she spoke could he identify what it was. *She's not smiling. Ruby Mae always smiles.*

"I just want to say that I'm glad you listened to my advice." Her eyes offered the smile her lips couldn't form. Ruby Mae waited for Amelia to catch her eye before she said, "You've got you a good man there. I'm glad he stopped being a stubborn fool about you."

"I am too."

The men exchanged amused but impatient glances before Avelino asked, "Why did Consuela come to you?"

"Well, we've been friends for a long time, Consuela and me. She's a nervous type—always fretting about things—but right now she's spooked, and she knew that Mr. Welton thinks a lot of you and would help. Don't you, Mr. Welton?"

"I do and I will."

Just tell me what it is! Why am I here? This waiting makes me feel like I'm about to be told I'm dying or something. Despite the desire to scream out his frustration, Avelino forced himself to take a calming breath and acknowledge the compliment. "I appreciate that, Mr. Welton. I hope I won't need to bother you, but the offer is kind."

Ruby Mae shook her head and waved her hands. "I don't mean no disrespect, Mr. Welton, but I've been off for over an hour now, and I gots work to do at home. I'd like to tell Avelino what Consuela said and go, if that's all right."

"Go ahead."

"Okay. So like we said, Consuela is kind of a nervous type—allus gettin' in a fuss about somethin'. Well, I don't usually give a lotta attention to her stories. They's usually just how she gets past things—talk 'em out and such. But today was different. She couldn't stop jumpin' at any noise, and she whispered, had to tell me things over again when I couldn't hear her aright."

"I don't remember her being like that."

"You was a kid, Avelino. You saw what you spected to see." She glanced at Welton for confirmation before she continued. "Now part a why she's havin' trouble is that there's a certain amount of confident'ality spected from housekeepers. We keeps our families' secrets. We respects that. But Consuela respects you and your family too. And, well, she may respect the job, but Lyndon's a hard man—"

Ed Welton interrupted her. "We know this, Ruby Mae. Just tell him what she overheard. He knows she isn't a gossip."

"Okay then. So he and that Baines were talking last night until the late hours. Consuela's not allowed to go home until all company's gone, so she had to stay. They kept wantin' things—drinks and sandwiches—so she was in and out of the room a lot. They never stopped talking."

"Tell him what they said," Welton urged.

"They were talking about how to get you to leave, sayin' that the vandalism and physical attacks weren't workin'."

"So it is Lyndon behind all this." Amelia sat up straighter. "Did they say why?"

"Sorta. They was talking about that agreement he made with Avelino, sayin' that maybe it hadn't been necessary, and how he don't seem to know that."

"Don't know what?" Avelino's mind tried to understand the convoluted thought processes.

"That's just it. They didn't say."

"Well," Amelia interjected, "Consuela was in and out of the room. She probably missed a lot while she was gone, and they couldn't say too much with her there."

"Now that's where you're wrong." Ruby Mae hesitated, picking at her apron with her fingers, before she squared her shoulders. "We're the help, Miss Kearns. We're invisible. The families we works for only sees us when they needs us. Otherwise, we ain't there. We're not *really* people when we're workin'." Ed began to protest, but she shook her head and waved her hands. "No, sir. It's true and it's fine. It needs to be that way. When I'm off work or if something is wrong, you're as kind to me as any friend of yours—kinder to me even than to your own son sometimes—but while I'm working I need to be invisible. I understands that."

"So were they speaking cryptically, or did Consuela just not understand?" Avelino spoke aloud but his question was more for himself than the room.

"Or did she just not stay around long enough to hear enough? It could be so chopped up that a perfectly innocent conversation sounded very sinister." Amelia blushed as the two men stared at her in evident disbelief. "I know it's not likely, but it is within the realm of possibility."

"Axchally, it ain't. Because Consuela stood outside the door and listened once she realized they was plottin' to get rid of you."

"You don't mean dead!" Amelia stared aghast at Ruby Mae.

"No—we don't think so. They's plottin' to lure him away. And this is what's so important, I think." Ruby Mae inched to the very edge of the seat and leaned her hands on her knees. "They said that they had to get you out of here before you figured out it wasn't legal."

"What wasn't legal?"

The woman shrugged. "We don't know. 'Suela thinks it's some kind of contract, since he was talkin' to Baines, but that's pure speculatin'."

CHAPTER THIRTY-FOUR

THE FIGHT BEGINS

They worked together—their hands moving in such rhythm it seemed to be a dance of fingers. Amelia chopped tomatoes, onions, and peppers while Avelino rolled out corn tortillas so flat she winced each time he scooped them onto the griddle. Each wince teased a smile from the corners of his lips. *She will learn to trust—learn confidence in me. She has it now but only in more important things. Backwards—*

Amelia stood staring at him. "I'd offer a penny for your thoughts, but you've proven stubborn in the area of money. Then again . . ." She reached into a small bowl and fingered a few coins before pulling out a penny. "There. The first deposit into the Kearns-Carrillo marriage fund."

As the coin dropped into his hand, Avelino kissed her forehead. "I wish I could tell you what you want to hear, *querida*."

"Hearing that's enough for now." Amelia nodded to the griddle, where smoke billowed from beneath the weight of a cast-iron skillet. "Your tortilla is done, I think."

Avelino scrambled to dispose of the charred mess. Coughing from smoke that billowed into his lungs, he fanned the smoke out the window. His fiancée stood laughing with a knife in one hand and wiping tears with the other. Onion juice on her hands made Amelia's eyes smart, producing more tears and even more laughter. He grabbed a clean dishcloth, soaked it, and offered it to her, ready to apologize for the smoke, but something in her expression stopped him.

By the time she'd stopped laughing, stopped crying, and started avoiding eye contact, he'd confirmed his suspicions. "You distracted me on purpose. You *wanted* me to burn the tortilla."

Her smirk said it all before she could speak. "I saw you over there feeling all smug about your brilliant tortilla-making skills. 'Pride goeth before a fall,' my dear Avelino."

"A fall you orchestrated. It doesn't count."

"It most certainly does."

There it was; Avelino recognized it—that deceptive quiet that seemed to indicate a lack of interest but instead hid great excitement. *She's enjoying this.* La encantadora. The word stopped his thoughts as Avelino gazed at the young woman who would someday be his wife. *"Encantadora."*

"It's a pretty word—I like it. What does it mean?"

"Enchantress. They said that about Cherith Tandy," he murmured as his fingers traced the curve of her cheek, leaving a smudge of batter near her temple. "Amelita . . ."

"Kiss her later, son. I'm still waitin' on those chips you promised me."

They turned to see Joe standing in the doorway. Reluctantly, Avelino dropped his hand and returned to the mess he'd made of the griddle.

Amelia snickered. "Did you hear that, Granddad? I am an enchantress. He just proved that I will not be a quarter of a century old before I'm married."

"She just proved that she underestimates me," Avelino growled as he scraped the charred remains in the garbage and oiled the griddle once more. "I am stronger than she thinks." He pulled her close and murmured, "If you only knew the tortures I feel when I think of six long years."

"If you only knew the tortures my stomach feels when it hears it'll be getting good food and then none appears!" Joe crossed his arms over his chest and scowled at them with mock ferocity. "Save your flirting for when you don't have a task to do—like feeding an old man."

Amelia ignored his orders and kissed Avelino. "Oh, Granddad. I forgot. A letter came for you—from Aunt Ella."

"She'd better not be telling me to come get David. I'm not doin' it." Joe muttered something more about those "can't-be-bothered Colberts" and their "lack of responsibility toward our nation's heroes."

Avelino rolled out another tortilla as the griddle heated, keeping one eye on Amelia. She waited until they heard the letter opening before whispering, "Granddad wants Daddy here, you know. He just hates that his own family doesn't *want* him."

"It must be hard to take care of a man that large, though. Maybe it's too much for a woman to do."

"Daddy's not a burden," she protested. "He does for himself—if you tell him anyway. Sometimes he'll forget to bathe or shave—brush his teeth or something like that—but he can do it himself, and he does when you tell him." Avelino stood frozen as she wiped tears from her eyes and wailed, "Why do I have to have this wretched hair, this face? Why couldn't I look like Daddy?"

His eyes met Joe's as the older man stood in the doorway, and he stepped forward at Joe's nod and wrapped her tight in his arms. "Shh . . . you look exactly as El Señor created you—perfect. Your despised red hair is my dream—*el pelo como rosas*."

"You'll make me grateful for my hair yet."

The banter continued as they finished their snacks and carried it all out to the table on the patio. Avelino recalled similar evenings as a boy, crunching on chips and salsa as his family chatted about the day's events. *I have a new family now. We won't be exactly like* mamá y papá—*and Paco—but we'll be like the first Carrillos. We'll live here, and my traditions will merge with hers. We'll have children and grandchildren, who talk about the pretty señorita from Oklahoma who waited patiently for their* bisabuelo *to stop being an idiot and accept* el don de Dios—*the gift of God—that she was.*

". . . lino!"

He blinked. And blinked again. A man sat across from him— Ed Welton. "I—"

"I let myself in. I hope you don't mind . . ."

"No, no. I was . . ." He swallowed hard and smiled at Amelia. "Lost in the past and the future. Did you get a drink?"

Ed gave a glass of ice water a little shake. "And I got a few of these chips too. Delicious."

"Ed, I don't want to be rude, but you said you had something important for us." Joe leaned forward, his hands gripping the side of the table. "Just what have you found?"

"It's not what I *have* found, but what I think we need to find." Ed dipped another chip in his little bowl of salsa and moaned with pleasure. "I must have Amelia show Ruby Mae how to make these. It's a perfect after-dinner snack on a hot day." At Avelino's failed attempt to repress his frustration, Ed laughed. "Sorry. Put good food in front of a man, and his ability to think evaporates."

Amelia laughed at the joke, but Avelino, his curiosity piqued, rerouted the conversation from its culinary detour. "What do we need to find?"

"It's the contract. I've gone over and over the situation with my lawyer in Napa, and we both agree that there must be something in it that has Lyndon nervous."

Avelino leaned forward and asked, "Do you mean the current contract, or the agreement I had with Lyndon before I joined the army?"

Welton's forehead wrinkled. "What agreement? You have two understandings with Lyndon?"

Avelino explained the agreement that Lyndon had offered, promising to let him work off the heavy debt he owed. "Paco lost it all trying to turn the vineyards into a commercial enterprise that would turn migrant workers into residents. He thought of himself as the FDR of Napa Valley."

"How much did he owe?"

Avelino winced as he whispered, "Six thousand dollars."

As silence grew heavy over the table, shame filled Avelino, choking him in its grasp. He tried to speak—to explain that Paco's intentions had been honorable despite his actions—but the words refused to form. Instead, he hung his head in a gesture that had gotten him repeated reprimands from Sergeant Miller.

"Look me in the eye, Private! Show me some respect!" The rebuke still reverberated in his memory.

I tried to show respect. My mamá *would have whipped me good for staring her in the face when I'd done wrong. I showed shame and remorse for my failure, but you saw it as cowardice.* When no response came, Avelino forced his head upward, ready to apologize, but found the others staring at him, jaws agape. "What?"

"The vineyards are worth many times more than that!" Amelia cried. "Why didn't you go to the bank?"

"I . . ." He stared at Welton, imploring the man to explain. "They wouldn't give a man a loan to pay for one we'd defaulted on. Tell them."

"I'd have given you the money at three percent for fifteen years, and my banker would have done it at four and a half—maybe five at worst." Ed leaned forward. "Why didn't you get a second opinion? Why—?"

Emotion overtook Avelino. He threw up his hands and cried, "It was done! Paco defaulted. The loan was past due. I begged Lyndon for more time, but he said no. I tried to explain that I didn't know about the loan or due date in time, that I would have tried to find the money, but I still don't know why Lyndon was so generous as to offer that agreement."

"We need to see that agreement," Joe interjected. "I suppose it's at the bank."

Avelino nodded. "I have a copy of the wording in my room, though."

He started to rise, but Amelia jumped to her feet. "I'll get it. Where do I find it?"

"In that trunk—the one that had the linens and the material for your dress. It's in a cigar box on the left-hand side at the bottom." Avelino touched her arm as she passed. "Can you grab the contract I have with Lyndon too? I wrote out a copy of that as well."

"Be right back."

When she returned, Welton and Joe both read the agreement and the contract more than once. As they read, Avelino watched the men's faces, trying to judge their reactions, but found it impossible. "Well?"

Welton leaned back in his chair, shaking his head. "It doesn't make sense. He should never have offered you this agreement. You clearly agreed that your brother defaulted on his loan. You're sure this was his idea?"

"Yes, sir. I admit that I begged him for some way to try to work it out, and he said no. I was out of the house and down the road before he sent Baines in the car to bring me back."

"So he *brought you back*?" The rise in Amelia's voice amused him.

"Yes. There was a rough sketch of that agreement waiting by the time I got there. It was just a few lines—that he would retain ownership of the vineyard until I returned from the war, and if I worked for seven years without pay, he would sign the deed back to me and only me."

"So if you married and died before the seven years were up, your wife wouldn't inherit the property."

Avelino's eyes met Joe's. "No. *I* have to work all seven years. If something prevents *me* from completing that work, *I* do not regain the land." He glanced at Amelia. "The contract is only with me."

"I bet he'd rewrite it to include a wife if you agreed to start the seven years over," Welton muttered.

Amelia, despite all her failed attempts to stay out of the conversation, spoke once more. "Why do you think that?"

"Because it gives him another year of profits. Why wouldn't he?"

Joe spoke, his tones cold and dreadful. "Because it's less suspicious if one person dies." He took a drink of his water and batted at a mosquito before adding, "I do not think Lyndon ever intended to allow Avelino to live out the full seven years. I suspect around year five . . ."

Panic rose in Avelino's heart as he listened. Several things made sense with that train of thought—several except for the agreement in the first place. "There's only one flaw in your suspicions."

"The agreement in the first place," Joe murmured. "Yeah, I thought of that. I just don't see any other explanation."

Crickets chirped, and a toad bellowed somewhere nearby. Avelino watched several bats swoop down from the *secoya* over the vines. *Eat those bugs. Save my vines.* Mamá *hated you, but* papá *was right. You are our friends.*

Ed spoke first. "It has to lie in the contract your brother had with Lyndon."

"What does?" the other three asked at once.

"The answer." Ed snagged another chip and dug it into his bowl of salsa. Not until he'd polished it off and washed it down with a few gulps of water did he speak again. "There has to be something in that contract with Paco that Welton is afraid of."

That doesn't make sense, Avelino protested to himself. *Why would he be afraid of a contract he had a legal signature on?*

Joe preempted him, asking, "So you don't think it was a legal contract?"

"I don't see how it could have been. It's the only thing that makes any sense. He doesn't want you to contest it. So he's doing something he knows he can probably control."

"What do you think 'not legal' entails?"

Avelino sighed. "I *saw* the signature. It was Paco's. He even signed his full name." He couldn't help but snicker. "It filled the whole line across the page."

"Was that usual?" Ed shook his head and rephrased. "I mean, did he usually sign his whole name? How many names does he have?"

"Francisco Diego Vallejo Ruiz Aguilar Carrillo."

"If Paco really did sign, then the problem has to lie within the contract itself." Ed Welton folded his hands on the table and leaned forward. "Do you have a copy of that contract?"

He shook his head. "No. I asked," he insisted at the disapproving look on Ed's face. "I did. But Lyndon said the contract was between Paco and him, and I didn't have a right to a copy."

"That's a lie right there. You most definitely do have a right to a copy of something that cuts you out of your inheritance. Paco did leave the vineyards to you in his will?" When Avelino didn't answer, Ed groaned. "He *did* leave a will?"

His thoughts had already spun into an ever-increasing spiral of confusion, but upon Ed's emphasis of "did," Avelino snapped out of his reverie. *"¡Sí! Sí. Lo siento, por favor."* The words sounded wrong, out of place, but Avelino couldn't pinpoint why.

Joe and Amelia snickered, but Ed shook his head. "I should understand more than just yes."

"He speaks in Spanish when he's emotional," Joe explained.

You've got to stay in control. Not everyone can understand you. "I am sorry. I didn't mean . . ." He sighed. "Yes, Paco had a will."

Several long seconds passed before Amelia asked the question Avelino couldn't. "How do we see it then?" She turned rosy. "I—I mean how does *Avelino* see—that first contract?"

Ed didn't answer immediately. He sat with his hands folded, his thumbs rubbing together in an odd pyramid, until he began to nod. "We ask."

"He's not just—"

"But he is." Ed laid his palms flat and leaned forward. "Think about it. We go to him with a lawyer—we can use mine if we need to—and we say we want to see it. He'll probably refuse."

"No probably about it," Joe muttered.

Ed chuckled before continuing: "But we'll be there with a lawyer. We'll look as serious as we are. He'll say no, and we'll tell him that if he doesn't present a copy in forty-eight hours, we're going to file for a motion for a judge to examine the contract."

"And he won't want to!" Amelia nearly bounced with excitement.

I've not seen this much animation from you—ever. "It might work," Avelino allowed.

"It'll work," Ed assured him. "The contract is the key to everything. It has to be."

It makes sense, I guess. Paco signs a contract that isn't legal in some way—that would invalidate it. Paco breaks the contract, losing the property. I come along, obviously anxious to do anything I can to regain it. I'm going off to war, so the chances of me returning—whole anyway . . . Avelino winced as he realized that he hadn't returned whole. *Well, mostly whole—whole enough to oversee the land. While I return, his plan for the vineyard—whatever that is—is shot, so he tries to convince me to leave by sabotaging my work and making me feel unwelcome in the valley.*

"Avelino?"

He sat up, wiped his sweaty palms on his pants, and nodded. "We'll do it."

"Good," Amelia murmured. "Now tell us about Cherith and Edgar. I want them to arrive in California."

"Well . . ."

Ed started to rise. "I'll go—"

"No, you should stay, Mr. Welton. The stories—they'll help you see what Avelino is fighting for." She smiled. "Please stay. I'll get my notebook and more salsa."

Avelino saw Ed hesitate, start to protest, but the man sank back in his chair. "I've always wanted to hear more about your family. Jacinta used to talk about her grandfather's stories and how the girl with hair like roses came to California to become the matriarch of the vines."

"That's *tía* Jacinta's version. I don't think Cherith Tandy would recognize herself in that statement. She was very *gringa* and traditional."

Ed pressed him further. "But didn't she save the rancho from squatters and fight for their right to retain the land? I thought Juana Briones helped her."

"Yes, but that is because the rancho was in her name."

Avelino hadn't even noticed that Amelia had left, but when she returned, bowl and notepad in hand, he took that as his cue to begin. "They arrived in San Francisco on January 4, 1841 . . ."

CHAPTER THIRTY-FIVE

YERBA BUENA

January 1841

They stumbled up the street, much to Cherith's dismay. "I thought since we weren't on the ship as long, we wouldn't be as wobbly."

Edgar pulled her out of the path of a growling dog and charged the animal. "Go away!" he ordered.

The dog yelped, whined, and ran, tail between its legs.

"Is that why dogs chase people? Because people run rather than charge?"

"Sometimes. Don't do it until you learn to differentiate between a dog with bravado and a truly vicious one." As Cherith swayed where she stood, Edgar steadied her. "Just a few days at sea would make you unsteady when you hit land again."

She blinked, stumbled, and blinked again as her mind tried to jump from unsteadiness to unfriendly canines and back to unsteadiness again. "Papa, sometimes I find it hard to follow your rabbit trails back to the main road." She hitched up her satchel and glanced around her. "Is that the saloon?"

Edgar nodded. "I think so. Captain Phelps said that the owner, a Mr. Vioget, has a few small rooms in the backs of his buildings. If we hurry, we might have a chance at one."

"I can't believe there's not a hotel or boardinghouse."

"There's not very many people here—just a couple hundred," Edgar reminded her.

"I know, but with all the ships coming in, you'd think . . ." She glanced behind them at the slow stream of people making their way up from the shore. "If we didn't have luscious vines waiting for us to manage them, I'd start one myself. I think there would be good money in a boardinghouse here."

"My daughter the keen businesswoman. You'll make a success of our vines by sheer pluck and determination."

"And you'll make a success of our beef enterprise. You know cattle. And didn't Marco say we had to use so much of the property for beef?"

"Well, or cultivation. Strictly speaking, the vines have culti-vated a significant portion of land too, but not nearly as much as is free for cattle." Edgar took a deep breath. "I hope the air is less heavy there. I think I've lost my appreciation for the salt air. It feels almost oppressive in this fog."

Jean-Jacques Vioget promised them his only semiavailable room the moment that its previous occupant vacated it. "I heard him say he is going to Monterey and would be out first thing this morning."

Cherith and her father exchanged confused glances. The morn-ing was well underway and rushing toward noon. But Edgar just asked permission to leave their satchels in a storage room while they went to find supplies. Before Mr. Vioget could agree, a man with red-rimmed eyes and unsteady gait lumbered toward them. "Well, Vioget. I'm off. What do I owe you?"

The men argued, Mr. Vioget insisting that the man owed for an unpaid bar tab, and the man just as insistent that he'd paid it.

In the end the saloonkeeper won and shook his head as the other man left. "I never let a man leave without paying his bar tab, but they all try it." He examined the Tandys for a moment before smiling. "But I do not think that'll be a problem with you. I suspect that you do not imbibe."

*   *   *

Welton's laughter interrupted Avelino's story. Even as he started to ask what was so amusing, he laughed too.

Amelia and Joe exchanged confused glances until Amelia's face shifted to show understanding. "That's funny, but it's true. The Tandys came here as teetotalers and built a wine empire."

The men snickered at her exaggerated description of la Viña de los Sueños.

Avelino shook his head. "Empire. You have an optimistic view of our world here."

"Laugh if you want, but I see you as being the premiere wine-makers in Napa—*the* Napa vintners. Like . . ." Amelia frowned. "You got me sidetracked. Tell about Cherith. We've finally gotten to her point of view. I want more."

Avelino winked at the men as he began his story again. "The tiny room became a burden Cherith had to bear . . ."

*   *   *

Her leg smarted as she bumped into the bathing tub—again. Cherith gave it a swift kick before remembering she hadn't put on her shoes yet. "Ooooowww! Unpleasant things! Thinking and not saying unpleasant things right now!" She clapped her hands over her mouth as she realized anyone close enough could overhear her through the thin walls. *That will teach me to lose my composure.*

Her pacing continued and stopped as a splinter imbedded itself in her foot. "Ooooh . . . more unpleasant things I will not say!"

The wound bled as she dug out the splinter. Unwilling to risk further injury, Cherith picked up the still-wet stockings she'd left to dry on the side of the tub and sighed as she pulled them onto her feet. "Disgusting."

The squishy feeling of soggy socks in her shoes made Cherith want to add more unpleasant things to her repertoire of unspeakable words, but the sight of yet another rough patch on the floor stopped her from losing the final remnants of her composure. The bathing tub still occupied most of the room—still full of dirty water.

"At least it wasn't as nasty as the water in Acapulco," she muttered to herself. "I've never been so filthy in my life."

She eyed the tub again and the bucket that stood beside it. Determined to get it ready for her father's bath, Cherith scooped up a bucketful of water and lugged it to the door. As she opened it, a servant's hand nearly connected with her forehead. The girl's astonishment prompted a slew of apologies, or so Cherith assumed, followed by scolding as the girl grabbed the bucket handle before Cherith could pick it up again.

Rebellion welled up in her heart as she watched the girl carry off the bucket—to freedom, it seemed. *Papa is being ridiculous! He wasn't like this on the ship or in Virginia. I could go anywhere I liked in Texas. He said himself there aren't many people here. So why should he lock me away in this room as if we've entered some den of iniquity or something?*

Each trip the girl made to empty the tub seemed to fill her with even more rebellion. *I'll have to address this with Papa.*

When the girl could no longer fill the bucket from the tub, she called out for someone, but Cherith shook her head and grabbed one of the handles. The girl protested, her hands making shooing motions, but Cherith stood firm. After several seconds passed, Cherith began dragging the tub toward the door. It worked. The girl, with a steady stream of apparent reprimands, hoisted the other end and backed Cherith out the door before taking the lead down the little hallway and out the side door.

Dread overshadowed the fleeting feeling of freedom as she followed the girl—overshadowed it the moment she heard her father call out, "Cherith Elizabeth Tandy!"

Her eyes met the girl's, and she felt her face flush with the heat of her embarrassment. The girl's smirk changed to a smile of sympathy and compassion as Cherith's panic became obvious. As Edgar neared, the girl dropped her end of the bathing tub and flew past Cherith, imploring him in Spanish to do something—what, Cherith could only guess.

She doesn't know Papa. He'll scold me no matter how much she pleads. I disobeyed.

As the girl reached Edgar, she cowered, putting her arms over her head in a preemptive protective movement. Cherith shrugged at her father, but Edgar just laughed. "She thinks I'm going to beat her for interfering. She thinks I'm going to beat *you* for being a disobedient and headstrong daughter."

Slowly, the girl backed away, her eyes darting back and forth between Edgar and Cherith. *"No comprendo,"* she said at last. With one last glance back at them, the girl retrieved the tub, dumped it, and carried it back to the well, where she proceeded to rinse it with fresh water.

All the way to their room, Cherith waited in dreadful anticipation for the scolding she knew she'd receive. Edgar didn't give orders very often, but when he did he expected them to be obeyed without question or hesitation. The moment the door shut behind them,

Cherith squared her shoulders, met her father's gaze, and said, "I want to be sorry. It's the best I can do right now."

His arms crossed over his chest, and he leaned against the door, watching her. Cherith tried not to squirm but found herself with jitters. Still he said nothing. Determined not to cave—not to apologize for wanting to be helpful and productive—she stood before him, growing more agitated and implacable with each passing second.

"Would you like to wash our clothes with the girl—the servant girl?"

All the arguments she'd formed in the past fifteen to twenty seconds dissolved in that question. "Wha—aren't you going to chastise me for my insubordination?"

"No, but I am going to remind you of something." He led her to the room's only chair and gently pushed her into it, before starting to settle himself on the bed.

Cherith jumped up and traded places with him. "You're so filthy, Papa—the coverlet . . ."

"Very wise." He smiled as she settled her skirts around her. "Cherith . . ."

Her eyes rose, and as much as she tried to repress it, penitence rose in her heart with it. "Yes, Papa?"

"Do I ever deny you anything I can give?"

The truth of his question pierced the remaining layer of her rapidly failing armor. "No, Papa."

"Do you think I would truly deny you the opportunity to wander free after being cooped up on a ship for the better part of a year? Am I such a hard and unsympathetic father?"

A tear splashed onto her cheek and rolled until she wiped it away. "No . . ." The word escaped as little more than a whisper.

"I have learned something about you in the past year or two." Edgar waited for her to meet his gaze again before he continued.

"My daughter can be a very stubborn, hardheaded girl, but only when she doesn't understand why she can't do what she wants. As a child, she just wanted to be in control . . ."

Cherith blushed. "I did. I thought myself so much wiser than you."

"But now," he continued, "her father exasperates her when he restricts her without understanding."

She had never considered the *why* of her random rebellious moments, but as her father explained that with maturity came the need to understand and choose to yield, Cherith began to see the wisdom of his words. "So please explain, Papa. Why can I not do basic household chores? I just emptied the bath—and with a girl. I wasn't even out there alone!"

"But you would have been, wouldn't you?"

How does he always know these things? I don't understand how he does it! He seems to have insight into my very mind! "That is hardly the point. You were angry at my disobedience for doing what you will permit me to do later. I don't understand the difference."

"The difference, my dear, is that I need to be able to trust that you'll obey me even before I've had a chance to explain. You know I don't like to restrict you. You know that I only want what's best for you. Give me the chance, darlin', to be a *good* papa to you."

Her eyes slid to the tiny window high in the wall. "Why, then. Now you can tell me why. What is so dangerous here—?"

"That's the problem. I don't *know* if there is *any*thing dangerous here. I don't know this place or these people. I don't know anything, and that terrifies me. They are probably wonderful people. Our Mr. Vioget seems to be an honest man. The storekeeper, Mr. Leese, also struck me as someone trustworthy, but there are sailors, natives, and others about whom I cannot be certain." He smiled. "But I did learn that Mr. Leese has a wife, María, who would be pleased to have you visit. I'll take you over tomorrow."

"So you think," Cherith asked by way of clarification, "that the men here might accost me. I thought that was the purpose in not teaching me Spanish until I arrived—to protect me from hearing unsavory things." At his silence, she nodded, understanding dawning slowly and uncomfortably. "You fear worse."

"I don't fear anything—not truly—but I do wish to be cautious and prudent. I know it's been a very long time, but if you can just wait a week until I can have everything ready for the trip to Napa—to home—you'll be free again."

Her mind screamed for her to stop, but Cherith heard herself say, "And you do not think I'll be in danger of someone carrying me off if I'm with the girl. No evil man could overpower a young woman, a beautiful one at that, to haul off a"—she winked—"'redheaded chit' like me."

"I'm sure they could, but I'm more concerned about that *vaquero* we discussed."

* * *

The crunch of a tortilla chip served as punctuation as Avelino finished his story. Amelia slowly flipped the cover of her notebook, while Ed chewed the last of the chips.

Joe nodded thoughtfully. "I kind of understand Edgar's dilemma."

"There are worse histories your granddaughter could tie herself to," Ed insisted. "I think Amelia will be a very blessed woman."

"I agree." Joe cleared his throat in an attempt to disguise the crack in his voice. "So who goes to Lyndon's tomorrow?"

"I'll see if the lawyer I spoke to in Napa can—"

Ed Welton shook his head as Avelino spoke.

"What?"

"Lawyer you *spoke* to? Who is he?" Ed didn't wait for Avelino to continue. "I'm not trying to be insulting, but you need the best legal counsel available."

"I can't afford the best, but Vernon Greer . . ."

A look of utter disdain flashed and froze onto Welton's face.

"What's wrong with Greer?"

Ed Welton hesitated before saying, "I wouldn't trust him to write a will for my dog—the already-dead one." Before Avelino could respond, Ed tried again. "Look, I know you have to do what you can do, but I'd rather you let me send my man with you. He's the best in the area, and he'll give you a good price. Consider it my apology for Ray's foolishness if your pride won't allow you to accept a gift from a friend."

Joe led their guest from the patio and left Avelino and Amelia alone at the table.

"He's right, Avelino. You need a good lawyer. Don't let your pride—"

"When you have lost almost everything, Amelita," he whispered, "sometimes pride is all you have left."

"And it's all you'll ever have if you don't learn to get over it." Amelia reached her hand across the table and covered his with hers. "I saw your Purple Heart in the trunk."

"I was wounded in action, Amelia. Most of the men I served with have one. It's nothing special."

"It's symbolic at least," she argued.

Avelino laced her fingers through his, squeezing them gently. "I don't understand, *querida*. What is symbolic?"

"You went to battle and were wounded. They gave you a Purple Heart. You've battled your own demons these past months, and I can feel it." He almost missed the quiet excitement in her voice. "You'll get *your* Purple Heart—the grapes and vines that *are* your heartbeat."

CHAPTER THIRTY-SIX

CONTRACTUAL EVIDENCE

Avelino, Ed Welton, and Ed's lawyer, Elton James, stood in the entryway at Gregory Lyndon's home. At Joe's insistence, Sheriff Callum waited outside in his car, just as a protective measure.

As he stood there, his posture deceptively relaxed considering the tension that boded ill for the health of his nerves, Avelino prayed. *I do not know, Señor, if this is the right course for me. Am I wrong to confront this man? There was a contract. Paco signed it. Paco agreed that he'd broken the contract. That is why he drank too much that night. That is why he's—* The memory of finding his brother brought his prayer to an abrupt halt. He took a breath—a slow, steadying breath—and tried again. *But if Paco didn't know he'd signed something illegal, isn't it acceptable to renegotiate?* Papá *would be furious if I tried to weasel out of paying a debt. The debt is valid, even if the terms of repayment aren't. Please do not let me be tempted by my desire for the land and for Amelia. Don't let me do what is wrong to gain what is right.*

"He is ready for you."

Consuela's voice startled him. He tried to smile at her—smile his gratitude—but she wouldn't look at him. She wouldn't look at any of them. But as he entered the office, Avelino glanced over his shoulder and found her staring back at them, apprehension in her eyes but a new air about her. *What is it? What is different?* As he seated himself, Avelino identified it. *Relief. She is scared for us—or maybe herself—but she knows she did what she needed to do. I need to remember that.*

"What brings all of you here today?" The calm, bored tone belied the nervousness Avelino saw in Lyndon's facial muscles. The man's jaw twitched, and his eyes shifted too quickly from one man to the next in an obvious attempt to discern the cause of the meeting. When they lingered on Ed longer than the rest, Avelino assumed it to be further confirmation that Lyndon had been behind the attacks on him and the vineyard.

He swallowed hard and leaned forward, gripping his hands together. "I would like to see the contract Paco signed."

"And your posse is here to do what? Keep me from destroying it before your face? Is this really necessary, Avelino? After all I've done to try to help preserve your family's heritage for you, this is the thanks you offer me?"

"They are here to help me read it—to be sure I understand it."

"As I explained before," Lyndon said, "the contract was between Paco—"

"Which is ridiculous, as you well know," Ed Welton interjected. "He has every right to know how he lost his inheritance and if there was a clause he could have used to save the land."

"If there was, would I have offered—?"

Elton James laughed. "Because your seven-year labor agreement is so very generous."

"The income he would likely bring to the vineyard would cover the six-thousand-dollar debt, plus interest. It was a risk on my part." Lyndon's eyes bulged bigger and redder with each word. "If he did *not* generate enough revenue on his own to cover the difference, I would have been out everything. It was essentially an extension of his loan!"

Avelino started as Ed's laughter erupted. "Defensive, aren't we?"

"For attacking my character when I've done nothing but try to help this unfortunate young man, yes! I gave him the chance to earn back property that was rightfully mine when his brother defaulted. I kept the land for him until it seemed that he would not return. Then I began the process of making it saleable. When he returned, I honored our agreement—one I offered freely and generously, in my opinion."

"Which is why I would like for my lawyer to read that contract with Paco," Ed said.

Lyndon's face fell. He called out, "Baines!"

The little man appeared almost instantly—reasonable proof that Baines had been listening at the door. "Yes, Mr. Lyndon?"

"Please bring the contract between myself and Francisco Carrillo regarding Viña de los Sueños."

As they waited, Avelino stared at his hands, unwilling to watch the ocular swordplay before him. *This isn't going to go well. That was too easy. We have no authority here. What is happening?*

Lyndon laid the contract across his desk and leaned forward, covering most of it with his arm. "As you can see, it is signed, dated, and witnessed." He picked it up again, ready to hand it to Baines, but Ed stopped him.

"As we said before, we want to *read* the document. We did not need proof of signature. We want to read the terms."

"Well, you'll leave here wanting, then," Lyndon insisted as he passed it to Baines. "Because I do not share private business deals with those not involved. It is a professional courtesy, and a basic one at that."

How he can make his actions sound so virtuous while you can see the deceit on his face is nothing short of astounding. Avelino would have gone—would have given up without question—but Welton's lawyer didn't waver. "Would you prefer we call in the sheriff? I'm sure Callum would like to know that you are withholding proof of your right to the property in question. I could go to the courthouse in Napa and file a—"

"Mr. Carrillo does not have the resources to pursue legal action against me, as you all well know. I have offered him the opportunity to regain his property—at great personal loss, I might add. I have been more than generous. Now get out of my house."

Elton James stood, saying, "Consider yourself as having heard from Avelino's lawyer. We'll file our grievance with the court first thing tomorrow. If you prefer to waste your money on legal fees, then we'll be happy to oblige. Good day."

The derisive smirk on Lyndon's face told Avelino that the man considered their actions to be little more than empty threats—a bluff. But when Ed pulled out a check and handed it to Mr. James as they left the room, he felt the air shift. *This is too much for me. I'm a vintner. I grow grapes. I make wine. I want to raise a family and be a good citizen. I want to teach my children about Jesus and their history. I don't want to be devious and clever.*

As they drove away, a curtain fluttered in the window. Avelino kept his eyes riveted to the spot, even as the car backed around the semicircular drive. Once more they fluttered, but this time a dark jacket sleeve showed before the blurry silhouette disappeared. *Baines. What does he think of all of this?*

* * *

Footsteps sounded behind him. A twig cracked. Avelino called out, but no one answered. He spun in slow, deliberate circles, his eyes panning the acres of vines before him, but he saw only a sea of large green leaves. A flash of red in his peripheral vision confused him for a moment.

"Amelia?"

No answer.

Avelino crouched low and tried to listen, but only the distant rumbling of a truck broke the early-morning quiet. *What is it? Who is it? Should I hide or leave?*

Another twig cracked. From the opposite direction. Avelino's heart raced, and perspiration beaded on his upper lip. Rapid shallow breaths sounded insanely loud to him. *They'll find me. I must keep calm.* Once more a flash of orange red in his peripheral vision made him duck. *Jap flag. They're out there again. Gotta find Ted.* He called out, imitating a wild turkey, but Ted didn't respond. Footsteps grew nearer.

Wriggling between the vines, he worked his way across the rows, watching for boots. *Strange how the vegetation is so orderly here. Feels like home. Did the Japs plant gardens before we drove 'em back? Did we drive 'em back?*

A voice called out to him—not Ted's. *What do I do?* ¡Ten misericordia, Señor! *Have mercy.*

He crawled, scrambled, fought his way through the vines. Scratches bled, his shirt slowly became shredded, and footsteps closed in on him no matter where he hid, no matter how fast he moved. *POW. They'll take me. I won't survive. I failed,* papá. *I lost the vineyards. A hundred years of history for our family—gone.* Perdónenme, papá y mamá. *Forgive me.*

". . . are you doing crawling along the ground like that? I've had to chase you every which way!"

He started to run—hide—but a small niggle in the back of his mind grew until it illuminated the words. *That is English—good English. Not broken, like the Japs'.* The green of the jungle morphed into beautiful grape leaves with purple clusters hanging protected by them. *I am home—Napa. Is it a dream?*

Two shoes appeared. Avelino raised his head and backed away quickly. "Mr. Lyndon. They'll know you've come—that if anything happens to me, you had to be behind it."

"I'm not here to hurt you, fool. I may be an opportunist, but I'm not an idiot."

His eyes scanned the rows of vines, looking for anyone who might have seen them, but the inspectors were in the south quadrant—far away from where Avelino stood vulnerable before Gregory Lyndon. "What do you want?"

Lyndon pulled a rolled-up paper from his back pocket. "Here," he said. "I'll show you if you insist, but I'm not sharing my business agreements with anyone not affected by them. Even this is a courtesy. No judge—"

"That isn't true, or Mr. Welton would not be paying for a lawyer to arrange just that." He sounded sullen—petulant—and he knew it. By way of concession, Avelino forced a smile to his lips and said, "I'll go down to the phone box at Hank's and call Mr. Welton after I've read this." He hesitated. "Or is this my copy?"

"That's an original—not the *only* original, of course. I can't let you have it, but I did bring it for you to read."

Avelino hardly heard as Lyndon muttered on about being misunderstood and the unjustness of how people treated him. Instead, he read and reread the terms of the contract, trying to burn them into his memory. *Six thousand dollars to be paid back in three years at 29 percent interest. How did Paco think he could do that? Three years? Even six years would have been almost all of our personal income from the vines. We wouldn't have had anything to live on—nothing to pay taxes with or to buy food. Even if they had been extragood years . . .*

"As you can see, he was supposed to pay in full by January 1, 1940. I gave him a six-month extension and then another three-month extension. What more did you want from me?"

"You were generous, Mr. Lyndon. I knew you'd extended the loan. I didn't know how high the interest rate—"

"He offered that amount," Lyndon protested. "I told him it wasn't necessary, but Paco insisted." He shuffled his feet. "I didn't want to loan him the money at all. Prohibition did a number on your family's finances. Your parents—so wise to save all those years. Your family—wise. But Paco wanted to give employment to the workers, something to count on beyond the harvest and pruning months."

As crazy as near 30 percent interest sounded, Avelino did not doubt that Paco had promised it. *"It's a sure thing, Avelino. We'll triple our money in no time. Mamá and papá would approve; I know it. We'll be the top vineyard in Napa, but we have to seize the opportunity."* The words had been burned into his memory by an enthusiastic brother with limitless enthusiasm and boundless optimism.

"Are you satisfied that I'm not out to swindle you or your family?"

"I didn't think you were. You offered me a way to redeem our land. I did not forget that."

"So—"

"You've also left me wondering why. Mr. Welton suggested that perhaps the contract wasn't legal, and I had to admit I couldn't prove it was or wasn't." Guilt cut at him as he spoke, but Avelino continued, forcing himself to speak only truth, although he chose to be a bit selective in how he presented it. "I wanted to prove that I hadn't made a foolish decision by trusting you to keep your word, especially when you didn't *have* to give it in the first place."

Lyndon offered his hand. "I'm glad we understand each other. I hope this will be the end of suspicion regarding my motives."

The proffered hand hung between them, but Avelino couldn't bring himself to take it. Not until Lyndon dropped it and turned did he speak.

"Mr. Lyndon, I'll be proud to shake your hand in six years and two months—at the end of our contract. I *will* honor my end of the contract. I *will* work and bring you the most profit I can, and I *will* regain these vines so that the Carrillo name can live in this valley for the next hundred years."

CHAPTER THIRTY-SEVEN

A POINT OF HONOR

"Twenty-nine percent!" Amelia stopped in the middle of the road and pulled Avelino close, searching his face for some hint of teasing.

He smiled. "Paco always was reckless like that—a visionary. *Papá* used to say that Paco would keep us moving into the future, and I would keep us rooted in the present and past."

"That's . . ." Her eyebrows drew together in concentration. "Well, it's close to eighteen hundred dollars! How did he expect to pay off two and a half times your usual income each year?"

They walked again, hand in hand, Avelino trying to concentrate on Amelia's questions but too lost in his own wonder that she was truly *his* to give appropriate attention to her concerns.

"Avelino."

"What?"

"Are you even listening? How could he possibly expect to have that kind—?"

"Oh. *Lo siento*, Amelita." It worked. *She becomes distracted when I speak low and call her Amelita. I must not let myself use it to manipulate her. It would be so easy . . .*

". . . is just common sense." She grabbed his hand again. "I don't understand."

"Paco didn't think logically. He thought in big dreams and grandiose ideas. It was my job to bring him down to earth and make what I could work, but . . ."

Amelia squeezed his hand. "But . . . what?"

"But he didn't tell me that time." Emotion welled up in his throat, choking him. "He knew I'd say no. He knew I'd prove that we couldn't do it, so he shut me out. And I yelled at him, Amelia. I blasted him with every attack I'd ever felt about his irresponsibility." He dropped his head as shame filled him. "One of the last things I said to him was so cruel. My *mamá* would have thrashed me for being so disloyal to family. *'Never use the fact that family is stuck with you as an excuse for rudeness. They are* familia*; treat them like the gift they are from God.'*"

"And don't we do the opposite? People say, 'But they're family, so they understand.'" Amelia sighed. "We feel safe with family because they *have* to put up with us."

"And that is what *mamá* despised. She would scold little girls who tattled on their brothers, and little boys who teased their sisters. Oooh, she would get so angry, so infuriated."

"I wish I knew your mama. I could learn so much from her."

"You will have my *tías* Lucia and Jacinta. You have your grandfather. Joe is a good and wise man."

She pulled her hand from his and slipped it around his waist. He seemed to float beside her as his arm dropped around her shoulders and they made their way to the phone box at Hank's.

Just outside, she stopped him and touched his cheek near his eye patch.

Avelino failed to hold back a wince. "I—"

"It's okay, Avelino. I understand. I just wanted to say that I'll also have you. And you will teach me all of your mother's wisdom—your father's too. I had Grandmom and Granddad. Mama tried, but she spent most of her time with Papa—or avoiding him."

The raw pain in her voice tore at his heart. His troubles forgotten for a short while, Avelino distracted her with stories of pranks he'd played on his brother and his cousins. "I have lots of cousins. You'll see at harvest. They'll all come this year. Last year—well, it was different." He squeezed her hand and swung their arms lightly. "I can't wait to see what the hombres say when they see you."

*   *   *

One simple phone call—just his assurance that the document was valid and the terms were clear—set a string of events in motion that left Avelino lying on his bed that night, his mind spinning in dizzying directions. *It's my land again. It's mine. I don't owe anything.*

His gut clenched at that thought. *We still borrowed the money, and Lyndon is out that money. I know what the law says—what a judge would do—but can I live with that?*

Elton James's words echoed in his mind. *"The interest rate is usurious. It doesn't matter if Paco offered it or not; Lyndon broke the law the moment he signed that paper. The minute a judge sees this, he'll return the deed to you, and you won't owe a thing. It's how it works."* Despite Avelino's protest, James had been adamant. *"It was a big problem during the Depression. People, desperate not to lose their farms and sure that it would end that year, would take out loans for taxes at exorbitant interest rates and then lose the land when they couldn't pay. Most never knew that the contracts weren't valid, or refused to tell anyone for fear for their safety."*

The stuffy room became almost unbearable. He tried sitting by the window, but the breezes he always acquainted with home and the vines had vanished in the heat.

"Crazy heat wave. It feels like the jungle tonight." Honesty forced him to admit that the jungles of the South Pacific had been exponentially worse. "I got soft."

The memory of hot nights under the cooling branches of the ancient *secoya* spurred him out of his room, down the stairs, and across the moonlit yard—almost to the edge of the vineyard. The air felt cooler, less stifling. *It's all in your head, you fool. The familiar brings comfort even if it's not comfortable.*

Had he expected an instant—or even gradual—epiphany sitting at the grave of his great-great-grandfather, Avelino would have been sorely disappointed. He sat at the base of the tree, his head bent, and tried to rest his mind and heart. Each passing moment dragged into another until he'd lost all sense of time, but it failed to keep him from rehashing the situation in his mind.

He felt her presence long before he heard Amelia or saw her. She waited half-a-dozen feet away, watching, but Avelino said nothing. He ached to call her to him as emotions welled up within him, but no amount of desire could overcome the restlessness in his spirit. *She will know what to do. She won't be selfish, won't be tempted. Not like you. Talk to her,* his heart ordered, but still he sat silent and alone in his thoughts.

Her first footstep startled him. He'd been so certain she wouldn't advance until he called to her. *She's more intelligent than that. You underestimate her. Shameful how you do that—it's shameful.*

"Couldn't sleep either?"

She settled beside him, curled her arm around his, and rested her head on his arm. "Not when I knew you wouldn't." When he didn't speak, she laid open the subject without further hesitation. "What will you do?"

"I don't know," he rasped. "Nothing seems right."

"Do you think you're the only man he cheated?"

It hurt to admit it, but Avelino spoke the thoughts he'd tried to ignore. "I don't know that he did. Paco didn't even pay him half the principal. Even if the interest rate had been one percent, we would still have defaulted on that loan."

Amelia's silence assured him that she understood his dilemma. She grew heavy against him, and Avelino assumed she'd fallen asleep. He slipped his arm from hers and wrapped it around her. Her voice should have startled him. "You want to know if it's right to pursue legal action."

"I don't want to lose this property. That's why I made the agreement. Lyndon offered it," he added in a rushed panic. "I did nothing to pressure him. It wasn't wrong for me to accept—to hold him to it—was it?"

"I don't think so. He made the offer willingly. He may have made it out of guilt over an illegal contract, but that's not your responsibility. You held him to it, but I don't think you would have pursued legal action if he had said no."

"I thought about it." Avelino dropped his head. "I wondered if I could; if a judge would consider it binding."

"But you wouldn't have," she protested. "I know you. You wouldn't be here torn over something that is really a nonissue if you would."

"What is a nonissue?" Hearing the belligerent tone to his voice, Avelino tried again. "I didn't mean it like that."

"I know." Amelia scooted closer—how, he couldn't imagine—and wrapped one arm around his middle. "I just mean that you're torn about whether it's appropriate to take possession of land that you'll own again in six years anyway." He started to protest, but Amelia shushed him. "Stop it, Avelino. Don't beat yourself up for something that wasn't your doing. The contract you have with Mr. Lyndon is legal, binding, and of his own offering. Maybe he's not the corrupt man everyone thinks he is. Whatever the reason, you're not responsible."

"Mr. Welton and Joe want me to turn him in, but how can I? I'd be no better than Mr. Lyndon—taking advantage of another person's mistake."

"But . . ."

He groaned. "It would mean we could get married now. We wouldn't have to wait."

"We don't have—"

"Don't, Amelia. I can't choose what is good over what is *right*."

Her laughter, soft and low, did unsafe but wonderful things to his heart, but a new thought sent it plummeting into his stomach. "I never asked," Avelino whispered. "I just assumed."

"Assumed what?"

"That you'd wait—that you were *willing* to wait."

"If I say no, can we go to the courthouse next week?"

The question brought a smile to his lips. *She understands. That's part of why I love her. She understands.* "You know I can't."

"Even if I say I won't wait. Even if I say I will only wait six months?"

"That's a moot question, isn't it?" Avelino kissed her temple, lingering longer than he knew he should. "You would wait another seven years—like Jacob and Rachel."

"But Jacob didn't have to wait for Rachel fourteen years. He just had to *work* fourteen years for her." She giggled. "I think you just made a good argument for my side. Thank you."

An owl swooped low. Somewhere a coyote howled. And beneath a great *secoya*, a man sat with his sweetheart and begged *El Rey de los cielos*—the God of heaven—for answers.

* * *

". . . think that the thing with the saplings was a test," Ed Welton said as he addressed the others in the room.

Avelino tried to follow the logic but failed. "But why? I don't see—"

"Because if you didn't notice and cancel them, or at least ask about it, then he would have a good idea of how closely you were watching the books. He could skim off quite a bit, lowering your profit margin and possibly using it against you to convince you that the vineyards couldn't recover from the effects of Prohibition and the Depression. James has made inquiries."

Elton James nodded. "There are rumors that the Whittles are trying to negotiate with Lyndon to purchase Viña de Sueños."

"Rumors?"

"I can only say that I would make business decisions based upon the information I received if I were in a position to do so." James's left eyebrow rose.

"Just take a copy of the law to Lyndon, show him, and tell him he can give you your deed without contest, and you won't turn him in—"

"I can't do that," Avelino protested. "I don't want to pretend I can. A part of me—a part I'm not proud exists—screams at me to do it, but I can't."

Joe threw up his hands, stood, and began pacing. "Why not? I don't understand you! This is your chance to get it back now. To be free. This is your chance to get married *now*."

"And this"—his heart squeezed as he realized how ungrateful he would sound—"this is my chance to be the man my parents wanted me to be. I can't fail them. Paco signed that paper. He defaulted—not on the interest but on the principal."

A dreadful stillness filled the room and began to smother Avelino.

"I respect you for that," Ed said at last. "But you may not be—likely are not—Lyndon's only victim. Regardless of your brother's ability to pay, he signed a loan for an illegal interest rate. There are consequences to breaking the law."

"But turning him in means that I do not honor our family's commitment!"

Amelia entered the room carrying five water glasses on a small tray—the very tray his mother had used to carry broth to his room when he was ill.

"You are all too close to this. The solution seems simple enough to me."

"Tell us, 'Melia, because I'm ready to slap this boy upside the head and knock some sense into him."

"He's right, Granddad. You know he is."

"Well, I don't want him to be right," Joe muttered in an obstinate tone that Avelino thought sounded remarkably like Amelia.

"Avelino will go to Lyndon with Mr. James and only Mr. James. They will tell Mr. Lyndon that they know the contract is not valid and would be reversed by the court. They will remind him that those courts would prosecute him for breaking usury laws and investigate all of his financial dealings—something I doubt Mr. Lyndon wishes to have happen."

"But Amelia—" Avelino began in protest.

"Hush. I'm not finished." The men chuckled at Avelino's chagrin as she continued: "And then Avelino will show the kind of mercy that Gregory Lyndon showed—regardless of the reason. He will tell Mr. Lyndon that he has no wish to take the issue to the courts. He will request the property be deeded back to the Carrillo family and will sign a new contract that provides almost exactly the same terms as the current ones. He will work the full seven years as promised. Mr. Lyndon will keep all but a very small percentage—three or four percent—of the profits. That three or four will keep

Avelino in clothes and food so that he does not have to work on his one day off."

"And you think Lyndon will agree?" Avelino asked just as Welton said, "It's better than the current agreement."

"I think if he knows that Avelino will keep the situation confidential, he'll be relieved to do so."

Elton James said nothing but sat smiling on the couch. Not until Ed asked his opinion did the man speak. "She's good; she's very good. It solves all problems—the issue of the deed, the issue of Mr. Carrillo's conscience, and the issue of consequences for breaking the law. She should study for the bar. I suspect she'd be an excellent contract attorney."

CHAPTER THIRTY-EIGHT

CASE CLOSED

August 1, 1946

His hands shook as he reached for the door knocker. Elton James said nothing, but Avelino felt the man's support and encouragement. *It's as if he's saying, "Go ahead. I'll protect you," but only You can protect me, Señor. Please be with me. Stop me if this is wrong.*

Lyndon opened the door himself with an instant explanation. "Consuela's off this afternoon. What do you need now?"

"To talk, Mr. Lyndon. We need to talk."

"About . . . ?"

Avelino swallowed the lump that filled his throat and tried to speak. He swallowed hard again. "Our contract."

Mr. James cleared his throat and added, "And the one you had with Francisco Carrillo."

The blood drained from Lyndon's face before rushing back and turning him red with anger. "After all I've—"

"Do you care to discuss your business affairs on the front step, or would you prefer a little more privacy, Mr. Lyndon?"

James shifted his briefcase—one Avelino suspected was only for show.

"Come in," the man growled.

Again Avelino found himself opposite Gregory Lyndon and discussing the issue of la Viña de los Sueños. The man tried to insist that he would only speak to Avelino, but when Elton James pulled a document from his briefcase and set it on the desk between them, Lyndon grew quiet. A moment later he called out, "Baines! Get in here."

The door to the other room opened slowly, and the little man crept out. "Yes?"

"Bring me my deed box from the safe."

"Sir?"

A vein between Lyndon's eyes bulged as he bellowed, "Just *do* it!"

Behind Lyndon a clock ticked with nervous precision as the three men waited for Baines's return. But what he'd expected to be swift became a long, drawn-out procedure. Paper after paper appeared on the desk. Elton James read each one carefully, occasionally striking out a line, and passed it to Avelino for signature. A negotiation began—for what, Avelino didn't quite understand—and he signed that as well, praying that his trust in James wasn't misplaced.

As Avelino signed the last paper, and James placed their copies in his briefcase, the lawyer said, "I'll file these with the court today."

Lyndon just nodded.

"I want to thank—" Avelino began.

"Don't play mind games with me, Avelino Carrillo. You've played this card very well. I thought I could find a way to protect myself from legal action *and* recoup my investment. I failed. You won. Just get out of here. I'll have Kearns out of the house by Monday. At least they'll have the weekend—"

"Don't punish them—" Avelino began, but Lyndon exploded once more.

"Punish them? Who is punishing whom? It's your house! Rent it out to them for all I care, but I'll give them notice by end of work today that they have to apply to you for permission to stay."

Avelino exchanged confused glances with James.

Baines spoke up. "Sir, did you read the contract they offered?"

"Yes. They demanded the deed to the property—"

"Did you read *all* of it?" Baines repeated.

"I—"

Understanding hit Avelino hard and filled him with shame. "This is not extortion or blackmail, Mr. Lyndon. I want the deed, yes, but that contract binds me to finish my seven-year agreement with you. I want you to have your money. Paco borrowed it, spent it, and did not repay it. I *will* repay my brother's debt. I will not tell others the terms of Paco's or our agreement unless required by a judge in some other complaint. I request the deed now only for my own protection and because what you did was wrong." He stood. "How many others have you exploited in this way? How many people have lost property because they came to you in desperation?"

He didn't wait for an answer. With James on his heels, Avelino turned to leave, but at the door he spoke once more. "I will honor and satisfy that debt as it should be or should have been. I am sorry you thought me capable of capitalizing on someone else's mistakes."

* * *

Amelia found him on the hill where he'd stood as he left the only place he'd ever known as home. Her hand slipped into his as naturally as if it had always belonged there, and her other hand curled around his arm.

"It's a beautiful home, Avelino. We felt very fortunate to have such a nice place when we moved here, and now that I know its history I'm doubly blessed."

"It's mine again. If I found six thousand dollars somewhere, I could satisfy my debt tomorrow. It's a regular mortgage—of sorts. The terms of payment are not so regular, but—"

"But you own it again just as you should. If you are wounded in an accident tomorrow, your family could scrounge the money together to pay the loan. *That's* what the old contract should have had and didn't. He knew he'd always have the opportunity to prevent you from taking it, even if he had to cripple you to do it."

"I don't think he would have, Amelita," he murmured. "He's a hard businessman—an unethical one in some ways—but he does have a conscience. There is a limit to what he will do to protect his interests. He'd beat me, but I—"

She squeezed his arm. "I didn't at first, but now I do. I think the limit was murder. Granddad said it well. 'If Lyndon would make the clause, then he had to have reason for it.'"

He wrapped both arms around her, holding her close and reveling in the knowledge that this young woman knew him, understood him, loved him. "Will you regret six more years of waiting?"

"Not as much as I'd regret seeing you not stay true to who you are. We're going to be fine together. Six years will be an age, and," she added with a smile in her voice, "twenty years from now I suspect we'll feel like it flew by. It's what people always say about things like that."

"I wish I didn't have to wait. I do."

Amelia extracted herself from his arms and grabbed his hand again, tugging him down the hill. "I decided to consider this my journey to the life of a Carrillo. Cherith Tandy had to travel from Texas to Virginia, down the coast of South America, around that terrible Cape Horn, and back up the coast to Mexico and then

California. Now, I don't yet know what happened from there, because *someone* has been a little preoccupied with silly things like contracts and property and livelihoods, but I bet there was a bit of a trek from San Francisco—"

"Yerba Buena," Avelino corrected automatically.

"*Yerba Buena*," she echoed, "as well. So if she went through all that just to reach this wonderful house and this amazing life, I can make it through six years of relative ease with you and Granddad close by."

As they reached the door, Amelia covered the knob with her hand and leaned up to kiss him. "And if you didn't notice, that was a hint that I want the rest of Cherith's story."

"Now? I—"

"Granddad's waiting. Let's go."

He found her stenographer's notebook at the end table by her usual place on the couch.

Joe sat relaxed in his favorite chair. "Amelia wants to hear how Cherith and Edgar Tandy arrived at la Casa de los Sueños, is that right?"

Without waiting for confirmation, Avelino, in a move much bolder than he'd ever imagined, lay on the couch, his head in her lap and hands folded over his chest. "It took nearly two full weeks to find everything that Edgar thought they'd need—two weeks in which Cherith thought she'd go mad cooped up in the small ten-by-ten room. Not even the occasional visit with Mrs. Leese took away the feeling that she'd become a prisoner in this strange place where few people spoke English . . ."

CHAPTER THIRTY-NINE

AT LAST

January 1841

Two weeks—long weeks—Cherith thought she'd lose her mind, knowing that just a few dozen steps outside her door lay sand and sea and trees: nature. Her father had grown weaker by the day since their arrival, but the locals dismissed her concerns. "It's normal," they said. "People often become ill after a long journey. Once he acclimates he will be fine." Or so her father assured her. She hadn't been able to speak to anyone but Mrs. Leese since their arrival.

But Edgar had purchased a wagon, along with two good, stout horses. He'd also purchased beans, cornmeal, flour, sugar, salt, salt pork, and lard. He'd traded with natives for potatoes, carrots, and squash. Their larder would be full enough until they could rely on a garden for produce.

She woke up that last morning in Yerba Buena ready to enter this final walkway to the gate to their new life.

"Ready, darlin'?"

"Yes." She didn't glance around the room, looking for stray articles of clothing or small possessions. Every item had been packed within minutes of arising that morning. "May we still see the otters before we go?"

"Of course. I promised."

They left the wagon behind the saloon and strolled toward the rocks where they often found otters sunbathing.

"Look, Papa. There's one. I think that's our Mr. Whiskers. See his foot?"

She wanted to stay—to watch the little sea animals play in the water and on the rocks—but her father sagged with inexplicable weariness. *Lord, I'm worried. He's so listless, and he tires so easily. Is it from being at sea for so long? We've had fresh beef several times since we arrived. We've been eating greens. Everything. What else can we do?*

Edgar pointed to a green patch along the path. "Those are the leaves for that tea the girl brewed for us. It's the namesake here— *yerba buena*. Good herb."

"I'll miss the scent. Every time we walk past and crush a leaf, I smell mint."

Cherith started to ask if they couldn't dig up a plant to take it with them, but a glance at her father stopped her. *We need to go before he hasn't the strength to drive the horses.* She looped her arm through his and steered him back toward the saloon. "We need to go, Papa. It's a long drive, and I'm anxious to see our new home."

"I think you just want a chance to walk to a privy without an escort."

Her laughter dissolved in the ocean breeze. "That too, Papa. That too."

* * *

Several hours into the drive to Napa, Cherith took the reins from her father and stopped the horses. "There has to be a way for you to lie down back there."

"There's not, and you'll need direction soon enough anyway."

She started to protest, but Edgar turned and hoisted himself into the wagon box. "There is a woolen blanket back here . . . Found it. I'll just pad the seat a bit and rest my eyes."

Her eyes closed as she waited for her father to make himself comfortable. *He's so weary. I need—*

A kiss on her cheek arrested Cherith's thoughts.

"Thank you, darlin'."

The terrain changed slowly; rolling hills dipped into valleys as the road wound its way to Sonoma and Napa. *"Marco says the property is close to both locales—Sonoma and Napa,"* her Papa had said.

"The names sound so beautiful and exotic," she'd mused. Cherith felt old now as she recalled the conversation. The romance of a life in California had given way to reality. *Life is hard wherever you are.* The green of hills and trees in the middle of winter amended that thought. *But it has its blessings too. How many places are so green in January? What will it look like once spring arrives? This will probably seem dead by comparison, but it's beautiful to me. I need to remember that.*

A gentle snore startled her. Cherith, arms already aching from the tension of driving, saw a small cleared patch near the edge of the road ahead and nudged the horses off the road, and pulled up to a stop.

Edgar awoke. "We can't be there yet."

"We're not. But it'll be dark soon, and you're tired. I think we should stop now."

"I should have pushed the horses faster. This wagon isn't too heavy for them." Edgar climbed down, his usual agility gone, and in its place he moved with a gingerness that made him seem almost frail. "I'll get them some water."

"Where . . . ?" She stopped as she saw a line of trees in the distance. "That is probably why this is clear here. People must stop here often."

Cherith jumped down and rushed to take one of the reins, but Edgar waved her back. "You find us something for supper and see if you can find the other blanket. I'd rather not have to unpack a trunk. I should have planned for this."

"We were just eager to go, Papa. One night won't hurt us. I have my shawl, and you have your coat. It's already warmer here than it was in Yerba Buena. I'll rearrange the back into a nice bed for you, and I'll sleep on the wagon seat. We'll be fine."

Once her father and the horses had vanished from sight, and the sun set low in the sky, Cherith no longer felt "fine." Horses clopped along the road, advancing closer with each passing second. Her heart raced as she tried to decide whether to hide or pretend bravery she didn't feel. Her father's shotgun lay beneath the wagon seat, and just as the horses and riders appeared over the gentle rise behind her, Cherith reached for it and hid it in her skirts as well as she could.

Words flew at her in Spanish as four young men rode into view. *Do I smile to show I am not dangerous, or do I ignore them and hope it'll turn them away?* The question became moot as she froze in fear at the way the men stared and gesticulated. *They're mocking me—or maybe worse. I am not safe alone here. I should have gone with Papa! How—*

"Cherith, can you come help me with the horses? I'm tired."

She fled, the gun left behind in her need to escape. *Papa will be angry about that.*

As Cherith reached Edgar's side, the man passed her the reins to the nearest horse. "I shouldn't have left you. I'm sorry."

"I—"

"Listen to me. Do not make eye contact with these men. Do not engage them, even if I seem to trust them. Be as invisible as you can be. They're probably harmless, but we can't know. Did you hear them say anything?"

"No . . . the words made no sense to me. I'm sorry."

"This is probably best. This is why I didn't want you to learn. They could have said anything—complimented you or insulted you."

Cherith nodded. *Or worse. You didn't say it, but I heard it in your tone, Papa. You're afraid for me. Oh,* why *did we come here? This was a terrible idea.*

They ate toasted cheese on bread for dinner. Something about it amused one of the young men, and he offered them pieces of jerked beef, but Edgar shook his head and said something that made them laugh. She sat as far from the group as she could, trying to read by firelight, until her eyes grew heavy.

I can't leave him alone with them. They could overpower him easily— not that they couldn't now, I suppose. What do I do? The memory of the gun her father had replaced under the wagon seat gave her an idea. She retrieved it and carried it to him. "I'm going to sleep now, Papa. You keep this to drive away all the wild animals—wolves or whatever live here." Her eyes met and held his.

Edgar kissed her cheek and squeezed her hand before turning back to the group of young men. She didn't understand the words, although she thought she heard "coyote," but the burst of laughter that followed told Cherith that her plan had worked. *He's teasing me about my insistence that he protect me. Now he's protected, and without insulting our "guests." Thank you, Lord. Thank you.*

* * *

Once more the sun dropped lower and lower in the afternoon sky and cast a golden glow over the valley below them.

"If Marco's map is worth anything—and it has been perfect until now—we'll be able to see the house and the vines at the top of that little rise over there." Edgar pointed to the left. "I think the Carrillo rancho and la Casa de Vida is on the other side of that hill." Edgar pointed behind them. "Marco said the properties almost border each other, but that one is in Sonoma."

"It's more beautiful than I expected. How can there be so much green in winter? I've never seen anything like it."

"Texas—"

"Yes, I know it was greener than Virginia, but many of these trees still have leaves, and there's green grass on the ground."

Edgar laughed, sounding more robust than he had in days. "There's a lot more brown, dry, dormant grass than there is green. I keep teasing you about your romantic notions about California, and you think I am exaggerating, but really, darlin', how can I help it when you give me such fine fodder with which to do it?"

"I was just making conversation, Papa," she retorted with more than a little indignation. "You don't have to worry about me losing my head over what will likely be a lot of unfamiliar and difficult work." She sniffed, her pride still wounded, and added, "And after our encounter with those cowboys last night, I can assure you that I will *not* be losing my heart to some local man with no couth and no way to communicate!"

"They were honorable young fellows, for all I could tell," he interjected. "They teased me about having a daughter and a mother all rolled into one. They commended me on your manners and your proper respect for your father—if they only knew."

"Papa!"

Laughter again; it felt good to hear it.

"But we didn't know, Cherith. It was a good thing that you couldn't understand them when I wasn't there to hear what they said. I think it was appropriate and complimentary. They do love your hair, and one definitely thought you were pretty."

She laughed. "And his comrades suggested that he consider spectacles at his earliest convenience?"

"No, another of the young men didn't seem fond of your freckles, but . . ."

That stung. Cherith's freckles had been a trial to her for as long as she'd realized that everyone doesn't have a speckled face. "Well, that should be no surprise."

"It wasn't that. He seemed affronted by you somehow, but his comrades brushed it off as his way. I think he's quite a ladies' man, and you gave him no attention."

"Well, I'm glad I did not then. Very glad indeed. The arrogance! The . . ."

Cherith's words died as the wagon came to rest at the top of the rise. A low, white house sat nestled among trees, and behind it several long rows of vines stretched spindly tentacles across their supports. It squeezed her heart until it ached from the pressure. "Is that—?"

Edgar pulled her close and held her. "That's it, darlin'."

"Casa de—"

The sun sank beneath the horizon beside them as Edgar nodded. "Sueños. House of Dreams. They were Avelino's dreams. Now they are ours, and someday," he murmured as he kissed the top of her head, "someday they will be your children's, grandchildren's, and even great-grandchildren's dreams. This is the beginning of something beautiful for our family, Cherith."

But Cherith hardly heard him. Her eyes scanned every detail of the house, from the small bush at the northwest corner to the barn off to one side of it. An enormous tree behind it all seemed to separate the house from the vines, and in the far fields cattle roamed. *We're home. This is home now. It's beautiful, Lord. House of Dreams. Mr. Aguilar named it well.*

EPILOGUE

THE LEGACY

Late August 1994

A hummingbird flitted about the feeder, zooming in for a drink and darting away again as laughter interrupted its meal. A pewter-haired Avelino leaned back in his patio chair, sipping iced tea—sweet tea, his Amelita had called it. *She succeeded in teaching me to love it better than I succeeded in teaching her to love jalapeños.*

"Tell us a story, *abuelito*," his great-granddaughter Lucy begged. "Tell us about the girl with *el pelo como rosas.*"

Little girls with blond curls and fair skin rarely speak with perfect Spanish inflection, but Lucy had learned at his knee from infancy. *The young ones now don't teach their children the old language, but I will. As long as I can speak, I will remind them of their roots, their heritage.*

"Which one, *querida*? Which girl with hair like roses?" He stood and wiped drool from his father-in-law's chin. "Are you thirsty, *papá* Colbert? Let's get you a drink."

As he seated himself again, a few little voices cried, "Yours! *Abuelita* Amelita!"

So Avelino told of his beloved Amelia and the father and grand-father who became family to him too. He joked about her ability to scold him without a word and soothe him just as silently. "She loved me more than anyone ever has—even my own *mamá*. She thought me handsome and charming. The only thing we ever truly disagreed on was whether we should wait to marry or not."

"And did you?" Lucy's wide eyes and charming smile reminded him of her great-grandmother.

Seated apart from the rest of his grandchildren, Marco listened and watched, trying to hide his interest in the story. *It's not "cool" to like the stories of an old man. It is only cool to wear patchwork plaid shorts and undershirts.* Avelino waited, knowing that Marco would ask if he waited for it. The question came sooner than he expected.

Marco turned to his father. "Did they wait the whole six years? I don't remember. Did he ever say?"

"Ask him," David Jr. insisted. "It's his story, not mine."

The question came. "Did you, Granddad? Did you wait, or did you get married? Who won?"

"We both won, Marco," Avelino said with just a little impatience in his tone. "We were married for thirty-five years. Not everyone is so blessed."

Undaunted, Marco pressed again. "But did you wait?"

Avelino nodded. "We waited. It was the honorable thing to do." He scooted forward with the slow, deliberate movements of an aging man. *I'm growing old. Growing?* he repeated to himself. *I am old.* "Be honorable, my boys. Above all, do what is right, especially when it's hard. You will have no regrets."

Impatient to hear more interesting tales, Lucy and a couple of her cousins clamored for more about his love story with Amelia. "What did she wear at the wedding? Was the church packed? Did she have a veil?" Lucy tugged at his sleeve. "*Please, abuelito.* Please! We want to know."

"There was no church," Avelino began. "Father Ortiz could not marry us. Amelita was not Catholic, and I was barely in his good graces. Pastor Fletcher would not marry us because I would not be rebaptized in his church."

"So where . . . ?" Marco slunk back and leaned against the pole and grew sullen and silent again.

"We went to Napa—to the courthouse. We thought about San Francisco, but Amelia wanted to stay here, 'where it all began.'" He squeezed two little hands and whispered as loudly as he could, "And she wore a veil—my mother's *mantilla*. Someday you will wear it if you like."

Squeals of excitement pierced even Avelino's dull hearing, and he thought he saw *papá* Colbert shift. *He hears so much, sees so much. My poor Amelia just wanted him to speak to her—to tell her he loved her. She never saw the change that came over him when she was around. How could she?*

Ami, one of the youngest of the little ones, wormed her way through the circle of adoring granddaughters and climbed up on his lap. Her hands cupped his face, and she asked, "What about the dress. Was it pretty? Was it white and poufy with lots of lace?"

He settled her against his chest and wrapped his arms around her. "She wore green, *mi* Ami. She wore the green dress she made for that first dance."

Several disappointed *aaaawww*s escaped, but Lucy grinned. "That's romantic—the real kind. The kind Mama says lasts."

Avelino nodded. "*Sí*, you are wise, little one. She was beautiful, my Amelia. She smiled and carried orchids. I saved for those orchids for . . ."

"Six years!" a chorus of boys and girls cried. Even Marco muttered his own response, but a smile hovered around the boy's mouth.

I'm getting through to you. You will listen, learn, respect. You will tell the stories someday, my Marco. You will tell of the first Marco and Avelino, of Edgar and Cherith, of my Amelia.

"*Abuelito!*" Lucy's indignant voice snapped him from his reverie.

"What? What did I miss?"

"Did you live happily ever after? After the wedding."

He thought long about how to answer the question. The children sat antsy in anticipation until he smiled and said, "We lived and we were happy together, and I've been as happy as I can be these past years without her. I have my family—my children, my grandchildren, now my great-grandchildren. God has been very good to me." His eyes met those of his little great-granddaughter. "She's gone now, and I miss her. But *she's* living happily ever after."

"With Jesus," Marco murmured.

"*Sí,* with Jesus." He leaned back in the chair again, his hands stroking Ami's hair. "I am not living happily ever—not yet—but when I join her in heaven with Jesus, then I will be 'happily ever after.'"

AFTERWORD

Rancho El Molino was a rancho in Sonoma County, situated along the Atascadero River and named for J. B. R. Cooper's Sawmill. Interestingly enough, Cooper did have a daughter, Ana Maria. However, that is where the accuracy within this story ends. The real Ana Maria married a German man, Hermann Wohler, who managed real estate from an office in San Francisco. I found this information particularly interesting because I discovered it *after* I wrote about my own Ana Maria in Sonoma.

Juana Briones is also an actual historical figure in California's state history. At eighteen she married a cavalryman, and she had ten children with him (seven who lived), as well as adopting an "Indian child." When her husband became a drunken abuser, she received a church-sanctioned separation from him and set up her own home in Yerba Buena. This woman was known for her charity and kindness to anyone—particularly in regard to medical issues. She was known as a *curandera*—a healer. After California was annexed into the United States, she waged a very clever war to keep her properties and fought for her husband's land after his death, taking that case all the way to the US Supreme Court. She is seen in this story as she could have appeared had my characters and the events been true. Juana Briones did travel to Marin County to help manage a smallpox outbreak there, so I don't think it's too much of a stretch to bring her to Sonoma for the purpose of my story.

There are others, of course—Mr. Leese, who built the first store in Yerba Buena (now San Francisco), and Jean-Jacques Vioget, who was the first developer and began with a saloon. I wrote the Battle of San Jacinto primarily from firsthand accounts by men who fought there as part of Santa Anna's army. The songs of the 1940s played through my head and my laptop as I wrote, and one inspired the "ballad" so dear to Avelino's heart.

I worked hard to keep every event as historically accurate as I could. Where I may have failed, I hope you'll forgive me.

ACKNOWLEDGMENTS

As I mostly write contemporary fiction, historical fiction opened up a whole new world of research. As well as checking simple things, such as whether they had toasters in 1900 or how long it takes to drive from Indiana to Chicago, I needed to get a feel for the era. In preparation for the writing of this book, I did a crazy amount of online research, and then I wrote. As the book neared completion, I made the seven-hour drive to Napa and spent the weekend driving the roads that I describe in the book. What I found astounded me. I had somehow described places that I'd never seen exactly as they are and were. In particular, the road to the Grange in Rutherford and the Grange building itself were so familiar that I felt as if I'd lived the very words I'd written. The trip into Yountville brought another surprise. There, exactly as I imagined it being (without knowing the name of the town when I wrote it), stood the little Catholic church St. Joan of Arc. I pulled into the parking lot and stared at it on a Sunday afternoon. I think I also concerned a few straggling parishioners.

But the best part of that trip was wandering through the Napa Valley Museum. The museum was changing exhibits the day I was there, but the staff went out of their way to accommodate me and help me get the information I needed. I'd like to thank Kristie Sheppard and Pat Alexander especially for their help in person and through e-mail.

ABOUT THE AUTHOR

© 2014 Braelyn Rae Photography

Chautona Havig is a prolific writer of fiction, including the popular Past Forward series and *Ready or Not*, among many other novels. When not writing, she enjoys paper crafting, sewing, and, of course, reading. She lives in a small, remote town in California's Mojave Desert with her husband and seven of her nine children.